THE
PERJURED
ALIBI

THE PERJURED ALIBI

by

Walter S. Masterman

RAMBLE HOUSE

First published (GB) 1935
Ramble House reprint 2009

ISBN 13 978-1-60543-345-5

ISBN 10: 1-60543-345-4

Cover Art: Gavin L. O'Keefe
Preparation: Gavin L. O'Keefe

"If there be trouble to Herward,
    and a lie of the blackest can clear,
Lie, while thy lips can move
    or a man is alive to hear."

Certain Maxims of Hafiz

RUDYARD KIPLING

CHAPTER I

MY VISIT TO CROWFIELD

TAKE small credit for my share in the strange affair of the Crowfield murder. Chance, and a somewhat churlish invitation from my friend, Kenneth Darent, took me to the village, and a series of accidents, rather than any particular shrewdness on my part, led me ultimately to the solution of the problem, where other and better brains had been baffled.

I was at a loose end in Town at the end of the season, limp and bored with life, and willing—Heaven knows—for any change from the sickly clamour of London.

Darent and I had soldiered together in the same regiment, though he was senior to me, and had every promise of a distinguished career, when the news of his father's death, and his inheritance of the small but very ancient property of Crowfield Hall, caused him to send in his papers. By chance my own father died almost at the same time, leaving me without any relation I had ever heard of.

My father, an Indian judge, had lived in that country for so many years that I hardly felt his loss as a personal sorrow, my recollection of him dating back to my schooldays, when he had paid breathless flying visits to see me: a hard, stern man, with little sympathy in him.

He had always made me an allowance, paid my small debts, and occasionally written me formal and concise letters of advice. But his death was the snapping of the last link with any family connexion, and made me realize that I was now completely alone in the world. It was our common loss and loneliness that drew Kenneth and myself together, and when I received a letter from my father's lawyers—Erskine, Martyr & Green—informing me that the amount left to me by my father would provide an ample income for a man of lazy habits and modest tastes, I decided to leave the Service, and Kenneth and I came home by the same boat from Egypt, where we were stationed at the time.

He was full of plans for the future: the estate had been in his family for centuries, and he meant to do great things there, for I gathered from hints he threw out that it had rather gone to pieces, and required careful administration.

We parted company in London, with a promise on his part that when he had been able to get things settled he would invite me to the Hall.

I stood on the platform with him, watching his sunburnt, handsome face, keen grey eyes and firm jaw, upright as a dart, a man who stood out above his fellows. A sense of complete loneliness crept over me as the train steamed out of the station.

But five years had passed since that day, and never a line had I received from him, and the promised invitation had never come. I had written to him several times, giving him my addresses, for I had been travelling a good deal, but had not even received an acknowledgement, so that when at last I did get his letter it came as a complete surprise to me. I did not answer the letter, as my plans were very uncertain, and I did not like the 'take-it-or-leave-it' tone, but a sudden hot spell in August made London intolerable, and so one morning I told Hoad, my man-of-all-jobs and formerly my batman, to pack my suit-case, and bring my car round. It was a sudden decision, taken on the spur of the moment, but I felt that if I was not welcome I could go on to the sea-side instead.

I knew that the town of Wickstead was the nearest of any size to Crowfield, and drove down there on a lovely August morning, through beautiful country of woods and old-world villages bright with flowers.

From this sleepy old market town I climbed up a long hill by a winding country road, little used, and found myself at the crest, where cross-roads marked the beginning of the little straggling village of Crowfield, sleeping in the sunshine like a contented cow.

At one corner stood an old stone-built church with a square tower, surrounded by a churchyard thickly dotted with tall yew trees, and at the opposite corner was a building that, at the moment, was a more attractive sight to me, an ancient inn, half timbered and covered with creepers. It stood back from the road, with a large space in front for vehicles to draw in, marked off by white pillars linked together by a chain. Two great chestnut trees gave ample shade with their wide-spread branches. A sign swung nobly overhead, depicting a crown, and on the lintel of the door the name of the inn was neatly painted, with that of the licensee—A. Willis.

Beneath the sign stood a long rustic table such as used to stand outside most English inns, with benches of rough, unpolished oak.

There was a homely atmosphere about the inn that attracted me after the garish cocktail bars of London, and my mind turned to thoughts of beer—a large, cool tankard of freshly drawn country beer.

The door opened directly into a large, low-roofed room with oak rafters, at the farther end of which there stood a huge sideboard adorned with highly polished pewter.

Two men were sitting at a small table; they looked up at my entrance and then resumed their conversation. A fresh-looking country girl entered from a farther door, carrying a tray on which were two of the very tankards I had visualized in my mind.

"Come on, Polly, m'dear, put 'em on the table—we're thirsty." The speaker was a stout, pleasant-faced man of middle age, with a yellow coat and drab gaiters. He turned his red face to me: "Perhaps you will join us, sir? I heard your car draw up outside—'tis a hot day."

I ordered a similar tankard, which the girl went out to fetch, and the man, whom I took to be a farmer, smiled affably.

"You are a stranger to these parts mabbe?" he asked.

I informed him that this was my first visit to the village, and noticed that the two men exchanged glances at my words. Some unaccountable instinct made me stop at that, and not mention Darent's name. My genial friend turned to his companion, a sallow fellow with a taciturn, shifty face, clothed entirely in black, who had remained silent, nursing a black dispatch-case.

"This is Mr. Turnbull, the lawyer from Wickstead, and my name is Hickmott, of Daly's Farm—now you know us both."

He picked up his tankard and took a mighty draught. The lawyer's face twisted into a wry smile, as though the process was one he found some difficulty in executing.

"Your health, sir," he said curtly.

"My name is Tracey," I replied. "I have just run down from Town, and stopped at this delightful inn for a drink."

Observing that Hickmott had emptied his tankard, I touched a brass bell that stood on the table, and the girl appeared. Hickmott extended a large, muscular arm and seized the girl by the waist. "And this is Polly Willis, bless her heart—I've known her since she was born, haven't I, Polly?"

The girl grinned at his clumsy gallantry, and I gave the order for the tankards to be replenished.

To my surprise the lawyer placed a claw-like hand over the top of his.

"Not for me, thank you—not for me," he snapped, as though fearing poison rather than good beer. The action was churlish, but Hickmott laughed boisterously: "Liver! He can't stand much, can you, Turnbull?"

"It's not that at all: I have had sufficient, and I have work to do—I am over-late already."

I suppose he read my looks, for he added hastily: "Hickmott will drink with you till closing-time, and after, maybe; he's nothing but a walking barrel, a cask to be filled as soon as it is empty."

Hickmott roared heartily: "Hear that now, Polly—it's all due to messing about with deeds and wills that's made him like that." He cast an amused glance at Turnbull, and smacked him on the knee—"And mortgages and marriage settlements, eh?"

Turnbull's face went black, and he shot a look of fury at the farmer.

"Never in forty years have I seen such a scandalous—" He stopped as quickly as he had begun, and pulled himself together. "I don't suppose our village gossip would interest Mr. Tracey," he added with a wan smile, shut his mouth tightly, and fumbled with his black case, while Hickmott picked up the newly-filled tankard that Polly had fetched.

"Are you staying long here, sir," he asked after wiping his large mouth with the back of his hand, "or just passing through, like?"

"I have nothing particular to do. I just came down for a change from London."

"You haven't come down for the wedding, sir?" Polly asked eagerly.

"What wedding?" An absurd idea came to me that Kenneth might be the bridegroom.

"Why, haven't you heard, sir?" The girl was agog with her news. "Sir John Barton at the Towers is to be married to Miss Browne, the rector's daughter, to-morrow, and there's to be a grand party at the Towers to-night."

It was all so much Greek to me, but further discussion was cut short by the entrance of Mr. Willis, a typical country landlord, large and stout and perspiring profusely.

"Well," he said, addressing the farmer, "thank the Lord that's over. Next time he gets like that I'll send him home in a cart."

"Drunk again, I suppose?" Hickmott asserted rather than queried.

"Drunk—he could hardly walk—and hung on to my arm like a lump of lead, and singing some Italian stuff all the way down to the Hall."

A sudden misgiving came to my mind at the mention the Hall, but I remained silent.

"One of these days," the landlord continued, "he'll fall into one of his own quarry pits and break his neck —why, what's the matter, Mr. Turnbull?"

The lawyer had been twisting his face into some sort of signal as Willis spoke.

"I am afraid," he said in a quiet, venomous tone, "this conversation will hardly interest an entire stranger."

The landlord noticed me for the first time, and his face went even redder than before. "No, sir," he said awkwardly; "we are proud of our village and we don't want Mr. Darent's name blazed abroad, so to speak."

"You wooden-headed fool," Turnbull exclaimed, "why go and mention names at all! With this wedding we shall have crowds of Pressmen and others coming down—perhaps Mr. Tracey is—er—"

"No, I am not," I said sharply. "I have no profession at all, and I certainly didn't come here to collect village scandal."

"Then may we inquire," the lawyer said testily, "for what purpose you have come to our village?"

"I came," I said slowly, looking steadily at Turnbull, "to stay with an old friend of mine—Mr. Kenneth Darent."

A roar of laughter from Hickmott greeted my words, and the fool slapped his thigh in coarse, uncontrolled merriment that made me go hot with rage. "Well, if that isn't real funny," he said between his bursts of laughing. I don't suppose I should have minded the asinine guffaws of this bumpkin, but the sneering bark that Turnbull gave and the sight of his eyebrows raised in supercilious contempt made me see red.

"I would be pleased to know the cause of this hilarity," I said sharply, addressing the lawyer.

"Oh, you'll find out quick enough," Hickmott gurgled.

"I am speaking to you, sir," I said, facing the lawyer.

"If I were you, young man," he said in a quick, dry voice, "I would turn my car round, and go back to London as fast as possible."

I stood up and faced them; I am afraid my temper is none of the best. "What's wrong with Mr. Darent?"

The landlord stood foolishly scratching his head, and Hickmott became suddenly quiet, and looked sheepishly at the floor, his laughter gone. The answer came from Turnbull, who leant forward over the table. "What's wrong, young man? I'll enlighten you. He's hardly ever sober, and when he is his temper is so bad that every one avoids him. He's heavily in debt, and never does a stroke of work. The Hall is a ramshackle old farmhouse falling to pieces, that ought to have been pulled down years ago; it's not fit to keep cows in. He's a drunken blackguard, a libertine and a thief—that's what is wrong with your old friend Mr. Darent!"

The words came in a thin stream of vitriolic abuse from the lawyer's cruel lips. He never raised his voice once, and even the bright sunshine through the latticed windows seemed to grow dark.

I could stand no more, not another word, and I saw he had taken breath to continue. I laid hold of his coat collar and dragged him over the table. If he had struggled, I should have hit him, but he only whined for help. I pushed him to the open door, and flung him into the yard outside; so that he fell sprawling to the ground, spread-eagled like some huge bird of prey. His precious dispatch-case, to which he had clung despairingly, as though he feared I should wrench it from him for some reason, had fallen open; and it did me good to see the papers flying in all directions, and the lawyer picking them up like a black hen pecking corn.

He got the papers into his case, and I saw that his hand was bleeding. I made a step towards him, meaning to see whether I had hurt him, but he gave one glance at me—a look of deadly hate—and rushed up the road as though the fiend himself were after him.

I came back to the group by the window, dusting my hands, and feeling better.

"And now, Mr. Hickmott, will you tell me in a more polite manner what is wrong with my friend?"

It was Willis, the landlord, who answered.

"It's a most unfortunate thing, sir; you couldn't have come at a worse time. Mr. Darent had an awful row with that lawyer this morning, and they hate each other like cat and dog."

"What was the quarrel about?" I asked sternly, meaning to get to the bottom of this matter.

"Well—you'll soon know, I reckon," Willis said haltingly. "Better have it said and done with. It was about this wedding."

"It's my belief," Hickmott said with heavy sincerity, "that that lawyer fellow's got a strangle hold on Mr. Darent—with them papers he had."

"Why should they quarrel about this wedding?" I was entirely in the dark in the matter.

"I should ask Mr. Darent if I were you, sir," Willis answered, with a glance at Hickmott. "All I know is that if I hadn't collared hold of him, he'd have half murdered that lawyer. He picked up a pewter pot, but Polly got between them, and Mr. Darent's always had a soft spot for Polly, and then I took him home."

"If you take my advice," Hickmott said, looking anywhere but at me, "you'll stay and have lunch here."

It didn't look as though I should get much lunch at the Hall, if half of what I had heard were true, and Darent would hardly be in a fit state to receive me. After all, I hadn't told him I was coming.

"We shall have lunch ready at one o'clock," Willis said, his instincts as a landlord asserting themselves. "But if you would care for it earlier, I'll ask Mrs. Willis."

I glanced at the clock and saw the time was half-past twelve. "That will do for me—I'll take a stroll round the village."

I wanted to get away from these people, and think what was best to be done. I had made rather an exhibition of myself, but the lawyer had angered me beyond endurance.

I felt better outside, and the sight of my car made me wonder whether it would not be wiser to take Turnbull's advice and to return to Town, but the very fact that the advice had come from him made me obstinate. I walked idly over the road to the old church, having a liking for ancient buildings. The churchyard was restful and cool, tall yews forming an avenue to the church door that reminded me of the Alyscamps at Arles. On each side were ancient tombs, and gravestones the inscriptions half obliterated by time. Among the lichen-covered tombstones, I saw something that set my teeth on edge. A large white marble vault stood out like an act of blasphemy, amid these simple village memorials, and above it was a vulgar white angel with hands crossed over her breast. It was as incongruous as the tables of the moneychangers in the Temple. I stepped between the grassy mounds to examine this thing.

The vault was surrounded by a space in which flowers were in bloom, with a white marble kerb and railings. In gold lettering I read the inscription:

Sacred to the Memory of
Elsie Barton,
beloved wife of Sir John Barton, Bart.
Died Aug. 23rd, 19—.
Aged 26 years.
'The Lord gave, and the Lord hath taken away.'

My gorge rose at this insult to the churchyard, and then I remembered the conversation at the inn. Tomorrow Sir John Barton was to marry the rector's daughter, and the date on the tomb was only three years ago.

And Kenneth had quarrelled with the lawyer over the wedding, and had nearly brained him. I decided that I would not return to London.

Here was some mystery that would relieve my boredom. The west door was open, and I entered the cool building and looked round. It was a fine old church; not large, but with massive stone pillars and rounded Norman arches. The east window was 'Early English,' probably added a century later to the original building, and the small deep-set lancet windows contained some good glass of the old dull blues and crimsons of the thirteenth century.

I walked up the central aisle towards the altar rails, when I became aware that I was not alone. A man stepped from behind a pillar, and his dress told me that he was the rector. Middle-aged, and of good proportions, with the high, intellectual forehead of a scholar, he seemed to be part of the church itself. In that dim light I could see little but the outlines of his face, but the hard, keen eyes and straight mouth gave me the impression of one who could be a terror to evil-doers in the village, as well as a masterful shepherd. These impressions came to me later, for after the glare of the sun outside the church was dark. He came forward to me with a smile.

"You are looking at our church, sir; it is well worth a visit, though few nowadays care to stop and admire churches."

"I have just run down from London," I replied. "I am afraid I came in here while waiting for my lunch, though I am much interested in old buildings."

"But not their uses, perhaps."

"That all depends on the uses to which they are put."

"My name is Browne, the local incumbent—All Souls, Oxford—were you at the 'varsity?"

"I was in the Service," I replied somewhat stiffly. "My name is Tracey."

"It is a treat for me—a real treat—to be able to converse with an educated man for a change—one is buried alive in this village; but let me tell you something about the church."

Without waiting for a reply he went on with the zeal of an enthusiast. "The tower now—doubtless you admired that twelfth-century tower, a landmark for miles. It has another claim to interest—a cresset burned on the tower to announce the coming of the Spanish Armada."

He went on with a description of the woodwork of the pulpit, and of the windows, when a shadow crossed the entrance, and a girl's clear voice called out: "Aren't you coming, dad? We shall be late for lunch." The speaker herself came into the church. I could only see that she walked with the free, springing step of the country-bred girl, and the easy grace that only comes from an outdoor life. As she came forward she saw me.

"This is Mr. Tracey—my daughter Margorie. I am afraid we must break off this interesting conversation, but I hope we shall see you again if you are staying here for any time—you must come to the rectory."

Even as he spoke I could sense that he was rattling off a formula of politeness rather than an invitation. I looked keenly at the girl. Even in that glimmering light I could see the perfect oval of a face eager and vivid, framed in a cluster of brown curls—for she wore no hat—and the perfect poise, as she stood there waiting.

So this was the cause of all the trouble—and she was to be married on the next day to Sir John Barton. I determined to force the issue.

"I am staying with my old friend Kenneth Darent."

The rector's mouth compressed to a straight line, and a slight frown appeared on his face, but it was to the girl that I turned in astonishment.

She opened wide her deep hazel eyes, with an expression of mortal dread.

"Mr. Darent?" she stammered. "Are you staying with him?"

I could not take my eyes from her face, but heard the rector say in a matter-of-fact voice from the gloom: "Dear me, that is most interesting. Margorie, we shall have to get off, or your mother will be scolding me."

The girl made no movement—she had leant against a pillar, cupping her face in her hands: only her great eyes were still fixed on me.

"You will be staying here over to-morrow?" she whispered.

"I hope so; I expect to be here for some days."

"You didn't come here especially for to-morrow?" She halted over her words.

"Of course not, my dear," the rector said impatiently. "I don't suppose that Mr. Tracey is in the least interested in your wedding."

"I am sure I am most interested," I said politely. "I shall certainly come if there is room for me."

There was no particular meaning in my remark; it was the merest politeness, to break off the conversation that I felt had become embarrassing.

The girl clutched my arm feverishly. "No! You mustn't come—you must keep him away—take him for a drive somewhere."

"Margorie," the rector intervened sternly, "you forget that you are talking to a total stranger." He addressed me: "Please take no notice of what my daughter has said—she is naturally a little overwrought— what girl would not be on the day before her wedding?" He took his daughter's arm, and almost hustled her from the church, with a hurried good-bye, and I heard his voice talking gravely as they rounded the corner.

Well, I had come to a queer village. I returned to the inn, determined to see the matter through.

CHAPTER II

AT CROWFIELD HALL

POLLY kept up a running commentary during my lunch, and informed me that the wedding was a great event in the village. She gave me the names of the bridesmaids, the number of wedding presents, and a list of those who were coming. She was going to help decorate the church in the afternoon, and 'Jack,' who was apparently the village constable, and a particular friend, was on duty at the Towers guarding the valuable presents.

It was only when I had finished, and lit my pipe, that the matter of the Hall was referred to.

"And now, Polly, will you direct me to the Hall?"

Her manner became serious at once. "If I were you, sir, I'd leave my car and bag here, and walk down—it isn't far over the fields. Then if you decide to stay, you can come up for the car, and if not, you can come back here and no harm done."

There was much shrewdness in Polly's advice, and I have no doubt she had one eye on the good of the 'house' —and after all, I hadn't seen Darent for five years, and there might be something in what these people had been saying.

"Very well," I said, smiling at the girl, "if you will show me the way."

We started along the village street that crowned the ridge, the ground sloping steeply away on both sides to the valleys. Stone-built thatched cottages were scattered along the road in irrational fashion, as though planted at random and left to grow. Every cottage had a garden that blazed with a mass of colours—dahlias and hollyhocks and late delphiniums. Crowfield was set on a hill, and was out of the beaten track of motorists, who avoided the rough, winding road and the steepness of the approach to the village. It was a 'man sanctuary,' from which the ferry-builder and the bungalow-fiend had alike been excluded. Away at the end of the straight, level street a mass of tall trees shut out the view, and arched over the road, so that it seemed to disappear into the round mouth of a railway tunnel.

We turned into a grass track on the right, and climbed a stile, and then went across a large meadow to the brow of the hill. Here Polly stopped and pointed down.

"That's the Hall, sir."

I don't know quite what I had expected to see after the queer talk of the morning—a huge house in decay, or a grotesque ruin. On the hill-side below, bedded in trees, was a square, substantial manor house of stone, little more than a farm-house, but suggesting comfort and home life. A short distance away were some farm buildings and stabling. There seemed nothing wrong about the place; it was as though one had expected a tiger and met a harmless cat. Polly evidently read my thoughts. "It looks all right from here, but it does want doing up badly."

"Does all this land belong to Mr. Darent?" I asked.

She pursed up her lips in a dubious smile. "M-yes, but it's heavily mortgaged, and my father says it's the worst land in England, and nothing will grow on it but grass."

There was something in her manner that made me wait. I had already learnt Polly's love of gossip.

"Mr. Darent won't sell an acre, and that's the trouble. He could have made a lot of money by selling some of it for building."

Her eyes had wandered from the Hall away to the left, and I followed the direction of her gaze. The cluster of trees that closed the end of the road no longer obscured the view, and I swore softly to myself. I am no artist, and I make small pretensions to a knowledge of modern architecture, but I am fond of the English countryside—the most beautiful, to my thinking, in the world.

The thing I saw—I can call it by no other name—had been mercifully hidden by the trees from the road, but now stood out in its naked hideousness, a blot on the landscape, an eyesore and an insult.

Imagine on the very crest of the hill a vast new red-brick house or palace glaring over the valley.

"Is that an hotel?" My gorge rose at the thought of any one defiling the countryside with this monstrosity.

"That's the Towers—Sir John Barton's house—that's what started all the trouble."

"Let's turn our backs on it, Polly, and sit down; you can tell me all about it."

The girl sat down with the easy motion of the country girl, and plucked a piece of quivering grass, which she put in her mouth like a cigarette.

"Someone ought to burn it down!" I remarked savagely, taking another look at the house, and then sitting beside her.

She laid an eager hand on my arm. "I wish you'd do it, sir—you didn't come down for that?"

"No, Polly; I am afraid that is not my vocation, but tell me about it."

She needed no urging. "The village was all right till he came—he's a brewer"—the contempt in her voice was amusing from a publican's daughter—"he's got a brewery in Wickstead that he inherited from his father, and owns about a hundred tied houses."

"Dreadful!"

She looked at me in doubt as to my sincerity, and continued: "One of his agents came over here some time ago, and wanted to buy the Crown, and make it a tied house."

"To whom does it belong?"

"Why, to Mr. Darent, of course—it's been in his family ever since it was built, and of course he wouldn't sell it. And then Sir John came over from Wickstead, and threatened that he would build another "house." He applied for a licence, but the magistrates refused it. That was Miss Morris's doing; she's the Lady of the Manor. He wasn't half mad about it, and said he would get his own back, and he built that—"

She jerked her finger over her shoulder in the direction of the Towers.

"He built that?"

"All this side of the road belongs to Mr. Darent, and the other to Miss Morris, and neither of them would sell him an acre at any price, but the Priory was up for sale, when old Colonel Jackson died, and although Miss Morris tried to buy it, Barton outbid her. He bought the property and pulled down the house. They say you can see the Towers right away at Crawfold."

I began to have considerable sympathy with my friend Darent.

"It's got forty bedrooms and a bathroom to every one, and he has all his food sent down from London," Polly said viciously.

"The brute."

"But he couldn't buy the shooting," she added triumphantly, "and no one calls on him."

"Perhaps he gets his friends from London, too," I said gravely.

"He does, and from Wickstead. The road hasn't been safe with cars since he came, and we hardly ever had any before. There'll be dozens of them to-night for the party."

"Well, Polly," I said, rising stiffly, "I must be getting on. I can find my way now, and thanks for coming with me. I shall see you later on."

"You can't miss the way now, sir—straight down, and over two stiles, and through that little wood—Spring Copse; but be careful how you go—Mr. Darent's a bit hasty with strangers, and might put a charge of buckshot into you."

A cheery prospect!

I watched the girl tripping lightly back to the village. She turned and waved to me at the corner, and I strode down the hill. The going was easy on the thin, dry grass— all meadow-land, plentifully sprinkled with stones; too thin for tillage. A few cows looked at me in mild surprise and then went on quietly grazing.

The path led through a little wood where nuts were ripening and holly bushes were interspersed with larches and hawthorn. On the other side the path bore away to the right, but a steep bank lay in front, and below me was the Hall, with a wide space of grass-covered garden before it. Weeds grew thick, but here and there a patch of flowers showed through the tangled mass, and a straggling herbaceous border marked the farther end towards the stables. The house was very old, and built of grey stone, with grey stone roofing. The walls were blotched with lichen, and green where the water had overflowed from the broken gutters. An indescribable desolation brooded over the place, as though the inhabitants were long dead, and merely haunted the scene of their living memories.

The windows were low, long and diamond paned, but many were cracked or broken, and the upper-story windows were grey with dust, curtainless and apparently unused.

There was no sign of life about the place, and the massive front door of unpolished oak stood wide open. As I approached it two hens, clucking violently, came running out, frightened at my presence. There was neither knocker nor bell, and somewhat doubtfully I walked into the stone-flagged hall, where a fine, broad staircase went up to a gallery that ran round the upper floor. A lantern in the roof was so grimed with dirt that the place was in semi-darkness. A round table stood in the centre, but there was no other piece of furniture, and the dark, oak-panelled walls were bare.

I paused irresolute, and then called loudly, but there was no answer. The shut doors stared at me on each side, as though mocking at my intrusion.

With sudden impatience I opened the door on my right at random. A large room faced me, evidently a library or study, for there were book-cases against the walls, half hiding the beautiful linenfold panelling, and between the long windows was a magnificent old fireplace, with dog-irons and a fine wrought iron fireback.

Before this fireplace stood a shabby, old-fashioned sofa, and the place smelt strongly of cigar smoke and spirits.

I was going to beat a retreat, when a head popped up over the back of the sofa, and a husky voice greeted me:

"Who the devil's that?"

In spite of all that I had heard, it was a shock to me. It was Darent without any doubt, but I was not prepared for such a change in him. His eyes were bloodshot, his hair tangled, and his face unshaven. He wore a threadbare old dressing-gown, and had no collar or tie.

"Hallo, Kenneth," I said as cheerfully as I could. "You asked me down, and I've come."

"The deuce I did.' He passed his hand over his forehead. "If I did, I suppose I did."

He stumbled towards me and held out a shaking hand.

"How are you?" He seemed to be trying to remember. "Damn it, man, you're Tracey, of course! What the hell are you doing here? I forgot—you say I asked you: I must have been sober at the time."

He gave a cackling, mirthless laugh, and shambled to a table, where a tantalus, siphon, and glasses were set out.

"Have a drink?" He fumbled with the bottles. "Curse that fellow John—there's not a drop left."

He went out into the hall and I heard him shouting for 'John,' and presently an old man in shirt-sleeves hurried in, carrying a bottle of whisky, and filled the tantalus bottle carefully. Then he saw me standing by the window and gave a start.

"Beg pardon, sir; I didn't know that any one was here."

"Mr. Tracey has come to visit me, and is staying—if he wants to after he's seen us. Tell Mary he'll take my room; it's the only respectable one in the house. She can put on some clean sheets if she can find any and get it ready. And we shall want dinner."

"Dinner, sir?" The old man seemed embarrassed.

"Yes—dinner. Didn't I say so?"

"Yes, sir; very good, sir." He went out quickly, as though glad to escape. Darent poured out about half a glass of whisky and handed it to me, then filled up his glass, and emptied it without the formality of adding soda-water.

"That's better. Do you know, Tracey, I can't imagine how the servants stay on—I have dismissed them time and again, but they won't go. Martin—that's the old fellow who came in—and his wife, and Mary, their daughter, were born on the estate, but goodness knows when they had any pay last—must be years ago. But you're not drinking."

A look of positive horror came to his face. "Don't tell me you are a teetotaller!"

I hastened to reassure him, though the strength of the fiery spirit, even diluted to the brim with soda-water, nearly choked me.

"It's a strange thing, Tracey, this loyalty to a family; you don't find it nowadays. By the way, didn't you bring any luggage?"

"I left my car and suit-case at the Crown—can I use your phone?" I had seen it standing on a side table.

"If you can, you'll be cleverer than I am; it's been cut off long ago. The insolent dog wanted payment, and now they are after me for tithes!"

"I'll go and fetch the car then." I wanted to get away from him, and from this house. I felt like running out of the front door and up the hill to the clean village inn.

"I'll come with you; I'd like a walk."

He seized a walking-stick, a great cudgel of holly with the root trimmed for a handle that he had cut in the woods.

In the hall Mary, a typical country girl, perhaps eighteen years old, strong, and with a tangle of red hair, was standing with Darent's coat and waistcoat. She wore a cotton frock which from her appearance was practically her only garment, and her feet and legs were bare.

Washed and properly dressed, she might have been passably good-looking.

"You are getting my room ready for Mr. Tracey?" he said, struggling into the coat.

I strolled to the door, feeling awkward before these domestic discussions.

"Then you must take my room, sir. It's the only other, and I can manage with a mattress on the kitchen floor."

"I'm damned if I do—I can doss on the sofa in the library—it won't be the first time."

"Anything will do for me," I ventured to say, but Darent turned on me.

"Shut up; it's not your house. If it's not good enough for you, go and sleep at the Crown."

He came after me, and started up the hill with great, easy strides, and I marvelled at the man who had been brought home drunk that morning. I could not keep pace with him, but followed him to the top of the hill, where he waited for me with an obvious contempt for my powers of walking. He pointed back to the Hall, a soft look on his face, and his harsh features relaxed.

"If I had to sell the Hall, or they took it from me, I should put a bullet into my head."

"I quite understand your feelings."

"I wrote to you, and you never came." There was a bitterness in his voice that I was at a loss to understand, but the meaning was to be only too clear, tragically clear, before very long.

"I didn't know it was urgent," I stammered. "I would have come at once."

"Never mind; I didn't expect you would." He suddenly swung round and pointed to the vast, red-brick house on the crest of the hill. The western sun was reflected from its rows of windows like fiery eyes.

"That swine Barton," he said, shaking his murderous-looking stick at the house, "has tried every dirty trick he could to buy up the mortgage on my estate, and now he's done it. Only to-day that damned lawyer was flaunting it in my face."

"Turnbull? I threw him into the road if that's any consolation," I said, smiling at the recollection.

"I'm glad you did, Tracey, but it was a dangerous thing to do—that spiteful little toad will get his own back on you."

He walked moodily on, muttering to himself, till we entered the main road. A car was coming along at a cracking speed, and I just had time to see my friend the rector inside with a swarthy-faced, stoutish man with a black moustache as they went by. Darent stopped dead, and swore violently. I looked at his face in surprise. He had gone a sickly purplish colour, and his eyes had become mere pin-points. His teeth were showing between his lips—his face was the face of a devil. And then he broke into a laugh so hideous that I felt a spasm of fear.

"That's Barton—Sir John Barton, Baronet, who's going to get married to-morrow—a fine match. . . Drink, Dennis—come on. Let's drink to their happiness."

We walked on in silence to the Crown, and I repented too late that I had ever come to this village.

CHAPTER III

THE TRAGEDY AT THE TOWERS

DARENT went to the back of the inn, and pushed open a door. A short passage led into the lounge and common bar, but on our left was a cool, airy sitting-room which Darent entered without ceremony.

A pleasant-faced woman was sitting by the empty fireplace, knitting, and the landlord was smoking in his shirt-sleeves, while my friend Polly was clearing away the tea things. The inn was not yet open, and the Willises were enjoying a few minutes' peace.

"Don't get up, please," Darent said, as Willis was about to rise from his chair.

From some queer twist in his mind, Darent was as invariably courteous to those beneath him in the social scale as he was rude to those of his own standing.

"Hello, Polly, busy as ever—Mr. Tracey has come for his car, but we are both thirsty, and I think a little whisky would do us good."

I saw a look of pity on Mrs. Willis's motherly face. "Let me get you some tea, Mr. Darent, we've only just finished ours."

Darent walked across the room, and sat down on the arm of her chair, placing his hand playfully on her shoulder.

"My dear Christian lady, don't you know that tea is rank poison? It contains two deadly drugs—tannin and caffeine, they are called. They are much worse than morphia, and the effect is to drive people mad, like those old cats who meet at the rectory to talk scandal and drink tea—quantities of it. Fact! It makes them stark staring mad. We were all healthier and better in the old days when we all drank good English ale: this tea makes sneaking, lying, scheming beasts, like the rector's wife."

"Oh, Mr. Darent, you do say such things," Mrs. Willis said with a laugh in which there was more sadness than mirth.

Willis set a bottle and two glasses on the table, and Polly disappeared with her tray. There was comfort and quiet happiness in this room: geraniums were set in the window, through which the country air blew freely. On the opposite side of the road the simple village shops were situated, for no 'multiple stores' had come to the village. The bus for Wickstead was waiting outside the grocer post office, and as I watched, three cars passed in rapid succession, heading for the Towers. Mrs. Willis saw them, and remarked: "There'll be a grand show up there to-night: they do say there's a band from London coming, and a troupe of singers."

Darent picked up his glass. "Here's luck to them! I'll give that parson a text for his sermon next Sunday—'Cast not pearls before swine'—pearls before swine." He drank off his whisky neat, and his face became suffused with blood. "I'd sooner kill him with my own hands than let him marry her."

"Oh, hush, Mr. Darent, please—someone may hear." She glanced apprehensively at the open window.

"I don't care who hears me." His voice rose in anger. "It's that damned mother of hers; just to have her called Lady Barton—she's been trying for that ever since poor Elsie Barton died."

"I wish you wouldn't say such things, Mr. Darent," Mrs. Willis said coaxingly.

"I would never disobey an order from you, dear lady." He patted her on the back as though she were a wilful child. "Come on, Dennis, my boy—it's time we were trekking."

"I'm ready," I said, trying wildly to think of any excuse to stop me from going back to the Hall.

The whole family came to see us off, a little worried and nervous, I thought. Two more cars rushed by, and Darent scowled at them as he took his seat beside me. The afternoon was perfect, and the sunlight through the leaves made a chequer-work of gold on the gravel, as we issued from the shade into the main road and went after the cars, which Darent had directed me to follow.

The hump of the downs hid the Hall, but on each side of the ridge was a glorious view over the wooded valleys to the hills beyond, which rose in tumbled heaps, misty and fairylike in the thin blue haze that had come up with the evening after the heat of the day.

The west was a glory of gold and crimson, with pale bars of greenish blue, transforming the vales and hills into such a picture as must have greeted the Pilgrims when they stood on the Delectable Mountains and saw the land of Beulah.

An exclamation of disgust from Darent broke my vision. On our left was a large, comfortable white house, with a well-kept garden and carriage drive.

"The rectory—the home of scandal and gossip," he said bitterly.

A few hundred yards farther on and we drove into the tunnel beneath the tall trees, their leafy arms thrust out as though in warning.

A red-brick wall six or more feet in height appeared on the right, with square supporting pillars at regular intervals, on which were set balls of stone. And then the wall receded inwards, disclosing a pair of massive iron gates, above which was displayed a newly painted coat of arms in red and gold. I caught a glimpse as we passed of a winding gravel drive, on both sides of which were formal beds of red geraniums, and a huge porch at which stood a flunkey in gorgeous livery.

"The dwelling of the hog," Darent said between his teeth. We turned to the left, following the high wall, and down a narrow road little better than a cart track, through a five-barred gate and past some farm buildings to the Hall. The farm showed the same marks of neglect as the Hall itself; part of a cow-shed had fallen in, and a large barn was in a state of decay. Darent was silent and moody, and left me abruptly in the hall, while I was guided by Mary to a rough shed that served as a garage. The girl was evidently sulky because her master had been turned out of his room for a visitor, but showed me to the room, and fetched hot water. She opened my bag and laid out my dress clothes, which rather astonished me, as I had no idea that Darent dressed for dinner.

The room faced south-west, towards the valley, for the Hall was built on the side of a hill, and below me I saw a stream marked by the trees that grew along its banks, and a small lake, red like blood in the light from the dying sun. The garden presented the same aspect of neglect and decay as the rest of the estate, and was a desolation of weeds and stunted bushes.

The room itself was clean and well furnished, but I gathered from Mary that not another room, except those used by the Martins, was fit for occupation, and there had not been a guest at the place for years.

Having settled in my mind to depart the next day at all costs, I made my way down the broad staircase, and saw Darent waiting in the hall. I thought I had had surprises enough for one day, and was unprepared for what I saw.

Darent had shaved and brushed his hair, and his evening clothes fitted him perfectly: he looked ten years younger, and even his manner seemed to have changed with his dress.

He had become the courteous, urbane host.

John announced that dinner was served. He also was wearing an old dress suit, shabby but clean, and looked more like a family butler than he had done in his shirtsleeves.

We entered the dining-room, a spacious place with three windows facing the garden and lake at the back. The table would have seated twenty people or more, but two places were laid at the head, with old lace doilies on the oak. But the most astonishing sight in this bizarre scene was a long strip of crimson velvet laid down the centre of the table, on which were displayed beautiful old pieces of silver plate, and the table appointments would have done justice to a ducal palace. It was a strange problem—Darent obviously deep in debt, the whole estate going to rack and ruin, and only one bedroom fit for occupation, and yet he dressed for dinner, and possessed magnificent silver, and, as I was to find out, a cellar stocked with choice wines.

"You are wondering, Tracey," he said, reading my thoughts, "that a drunken beggar can still keep a gentleman's table. When my cellar is empty, and the Jews come for my plate, I shall set fire to the Hall and shoot myself." He spoke in the smooth, polished tones of an educated gentleman, without a trace of excitement. "It has been in my family for four hundred years, and no one else shall have it."

The old butler placed before us some delicious vegetable soup, a rather tough chicken, with vegetables from the garden, and stewed fruit, and I suspected that the whole household lived on the produce of the estate. Old John served the dinner with the same care as he would have taken with a seven-course affair.

"John, uncork the Bollinger," Darent said, and the wine sparkled in our glasses. Kenneth drank delicately, like a connoisseur, but of two bottles at least one and a half had gone down his throat before John set dessert, and placed a cut-glass decanter of port before his master, as though handling a baby at a baptism, and withdrew.

"I brought some rather good cigars with me," I said thoughtlessly.

"If you prefer to smoke your own, you are welcome. Are you sure you did not bring your food as well?"

I apologized at once—touch him on the subject of his poverty and his feathers were up like an angry peacock.

"Cigars and coffee will be in the library when we have drunk our port—you should know that, having been an officer."

I raised my glass. "Here's luck, anyway, Kenneth."

"Luck! Ye gods—" He said no more, but I looked anxiously at his face—the man was suffering dreadfully, and holding himself in with an effort of will. He had half emptied the decanter, and his hands were closing and unclosing.

"Drink, man—drink! What does old Omar say?"

" *'Drink, for once dead you never shall return.'* "

I watched him narrowly, for he was in a dangerous mood. If the control snapped, he was capable of anything. In the library I tried to talk of old times, and to get him interested, but although I could see that he made an effort, his mind was wandering. His answers became monosyllables, sometimes quite irrelevant. It became hopeless after a time, and I gave it up, watching for some fearful thing, I knew not what, to happen.

He paid frequent visits to the brandy decanter, declaring that, like all good drinkers, he never took whisky after champagne. Then he began to mutter to himself, still pacing the floor like a panther in its cage.

"The dirty, low-down dog . . . isn't it enough that he's ruined the country with his house, and ruined me by buying up the mortgage, but he must set his beery eyes on Margorie? . . . What right has he to a thoroughbred? . . . House gone—Margorie gone . . . it's time to make an end."

I took him by the shoulders—his restless pacing was driving me mad. "It's no good going on like this, Kenneth. Tell me what you wanted me for—perhaps even now it's not too late."

His laughter was like the croak of a monstrous bullfrog.

"You must have guessed unless you are a bigger fool than I took you for. I knew you were a bachelor, with a fair amount of money, and no ties. I wasn't trying to sponge on you—don't imagine that—but I thought you might have bought up the mortgage on this estate, as fine an investment as you could wish for. . . . Now Barton's got it. . . . What the hell does it matter? . . . What does anything matter?"

He stopped suddenly—the perspiration was standing on his forehead—the man was in hell fire.

He suddenly pulled himself up, and laid a hand on my arm, and his voice changed. "Dennis—she's the best little girl in the world; there's never been another like her. . . . I remember her as a schoolgirl, like a fairy child: she used to come here and I taught her to ride, though she didn't want much teaching. It's rape, I tell you—nothing less. They are celebrating in his pigsty, the night before the wedding, and her mother, damn her, smiling and smirking—I can see her: "You know, dear, Margorie is *so* happy"—and that swine swilling away with other hogs like him, birds of a feather. The Towers—did you ever hear such a name?—the Brewery, I call it. I'll stop it somehow if I have to kill the brute."

I was thoroughly alarmed; he was working himself up into a frenzy.

"For goodness' sake sit down, and try to forget it—you can't help it now."

It was about the worst thing I could have said. "Forget it, you fool! You were always a soft easy-going sort of ass, of the 'take-it-lying-down' type. What do you know about life, anyway? Everything's gone well with you—plenty of money, popular, good-looking fellow— you've never faced a crisis—what do you know of love—?" He broke off suddenly and seized his glass. Every word stung me like a whip: it was all true. Here was a smug, contented man, lazy and with no object in life, up against a raw, ghastly tragedy—the tragedy of a proud, sensitive nature faced with the loss of his estate and the girl he loved, and sinking lower and lower, hiding his self-contempt under a show of surliness and drinking to drown his loneliness and grief.

"I can't stand it any longer—I'm going to the Towers."

"For God's sake don't play the fool—what good can you do? There will only be a scene, and he'll get his servants to throw you out."

"Throw me out," he snarled. "No, Dennis Tracey, I don't think they will do that."

He turned without another word, brushing me on one side, and strode out of the room, I ran after him into the hall, where it was dark, and called him, but I could only hear the creak of his footsteps as he went up the stairs.

I opened the door to the servants' quarters and shouted for John, and the old man hurried in with a lamp, which he set on the table, thinking that that was what I wanted.

"Mr. Darent is going to the Towers; we must stop him somehow," I said wildly.

Old John saw to the trimming of the lamp, and then looked at me with an expression of stony contempt.

"I shouldn't interfere with the master, sir. I expect he knows his own business."

Darent came down the stairs without hat or coat, and for a moment I wondered for what purpose he had gone—then I guessed.

"Won't you let me come with you?" I cried desperately.

"I don't want you mixed up with my affairs, thank you. John, don't wait up for me; I may be late."

He went to the open front door, and I sprang after him. "You are not armed?"

Involuntarily his hand went to his hip pocket, under his dress coat. "What's that got to do with you. Go to bed, baby. John, take care of him."

Even then I tried to follow him. I ran up for a light overcoat, as the nights were chilly, but I had not got more than a dozen yards from the door when I saw a bulky figure in the gloom, and by the light of my cigar I made out the stalwart form of Jilkes, the bailiff, whom I had met in the afternoon.

"Good evening, Jilkes," I said casually, and tried to pass him.

"Beg pardon, zur, but maister said as 'ow you was not to follow un."

"I suppose I can go for a walk if I like!" I retorted angrily.

"I'll come with 'ee, zur; there be them poachers about, most times."

This was more than I could stand, to be led about like a dancing bear. I turned back, feeling an arrant fool, but I was certain I couldn't shake him off, and these loyal servants could not be bribed. John was waiting in the hall, respectful but alert. "Will you be wanting anything, sir?"

"Nothing—you can go to bed—leave that lamp burning."

I had half a mind to fetch my car and go to the Towers, or even back to London, but a feeling of pity for Kenneth and loyalty to an old brother officer compelled me to stay.

I returned to the library, and tried to interest myself in Darent's books, for bed was out of the question. I picked up first one and then another, and fretfully replaced them. My ears were strained to catch the least sound, though common sense told me that he could not have got half-way by now. I could picture that grim figure, hatless and coatless, striding up the hill, and across the dark meadows, with death in his heart and a loaded pistol in his pocket. Peering about among the books I came across a Bible, on the fly-leaf of which, in faded writing, was the inscription: 'Kenneth, on his sixth birthday, from Mother.' In my feverish mood anything was a welcome relief from thinking. I recalled an old custom in which the good people of a century ago used to believe firmly.

They would open a Bible at random and put their finger on a text 'to seek guidance.'

I opened the book, laughing at myself in an hysterical manner, and, shutting my eyes, placed my index finger on the page.

It was the book of Esther, and the words were: 'Who knoweth whether thou art come to the kingdom for such a time as this.' The words seemed to stare at me and impatiently I closed the book and replaced it in the shelf. I was angry with myself for the trick— the quotation seemed ominously apt to the situation. Had I come when he had written, I might at any rate have saved his estate, and lessened his anxiety, but it was too late to think of that now. My fears grew as this bitter vigil passed slowly. A sense of dread, and of expectation—the hardest thing to bear—held me in its grip. The house was very still, not a breath stirred, though the windows were standing open. I felt I must have air, and went to the huge front door, still widely opened, as though waiting for the master to return. The lamp burnt steadily on the table, throwing its beams on the dark, tangled garden outside. The grandfather clock in the library behind me ticked noisily, and even as I stood there it struck the hour of midnight.

Midnight! He had been gone over an hour. The servants had all gone to bed—evidently they did not share my alarm. The night was pitchy black, without moon or stars, and I could feel the perspiration trickling down my back. I felt that I must do something, and returning to the library, helped myself to a stiff brandy. I was bending over the siphon, when a slight noise made me turn quickly. Darent was standing in the doorway, very white in the face, and the drink seemed to have been knocked right out of him. My heart missed a beat when I saw blood on his right hand and on the cuff of his shirt.

"What is it?" The words hardly seemed to be my own. I put the glass to my lips and heard it click against my teeth in the frozen silence.

Darent made no answer, but came forward to the table, limping slightly, and helped himself to brandy.

"That's better," he said coolly, and proceeded to light a cigar with a steady hand.

"Dennis," he said quietly, "you were sent down here for a purpose. Don't misunderstand me—I don't mean any religious slop—but Fate."

"Tell me what happened." I seized his arm and shook him in a frenzy of foreboding.

"Steady, Dennis; don't lose your nerve—you will want it all before we've finished. Happened? I'd give a lot to know."

"Barton?" I gasped.

"John Barton has been murdered."

CHAPTER IV

THE ALIBI

I SUPPOSE his words did not come to me as a surprise, for I had guessed from the moment that he had entered the room that such a tragedy had taken place. For a moment my mind was a blank—as Darent had taunted me, I had never really faced life.

He was speaking in a hard, dry voice.

"Don't make a mistake, Dennis. If I had murdered Barton, which of course you think I did, I should have said so at once, and would have been proud of it, but our difficulty lies in the fact that I did not."

"Thank God for that."

Somehow from the very beginning I never doubted his word. He was quite capable of murder, but not of lying—not to save his life.

"You may think it strange, but I didn't kill him, and I have not the faintest idea who did. If I had done so, I should have put a bullet into my brain, for you don't suppose that I should allow myself to be arrested and hanged." He drew a small automatic from his pocket and flung it on the table. "You see, I haven't even fired a shot."

I left the thing untouched, and he went on

"I went to the Towers, not quite knowing what I was going to do, but I couldn't stay here listening to your boring conversation; it nearly drove me mad. Sorry to hurt your feelings, Dennis, but it did, you know. I suppose I was nearly drunk; anyhow, when I got into the grounds I saw the whole place lighted up, and a jazz-band was making an infernal noise. The windows were open, and I saw Margorie dancing. I had an insane idea of going straight in and taking her from under the very nose of the brewer, but these things can't be done nowadays, and I don't suppose Margorie—" He stopped suddenly, and poured out another drink. I saw that at this rate he would soon be incapable of movement.

"What happened?"

"There was no sign of Barton, and I expected he had gone into the smoking-room with some of his companions for a drink. I was walking across the lawn to get a glimpse inside, when I stumbled over something. I thought it was a raised flower-bed—it was very dark in contrast with the brightly lighted house—but when I put my hand down to feel—"

He showed his hand and cuff covered with dried blood.

"It was the body of a man in evening dress, with his head smashed in. I had only my cigarette-lighter, but with that I examined the body. It was Barton, all right, and by the look of things someone had hit him pretty savagely."

My mind was dumb with sheer horror at the calm, deliberate way in which Darent told the story. He was searching my face for any trace of doubt; I could feel that.

"I came away—I could hardly go to the house and raise the alarm with blood on my hands and a loaded pistol in my pocket; and every one knew how cordial our relationship had been!

"The evidence would have been damning against me. Every one knows of the threats I have uttered against this man—you heard this afternoon at the Crown Inn. Now you may have noticed that I have a strong sense of family pride, and I am certainly not going to the gallows for a crime I never committed."

"What are you going to do—get away?"

He laughed scornfully. "Do you think I'm going to play the fox in a man-hunt, chased by police and civilians, like a gangster? No, Dennis; I'm going to bed."

"But the police may come here—they may suspect you."

"If they do, I shall say nothing—it's no business of mine." He drained his third glass of neat brandy, and his head sank back on the chair. He had fallen fast asleep.

I dragged him to the sofa and laid him there, my mind in a whirl.

The fool—of course they would suspect him, and probably come to the Hall, and find him like this. I felt I must do something, and there grew in my mind that monstrous imprudence that was to involve us all.

If Darent was innocent, and I firmly believed him to be so, then his fatal visit to the Towers must be concealed by some means.

My blood went cold at the thought of the risk we were taking, for the servants would have to be brought into this, but it seemed the only way out. After all, I might be unduly alarmed. The police might find the murderer, and vague threats were not enough to convict.

I stood undecided, wavering as to what was best to be done. His stinging words to me still galled me, and here was a chance to show that I was not quite the soft fool he thought me.

I don't know to this day how I should have decided, but a slight sound came from the hall, and I heard the old butler calling me softly from the first story. I went into the hall, and saw him leaning over the gallery railings in a shirt and trousers, with a scared face.

"Has the master come back?" he asked in tremulous tones.

I saw through the crack of their door the face of Mrs. Martin, holding a lighted candle.

"Put on some clothes and come down to the kitchen at once—both of you."

I had no mind to discuss matters with that drunken man snoring loudly on the sofa.

The servants all slept on the first floor, as Darent had explained to me that he didn't believe in putting old and trusted servants in leaky attics, and I saw Mary's room door open, with a candle burning ready for Darent.

I went along to the kitchen, where a fire of logs was still smouldering in the huge old fireplace, carrying the lamp from the hall with me. I was setting it on the table, when I became aware that a mattress had been placed on the floor, on which Mary was sleeping. The light woke her, and the girl started up to her feet in a moment, clad in a cotton nightgown.

"Has anything happened to Mr. Darent?" she asked. John and his wife hurried in, having donned a few clothes.

"Listen carefully," I said. Somehow a cold, decisive feeling had come over me, and I felt that everything rested on my orders, and that I must direct. They were all watching me, silent and waiting.

"Mr. Darent went to the Towers, and there he found Sir John Barton dead in the garden—he had been murdered. Mr. Darent had nothing to do with it at all—you understand that?"

I felt as though I was talking to children; teaching them a lesson that had to be learnt by heart.

"Why, of course he didn't," Mary said confidently.

"But, you see, he may be suspected: you know how he has talked about Barton—and the police may come here and make inquiries. We must have an alibi ready—you know what that is?"

"Why, yes, sir," said doubtfully.

"What it means is this. All of us must swear that he never left the house during the whole evening."

"That's easy enough," Mary said with unmistakable relief.

"Of course we will," Mrs. Martin chimed in. "We'd do anything for the master."

I was taken aback by the staunch loyalty of these servants. I was quite certain that they did not believe my story, that they thought Darent had killed Barton, and yet they never hesitated for a moment.

It made me ashamed of my own vacillation.

"You tell us what to do, sir, and we'll do it right enough."

"Very well then. Mr. Darent is lying on the sofa, quite drunk. You and I, John, must undress him, and get him to bed."

A faint smile crossed the face of the old butler, as though there was nothing new in this suggestion.

"We must say that he was so drunk that he couldn't even stand, so he couldn't have gone out. Wait a moment, though—"

I saw that matters were not going to be so easy as all that. "His dress clothes—I forgot—he's got blood on his sleeve and cuff, and his pumps must be wringing wet with dew. Mary, you must burn the shirt and hide the clothes—there's no time to clean them now, and hide his pumps till they are dry. We must all say that Mr. Darent and I did not dress for dinner—do you understand that?"

We all moved rapidly and silently. Mary fetched Darent's pyjamas from her room, and John and I took off his clothes—he might have been a block of wood for all the signs of life he gave.

Mary took his clothes and fetched a basin of water with which we carefully washed the blood from his hand and wrist. Then we carried him to bed, Mrs. Martin following us up with the lamp from the hall. I placed the guttering candle by his side, and quietly closed his door. John shut and bolted the front door, and we stood breathless in the hall. I glanced round to see whether there was anything we had forgotten. Mary was going to burn the shirt, and John was going to slip round to the bailiff's cottage to tell Jilkes, who we all knew would fall in with any plans we made. At last everything was done, and we separated to our rooms for what rest we could get.

I peeped into the room where Darent was sleeping, and heard him snoring loudly, and then went to my own room, and sat down on the bed to think things out. I had read that criminals are supposed to leave some small item omitted, and get themselves hanged in consequence, and the thought was not pleasant. Had we left a loop-hole anywhere? I took off my dress clothes and carefully packed them away in my suit-case, as it must not appear that I had put them on. The enormity of the offence of perjury came vividly to my mind. Suppose we were bowled out? Then a moment of confidence returned. After all, why should the police come here at all, when there would be investigations to be made after the finding of the body?

If they came to-morrow, it might be more difficult for us, as Darent would presumably have slept off his drunken bout. I had hardly slipped into bed when out of the stillness of the night I heard the ominous sound of a car. I waited, scarcely daring to breathe, and then there came a crashing knock on the front door, followed by a succession of blows. Panic seized me—'that terrible, trivial knocking' in *Macbeth*. My first thought was to rush downstairs, but I saw the folly of such a course, and instead crept to the window and looked cautiously out. The night was very dark, but I could make out the flash of a bull's-eye lantern searching out the lower windows, and the dim figure of someone who held it.

By this time I heard noises from the hall, and slipped on my dressing-gown. There was a light in the hall, and old John called out to know who was there.

"Police officers—open the door!"

John was fumbling with the bolts as I descended the stairs, and Mrs. Martin was peering over the gallery. The door opened, and an inspector in uniform came in, followed by a constable.

The former was a stocky man about forty years old, as I judged, with a reddish moustache and a not-overintelligent face. He glanced rapidly round the hall, and addressed John.

"I wish to see Mr. Darent—where is he?"

"Why, in bed, sir, and has been this many hour," John said innocently.

"Humph! We'll see about that."

I felt it was time that I took a hand, and advanced into the hall.

"What's all this, John?" I said with an assumption of swagger I was far from feeling.

"Who is this?" the inspector asked sharply.

"Since you have come into this house, and at this time of night, inspector, I think I am entitled to some explanation of your business. My name is Tracey, and I am staying with my old friend Mr. Darent!"

"I'm Inspector Watson from Wickstead," he answered gruffly. "I may want to question you afterwards; at present my business is with Mr. Darent. Which is his room?"

"He's fast asleep, or he would have come out, but there is a good reason for that, eh, John?" I laughed as brightly as I was able, and John grinned in answer.

The inspector's eyes narrowed. "Never mind that now—I am going to see him."

"One moment," I said. "There is not the slightest reason why you should not see him if you wish to, but we are surely entitled to know a little more about this visit—please remember that Mr. Darent is a county magistrate, and some respect is due to him."

The shot went home—he glanced at the constable, who had stood rigidly by the door.

"I wish to interrogate him with regard to the murder of Sir John Barton."

Well, I am no actor, and I expect I should have betrayed myself right away by saying the wrong thing or exaggerating my surprise. I felt myself turning red, but a timely diversion occurred. Mary, whom no one had noticed rushed at the inspector. "What's that you say? Sir John Barton murdered. What an awful thing! When—"

The inspector patted her not unkindly.

"There's no need to get excited, my girl; I should go and get some clothes on if I were you, or better still go to bed."

He turned to me. "He was found on the lawn outside the Towers with his head battered in, and there are grave suspicions that this is the work of Mr. Darent. It's strange he doesn't come out of his room." He took a step towards the staircase.

"If you had seen him last night, you wouldn't think it strange, inspector. John and I had to carry him to bed. Drunk! I've seen drunken men, but he was speechless —couldn't even walk, could he, John?"

"He was pretty bad, sir; we had a job to get him up between us."

The inspector looked keenly at each of us in turn. "What time was this?"

"About eleven o'clock," I said unguardedly, and could have bitten my tongue. I saw the inspector's face clear, and he smiled grimly as he produced a pocket-book and a pencil.

"Eleven o'clock, you say—you are prepared to swear to that?"

There was no help for it now. Why had I not said twelve, or even one? But it was no use prevaricating now.

"About that—I couldn't swear to the exact time."

"And you?" The inspector whipped round to John.

The loyal old fellow, not seeing the danger, backed me up.

"Yes, sir, that was the time. I went in to ask if I could get anything more for the gentlemen, and Mr. Tracey asked me to help him carry the master to bed. He was lying on the sofa fast asleep."

"I see," Inspector Watson said with a grin. "You took him to bed at eleven o'clock—neither of you know whether he went out again!"

I tried to laugh it off. "My dear inspector, he was utterly incapable of standing, far less of going out. If you'd seen him—"

"I didn't ask that: I said neither of you can swear that he didn't dress again and go out. Drunkenness can be assumed, you know!"

Our hastily devised alibi was crumbling to pieces. I had a frantic idea of saying that I had been in to see him, but knew that the inspector would see through me and doubt the whole story. A girl's sob broke the strained silence—we had again forgotten Mary for the moment. She was standing there shivering, and covering her face with her two rough hands, coarsened by hard work.

"I know he didn't go out again," she sobbed.

"You? How do you know? Stop that crying, girl!" the Inspector said brutally.

"He—came into my bedroom—he—he's there now, in my bed."

Mary had told nothing but the literal truth—he was in her room—but her quick brain had grasped the only means of clinching our shaken alibi. At the expense of her reputation she would save him.

"Are you telling the truth, girl?" He took her by the wrist, and twisted her round to face him.

"Yes sir, it's the truth."

"Then why didn't you shout out? Or perhaps you didn't mind?" he sneered.

"He was drunk, sir, or I am sure he wouldn't have come—and I didn't dare move."

He dropped her wrist. "We'll look into this—take me to your room at once."

Mary ascended the stairs, her shoulders heaving with sobs, though whether simulated or due to fright, I do not know. She opened the door and flashed a candle on the sleeping man. His face was a mottled red colour, his lips half open, and he was breathing heavily.

Watson bent down and sniffed at his breath, and then looked round the room keenly. It was obviously a servant's room, though of good size and very neat and clean. He threw open a cupboard, disclosing Mary's poor finery—her Sunday clothes and hat, and a coat. There were a few books on a tiny shelf, which the inspector examined. One was a Sunday-school prize, with the girl's name inside.

Watson went to the bed, and opened the eyes of the sleeper roughly with his thumbs; a muttered curse came from Darent, and he moved his head impatiently. The inspector shook him violently. "Here, wake up!" he shouted in his ear.

"What's matter?" came in thick, guttural accents. Darent's bleary eyes slowly opened, and he looked round in a dazed way. Mary leant forward, searching his face anxiously, for everything hung on his words.

He saw the girl; the rest of us were in partial shadow, as she had purposely held the candle before her face.

"Hello, Mary m'dear," he said thickly, "what'yer doing in my room? You'll catch a cold out of bed." He rolled over as though the problem was too difficult to solve, and fell asleep.

"Wake up, Mr. Darent," the inspector shouted. "I am a police inspector—"

"All ri't; carry on, 'spector—tell the clerk I'll be there i' morning."

"Drunk!" Watson exclaimed. "We shan't get anything out of him till the morning. Smith"—he turned to the constable—"stay here by his bedside and take down anything he says—you understand?"

"Very good, sir!"

He stamped out of the room and down the stairs.

"You'd better go to bed, my girl," he said grimly to Mary as he passed. I followed him, as the saying is, on tenterhooks. I was desperately afraid that he would want to see Darent's own room, and thanked the stars I had not to do with a Scotland Yard expert, who would have driven a horse and cart through our flimsy alibi.

In the hall he paused irresolute.

"I must get back to the Towers at once." He was evidently shaken, though not convinced. He had come expecting Darent either in hiding or gone. To find him sleeping off a drunken bout was unexpected.

"You've had a tiring night, inspector," I said affably. "May I offer you a whisky in the library? I must act as host."

"That's very kind of you, sir," he said in a more conciliatory tone than he had adopted up till then.

"Mr. Darent has finished the whole of the brandy," I said with a laugh, holding up the empty decanter. I poured him out a good stiff whisky, and handed it to him.

"Thank you, sir," he said, drinking it with appreciation. "This case is going to be a puzzle—it'll be a Scotland Yard affair as sure as mabbe. They'll take it out of our hands on account of the parties—Sir John being a baronet and a big man about here, and this happening on his wedding eve, too." He glanced keenly at me, but I had taken his measure, and felt I was a match for him.

"Look here, inspector, let me be quite frank with you. I only came here yesterday, and I haven't seen my friend Darent for five years. It was a great shock to me to find him—well—as you saw to-night, and to see the state of things here. He's hardly been sober since I came, and that is a fact. I have no interest in the matter, and have never met this man Barton in my life to speak to."

"I am glad to hear it, sir," he said genially. "I did hear in the village—but never mind. I'm rather in the same position. They phoned me from Wickstead to come over at once, and I ran over with Smith, whom you saw, and brought the local constable, Jack Oliver, along with me. So I don't know much about the crime yet."

I refilled his glass, pouring in soda-water. "Thank you—I really don't think I want any more, but since you've taken the trouble to pour it out—my best respects."

I waited till he had assimilated the spirit, and then said as casually as I could: "What I don't understand, inspector, is why you suspected Mr. Darent and came down here at once?"

He looked at me queerly. "Well, I suppose there's no harm in telling you, as it will all come out at the inquest. Sir John was killed with Mr. Darcut's walking-stick—there were plenty who identified it."

I could have shouted—I nearly blurted out: "But he never took it with him," and then our alibi would have been blown sky high. I just stopped in time, but a great sense of relief came to me, for Darent had left his stick at the Crown Inn, and had been grumbling about it all the way back. If I could ascertain who took it from the inn, I might solve the problem right away, but I decided to keep my own counsel.

"You see," the inspector went on, becoming more communicative, "those idiots at the party, when they missed Sir John, all rushed out and trampled and stamped like a herd of buffaloes, searching with electric torches. You never saw such a ballyhoo, and to make matters worse, of course, they carried the body into the house when they found him, instead of leaving him when they knew he was dead."

"Who found him?" I asked.

"Mr. Robert Barton, his younger brother—I suppose he knew the place better than the others."

"Well, the sooner you lay your hands on the murderer the better, inspector. It'll be a score for you if you can do it before the Scotland Yard people come along. It should not be beyond your powers."

He seemed pleased with my flattery. "I don't mind telling you, sir, there are other things beside the holly stick that have thrown suspicion upon Mr. Darent. The people up at the Towers seemed to have no doubt about it, and young Mr. Barton told me to come down here straight away, and find out all I could. It is said that he had threatened Sir John and that there was some quarrel between them—at least, I gathered something of that sort from Mr. Turnbull, the lawyer from Wickstead." He looked at me inquiringly, but I merely repeated that I knew nothing, and went towards the door, for to tell the truth I was anxious to get rid of him.

John came in, now fully dressed, and spoke to me. "I took the liberty, sir, of taking some sandwiches and coffee to the officer in Mr. Darent's room, and I asked Oliver, who is of course, a friend of ours, into the kitchen for some beer and bread and cheese. I hope I did right?"

"Quite right, John—I'm sure Mr. Darent would have wished it."

Watson looked uncomfortable—hospitality was all right in its place, but he had come on an unpleasant duty, and was not quite sure whether the authorities would approve of this. I set his mind at rest, telling him that this, like our talk, was strictly private.

We had got him as far as the hall, and John had gone to fetch Oliver from the kitchen, when the inspector turned to me and said rather stiffly: "By the way, Mr. Tracey, I haven't seen Mr. Darent's bedroom yet. I would like just to have a look at that."

Damn the fellow! I thought I had headed him off from that, but hesitation would be fatal.

"Come along, by all means," I said.

I racked my brain as we went up the stairs for some excuse for the presence of my suit-case and clothes in the room.

The door stood open, as I had left it, and I led the way in, carrying the lamp from the hall. One glance was sufficient, and I blessed John and Mary, for I guessed it was their work. John had taken food into Darent's room for Smith, and got Oliver safely in the kitchen to be entertained by Mrs. Martin, while Mary had removed all traces of my occupation from the room, and placed Darent's morning clothes on a chair and his brushes and other things in their places.

"I see," Watson said. "You put him to bed in here, and he must have got up again when you had gone, if that girl is telling the truth. She's either a liar or a pretty bad piece of work."

"Come, inspector; you know what a drunken man is like—there's no accounting for what he will do."

He grunted: "Do you suppose that's the first time?"

I was about to make an indignant denial, when I saw the danger. If we made out that this was a drunken mistake, *made for the first time*, it would sound terribly suspicious. Poor Mary—I was afraid she had not realized what she was saying when she told that heroic lie.

The inspector glanced into Mary's room, and learnt from Smith that Darent had not spoken a word. He collected Oliver in the hall, and went out to his car.

"I shall probably see you later," I called after him cheerily, and returned to the house feeling quite done up.

CHAPTER V

AT THE CROWN INN

I CANNOT account for my actions that night. After a quiet, uneventful life I had been plunged into this grim adventure, on the very first day of my visit, and I felt a sense of being driven along impotent and helpless by some power outside myself.

I thought the matter carefully out, running over the conversation with the inspector, and considering our brazen alibi.

It seemed to me that the crime centred round the holly stick that had been used for the murder, and that if I could find out who took it from the Crown, I should be on the way to discovering the criminal.

At the same time an uneasy suspicion would intrude itself upon my mind that Darent might have gone to the Crown on his way to the Towers, but I tried to banish it from my mind. The constable was safely out of the way in Darent's room, and the house was open to me. There was nothing to keep me here, and then like a flash I saw the course I ought to follow in Darent's interests. The first necessity was for clothes, and I made my way to the kitchen, where the Martins were seated round a crackling fire, for sleep was out of the question for all of us that night.

They were discussing the affair in low tones, very scared, but determined to see it through.

I accepted, with gratitude, a cup of hot coffee from Mrs. Martin.

"I am going to the Crown Inn," I said, and saw a look almost of contempt on Mary's face. "Let me explain—I'm not running away, but our best chance is to find out who took that stick of Mr. Darent's from the inn. Perhaps you don't know that Sir John Barton was killed with Mr. Darent's holly stick—and I know for a fact that he left it at the Crown in the afternoon."

"Oh, Lord, sir!" Mrs. Martin exclaimed.

"That's a good job, sir," old John said, looking at me intently, "but do you think he went and fetched it? He'd had a drop, and perhaps he didn't rightly know."

"That's what I'm going to find out," I said peevishly, for his suspicions were perilously like my own. "I can be of far more use to Mr. Darent if I am not here. Now listen carefully, because what I am going to say you will probably have to tell the inspector, and you must, of course, let Mr. Darent into the secret. I came here yesterday, as you all know. I hadn't seen my friend for five years, and was disgusted at the change in him and with the Hall and the accommodation."

"I'm sorry, sir—" John began.

"Don't be foolish, dad," Mary interrupted. "This is what Mr. Tracey wants us to say—not what he really thinks."

I nodded to the girl. "That's right. Now follow me —Mr. Darent got very drunk and abusive to me, and he got angry with me because I suggested dressing for dinner—don't forget that—and you know the rest. We put him to bed in his own room, mind. Then I asked you where I was sleeping, and you showed me a dirty old room that hadn't been occupied for years—damp and musty. You'll have to get one ready when I've gone. And then the police came and there was all this fuss, and I said I was sick and tired of the place and of Mr. Darent and wouldn't stay another hour, and went off to the inn."

"What good will that do?" Mary asked, staring hard at me. She evidently thought I wanted to slip off to London and get out of the whole business.

"I'll tell you, Mary. If I stay on here as a friend of Mr. Darent's, they might suspect that we had put our heads together and made up this plot to screen him, but if I go off in a temper and angry with him and his treatment of me, they are much more likely to believe my story. I shall not desert you or leave you in the lurch—you may rely absolutely on me. I shall keep you informed, and find out all I can, but I can do no good here. Now is that quite clear?"

"I think you are acting as a friend to the master, sir," John observed, "and I only hope you won't get into any trouble over it."

I hoped so too, but was not sure by any means and I departed into the scullery to dress, Mary having fetched my bag from some secret hiding-place. I did not trouble about shaving—it would look more natural not to have stayed for that—but had a sluice under the scullery tap, and hurried into my clothes.

I left the Martins standing rather forlorn at the door, but reassured as to my fidelity, and reinforced with some money that I insisted on them taking, telling them I would get it back from Darent.

If only he did not blurt out something before he could collect his thoughts after his drunken sleep, we might be able to cover things up till the real murderer was found.

The Towers was brightly lighted, and as I passed I saw figures moving about within, throwing their shadows on the blinds. A constable stood at the gate, a reminder of the gruesome tragedy that had taken place on the lawn.

I had expected to find the inn in complete darkness, but lights were showing behind the curtains, and several cars were standing in front of the door. Remembering that the front door opened straight into the bar-parlour, I took the car round to the back, and walked to the back door by which Darent and I had entered.

Receiving no answer to my knock, I pushed open the door, and entered the sitting-room, where Mrs. Willis was cutting sandwiches. She looked up quickly, saw me, and dropped her knife.

"Good morning," I said. "I have just motored from the Hall."

"The Hall!" Her voice spoke volumes. She could only stare at me, and then going to the door, shouted for her husband.

Willis came in looking worried, and glared at me as though he had seen a ghost. "Mr. Tracey—you here?" he gasped.

"Why shouldn't I be here? I want a room. There's not one fit to sleep in at the Hall?"

"They are all saying in the parlour that you and Mr. Darent did the murder and have been arrested. Our Polly has just come back from the Towers; she went to watch the dancing."

"What nonsense!" I slapped him on the back. "From what I've seen of your village, it's a hot-bed of gossip. Why, Mr. Darent and I never left the place the whole evening, and I am sure he was far too drunk to move."

"But it was done with his stick," Willis muttered, gazing fearfully at me.

I went to the door and shut it, and faced the two. "That stick was the one Mr. Darent was carrying yesterday when we came here—do you remember?"

"He had it in this very room," Mrs. Willis said excitedly. "He put it down in that corner when he came in."

"Well," I said with as much emphasis as I could put into the words, "he never brought it back to the Hall with him. You haven't seen him since then, I suppose?"

They both shook their heads, and I breathed a sigh of relief.

"He's never been near here—we locked up as usual at ten, sir, and went to bed, and then Jack Oliver roused us up to tell us about the murder."

"How did Polly get in then?"

A smile crossed Mrs. Willis's face. "Our Polly is walking out with Jack, and went with him—he was on duty there. She had a key of her own."

"We must find out who took that stick, but mind, not a word to any one above it."

"I'll ask Polly when I can get hold of her," Willis said. "She's very busy." A clamour from outside confirmed his words. "I must get back to the bar, sir."

Mrs. Willis returned to her sandwich-making, but I heard her murmur: "Poor Mr. Darent." She evidently did not set much store by my story of the stick.

I went down the passage and the three steps that led to the parlour.

The loud buzz of conversation ceased as if by magic as I entered, and every eye was focused on me. If the devil himself had made an entry, he could not have wished for a better reception. I could see Hickmott, with his silly red face struck dumb and his mouth half open, but the rest were strangers, guests from the Towers.

A diversion occurred—Polly entered with a tray full of drinks, and set it down on the sideboard. The homely, familiar action and the clink of the glasses seemed to break some spell—the faces turned away from me and conversation broke out again in subdued tones. The incident had lasted perhaps ten seconds, but left a vivid and ugly impression on my mind. How on earth did they know me, and of what interest could I be to them?

I advanced with what assurance I could muster to a table at which one man was sitting alone, with his back to me, and beckoned Polly, who gave me a glance of recognition, her father having evidently told her of my arrival. I ordered a drink and took my seat with a courteous word to the occupant of the table, who looked up; and I found myself staring into the face of Turnbull —a face black with passion, hardly disguised. I noticed that his right hand was heavily bandaged.

"And so we meet again, young man!" he exclaimed loudly for all to hear. "I hope you are pleased with the work of *your friend* Darent now."

I saw that infinite tact was needed, and to lose my temper would be disastrous. I was here for information, and in this crowded room the less I said the better. I suspected—and found afterwards that I was right—that Turnbull had told the whole company that I had arrived and was coming into the room.

"I owe you an apology," I said suavely; "I hope I did hurt you badly yesterday."

He cast a venomous look at Hickmott who had tittered boldly at my remark.

"Hurt me?" He held up his bandaged hand. "That was your work, and you'll hear more of it later."

For a moment I stared at him. Polly had brought me a drink, and I picked up the glass mechanically, but my mind was not concerned with the room or its occupants.

I saw again the lawyer sprawling on the ground, and his scratched hand. But the hand he had scratched had been the left and the bandaged hand was the right. I would have moved from the table, but I could see that every one in the room was furtively watching us, and listening intently.

"I am very sorry—I hope the damage was not great. I rather fancied it was the other hand, Mr. Turnbull."

"You sprained my wrist," he snarled, but less aggressively.

"I have come here on my way back to London," I said steadily and loudly enough for all to hear. "I have had enough of the Hall to last me for the rest of my life. What a place!"

"I can quite believe that," he said with meaning underlying his words that there was no mistaking.

"I am afraid you still bear me ill-will for what occurred yesterday, Mr. Turnbull, but don't let your feelings carry you too far. You were right, and I was wrong, I'll own to that. It would have been better if I had taken your advice and gone back to London."

The very boldness of the attack took the wind out of his sails, and curious eyes were turned on us: someone had recounted the story of our meeting.

"Five years makes a lot of change in some people," I went on calmly. "The last time I saw Darent was at Charing Cross, and then he was a fine looking man, bronzed and fit. Now he's a physical wreck through drink, and the reason I suppose some of the village gossips know, but I'm sure I don't. He was drunk the whole time I was with him, and the place isn't worth calling a house, so I came away. It was a sad disappointment after expecting to meet a friend."

Turnbull gave all unpleasant laugh. "And so you came away at three o'clock in the morning—you took a long time to make up your mind."

"Look here, Mr. Turnbull," I said, leaning forward, "I've told you this merely because I was unfair to you yesterday, and I felt I owed you an apology, but I'm damned if I'm going to stand any insults from you, so you can take that from me."

The little whiff of temper cleared the atmosphere.

"I suppose you know that Sir John Barton was murdered to-night at the Towers?" he said slowly. I could see that he was setting a trap for me.

"Of course I know—these people would not be here otherwise. It's common knowledge that he was found dead, but was it murder?"

"Aye—it was black murder true enough," Hickmott interjected. All eyes turned to the farmer, as though in relief from the duel of words between me and the lawyer.

"And no one knows that better than you do, Mr. Tracey," Turnbull exclaimed, glaring as me. I rose to my feet, and saw a look of fear spring up to his face.

A man walked across the room, dressed in a neat blue suit, and with an air of authority about him. He was past middle age, but erect and with a finely chiselled face, and grey hair.

"You will excuse me," he said in a clear incisive voice. "I could not help overhearing your conversation—I suppose every one in the room did the same. My name is Peters and every one here knows me, I think. In my opinion there has been far too much wild talk going on in this room to-night, and your name has been freely bandied about, behind your back, which is unfair." He glanced severely at Turnbull. "It's a pity these things are not left to the proper authorities, the police; they can get all the evidence they require by legitimate means."

I was not quite certain whether to be glad or annoyed by his interruption. His voice had a tone of command that I hardly liked, but what he said was fair enough, and somehow his face was familiar to me, though for the moment I could not place him.

"I entirely agree with you, Mr. Peters. When I drove up here, I had no idea that I should find a soul in the place. I merely wished for a bed."

"Then perhaps," he said with a singularly disarming smile, "you will join me at my table, as I would like a word with you, if I may."

He turned sharply to the lawyer. "Turnbull, in your position, I am surprised at your conduct. I shall not forget it."

To my astonishment Turnbull seemed to shrink into himself, and mumbled some sort of apology.

I followed Peters to a small table in the corner of the room, and general conversation broke out, as though the tension had been relaxed.

"You may have heard my name before," he said when we were seated. "I am a barrister by profession, and I used to know your father—Sir James, the Indian judge—he was, I may say, a very great friend of mine."

Light dawned on me: of course he was the celebrated K.C., and I had heard his name when quite young from my father.

I had left my drink practically untouched on Turnbull's table, and Peters summoned Polly, and ordered a fresh one for me, and coffee for himself.

"I hope you did not resent my intrusion," he went on. "Your name as I told you has been freely mentioned here, as being in some way connected with the murder."

"So I gathered," I said dryly. "I am delighted to meet an old friend of my father's, and if I may say so, such a distinguished barrister."

I have often noticed that the more distinguished a man or woman may be, the more amenable they are to flattery, and Peters was no exception.

"I ought to explain my position here," he said in a friendly manner. "Every one in the village, of course, knows, but you are a stranger. Sir John Barton married my daughter Elsie. She died three years ago."

I murmured my sympathy.

"No doubt you will wonder why in that case I, of all people, should come to his second wedding, but I must tell you that my other daughter, Mabel, is a very great friend of Margorie Browne—they were at school together—and one has to put personal feelings on one side. I had in any case to come officially, as I am Margorie's trustee and godfather, but, of course, I refused the invitation to this party. My wife and daughter went for Margorie's sake, and they have returned naturally very upset, and have gone to bed."

"They were there when the murder took place?"

"It has been a terrible shock to them—I suppose it was to every one—and Mabel is almost hysterical. But you, Tracey—I understand that you were staying at the Hall?" He looked at me with those piercing eyes that had forced the truth from many a reluctant witness.

"I fled from the place."

"I don't blame you. I know all about Darent, and have a good deal of sympathy for him, but this is another thing."

"You are jumping to conclusions, like the villagers," I exclaimed angrily. "Because a man is addicted to drink, he is not necessarily a murderer. As a matter of fact, I have the clearest proof that he did not murder Barton."

"I should be glad to hear it—truly glad," he observed gravely, and a little doubtfully.

"I hold no brief for Kenneth," I went on firmly, glad of the opportunity of testing myself before such an expert. "He treated me very badly, asking me down to such a place and then getting drunk, but as he never left the Hall during the whole evening, I know that he did not do the murder."

Peters became thoughtful, resting his head on his hand. I was going to take a formal good night, and seek my room, when he spoke.

"I don't doubt your word for a moment, Tracey. Darent is fortunate in the fact that you were there. As a lawyer myself—though I ought not to express an opinion—I must tell you that there are very grave suspicions concerning him."

"I know nothing of the circumstances, Mr. Peters, I only know that Barton was killed—nothing more."

"From what my wife tells me," he said, choosing his words carefully," I gather they were dancing and generally celebrating the occasion, when Barton was missed. There had been a draw for prizes; John was rather vulgar in his tastes—one does not generally give away expensive presents at one's wedding. No one knew where he had gone, and he was wanted to give away the prizes with Margorie. The first intimation that anything was wrong came from the butler, who stated that about half an hour before, John had received a note. The butler had no idea from whom it came or who brought it. He saw his master reading it in the hall, and he seemed to be agitated. He told the butler that he would not be long, and went out, just as he was, into the garden."

"I see," I said. "He went alone. Did he take a weapon with him?"

"You are smart, Tracey—he hadn't got one when he was found, but the murderer might have taken it away; on the other hand, he may not have suspected anything."

"Come, Mr. Peters; you, an eminent counsel. If the note was from Darent, his enemy, would he have gone out unarmed and alone? Wouldn't he have taken someone with him, or have refused to see Darent?"

"You should have been a lawyer, like your father," he said, though whether in irony or not, I could not guess. "Unfortunately for your theory, the butler declared that Sir John said to him: " 'It's a nuisance. Mr. Darent wants to see me about something!' "

The blow was a shrewd one, and I confess I was taken off my guard. Peters gave me time while he smoked his cigar in silence, and then said very quietly:

"So, you see, it looks as though he did leave the house after all."

He read the indignation in my face, and placed a kindly hand on my shoulder. "Come, my boy; I knew and respected your father. May I give you a word of advice as an older man, and one of some experience? Don't get yourself mixed up with this business—you will only regret it. Best leave it alone."

The place was almost empty now—only Turnbull sat still at his table, and Polly was clearing away the glasses and plates. The guests had either gone in their cars, or to bed. The party had broken up in confusion, and the departing guests had come to the Crown for refreshments.

Peters's eyes wandered to Turnbull. "A dangerous fellow, that," he whispered confidentially to me, as though wishing to change the conversation. "For some reason he doesn't seem to love you."

"I threw him into the road yesterday," I said.

"Well, of course, that may have something to do with it—still, I should avoid him if I were you. Before you came in he was telling every one in the room that you had come down to stay with Darent, and suggesting that it was a strange coincidence that Barton was killed the same night."

"Was he, by Jove? To put it plainly, he was hinting that I was a hired gangster who had come down to bump off Sir John—I believe that is the correct expression?"

"You are quick at taking a point," he said with quiet irony. "Of course, I did not connect you with my old friend then, and when he announced that you were in the inn—I suppose Willis had told him—I certainly expected to see a sort of thug come in. I think every one did."

I burst out laughing—rather a forced laugh, I fear. "He's certainly taking his revenge for the shaking up I gave him."

Peters did not respond to my mirth. He gave me one keen glance, and then rose. "I suppose I must try and get some sleep. I must go to the Towers to-morrow. I shall hope to see you before you go."

"I don't expect to be going at once," I said lightly. "I shall stay and watch this case."

We had strolled together to the steps leading to the upper floors, ignoring the lawyer, who was greedily examining some papers, as though searching for something.

"I should not be too insistent about that alibi," Peters said gravely. "Don't be offended at my advice. Perhaps when you learn a little more you may reconsider the matter. You haven't told any one yet, except me?"

"On the contrary, I told the inspector when he came."

A look almost of horror came to his pale, ascetic face. "Heavens, and Darent's footprints were on the grass!"

I was dumbfounded, and remained silent while he went slowly up the stairs. Every fresh fact told against Darent. It was one thing to stand by him in his own house, with the loyal servants backing me up, though the place was sordid beyond words, but quite another when in the company of a polished, educated man like Peters. Dawn was breaking and I suddenly felt very tired and limp.

Polly was waiting in the passage and showed me to my room, which was the best she could do for me, as several persons had decided to stay the night at the Crown. It was really only an attic, but quite comfortable for a man as weary as I was, and Polly had kindly unpacked my bag, for which I afterwards was profoundly grateful.

"I can't think who can have taken that stick," she said, standing in the doorway. "You are quite sure, sir, that Mr. Darent did not take it with him?"

"Absolutely—and don't you see, Polly, how important that is?—because as he left it here, and did not fetch it, whoever did take it was the murderer of Sir John Barton."

CHAPTER VI

THE RECTOR OF CROWFIELD

WOKE with what is called a thick head and an intense feeling of depression. I had mixed my drinks on the preceding day in a disgraceful way, to which I had been a stranger since my old army days. And the crowning folly of whisky after champagne in the early hours of the morning had brought upon me a just punishment.

My first feelings were all physical, and very unpleasant, but as recollection returned, and my mental faculties became clearer, I was tortured by the worst of demons. I could hardly remember what I had said or done, and had to go over the events of the day before, step by step, in order to sort out what was real from the nightmares that had haunted my sleep.

When a knock came at my door I trembled like a coward, expecting to see the inspector coming to claim my vile body.

To my relief it was Polly with a cup of hot, strong tea. My watch had run down, but she informed me that it was after ten o'clock, and inquired about breakfast in a practical, reassuring manner.

Food did not appeal to me in the least, and I asked for news.

"Mr. Darent was arrested this morning, sir, on a charge of murder."

I felt an awful sinking sensation. "Tell me about it," I managed to say.

"That inspector went down to the Hall early this morning and arrested him."

"How do you know, Polly?" I hoped that it was only village gossip.

"I went down to fetch the milk that we always get from the Hall. There was a constable from Wickstead on duty, and he wouldn't let me into the house, so I had to go round to the dairy, and Mary came to see me. She gave me this note for you, sir."

She handed me a bulky package.

"I'll dress," I said anxiously. "You can tell me the rest when I've read this letter."

As soon as the girl had gone I tore open the rough brown paper in which the letter was wrapped. Inside were a number of sheets of paper torn from an exercise-book; the writing was large and the spelling atrocious, but translated into ordinary language it ran as follows:

"SIR,

"I am writing to you in the lavatory, as the policemen are in the house, and I dare not let them see me writing. I am giving this letter to Polly to give to you. An awful thing has happened. Mr. Darent has been arrested. He woke up in an awful temper, and found the policeman asleep by his bed. Mr. Darent tried to push him down the stairs, and the policeman stunned him with his truncheon. Then the inspector came, and there was an awful row. They handcuffed Mr. Darent, and took him into the library. Then the inspector had mother, dad and me into the kitchen, one by one, and took down a statement from each of us, which they made us sign. They searched the whole place, and asked all about you and where you had gone, and we told them exactly what you told us. I showed them where you had slept, as I had made up a bed in one of the spare rooms, and said you had made an awful fuss and gone off to the Crown. They wanted Mr. Darent's dress clothes and pumps, but I told them that neither of you two gentlemen had dressed last night, but they in-sisted, so I had to get them. I had cleaned them, and put them away, so that will be all right. They took Mr. Darent to their car, and he was swearing something awful about being handcuffed, but they wouldn't let us speak to him, so we couldn't tell him about last night or anything, or about what you had said, and then they told us to take our things to the bailiff's cottage, as they were locking up the Hall. So I am writing to you, sir, to ask you not to come here or try to see us at all. Polly will bring any message when she comes for the milk. Mother is very upset, and we want to know what we are to do. Don't leave us, sir, will you?

"Yours respectfully,

"MARY MARTIN."

I read the letter through twice and the horror of the situation dawned on me. Darent knew nothing about our alibi, and nothing of what Mary had said. Our only hope lay on the chance that he might have forgotten everything that had happened the night before, and in his statement to me that he would tell the police nothing. "They could damned well find out for themselves," as he had expressed it.

I dressed hurriedly and went down into the lounge, which was now empty, all the visitors having gone; only Polly was busy cleaning the room for opening-time.

"I'll get your breakfast, sir," she said briskly.

"No, thank you, Polly, I couldn't eat anything. I've read Mary's letter; she was very foolish to write it, as it might have fallen into the hands of the police. You must tell her not to write again; but send messages by you. You can tell her I am doing everything I can for Mr. Darent.”

“Yes, sir.” She appeared to hesitate. “I don’t know as I ought to tell you.”

“Go on, Polly tell me all you know.”

“Well—Mary told me they wouldn’t let Mr. Darent speak to them, but he was going on something awful about you—calling you a rotter and a cad and a coward, and Mary says the detective was standing there taking it all in.”

“That may not be a bad thing—it bears out my story.” Here was a desperate situation. Thanks to his ill-timed attack on the policeman, Darent was entirely ignorant of what I had done or said. He probably thought that I had bolted as soon as he had gone to bed, and left the servants to do what they could. Another and more sinister thought came to my mind—perhaps he thought I had gone straight to the police and told them all I knew.

The very idea made me furious with indignation—that he was now in prison thinking me a Judas, who had betrayed him.

Everything seemed to have gone wrong, and our hopeless alibi appeared to have done more harm than good.

“You know nothing more?” I asked.

“Nothing, sir, except that the policeman came and ordered me off, but Jack Oliver—that’s our own constable—told him to mind his own business.”

“You know Oliver very well then, Polly?” My smile produced a blush on her cheeks.

“Yes, sir, very.”

It was always well to have inside information, and I saw that our little Delilah might get information from our uniformed Samson that would be extremely useful.

“Where is Oliver now?”

“He went to bed, having been up all night, and they have a man from Wickstead now on duty, but Jack will likely be round to-night, as he will be off duty at six, and they have taken this right out of his hands.”

“Then perhaps you may be going out with him this evening?”

“It’s my night out,” she said simply. “We thought of going to the pictures at Wickstead, by the bus.”

“Now listen, Polly—you want to help Mr. Darent and Mary, don’t you?”

“Yes, sir, indeed I do!”

“Well, try and get all the information you can out of Oliver, and what happened at the Towers when he was sent for, and what the police think about it.”

"I am sure Jack will tell me all he knows," she replied with a toss of her head. "Do you think that they will keep Mr. Darent for a long time?"

"I hope not, Polly: it all depends on how long we take to find the murderer."

She looked at me queerly. "They do say in the village that you and Mr. Darent did it between you."

I tried to laugh it off as a joke, but the idea seemed so widespread that I began to have misgivings about my own position.

"All right, Polly—you can take a message to Mary for me. I must go for a walk, and try to get an appetite."

I went out into the sunlit road, now deserted, and walked in the direction of the Towers. The large, white house that Kenneth had pointed out to me as the rectory was on my left. The rector had asked me to call, but this was hardly a suitable time, and I was going on, when the man himself came along briskly from the village, and greeted me a little coldly. "You were coming to see me, perhaps?" he said.

"Yes and no, Mr. Browne. I did think of looking you up, but then I thought the occasion was hardly suitable."

To my surprise he took my arm firmly. "Come along then," he said. We walked up the well-kept drive to the front door, on which were chromium-plated knocker and fittings, and electric bell push. A fairly large hall faced us as he opened the door, and the rector conducted me into a plainly furnished room that reminded me of a doctor's waiting-room: evidently the room in which interviews took place.

He pointed to a seat, and sat down himself opposite to me, as though I had come to beg for money.

"What can I do for you, Mr. Tracey?"

"This is a dreadful business, Mr. Browne," I began nervously.

"Yes, of course it is, but, pardon me, you did not come to tell me that, and you have hardly known me long enough to call and express your sympathy."

I was getting rather annoyed. In this better light than in the church, I could observe his intellectual face, hard, shrewd eyes, and determined mouth. Here was a man who would sympathize with a sinner, but be ruthless to the sin, and one who would stand no whining or lying. I went straight to the point.

"You are right, Mr. Browne, I had no real reason for intruding upon you, but you are the only person in the village whom I know, apart from the landlord of the Crown and his wife. I came to you for advice."

"You will pardon me again, Mr. Tracey"—his voice was coldly polite—" you did not come here for advice, you came for information."

My evident confusion made him assume a kindlier tone. He touched me lightly on the arm.

"Mr. Tracey, I don't know whether you are a religious man, but you are an educated one. I am a priest, and like a doctor, a specialist. In the many—sometimes very painful—interviews that I have had in this room, I always believe in prayer before discussion. Would you care to join me in a few words to ask for guidance in this matter, and that the truth about this murder may be revealed?"

I looked at him—speechless. His face was calm and stern, and I felt that he was no fanatic, but a sincere believer, and one who would stand no nonsense. He read my thoughts and his mouth became hard.

"You need not say anything, Mr. Tracey. I would not insult the Deity by praying with one who is an unbeliever. We will continue the conversation. I never turn my back on a man or woman because they cannot see eye to eye with me in religious matters."

"Thank you—I won't argue the case, but frankly I'm not going to pretend to beliefs I do not hold—that would be sheer hypocrisy."

He produced a cigarette-case and handed it to me. "In that case, we will smoke: I always prefer a pipe myself, and I find it a comfort when talking."

He pulled out a pipe and a worn tobacco-pouch from his pocket, and filled his pipe.

"I did come for information," I said. "You know the facts, as you were at the Towers last night. Darent pointed out this house to me yesterday as being the rectory, and it was a sudden impulse that made me stop at the gate."

The conversation had begun so strangely, that I had entirely forgotten what this tragedy must have meant for his daughter—my mind had been absorbed with the question of Darent.

"I beg your pardon," I hastened to say, "I should have asked after your daughter—it must have been a terrible blow for her."

"If you don't mind, Mr. Tracey, I prefer not to discuss Margorie or her position."

For a brief moment there came into his eyes a look that was neither pain nor sorrow, but rather a flash of anger.

Then his face assumed its normal self-possessed appearance. "I understand that your friend Darent was arrested this morning on a charge of murder."

The change in the conversation was sudden and disconcerting.

"I have been told so; I know nothing of the details."

"I was at the Towers last night, Mr. Tracey, you know," he said with quiet emphasis. There was nothing to indicate in his remark whether he was merely giving me information, or hinting at something more.

"I understand that Sir John was called from his house, and that it was some time before his absence was discovered."

The rector puffed at his pipe without replying for a few minutes, and we looked at each other in gloomy silence—he seemed in no hurry, though he must have been extremely busy after the events of last night.

At last he said—measuring each word: "You will be returning to London at once, I suppose, Mr. Tracey?

Every one seemed to be anxious for me to go back to London, and of course it was the obvious thing to do, but I have a certain vein of obstinacy, and I hate being driven.

"I am not leaving this village till I have found out who murdered Sir John Barton, if I have to stay for a year," I cried somewhat bombastically.

The rector got to his feet and walked to the window, looking out on his beautiful garden, one of the loveliest I have ever seen. My mind was confused—there was a hint of suspicion in his manner, as though he were holding something back from me. I had almost made up my mind to terminate the interview, when he came back and resumed his seat.

"Mr. Tracey"—his voice was not quite so steady as before—"when I met you at the gate, I brought you in here because I believed that you had something to tell me, but wished first to find out exactly how much I knew. I hate subterfuge in all its forms, and I tell you honestly that I had determined to tell you nothing, but if you had anything to say, I would have listened, and treated your information in the strictest confidence. I hold very strong views with regard to the position of an ordained priest, and rightly or wrongly I have always treated anything imparted to me as sacred, as well as secret. If I can help in any way, I always try to do so, but I regard sin and crime as a matter between the sinner and God—we differ probably about that—"

He paused and gave me a searching glance, then resumed: "I can assure you, Mr. Tracey, that if the murderer walked into this room, and confessed to me, I should say nothing to the police, although I might urge that person to clear his conscience by a frank confession. If he refused, I should still hold my peace, but I should not help him or her if they continued in unconfessed sin."

There was a clear sincerity in his words that assured me that he was no canting hypocrite, and more than that —he was throwing out an invitation to me, as plainly as he could.

"I admire your principles," I said, accepting his challenge. "In that case, may I ask whether you think I did the murder?"

The direct attack took him by surprise.

"I attach no importance to village gossip."

My temper rose at his words.

"You have been straight with me up till now, Mr. Browne; please don't prevaricate. I asked you a plain question."

"And I will answer it," he said sternly. "I don't think you did the murder, but I suspect that you know more about it than you care to say."

"May I ask why?"

"Are you prepared to tell me all you do know? If so, short of screening the murderer, I will do all I can to help."

I took a quick resolve—I was all alone in this business, and badly wanted a confidant and adviser.

"If you will tell me all *you know*, I give you my word of honour that I will tell you everything. I think that's fair."

He smiled at me, and nodded. "Now I think we begin to understand one another. Let me tell you at once that grave suspicion rests on you as accessory to the fact, as they call it legally, and that is equivalent to a charge of murder."

"Then why haven't they arrested me with Darent?"

"My dear sir, if you had followed criminal cases, as I have been compelled to do in my study of human nature and crime, you would know that very frequently the police prefer a really good first-hand witness, who could clinch the evidence."

My face went crimson, and I clenched my hands. "You are suggesting that they will try to use me as a witness—what they call turning King's evidence—a dirty form of treachery!"

"You have taken my meaning exactly," he said calmly. "I will go further. If you had remained at the Hall, instead of coming away, you might have been arrested on suspicion, and examined."

"But look here—all these suggestions and hints lead nowhere. We have agreed to be quite open with each other. I tell you straight, I had nothing whatever to do with the murder, either actively, or what you call as accessory."

"I am delighted to hear it." His face cleared at once. "Then I can help you. In the first place, you have already made an enemy here, I don't know how, in Turnbull. I know he made a statement to the police about you directly the murder was discovered, and he has been spreading rumours about you in the village."

"I'll tell you all about Master Turnbull presently," I said, laughing, for somehow this quiet, strong man inspired me with a sadly needed confidence. His face was still very grave, and the laugh met with no response on his part.

"The next point I have to mention will give you a shock. There were two pairs of footmarks quite clearly marked in the dew on the lawn, both made by evening dress pumps, both leading from the body of the murdered man, in the direction of the Hall."

That knocked the stuffing out of me. I was firmly convinced of the truth of Darent's story, and one set were undoubtedly his—but the other set? It looked as though someone had followed him—probably the murderer.

"There were two sets, you say?"

"I will make it clear to you. Naturally, as Margorie's father, I was one of the chief actors in the discovery of this tragedy, and, in fact, took charge, as every one seemed to lose their heads. The ground all round the spot where the murder took place was trampled down. When I had got the guests back, and telephoned for the police and a doctor, I went out again alone, and on the smooth lawn covered with dew that almost resembled hoar frost I discovered these tracks. You understand that they led away from the body—there were no corresponding traces of any one coming across the lawn from the opposite direction. When Watson returned from the Hall I took him out and showed them to him. Had he seen them before, it is likely enough that he would have arrested you both at once. If I had waited till the morning, the dew would have been off the grass, and there would not have been any footprints. As it was, the inspector was able to take tracings of them, and can identify the size, at any rate, of the shoes."

"You saw Watson, then, when he came back from the Hall the first time?"

"He came straight to me and told me everything, and I am bound to tell you that I was astonished."

He looked hard at me, waiting.

"All right—I accept your challenge, and trust to your word."

"Mary was in my wife's Bible class, and I prepared her for confirmation," he said with meaning. "There is something all wrong here."

I began from the beginning, hiding nothing, and told him everything from the time when Darent and I had soldiered together. It was a relief to get it done, and a burden off my mind.

He never moved a muscle during the recital; only once he refilled his old brier pipe and relighted it.

"There—that's the truth, on my word of honour," I concluded, prepared if he started preaching to walk out, relying on his promise of secrecy.

"I think you and the servants behaved in a truly Christian manner, and did the only possible thing," he said, to my utter surprise. "I won't say anything about the mess you have got yourselves into, or the question of perjury—none of you have done that yet, as nothing has been taken on oath. I am human, and there are cases in which it may be even necessary to tell a lie. That is not for us to judge. In the old days, when Darent's ancestors were fighting for King Charles, and had to take refuge from their pursuers, the faithful retainers who swore that they had never seen them, while they were hiding them, were telling lies, but they were right. As Bassanio says: "to do a great right, do a little wrong"—it is sometimes the lesser sin. I am glad you have told me this; it is the story of sacrifice for a friend, especially on the part of Mary, a story after my own heart."

I was completely taken aback, and immensely relieved at his attitude, which was that of a broad-minded gentleman.

"It's going to be very difficult, Tracey." I noticed at once the change in his tone. "At present there is enough evidence to hang any one. There is the damning evidence of the weapon with which Barton was killed, the foot marks, and the known quarrel between the two men. Then there are the words spoken by Barton to his butler, and another thing that I have not mentioned. Only yesterday Turnbull brought the mortgage deeds on the estate and handed them over to Barton. They are missing, although a thorough search has been made for them everywhere. It's going to be a tough fight, but there's one man I am afraid of more than any one else."

"Turnbull?"

"No! Kenneth Darent. I know him a good deal better than you do. I thought that he had done this crime—I won't call it murder at present—in a moment of drunken fury, and possibly under great provocation. Now that I have heard your story, which I believe entirely, because I can generally judge accurately when a man is telling the truth, I am afraid that Darent himself will be the first to repudiate the alibi. If he thinks that Mary's reputation is at stake, he is of that type to which chivalry counts for everything, and he will blurt out the whole story rather than let a breath of scandal rest on this girl. I know him only too well."

His warm advocacy of Darent took me by surprise, and he must have read the look on my face.

"We are confiding in one another, Tracey, and I am going to tell you what I know about your friend. When he first came here, as you are aware, he was a fine type of soldier, and we all hoped he would retrieve the fortunes of the estate, which his father had let go to ruin. He did try—tried hard, and became, like all his ancestors, a county magistrate, and a leader in the village. I had many talks with him, and I knew how hopeless the position was unless he sold some of his land on the main road for building purposes. But then Barton came on the scene, and they quarrelled at once. They were opposite in character in every way, and neither could see a shred of good in the other. While Lady Barton was alive there was an armed neutrality, for she understood Darent, and always stood for him, but when she died things got worse, and Darent started drinking heavily, not because he is naturally a drunkard—he is far from that—but he has a melancholy, introspective nature, sensitive to a degree, and imagined insult where none existed. Then, thinking that every one was against him, he drank from sheer bravado, openly showing himself drunk in the village street. I am no bigot, but I had to ask him to resign from the choir, although he has a beautiful voice, but the example was doing a lot of harm."

For the first time that morning he showed signs of emotion, and his voice shook.

"And then came rivalry."

"He loved your daughter," I said, remembering Darent's wild words the night before.

"Poor fellow, he did, but was too proud to say a word, on account of his position financially, and I am sorry to have to tell you my wife did her best to keep them apart. Elsie Peters had been a great friend of Margorie's, and they were always together, and Mabel Peters, the younger daughter, used to stop here. The three were inseparable. They made up a party to go to Switzerland with some young fellows they knew, and there was a terrible accident. Elsie was killed and Margorie was badly injured. Barton went straight out there, and fetched his wife's body home—she is buried in the churchyard. Margorie was in hospital, and as soon as I could leave I went to Meiningen, and when she was well enough to travel I brought her back."

He paused for a moment and I did not interrupt.

"It was then the mischief began. Margorie used to go to the Towers, as Barton seemed heart-broken and wanted sympathy, and gradually he started making love to her in subtle ways, expressing his sympathy with Darent, and hinting to my wife that he would be willing to pay Darent's debts and also try to buy the mortgage, and so prevent the holders from foreclosing."

"In other words," I remarked bitterly, "he was trying to buy your daughter by promising help to his rival."

"I fear that is so, but I am sure he never saw it in that light. He had the business man's mind, and saw everything from a financial point of view. I am sure that Margorie never suspected his motives. Barton was far too clever for that. He used my wife as an intermediary, gave liberally to village clubs and institutions, always insisting that his gifts should be anonymous. Darent saw through it all, I believe, and avoided our house altogether. Margorie was hurt by his treatment, but I never meddled with her affairs. And then the crisis came. Barton proposed to Margorie and she refused him. I can't tell you the wretched time we went through. Her mother was at Margorie every day, and Barton had the sense to keep away and merely continued to be kind and generous. Margorie is not the kind of girl who can be coerced or bullied, but for some reason she gave way, and consented."

"I think I can guess," I said. "Your wife had told her that it was the only way to save Darent from ruin and disgrace, and a drunkard's death."

"You are shrewd, Tracey," he commented dryly.

"I can tell you more. Darent told me that if ever the Hall was sold over his head, he would burn the place down and commit suicide. Perhaps your daughter knew that."

"I wonder—if so she was fonder of him than we knew, but these heroic sacrifices are not made nowadays. Anyway the news was all over the village, and Darent took it badly. I expect that was when he wrote to you."

"I wish I had come at once—I might have helped him."

The rector looked up quickly, as though to ask a question, but after a moment's hesitation went on "That is the miserable story, known to the whole village, I am afraid. What more damning motive could you have? Darent, drunk or half-drunk, going to the Towers to try to stop the wedding, sends for Barton—"

He paused and looked at me, as though seeking my opinion.

"And against that we have nothing but the bare statement he made to me, and the fact that he never had that stick with him."

"Come, Tracey." He rose briskly. "We have talked enough. We must try whether we can't get some indications as to the real murderer. We will go to the Towers; they will admit me; and then you must come back here for lunch—I insist on it."

"But would your wife like it? They must be very upset at present."

A curious smile flittered over the rector's face, half sad and half quizzical.

"My wife has gone to the Hall to see the Martins, and taken Margorie with her. They will be back for lunch. We shall not be a very merry party, but it will be better for you than the Crown Inn; I don't think you should go there just now."

I quite agreed with him.

CHAPTER VII

AT THE TOWERS

A T the entrance gates of the Towers, a constable was standing on duty, an officer from Wickstead.

He was about to stop us when the rector said: "Good morning, Thompson, you know me by this time I have business at the house."

"Yes, sir, I know you by sight, but not the gentleman with you, and I was told to allow no one inside but officials and members of the family."

"He is a friend of mine, and I will answer for him." The rector spoke in his grand manner, and the constable allowed us to pass.

As we proceeded up the drive, the rector chuckled softly. "You would not have stood much chance of getting in, Tracey, by yourself."

The blinds were drawn, and not a soul was in sight.

"We are only just in time—the inspector will be here presently. He has gone to meet a Scotland Yard official who has been sent down. I have to see the brother—young Barton—about the funeral arrangements, and Peters on business. Take your opportunity and have a look round. With the knowledge you have already, you may find out more than you think possible at present."

He disappeared inside the pompous front entrance, while I slipped round the massive structure to the back. Lawns had been laid out in front of a terrace at great cost, for the slope had been steep, and Barton had banked up the ground, so that at the farther end there was a huge ramp of earth, on the slope of which were planted shrubs and quick-growing trees.

Whatever I might think about the house, the gardens had been laid out by an expert I could see, and apart from their newness, were delightful. Tennis and croquet lawns were in front, divided by an alley of young yews with a wide grass ride down the centre, almost big enough for a bowling alley. Beds of roses and borders of herbaceous plants gave a mass of colour to the gardens.

But I had not come here to admire gardens, but upon a grimmer matter. In the lawn on the right, as one looked from the house, was a roped square resembling a boxing ring. This was evidently where the body had been found, and the distance from the house was perhaps fifty yards or so. There was a line run out from this spot, and marked with croquet hoops, right across the lawn to the ramp, and I had no difficulty in guessing that this was the track of the footprints, leading in the direction of the Hall. I dared not approach nearer to investigate, in case any one should observe me from the Towers. It was exactly as Darent had described, and the first thought that crossed my mind was that no one but a madman, having done a murder, would have retreated straight across the lawn, but would have rushed to cover in one of the many bushes nearby and into the woods.

The second line of footprints was a complete mystery. I tried to let my imagination have play, and visualized the scene. This second line came from the spot where the body had lain, and had followed the first. Had someone found the body, and followed the tracks by himself, while the guests were stampeding the lawns near the house? If so, why had the mysterious person not imparted the information to the police, and why had he not retraced his steps?

Then, again, why should Sir John meet the writer of the note on a dark night in the middle of a lawn? There were two explanations to my mind. Either the writer was a woman, and he wanted a dark place in which to hold their consultation, or the person he was meeting was one whom he would not suspect of any evil intentions.

The police and I were approaching the problem from different an-gles. They were convinced that Darent had done the murder, whereas I was convinced that he had not, and was trying to find the truth. It seemed fairly obvious that no one in the house among the guests could have done it, for, in so large a house, if any one had sought an interview it would have been perfectly simple to have found some private room. I could not take my eyes off that square of rope; there was something all wrong here—I felt it by instinct.

I could visualize the scene. The sounds of music and dancing coming from the house, and a silent figure in evening dress, the host—the principal person at the Towers—stealing out into the bitter night, flitting from cover to cover, lest he be discovered on his own lawn. Surely some evil purpose must have taken him out. And then what took place?

Was it a frenzied attack, unexpected and out of the dark night, or was it when some bargain was offered, and refused, that the fierce anger of the mysterious visitant had broken out, and the baronet left dead on the grass? Then silence, until someone from the house had come stumbling on the corpse unawares, or did that someone *discover* the body, knowing all too well where it lay?

In spite of the heat of the sun beating down on me, I shuddered. My time was short, and I had wasted too long in idle speculation. I turned back, and wandered down a path that led to the out-buildings and came upon a yard, from which opened the garages, large enough to accommodate at least twelve cars. High walls surrounded the other three sides. A man in shirt-sleeves and gaiters approached me, and touched his cap, thinking me one of the guests who had come for his car. I could see that nearly all the garages were empty, and felt that I must bluff, or he might become suspicious.

"I told my man to take my car to the village. I don't know whether he has done so?"

"What name, sir?"

"Peters," I said, naming the barrister.

"Yes, sir, his car is here; he is up at the house." There was a touch of suspicion in the man's voice.

"Then that's all right." I smiled at him. "I'll join him there." There seemed no reason for remaining longer, but the man stood stolidly waiting. Two cars were visible to me, one with the bonnet protruding from the doors of one of the garages, and another standing in the open. I have a curious habit of being able to remember numbers, and I had instinctively noted that of Barton's car when I had seen it the day before.

"Here is poor Sir John's car," I said, advancing towards it, more for something to say than for any real object. I wanted to get into conversation with the man, for one never knows what may leak out.

"You knew him, sir?"

"Only yesterday he passed me in the village," I prevaricated. "We little thought then that he was on his last ride."

"Not his last, sir; he went out again in the car."

I pricked up my ears at that. "Indeed—I had no idea," I remarked casually. "When was that?"

"I don't know, sir; only he came out here and took the car when I was busy with all the guests arriving, and brought it back about seven o'clock. Half the yard was blocked with cars, and he left it there and hurried off to the house. What with all that's happened since, I haven't had time to clean it again."

"You must have had a busy time." I opened the door of the car, as though in idle curiosity. The inside of the saloon was elaborately decorated and upholstered in crimson leather, and there was a piece of tapestry carpet on the floor.

"Nice car," I said, "and beautifully kept; it's as clean as a new pin."

"It's good of you to say so, sir, for, as I told you, I haven't had time to clean it."

"But you cleaned it when he came back the first time?" I said quickly, for my eye had caught something on the floor. I stooped forward and picked up a cigarette, half smoked, and held it up.

"Well, I never!" The man stared at the simple thing as though he had never seen a cigarette in his life.

I held the thing in my hand; it had not been crushed or trodden on, and seemed to have gone out and been dropped. But the end that had been in the smoker's mouth was dyed vermilion, just where the lips had touched it. The man groped inside and produced two cigar-ends. "Here's the master's smokes—I never knew him to smoke a cigarette in my life."

He looked at me queerly, as though unspoken questions were on his tongue.

"I suppose," I said slowly, "no one could have got into the car last night—I mean a young couple having a lark?"

"I was here the whole time, and the electric light was full on, and then they came rushing in here for their cars when they found the master murdered—that inspector asked me if I had left the yard, and I told him I hadn't." There was a note of indignation in his voice. I took an envelope from my pocket, and slipped the cigarette and the cigar-ends into it, and a coin into the man's hand.

"Thank you, sir," he said, looking doubtfully at the car. "It looks to me as though the master had gone for a joy-ride; funny sort of time for that sort of thing."

He evidently had no great respect for the dead man.

"I'll find Mr. Peters," I said, not wishing to enter into a discussion with the man. I walked up the drive towards the house. So Barton had made another, and secret, trip when his guests were arriving, and his companion had smoked a cigarette that had gone out half consumed. Moreover, the companion had vermilion-painted lips. A group of people were standing before the door as I approached; the rector and Peters, and two men I had never seen.

One was a youth with black hair plastered down on his head and the same swarthy complexion I had noted in Sir John in my fleeting vision. He had a tiny tooth-brush moustache, which gave him an unpleasant, sneering look, and lounged against the porch with his hands deep in his trouser pockets. He viewed me with insolent black eyes. The other was an inconspicuous youngster who appeared rather frightened.

Peters greeted me cordially, with a smile, but continued the conversation with the others.

They were discussing the inquest, and I noticed that neither of the young men showed much signs of sorrow at the death of Sir John.

"You understand," Peters said, "under the new law the inquest is purely formal, as there has been an arrest, and will be adjourned until after the police court proceedings."

"Quite so," the elder of the two said languidly. He had an annoying habit of hanging a cigarette to his lower lip, as though too bored to hold it in his hand.

"I don't think we can do anything more here," the rector said, glancing at Peters with a meaning look. I could see that both were anxious, for some reason, to get away.

"May I ask the name of your friend?" the elder youth said rudely. "I thought only people on business were to be allowed here?"

Peters frowned. "I ought to have introduced you. This is Mr. Robert Barton, Sir John's younger brother, and this is his cousin James Vickers—Mr. Tracey, whose father was a great friend of mine years ago."

He spoke lightly, and was on the point of turning away, but a sour look came to young Barton's face. "Oh—so this is the man we have been hearing about," he said to his cousin with a contemptuous laugh. "You knew this wretched creature Darent, I understand?" he added, turning to me.

"Mr. Darent was a great friend of mine once," I replied firmly, "but I had not seen him for five years."

"They'll sling him up all right—clearest case I've ever seen, and when I was young I used to amuse myself by solving murder problems. There's not much difficulty here, eh, Jim?"

The cousin nodded without speak speaking: he was obviously overawed by the stronger personality of the other.

"If the fool's got any sense, he'll plead that he was drunk, and didn't know what he was doing, but, of course, there was a second pair of tracks, so he must have had an accomplice," he said, staring insolently at me.

"Tracey is lunching with me—could you give us a lift to my house?" the rector said hurriedly to Peters.

"Certainly, but you must come at once, as I can't wait much longer," Peters replied.

I was not to be rushed off, and stood my ground.

"I am sure," I said, meeting Barton's stare fairly, "half the village gossips think that I was the accomplice, and came from the Hall with my friend for the purpose of murdering your brother, and then walked back on the grass, in order to show our tracks to every one."

Barton would not meet my look, and his eyes dropped, while Vickers looked away uncomfortably.

I heard Peters swear under his breath.

"You see," I went on quietly, "the tale sounds so plausible, the sort of detective story that you read when young, Mr. Barton—or is it Sir Robert now?—but let me give you one tip. If Mr. Darent and I murdered your brother, wasn't it rather a mistake to leave the weapon on the spot? I mean, it's the kind of thing that's not done —it's so obvious."

He writhed under my sarcasm. "It's those mistakes that hang a man," he said rudely.

I laughed outright—I meant to upset as far as I could the cocksureness of the man, for I knew that he would be the first to see the detective from Scotland Yard.

"A rather fundamental mistake, wasn't it? But if someone had wanted to pin the murder on to Mr. Darent, it would have been a very fine bit of corroborative evidence."

"Ingenious," Peters interrupted. "But I think we had better leave all these points to the official police."

But I had not done with Barton.

"They always say in crime investigation—and you will agree with this, Mr. Barton—that the first thing to do is to find out who would benefit by the murder."

Barton flared up, and his face turned crimson. "Are you suggesting that because I am next-of-kin, and if my brother had not married I should inherit, that I had a hand in his murder?"

I don't think that any one was more astonished at this outburst than Peters—he strode away down the drive after casting one glance at the angry man.

"I'm sure Mr. Tracey never suggested such a thing," the rector observed quietly.

"If I had," I exclaimed, "it was only what he was hinting about me."

Barton took his cousin's arm. "Come along; we can't stay here all day. We've got to see about sending back all the wedding presents, and there are about fifty Pressmen on the phone waiting till the line is 'disengaged.' Good morning."

They went into the house, and the rector and I walked down the drive in silence, to the place where Peters was waiting with his car.

As we passed through the gates a car drew up to make room for us to pass, and the policeman on duty saluted. A glimpse inside showed me Inspector Watson and a keen-faced man in plain clothes—the Scotland Yard expert, I guessed. Another was sitting with the driver, carrying a camera.

Peters dropped us at the rectory, and as I got out he said: "I would like to have a few minutes' talk with you, Tracey, and you must meet my wife and daughter. Will you be coming back to the Crown after lunch?"

I replied that I should be doing so, as my car and suit-case were there.

"Then perhaps you would come to our private room?' He drove on with a nod to the rector.

Mrs. Browne and Margorie had returned from their visit, and were waiting for us. I had only seen the girl in the dim church, but my impression of her was confirmed when we met in the dining-room.

She was very pale, and there were dark rings round her clear, fearless hazel eyes, but she possessed a haunting beauty I am unable to describe. She had her father's clean-cut features and firm mouth, softened and more delicate; giving an indication of a strong will, but ready sympathy. She was clothed in a simple jumper and skirt, with no signs of mourning. Intense sadness marked her face, and she had the appearance of one who had been through hell, and come back unscathed by the fire.

She shook hands with a firm, friendly grip, and a faint smile of recognition. The mother fully came up to my expectations from what I had heard already. She was a tall, dominant, almost scraggy woman, with the curved nose of a bird, thin-lipped and with piercing black eyes. She wore a black dress without ornament of any kind, and held herself with a dignity of carriage and expression that denoted a haughty, dictatorial nature.

She greeted me coldly, though with scrupulous politeness, as though I had to be endured, but must be kept in my place—I saw in her an enemy.

The meal was a most uncomfortable one. Mrs. Browne had obviously determined that the vital subject of the murder should not be referred to on any account, and kept up a conventional conversation that nearly drove me mad.

"You belong to the Norfolk Traceys—dear me, that is interesting. My uncle—Lord Dunmow, you know—was acquainted with a Sir William Tracey, or was it Walter? I forget." And then without waiting for an answer: "And you live in London—how interesting. The country must look very beautiful to you. The rector takes a great delight in our garden, and we frequently give parties to the poor of the parish, but they fail to appreciate it . . . really the lower orders are most ungrateful—they will take gifts but do not come to church."

I will not bore my readers with more of the trivial and banal talk of which this is a sample!

"You are eating nothing," the rector said when he could get in a word. "That doesn't do credit to our country air."

He looked round the table. "My dear, Mr. Tracey is not an abstainer. Would you prefer burgundy or claret?"

I was going to refuse, but the acid look on Mrs. Browne's face roused my natural mulishness.

"Thank you—either will do."

The rector ordered claret, and a good wine it was. He helped himself, an act of courtesy that I appreciated when I saw his wife's face. He turned to Margorie, "I think a glass of this would do you good, my dear."

"Really, John!" Mrs. Browne protested. Margorie looked up and our eyes met. I saw a kindly and amused expression in hers.

"Thank you, dad." She passed her glass.

The rector's wife assumed an attitude as though someone had just told a particularly vulgar story, but she lapsed into silence, for which I was thankful.

I was glad when lunch was over, and the rector suggested a smoke in the garden. Mrs. Browne shook hands formally with me, remarking that she had a round of parish visits to pay, and should probably not see me again. She might have added truthfully that she had no wish to do so, a sentiment with which I would have been in complete agreement.

It was truly a wonderful garden—old and natural. Some of the trees were as old as the church itself, and the rector was as much an enthusiast over his flowers as he had shown himself to be over the beauties of his church. Margorie was very silent, and walked with us, I think, to avoid the necessity of accompanying her mother. We had taken a seat under a gigantic elm, and were smoking contentedly, out of sight of the house, when the same trim maid that lead waited upon us at lunch came across the lawn where village fêtes were held, and approached the rector.

"Two gentlemen want to see you, sir," she said, and I noticed that her face was flushed, and that her eyes strayed in my direction.

"Who are they, Sarah?"

"They would not give me any names, sir, but said they must see you urgently."

"Very well, I'll come. I'm sorry, Tracey, I have frequent visitors, and in my position I never turn any one away. I shall not be long, and Margorie will entertain you."

He spoke lightly, but I observed an anxious look on his face, and his mouth set in a straight line, a sure sign that he was troubled.

We saw his solid figure striding across the lawn, massive beside the maid who tripped lightly beside him.

I was on the point of making some trivial remark when he had disappeared and we were alone, as the silence was becoming awkward. Margorie laid her hand on my arm, and spoke quickly:

"Mr. Tracey, I must see you—I can't tell you here as my father may be back at any moment. You must think what you like of me. Meet me in the church at ten o'clock to-night. You won't fail me, will you?"

The words took my breath away. I saw the intense earnestness in her beseeching eyes.

"Certainly. I will be there," I stammered.

Don't forget—come to the west door, where you went in before. I shall have the key. Not a word to any one, mind."

I gave her my promise, and she smiled in acknowledgement.

"We can talk about the garden, and you can give me a cigarette."

I took out my case and handed it to her. The recollection of the half-burnt cigarette in the car made me glance involuntarily at her lips, that showed no signs of colouring matter. Such lips as hers required no other red.

"I'm glad you don't use that horrible paint that some girls think it necessary to use," I said, greatly daring, as I held a match for her.

"I abominate the stuff—I'm glad you do," she said frankly, and I knew that it was not Margorie who had been in the car with Sir John the night before, and somehow felt glad that it was not she.

With a sense of foreboding I saw the rector hurrying across the lawn in our direction. The quickness of his return was ominous.

He was walking fast and with determination, and did not call to us. Margorie and I went to meet him, and I whispered to her:

"Whatever happens I shall be there."

She gave my hand a tiny squeeze in assent.

The rector stopped—he was hot and had an odd, disturbing look on his determined face.

"Tracey," he said at once, "Detective-Inspector Pyke from Scotland Yard is here, and wants to see you."

"I will come." I shook hands with Margorie, who smiled bravely, and the rector and I returned to the house together.

CHAPTER VIII

UNDER SUSPICION OF MURDER

KEEP your head, and be careful in your answers: and above all don't lose your temper—you are rather inclined to take offence."

He opened the library door, and I found myself in a large, comfortable room almost entirely surrounded by books. Over the mantelshelf two oars were crossed—relics of the rector's rowing days, and below them, a fine reproduction of 'The Agony in the Garden,' to a stranger might appear incongruous, but to my mind represented the two sides of the rector's character—sportsman and Christian.

Two men were standing by the window as we entered, Watson and the stranger I had seen in the car.

"This is Detective-Inspector Pyke—Mr. Tracey." Pyke bowed stiffly.

"You wished to see me," I said.

"I wanted a word with you, Mr. Tracey," he said politely enough.

"Won't you sit down?" the rector said, and I saw the inspector was looking for a seat by the window where he could have his back to the light, and my face in the full glare of the sunlight, but I was up to that trick, and went to the window-seat carelessly and sat by the open window. Whether he saw my purpose or not I do not know, but he smiled grimly, and took an arm-chair. He had a sharp incisive manner, and a piercing eye that he focused on me in a disconcerting way.

I took one of the rector's cigars from the box he passed round, and puffed clouds of smoke defiantly. Watson had taken a seat behind Pyke and was evidently a very secondary figure now.

"We wanted to see this gentleman alone. Is there any place where we could interview him privately?"

"I would rather that Mr. Browne should be present," I replied.

"I am afraid that I cannot permit that."

"Look here, Mr. Pyke," I said with some heat, forgetting at once the rector's warning. "If you want to question me, it's here or nowhere, unless you wish to preface your remarks with the usual formula that anything I say will be used as evidence against me."

I saw Watson smile, and wipe his moustache to hide it. I guessed that he was not overpleased with the intervention of Scotland Yard.

"We have not got to that stage yet," Pyke said with a smile, "and I hope it will not come to that. If Mr. Browne stays I must insist on his complete silence, and also that he will regard this conversation as strictly private."

"I will certainly give you that promise," the rector said suavely.

I remembered his words to me about being called as a witness against Darent, and felt that I must be on my guard.

Pyke was in no hurry to begin: he had selected a cigar and bitten off the end, and now lighted it in a contemplative manner. Perhaps this was part of his stock-in-trade, I thought.

"You had a letter from your friend, Mr. Darent, asking you to come to see him," he fired off without warning.

"That is so."

"What was the date of that letter?"

"I really can't remember; about three months, ago I should say."

"You can't remember—just think now, Mr. Tracey."

I was utterly at a loss to understand at what he was driving. The questions were so different from what I had expected.

"I couldn't say—I didn't take much notice; in fact, I never answered the letter at all."

"Where is it now?"

I laughed easily. "I am sure I don't know—at my flat in London, I expect."

Pyke placed his hand in his pocket and produced a letter. "That's not it by any chance?"

Hoad must have put it into my bag with a pile of other letters all requiring answers. I opened it, and read Darent's scribbled invitation.

"That's it—I suppose you stole it from my bag."

"There was no question of stealing—I had a search-warrant," Pyke said quietly. I shrugged my shoulders, wondering what on earth the letter mattered to any one.

"You can now tell me the date."

"You can see it for yourself," I replied; "June 2nd."

"The date doesn't suggest anything to you?" His piercing eye was boring through my brain, but there was nothing alarming in this line of examination.

"Nothing whatever—it means no more than any other date."

The detective turned to the rector, who was quietly smoking in his arm-chair.

"Do you mind telling me the date on which the engagement of your daughter was announced?"

Browne seemed as surprised as I—he answered readily. "It was in the papers on June 1st."

"The day before Mr. Darent wrote that letter—you still say that there is nothing of any consequence about the date?"

"I see no connexion whatever. I never saw any announcement, and I did not even know of the existence of Mr. Browne, his daughter, or of Sir John Barton."

"Possibly not—you did not come at once."

"Really, inspector, I think some of your questions are bordering on impertinence. What have my affairs to do with you? As a matter of fact, I was not coming at all, but the heat drove me from London, and I remembered this invitation—that's all."

He was not in the least put out. "And so, by pure accident, you arrived the day before the wedding?"

I remained silent; the remark called for no answer, and to tell the truth I was rather relieved at the line he had taken, and scented Turnbull a mile off.

"I know your subsequent movements, and have a report from Inspector Watson. I need not trouble you with that now."

I was amazed; but my smug complacency was soon to be shattered. "You didn't go outside the Hall at all after you had dressed for dinner?"

"No—I never went out; neither did Darent."

Fool! He had trapped me—our whole case rested on the fact that we had not dressed for dinner. To try to amend my answer now would have been worse than useless. He gave no sign, but I knew he had gained his point.

"Just give me those pumps, Watson."

A cold shiver went down my back as the inspector drew a pair of pumps from the case he was carrying, and handed them to the detective.

Pyke produced two paper tracings from his own pocket, and laying them on the table by his side, placed the pumps carefully over the left and right tracings—they fitted exactly: there was not a space the size of a pin's head between the traced line and the soles of the shoes. "You will observe," he said coldly, "these pumps fit exactly. The tracings were taken from the footmarks on the lawn, before the dew dried them out, and there were also marks in the soft earth at a point in the fence where two people, shall we say, climbed the fence that divides the property of Sir John Barton from that of Mr. Darent."

He spoke very deliberately, as though to a child or a rustic, and his eyes never left mine.

"I know nothing about the matter," I said doggedly.

"Would it not be better," Pyke said slowly, "if you would be quite frank with me? Believe me, Mr. Tracey, it is the wisest course, and I

am giving you every chance —I can assure you you will not get another."

"I am afraid I don't follow you," I said, genuinely nonplussed by
the questions he was putting.

"Would it surprise you very much if I told you that I myself took
those pumps out of your suit-case this morning, on my way to the
Towers?"

I saw the rector looking at me in perplexity, as though doubts about
my veracity were growing in his mind, and I saw the detective bal-
ancing one of the pumps in his hand—yet it was as much a mystery to
me as to them, for the pumps had never left my feet till I had packed
them in the suit-case at the Hall. I leant forward and snatched the shoe
from the detective's hand, and examined it closely. Then I laughed in
his face.

"Somebody has been making a fool of you, Mr. Pyke —these are
not my pumps."

"That is merely a statement—it will have to be proved."

"I might reply that the onus of proof is with you," I said smiling,
now that I had scored a point off him, "but as a matter of fact the proof
is easy. I always buy mine at Croxall's, in Burlington Arcade, and you
see these are by a different maker, and my man can tell you they are not
mine; but the surest proof is this." I took off the brown shoes I was
wearing, and tried to squeeze my foot into the pump, which was at least
two sizes too small. The detective took the others and placed them sole
to sole with the same result.

I expected to see him crestfallen at the discovery, but he smiled
pleasantly. "They are certainly not yours, Mr. Tracey," he said.

"Somebody must have put them into my suit-case," I said angrily,
my suspicions resting on Turnbull as I spoke.

A look of understanding passed between the two sleuths, and Pyke
remarked quietly:

"Exactly, Mr. Tracey—as you say, somebody must have put them
into your suit-case. I wonder why?"

He rose and took his hat, and Watson did the same, going to the
door to open it for his superior.

"As these shoes do not belong to you, I will take them for the present. I don't think I need detain you any longer."

He shook hands with the rector and myself in a friendly manner,
and followed Watson from the room.

"Poor Tracey," the rector said kindly when the door was shut, "you
will never make a good liar as long as you live."

"What have I done?" I asked uneasily—that detective had upset my
temper.

His manner became grave. "Unless a miracle happens, you have put a rope round Darent's neck."

I stared at the rector in absolute horror.

"I did not interrupt, as I had promised not to do so, but in any case I could have done no good. You were telling the truth, and I fail to see why you should be accused of a crime in which you had no part. You have cleared yourself in Pyke's eyes of being anything more than a tool, but you will be a damning witness against Darent."

"What exactly have I done? I thought his questions were ridiculous."

A sense of futility came to me, as I had tried to be careful and guarded in my replies.

"My dear fellow, you couldn't help it, but don't you see that he has now got what he wanted? If you had said nothing about the pumps, they would have held this as a trump card for the trial, and then your evidence would have been destructive to their case. I am going to give you the case as I am sure Pyke has constructed it after this interview. Darent is desperately hard up, and fears that the mortgage on the estate will be foreclosed, as he had failed to pay the interest, and the property sold up."

"He told me he would burn the Hall and commit suicide if that happened," I interrupted.

"That must not come out—but to proceed with our hypothetical case. Darent knows that you are a bachelor, with no ties, and fairly rich. He writes to you, hoping that you would take up the mortgages, but will not ask in a letter. He wrote the very day after the engagement of Sir John to Margorie was announced."

"But why? I can't see the connexion."

"I am afraid, Tracey, because he had somehow become acquainted with the fact that Barton was trying to buy them and hold them out as a bait to catch Margorie—it's all very sordid, and I hoped that it would never be necessary to bring out these things, but the fates are against us. The delay was fatal to Darent. You did not come, and Barton got Turnbull to buy them up, and Kenneth became more desperate as the time for the wedding approached. Remember, I am trying to construct the police view. He sends for you—and you come the very day before the wedding—remember that. Turnbull has told Darent that he has the deeds—flaunting them in his face, and you appear and pick a quarrel with the lawyer. Oh, I know you didn't," he said, as I was about to interrupt, "but don't you see the implication? You had met Darent, or been in communication with him—he had told you Turnbull was at the Crown and had these papers on him, and you throw the man into the yard, where all his precious papers were scattered about. No wonder he collected them with all the speed he could and rushed up the road. Here are two attacks made on Turnbull, and he will make out that Darent would have killed him if Willis hadn't intervened—which I am not at all certain he would not have done."

"So I understood," I answered, picturing to myself that scene in the sunlit lounge.

"These efforts having failed," the rector continued, as though telling a fantastic fairy story, "there remains one course only for Darent. He must get hold of Barton and get those papers somehow, possibly only that they might be transferred to you, and save his estate, and he arranges an interview. Either Barton brought the deeds with him, or he came without them—they are gone; and a quarrel resulting in Barton's death takes place. That's the police case, and Pyke thought that you had accompanied Darent to the Towers."

"But now he knows that I didn't."

The rector looked at me in a peculiar way. "Pyke wanted to know whether you were an accomplice or merely a tool used by Darent."

"A pleasing alternative."

"Now follow—you first slipped out that you had dressed for dinner, though your alibi turned on the fact that you didn't. Then you proved to him that the pumps were not yours—and actually said that someone must have put them into your case. He concludes that that somebody was at the Hall, and that the pumps were placed in your case, because they were Darent's and not yours, and therefore the marks on the grass were made by him."

"I am certain that was not the case. I packed my own suit-case," I asserted.

"I did not say it was—I said that is Pyke's case. The question is now whether Darent's own pumps made the other track or were these his?"

"Good Lord, what a mess!"

"One other matter and I have done." The rector rose and paced the floor, and I was surprised to see that he had become agitated. "Up till now we have dealt only with the matter of the mortgages, a mere financial matter, though serious enough; but there is the other—that is known only to a few at present—the rivalry between the two men, and Darent's bitter jealousy at Barton's victory. That must be kept out of the case if we can possibly manage it, for Margorie's sake as well as for Kenneth's; for here is a deadlier motive for murder."

"I shall do all I can to help there," I said fervently.

"I know you will, and short of lying I shall do the same. In one way this interview may do good, indirectly—I think you have cleared yourself in the detective's view, though he will try and get more out of you. I should get hold of a good lawyer, and only see Pyke in his presence."

"I intend to do so at once—a very old friend of mine, and just the man for the job."

"Good; then I think we can go no further at present. You will, of course, keep in touch with me?"

I thanked him for his help and advice and gave the promise.

"I'll give you a lift to the village if you like: I find in such a scattered parish a car is absolutely necessary."

He fetched his little two-seater, and ran me down to the village. My mind was fully occupied with the interview, and already I saw the necessity of keeping my own counsel. The rector and Pyke were of the opinion that the pumps had been put into my suit-case at the Hall, but I knew that they had not, and that someone had deliberately placed them there at the Crown, in order to implicate me in the crime. I had my own ideas as to who that was!

We stopped at the lich-gate at the entrance to the churchyard, and walked towards the church, for he had business there. He pointed to the white marble vault. "That is Lady Barton's grave."

"I've seen it. Pardon me for saying so, but I wonder how you could have allowed such a thing to be put up?"

"I did not, Tracey," he said, and his mouth set hard. "I was in Switzerland with Margorie at the time. My wife gave her consent, as she did not want to offend Sir John: it's a terrible eyesore, and I expect Sir John will be buried there." He walked in silence, and at the little door of the vestry paused. "If Elsie had lived this would never have happened, Tracey." He was more disturbed than I had seen him before. With a sudden change he said: "I often think that one is nearer to death, and nearer to God in a village than in a city. There people are hurried away to some far-off cemetery, and forgotten. Here they are present and real, and living still among us."

There was something at the back of his mind that I could not fathom, and a deeper meaning in his words than the bare statement.

I crossed the road to the Crown Inn, and noticed an unusual crowd of villagers round the place, and the eyes that were turned in my direction. I had become a celebrity in one day, though whether as a murderer or deliverer I could not guess. There were several people in the lounge, and the noise from the bar denoted that the murder was being discussed there. I saw the grinning face of Hickmott in the corner, red and foolish. He waved his hand in welcome, but I had no time to waste on him, being already late for my appointment with Peters. I was just going to ascend the three steps from the lounge, when a young man in plus-fours intercepted me. "Pardon me, but are you Mr. Tracey?"

I told him coldly that such was the case.

"I represent the *Daily Echo*—I wonder whether you would mind giving me a few particulars—"

A demon of malice seized me. "That's the man you want," I said confidentially, "that man over there, Mr. Hickmott of Daly's Farm. He can tell you more than I can, and, between ourselves, you will get information from him that the police would give their eyes to have."

I watched with satisfaction the newspaper man settling on Hickmott like a blowfly on a joint, and heard him order drinks. Then I fled up the steps to the private room the Peters were occupying.

CHAPTER IX

I MAKE A DISCOVERY

IN answer to my knock, Peters himself opened the door. "Come in, Tracey—we were wondering what had happened to you."

Beneath his quiet words there was a note of relief.

"I'm sorry—the rector kept me, showing me his garden."

Mrs. Peters was seated at the table, from which the luncheon had been cleared, sipping coffee, and smoking a cigarette. She was a well-preserved fine-looking woman with white hair and a kindly face, and I felt at home with her at once.

Mabel was a good-looking girl—though she would never come up to her mother's standard—but rather over-doctored with make-up, and appeared desperately nervous and tired. Her face was haggard and there was a haunted look, as though the tragedy had affected a mind not over well-balanced—at least such was my impression.

"Come and sit down, Mr. Tracey," Mrs. Peters said. "How did you get on at the rectory?"

"Very well," I answered guardedly.

"How is poor Margorie? This mist have been a terrible shock for her."

I could hardly say that she was showing no signs of grief, but replied that she was bearing up as well as could be expected. And then I had a shock myself. Mabel was smoking a cigarette that had gone out, half consumed. She took it from her mouth, and I saw that the end was coloured with vermilion from her lips. She held it in her hand, looking round for an ash-tray. "Allow me," I said, taking it from her, and carrying it to the fireplace I dropped it behind a copper scuttle that stood in the empty grate. I pulled out my case and offered her one of mine.

"Thank you, Mr. Tracey, I waste more cigarettes than I smoke; I can't keep them alight."

Dimly I heard Mrs. Peters speaking, though my mind was wandering to the envelope in my pocket.

"You got on well with Mrs. Browne?"

There was a smile on her face that told me she knew the lady.

"She is rather difficult."

"She's an old cat," Mabel said viciously, "she's done more mischief in this village—"

"My dear," Peters said laughing, "never take people's characters away—they have only got one, you know."

"That's just what she does—no one is safe from her. You wouldn't believe it, Mr. Tracey—if a boy in the village goes for a walk with a girl she sends for him, and asks him 'what his intentions are, and whether they are strictly honourable.' She makes me sick—why, if it hadn't been for her I don't believe this murder would ever have taken place."

Silence fell on all of us, and I saw Peters give his daughter a glance of disapproval.

"It's no good, Mr. Peters," I said, coming to the girl's rescue. "We've got to discuss this matter. I am sure you asked me here for that purpose."

"I quite agree," Mabel chimed in feverishly. "We were discussing it when you came in. Dad thinks you've got yourself into a mess. Bother! this cigarette has gone out—no, Mr. Tracey, I'm going to relight it just to cure myself of the habit, and it's too good to waste."

Mrs. Peters smiled indulgently at Mabel. "You smoke too much, my dear, at your age."

Her object was plain, but I was not to be put off. "So," I remarked, smiling at Peters, "dad thinks I've got myself into a mess?"

"I think your friend Darent is in a serious position, but, of course, we must not judge hastily."

My heart sank at this opinion, coming from a barrister of so great a reputation.

"He must have a solicitor at once," Peters declared. "That's what we were discussing when you came in. He's so stubborn that it is quite likely that he will refuse."

"Surely there must be some family lawyer?" I asked.

"There was," Peters said grimly. "Notcutt and Baines, a very old and respected firm, but Darent quarrelled with them, and told them they were a pack of swindlers. They merely wanted him to sell some of his land for building—a sensible thing to do—he could have paid off his debts and put the place in repair. He wouldn't do it—"

"Sir John Barton wanted to buy the land, I believe," I commented.

"You are right. I tried my hardest to get him to sell—of course, as John's father-in-law, not in a professional capacity—but he simply would not hear of it. It was a pity, as that started the quarrel."

I was getting a little tired of all this question about the quarrel. "Then I suppose we must get him another solicitor," I said briskly.

"Quite candidly, when I asked you to come and see me, Tracey, I was wondering whether you would be prepared to help, but this matter has now been settled. After I left you I called on Miss Morris, the Lady of the Manor, who is a queer old thing, but has a heart of gold, and was one of the only people of standing here who believed in Darent and liked him. They got on splendidly together, both being thoroughly rude by habit. She insists on paying for a solicitor, and when she makes up her mind to a course of action nothing will move her."

"I'm very glad to hear about this, for I was going to offer to help, but wondered how Kenneth would take it; he's so touchy. The solicitor will, of course, brief the best counsel he can get."

Mrs. Peters smiled at me, and laid her hand affectionately on her husband's arm.

"He is going to have the best: my husband has told Miss Morris that he will be pleased to act for the defence without charging any fees—that is, when the solicitor has given him the brief."

I confess I was startled at this news. I had not observed any particular affection for Darent on Peters's part, and he had been Barton's father-in-law, but perhaps I had misjudged him.

"That is very generous of you, Mr. Peters."

"Not at all—I am sorry my wife mentioned it," he said testily, and in that pompous manner I had objected to the night before. "I feel that if any one can make out a case for him, I can, because I am acquainted with all the circumstances and the difficulties."

"Perhaps you will defend me as well," I remarked, I fear, to pull his leg, but he did not respond to my mood.

"I hope it will not come to that. Certainly you will be called as a witness—a very important one."

"On which side, Mr. Peters?" I challenged him.

"I am afraid I mustn't discuss the case at all under the circumstances. Now that Miss Morris and I have arranged matters I can no longer speak freely to you—I hope you will understand."

His tone annoyed me.

"I expect they will try and get me to give evidence against my friend," I said to tease him.

Mabel, who had remained strangely silent, suddenly broke in. "You wouldn't do that, Mr. Tracey; you're not that sort—you'd sooner lie to save a friend."

I am certain my face went scarlet, in spite of my efforts to control myself.

"You mustn't talk like that, Mabel," Mrs. Peters said gently.

Mabel was getting rather near to the truth, but she was not going to be shut up. "Why not? I'd lie like a trooper to get any one off—if it happened to be a friend of mine. Suppose dad killed Mr. Turnbull—"

"Which," I remarked with relish, "would be a most excellent piece of work."

"Really, Mr. Tracey, you are as bad as Mabel," Mrs. Peters said, but her husband was watching me closely.

"I think he's a wretched little worm—I'm so glad you threw him out of the Crown," Mabel observed.

"I'm not," her father snapped.

I felt the conversation had lasted long enough. "All these arrangements may be quite unnecessary, Mr. Peters, if the police can lay their hands on the real murderer."

"I profoundly hope they will, but I see small chance of that at present."

Our eyes met, and in that moment I realized that Peters was of opinion that Darent would have to take his trial, and that we must be prepared for it.

"Oh, by the way—I'm sorry." Peters produced an envelope from his pocket. "Miss Morris gave me this note to give you, but I quite forgot it."

I thanked him, and was putting the letter into my pocket.

"Won't you read it? It may have some bearing on this case. I am sure Mrs. Peters will excuse you." I broke the seal, and read this extraordinary missive

"The Crest,
"Crowfield.

"DEAR SIR,

"You have probably heard of me; if not, it doesn't matter in the least. I am Rosie Morris, and happen to be the Lady of the Manor of Crowfield—I am also old and extremely ugly. Of course, I am interested in this murder, and I can't say I am very sorry, for I couldn't stand the man.

"My maid tells me that you and Kenneth Darent did it between you, but that's all damned nonsense. I want to see you and have a talk, but not here, as there are too many gossiping old women of both sexes in the village. I am going up to Town to see about getting a lawyer for Kenneth, as I know he won't trouble about getting one, the idiot!

"Come and have lunch with me to-morrow at 1.30 if you don't mind my company. I rather liked the look of you when I saw you in the village yesterday. The address is 39 Yorkshire Terrace, Regent's Park.

"Don't make excuses, as I know you have nothing to do, and it's no good your mooning about this village, as you won't find out anything here.

Yours truly,

"ROSIE MORRIS."

"Miss Morris wants me to lunch with her to-morrow in Town," I said shortly, not wishing to read the note aloud.

"You'll find her a strange being, Mr. Tracey," Mrs. Peters said. "I am too old-fashioned for her, I am afraid."

"She seems a rum bird," I remarked.

"We really must be going," Peters said—rather hurriedly, I thought. "I hope we shall see you in Town—you must let me know how you get on."

"Will you settle up with the landlord, James? Mabel and I will go and get ready."

Miss Morris's letter seemed to have broken up the party abruptly. Peters shook hands with me, but there was an expression on his poker face that I could not read—whether hostility or friendship. I saw him make his way down the passage to Willis's private room.

When they had gone I darted to the fireplace and picked up the half-burnt cigarette, and then from the envelope took the one from the car, and laid them side by side. They were both of the same length, and of the same brand, and both were stained with vermilion at the tip.

I heard the sound of the Peters car starting, and Polly's cheerful 'good-bye,' but stood staring at the two cigarettes, trying to find an explanation. I was unaware of Polly's presence in the room until she spoke.

"I beg your pardon, Mr. Tracey; I didn't know you were here."

"I was having a think, Polly. Any news?"

I was beginning to understand my young friend, who was a born gossip and enjoyed a talk at any time. "Nothing at all, sir. May I take these?"

She was just going to sweep up my cigarette-ends, but I closed my hands over them. "No, Polly; I always make a point of collecting old cigarette-ends, and smoking them in a pipe—it saves money."

She looked at me doubtfully. "You wouldn't smoke those; she always throws them away half smoked, and red at the ends."

"Who smokes them?" I asked innocently.

"Why, Miss Peters. She's always smoking—ever since I first knew her, and she was only a schoolgirl then. She gave me the first one I ever had, and her bedroom's a sight in the morning."

"Don't you ever put lipstick to your lips, Polly—not even when you go out with jack?"

She tossed her head. "No, sir; he doesn't like it."

"I quite appreciate his taste," I replied, laughing. "You are sure these are Miss Peters's?"

She examined the two ends. "Certain—she asked for a box last night when she went out. Oh, she asked me not to say anything about it."

"But it's very important, Polly, and I won't tell tales. When did she go out?"

"You won't tell her, sir?

"Honour bright."

"Last night, sir; she got dressed before Mrs. Peters, and came down. I was laying the table for their dinner. They were dining here first, as Mr. Peters wouldn't go there, and I can quite understand that, after poor Lady Barton's death. Well, as I was saying, sir, Miss Mabel asked me for cigarettes, and I fetched a box from the bar. She filled her case and told me I could keep the rest. Then she said she had to go out, but wouldn't be long, and would I tell her mother, if she asked, that she was still in her room."

"How long was she out, Polly?

"About half an hour, I should say. I think she went to see Miss Margorie; but something had upset her—she hardly ate anything—"

"All right, Polly. I shall be going to London to-night: I've had enough of Crowfield for the present. I expect I shall be back shortly. Now get my bill, and I'll go into the lounge and wait."

"Won't you go and say good-bye to my mother?' she said, and was almost pushing me out of the room.

"There's plenty of time for that. What's the matter, Polly? You seem in a great hurry to get rid of me." A thought struck me, and I stopped at the doorway.

"Is there someone in the lounge you don't want me to meet? I think I'll go and see."

Her face betrayed her. "It's Mr. Turnbull—please don't go—there are two men with him—I shouldn't go, sir." She placed a detaining hand on my arm.

I strode, laughing at her fears, down the steps to the lounge, and saw the lawyer in deep consultation with two men of unpleasant appearance. He looked up and saw me, and a sour expression came to his sallow face. With these two supporters he felt safe from physical violence.

"So, Mr. Tracey," he croaked, "you are still here? Polly informed me that you had gone to London. I am afraid truthfulness is not a strong point with these villagers."

"Nor honesty with you lawyers," I retorted.

He scowled at me. "This is Mr. Tracey about whom I was speaking," he said to the other two men, who merely stared rudely at me.

"I think I am correct in saying that you two are here in connexion with the affairs of my friend, Mr. Darent?" I asked.

They looked for guidance to the lawyer, who gave a smile of amused contempt. "Really, Mr. Tracey, you are behaving like an overgrown schoolboy; I fail to see what concern it is of yours."

"I should not act hastily if I were you," I said, ignoring Turnbull. "I am instructing my lawyer with regard to all the outstanding debts of Mr. Darent's, and he will take action at once, so that he will be relieved from all financial worry until he is released."

My bluff seemed to have some effect on the two men who were obviously acting under Turnbull's orders.

"If there is any distraint on the property, I shall apply for a stay of execution," I said, using the first phrase that came into my head, and I saw the sneer on Turnbull's face. I could not refrain from giving him one parting shot.

"Let me give you one piece of advice, Turnbull. Many a murderer has been caught by trying to fix the crime on another man—it's a risky game."

I marched triumphantly out of the room, as he sprang to his feet, and I saw the sickly green colour of his face. I had already made up my mind that it was the lawyer who had taken my pumps, and had an idea that he had removed the stick from the Willises' room the night before. Whether he had actually done the murder or not, I had not made up my mind—on the whole, I thought he was too great a coward, but I was pretty certain he knew something about it.

At the same time I had an uneasy feeling that he was going to make a bad enemy.

CHAPTER X

THE MEETING IN THE CHURCH

HAD decided to take no risks with regard to my meeting with Margorie, being certain in my mind that my movements were being watched. I announced openly that I had to return to London, paid my bill, and brought my car round to the front, placing the suit-case on the back seat. I had studied the map and found that at the bottom of the hill where the railway ran along the valley, there was a little village called Waddington. Although some distance from Crowfield by road on account of the steepness of the hill, there was a footpath marked on the map that led from the village to Crowfield and came out close to the church, making a short cut.

I had time to slip up to London, and reassure my man as to my existence, and then get in touch with my friend Charles Erskine, whom I had known all my life, and arrange for an appointment for the next day. His father and mine had been lifelong friends, and now that he had retired from business, Charles was nominally, at any rate, at the head of the firm of solicitors that bore his name. He was just the man I wanted for an emergency like this.

I was glad to get away from the village, and feel the breeze blowing freely around me. And only yesterday it seemed incredible—I had been speeding down for a pleasant holiday with my old friend Kenneth.

My thoughts came back to the grim problem, in spite of all my efforts to concentrate on driving. Of course there was always the possibility that some entire stranger had been the murderer—someone who had a grudge against Barton, or who was out for blackmail on the eve of his wedding. From all accounts he had not been a very pleasant character.

But there were the footmarks of the pair of pumps that had afterwards appeared in my bag mysteriously; and Darent's stick!

And then there floated before my eyes the face of the girl who had come into my life—it was no good disguising the fact—whose image would never be out of my mind. I had never looked upon a woman with anything but a passing interest in my crabbed, rather selfish life, and then I must needs meet one who belonged to another man, for whom I was risking my liberty and reputation.

For I knew quite clearly now that I would not have gone on with that alibi for Darent's sake—though I would not have betrayed him—if it had not been for Margorie's pleading look, and her request for a secret meeting, which could only be about this very business.

My work in Town was soon over—a telephone call, and a brief visit to my flat, and I went back by a different road, and arrived at half-past nine at the tiny village of Waddington, where all the good people had already retired, and the miniature station was shut up and in darkness.

I left the car under some trees, in charge of Hoad, whom I had brought with me for company, and made my way to the pathway which started close to the station yard.

Darkness had come on, but there was an afterglow in the sky, deep purple above, and pale green and saffron in the west, and the moon was showing above the skyline, pale and gibbous. On one side were fields enclosed by a wire fence, and on the other dense woods, and the path was steep and stony in places. I toiled up, hanging on by the wire of the fence, and thankful that no rain had fallen for days.

At length I reached a spot where the wood ended, and away on my right the church tower rose black above the black yew trees, against the greenish glow of the sky.

The moon rose above the wood, and flooded the place with light. A low wall was before me, which I climbed, and found myself in the churchyard. My watch showed me that the time was ten minutes to ten, and I crouched down among the tombstones. It was eerie work waiting there, for a churchyard is not the cheeriest place in which to keep a vigil, and bats flickered round from time to time like lost souls. The air was very still, and the night noises of the countryside came sharp and clear to my ears. The sound of a train shunting somewhere and the clank of the trucks as they struck one another mingled with the hum of an aeroplane in the distance, as though the triumph of man's inventions mocked the dead that lay so still.

I crept forward and found myself opposite the massive vault that the dead baronet had erected for his wife, and the angel surmounting it stood gaunt and white in the moonlight.

The rector's words came back to me: "If she had lived, this would never have occurred." Was it merely a catch-phrase, or was there some deeper meaning underlying his words?

A faint sound in the still night made me look round sharply, and I could not refrain from a shudder when I saw a black form flitting from stone to stone, though I knew it must be Margorie. All doubt was removed when she made for the west door, and I heard the grating of a key in the lock. I rose stealthily and glided forward, and she turned and saw me. Without a word we entered together, and she locked the door behind us. Taking my hand, in case I should stumble against one of the pews, she led me to the north side of the church, along an aisle to a small side chapel at the end. My eyes were getting used to the dark, and by the fitful glimmer of the moonlight through the windows I could make out patches of white by the stone pillars, the meaning of which I did not for a moment grasp.

We stopped at the altar rails of the side chapel, and Margorie removed the dark shawl she was wearing over her head, letting it fall round her shoulders, so that the perfect oval of her face showed white against the dark ring of her hair. Her great eyes shone in the dim, uncertain light, calm and clear, though the hand that still held mine was trembling.

"It was very good of you to come, Mr. Tracey," she said in a low, steady voice, and the echoes seemed to whisper round the building.

I started as the clock in the tower above us boomed the hour of ten. "Of course I came."

"We haven't much time. You will wonder why I asked you to meet me, especially in this place, where the flowers for my wedding have not even been removed."

I shuddered as the meaning of those white patches dawned on me. Her voice had almost an hysterical note, but she pulled herself up sharply.

"There was no other place—my mother is watching me all the time, and you too are under observation. No one saw you come?"

I told her about my movements briefly.

"I am not going to keep you long, but I believe you are the only man who can save him."

I had no need to ask to whom she was referring, and I felt a pang of petulant jealousy, but I answered her firmly enough: "I mean to do so."

"I know everything," she went on in quiet, even tones. "My mother took me to the Hall this morning, saying that she must see the servants and give them 'what comfort she could,' but really to find out all she could get out of them. While she was talking to Mrs. Martin I took Mary aside. I have known her all my life, and she knew she could trust me." Margorie paused, as though she could hardly go on, and her eyes turned away from me. "She told me the whole story of what you did last night, and I think it was splendid of you all, but especially of you as a stranger; and you had been treated badly."

"A friend," I corrected her.

"A true friend if ever a man had one," she cried passionately.

The very sound of her voice was like music to me, and I could have listened all night, like a lovesick fool. "When I heard this from Mary I knew that I must see you, not only to thank you, but to tell you everything I can to help."

"Don't tell me anything you would rather not," I said foolishly.

"There is nothing to hide—I want you to know the truth. I shall never forgive myself as long as I live. It was all my fault."

"You must not blame yourself—your mother made you do it."

"You know that—but nothing can alter my crime, though I acted for the best." She drew away from me slightly, and her manner changed. "You think me a cold-blooded, heartless gold-digger, selling myself to a rich man, and now speaking like this in the very place where we were to have been married."

"I don't," I said stoutly. "You never loved him."

"That makes it all the worse. I know that few girls now marry for love, and any romance is laughed at—my mother was always rubbing that in. I can't help saying this, and you must think what you like of me, but I have a positive sense of relief—horrible, isn't it?"

"I don't agree—he ought never to have tried the methods of a cad; bribery, and blackmail, that's what it amounted to."

My heat seemed to astonish her.

"I don't know how much you have been told, but I won't hide anything from you. I loved Ken from the first day we met, when he came to the Hall after his father's death. I was only a schoolgirl then, but he was so fine and strong, and full of all he was going to do; and he was so chivalrous and brave. He once rescued me from a savage bull, and he hadn't even a stick, but waved his handkerchief in the animal's face. I never forgot it. And then I saw him gradually going to pieces. I knew that he loved me—he does now . . . If only he had told me, it would have made all the difference. I don't suppose many girls have gone through what I have. I didn't know how bad things were with him at the Hall, but I do now."

I could visualize the drama that had been enacted in this quiet village—a proud man stricken with poverty and afraid to tell the girl he loved her, and she hurt beyond measure at his treatment of her.

"He quarrelled with my mother," she went on dreamily, as though talking to herself, "and I never guessed the reason until too late. He never came near us, and seemed to shut himself up more and more at the Hall, and he was drinking—"

"I know," I said quickly. "Your father told me about that, and the reason."

She gave me a look of thanks, as though glad that she had not to explain.

"All the time I was going to the Towers with Elsie and Mabel, and having a good time. . . . I heard by accident that Ken had actually had a tennis court got ready, and was going to ask us down, but was too shy and proud to go on with it. . . . I nearly cried when I heard about it—it was so pathetic when he had no money to spare. And then came poor

Elsie's death, and from that moment everything got worse. I never guessed—"

A sudden conviction came to my mind, born of what the rector had said.

"Barton was in love with you before his wife died," I said almost sternly.

"I never dreamt of such a thing—they appeared quite happy; but afterwards I came to know that it was so. I wouldn't have gone near his place if I had known it, but he seemed so broken-hearted at her death, and so miserable and wanting sympathy. He hadn't the strong character of Ken, who could suffer without complaint, and mother told me I ought to go and talk to him, with Mabel. He was so clever." Her voice assumed a bitter tone. "He would talk so nicely about Ken, and ask how he could possibly help him without him knowing, and suggest all kinds of ways, and I foolishly fell into the trap, and told him about the mortgage, and how I knew Ken was worrying, in terror that the people would foreclose on him. Then he suggested that he should buy it, and I told him Ken would be furious. I can see now what he was leading up to—but I thought it rather fine of him at the time. And all the time he was scheming with my mother, and at last he proposed to me."

"You refused him."

"I did at first, and he kept away, but wrote me a letter, so charmingly worded, saying that my refusal would make no difference to what he proposed to do to help Ken, and that he had a plan to help him. And Ken was getting worse, and I thought he had ceased to care for me, and a girl can't stand throwing herself at a man who doesn't want her. Now I know I was wrong, but it seemed the only way to save the Hall and him, and I had heard that he would sooner kill himself than give up his estate. I didn't care what happened, and mother was always saying that nowadays people married simply to get a position and that no one cared whether they were fond of each other or not. But I would have done what I could for him if I had married him—I don't know whether I could have gone through with it."

"I know," I said. "I saw you yesterday in this church."

"I must tell you—it is very important. Yesterday he called to see me in the afternoon, with the mortgage deeds of the Hall, which Mr. Turnbull had bought for him, and gave them to me. He had had them made out in my name, and the transfer was to me. He said I could do what I liked with them—either give them back to Ken, or if I destroyed them, the property would revert to Ken. He asked me to take it as a wedding present, though he had already given me far too many."

Turnbull's words about a 'monstrous document' came back to me.

"Does any one know about this?" I asked.

"Only Mr. Turnbull, who arranged the whole thing—not a soul otherwise down here."

"So you have the deeds?"

I destroyed them last night before the murder. I wanted to make sure that Ken should have his property back, and I knew he would never take it from me."

"That's going to make things awkward, but how can I help you?"

"I wanted to tell you all this; let him know if you can that I am going to stand by him. We must save him—"

Something in her manner gave me a hint of the truth. "Will you answer me if I ask a question, and not be offended?"

"What is it?" She spoke in a whisper and her eyes had terror in them.

"Do you believe that Kenneth murdered Sir John? Oh, not murdered—he would never have done that, but if they had quarrelled—Ken had a hasty temper. Didn't Mary tell you about the stick?"

"Yes, but,"—she hesitated—"I thought you had made that up to screen him—I thought all the more of you for that." There was a tremor in her voice and she hung on my next words. In her excitement she had gripped my hands.

"It was true," I said slowly; "absolutely true. Kenneth never had that stick."

She buried her face in her hands, which she had torn from mine, and sobs shook her body. I felt too helpless to say anything. I knew what her feelings must be.

Then she looked at me, and her face was calm. "I wish I could believe you, but I saw him myself."

She spoke with the calm of despair.

"You saw him?"

"They were asking for John, and I was worried—I feared that Ken would come, somehow, and I slipped out at the back. I saw Ken moving across the lawn, I could not possibly mistake him—I know his walk so well. I ran in and asked where John was, and then they searched—"

"I know. Did you see anything else?"

She would not look at me. "I fancy I saw another figure crouching and moving after him."

"And you thought that I was the other?" I said with a laugh which sounded hollow in the darkness of the church.

"I didn't know—" she stammered.

"Margorie"—the Christian name slipped out, but she took no notice—"you must believe me—I swear to you on my honour that every word I have told you is true— that Kenneth found Sir John dead, and that the crouching figure you saw was the murderer."

"I do believe you; I do really now, but what must you think of me?"

"All the more," I said lightly, "for you met me here, and were going to stand by Kenneth."

"I am so glad—you know what I mean—it's such a weight off my mind. We must find out who did it." She hardly seemed to know what she was saying.

"What did you do?" I asked, to give her time to collect her thoughts.

"I went back to the house, and asked my father if he had seen John, and then the search began, and Robert came in to say that he had seen the butler, and that Ken had met him somewhere by appointment."

"One more question—who found the holly-stick?

"Robert Barton—it was lying beside the body, he said."

"Thank you, that's most valuable."

She seemed to realize how time was passing. "I must get back, or I shall be missed. You must leave me now. You are a true friend to Ken—and to me," she added softly. "Write to Polly, and I will fetch the letters; it's the only safe way. Here is the key; you can leave it in the lock. I shall wait here till you have gone."

I took the key and bending down, kissed her hand lightly.

"I thought that courteous custom had gone out of date," she said with a low laugh, and I saw she was near to tears.

She turned from me, and knelt at the altar rails. I tiptoed out of the building, with an agony of bitterness in my heart, for I knew that I must fight and lie to save the man she loved from the gallows, without hope of reward. I am no hero—I could not rise to heights of unselfish exultation at the thought that I was fighting for her happiness. I could only curse Darent in my mind for ever having brought me to this village, and to a lifetime of misery.

CHAPTER XI

MISS MORRIS GIVES ADVICE

WILL not dwell upon the night I spent after returning from Crowfield, for my personal feelings are of no interest in this tale.

I drove to Yorkshire Terrace the next morning, rather curious to meet the writer of the eccentric letter I had received.

No. 39 was one of the few large houses in the terrace facing Regent's Park, that had not been converted into flats or boarding-houses of the more exclusive kind.

A butler, looking as though he had stepped straight out of the eighteenth century, with mutton-chop whiskers and a bland manner, opened the door and ushered me in with a low bow.

"I will inform Miss Morris that you are here, sir, if you will not mind waiting in here for a few minutes," he said with a carefully modulated voice, and waved me into a sitting-room, half drawing-room, and half lounge, with windows both at the front and back. The latter opened to the garden, with iron steps leading down from the French windows. Two enormous boar-hounds rose at my entrance and sniffed at me suspiciously.

"They won't bite, sir," the old man said reassuringly, and softly closed the door. I walked to the window and looked out at the garden, which was of considerable size for London, and contained a tennis court. The aged butler was waddling down a gravel path, and he disappeared behind some tall bushes, from whence came the sound of voices.

A figure emerged and came towards me. I say a figure advisedly, for seldom have I seen anything so grotesque outside a fancy dress ball. Miss Morris—for I was sure that it was she—was clothed in a very short tweed skirt, a green jumper, and a straw hat, very old and shabby. Her grey hair showed in straggling wisps beneath her hat, and from the brim there hung an eyeglass attached to the hat by a metal fastening.

She carried a tennis racket, and her face was the colour of a beetroot from violent exercise. She hailed me in a deep contralto voice, almost amounting to a bass.

"That you, Mr. Tracey? I've just been playing tennis with Miss Baines, my companion; there's nothing like exercise to keep one fit." She came up the iron stairs like a young girl, and shook hands with a man's grip. "Down, Dirk," she said to one of the boar-hounds, who had put his two paws on her shoulders, patting him on the nose with her racket. On close inspection I saw that she had a squint in one eye, and a perceptible moustache.

She removed the straw hat and flung it on a chair. "Ugly looking brute, aren't I? Just give me a minute to wash, and we'll have lunch. I told Miss Baines I wanted to talk to you alone."

She gave me no time for a reply, but hurried out of the room, returning in a few minutes.

"Come along—what do they call you—I can't stand all this 'mister' business?"

"My name is Dennis Tracey," I replied, leaving her to take her choice.

"All right, I'll call you Dennis." She led the way across the hall to the dining-room, the furniture of which was in keeping with the house. I don't suppose it had been altered for a hundred years. There were portraits of former Morrises on the walls, old men with bald heads and white whiskers, and one in the uniform of the Crimean War period. The two huge dogs had solemnly followed their mistress, and lay down on each side of her in quiet expectation. She dismissed the old butler, and started her lunch with the appetite of a navvy, after placing two plates on the floor for the hounds. She pushed a decanter across to me. "Help yourself if you like burgundy—have anything else if you want it. I drink whisky—wine is too acid for me."

I set-to with a good will, having had no breakfast, and she smiled her approval. "I never trust a man who won't eat. Now about this murder—I never believe in beating about the bush. Kenneth has got himself into a hell of a mess, and we've got to get him out of it."

"I'll do anything I can."

"Of course you will—I wouldn't have asked you here if I hadn't known that. He's been a damned fool, but he's not a murderer, you can take that from me."

"I know he's not," I said with all the assurance I could muster.

"Don't be a fool, you can't know! I've heard all about that alibi of yours, but I'm a county magistrate, and you can't spoof me so easily."

"Then may I ask what is the use of this interview?" I said stiffly.

"Now don't go and lose your temper—that's the worst of you young men, you are so touchy you go off the deep end at the least thing. We have got to get Kenneth out of this somehow, and it's going to be a tough job."

"The first thing is the question of his defence, in case he will agree to have a lawyer." I was thinking of Darent's mulishness.

"You need not worry your head over that; I've put a firm of solicitors on the track—the biggest collection of scoundrels in London, but if any one can make out a case they will, and I'm settling all that, as Kenneth hasn't a bean."

"That's very good of you."

"Stuff and nonsense—I couldn't stand that Barton man. I did my best to keep him from coming to the village."

"I was thinking that Kenneth won't allow any one to help him," I said humbly.

"Won't he? Let me hear him dare to refuse. I'm going to see him."

"I would like to come, if I may."

She gave a deep laugh, like the bay of a hound.

"You're not going to; make your mind easy about that. In the first place he wouldn't see you, as he thinks you've 'done the dirty' on him, and in the second place you will be an important witness, and must on no account hold any communication with him. You can leave all that to me. Now there's the question of the Hall while he's away."

"I am seeing to that."

"You are what?"

"I am meeting my lawyer to-day, and will arrange to settle up what is owing."

She gave a grunt. "He won't like that—you'd better keep out of it."

"I shall certainly not." I had begun to appreciate this strange creature, and was not going to be browbeaten. "I have it all fixed up; he won't know anything about it, and it will not be in my name even."

"Humph! Can you afford it?"

"It won't run me into bankruptcy, and I haven't a relation in the world that I know of, so my money will only go to some institution."

"You'll probably marry."

"Have you?"

"That's better, Dennis; I was afraid you were one of those fools who couldn't be rude."

"Then that's settled, but I should have thought the best way to help Kenneth would be to find the murderer."

"Marvellous brain you've got. It would help considerably, but we can't bank on that—we must be prepared for Kenneth going for trial."

"The police seem so convinced that Kenneth did it, that they are not worrying about any other explanation they are just trying to pile up evidence against him."

Miss Morris seized my plate and her own, slapped them on the ancient sideboard, and returned with fresh supplies. The dish she emptied into the plates on the floor.

"That's the best thing that could happen," she said when this had been done; "it'll give the murderer a sense of security."

"And give him time to get away," I grumbled. "It might have been a tramp, of course, or a burglar who was trying to take advantage of the party."

She interrupted me: "Do talk sense—of course it might have been any one. Have we got any clue at all?"

"Kenneth's stick—someone took it from the Crown Inn."

"You're certain he left it there—it's not part of the alibi?"

"It was undoubtedly left behind by the man who killed Barton, in order, I am sure, to fasten the crime on to him."

"You use the word 'man' —it might have been a woman."

"Hardly with those injuries—the head was terribly battered about, and the face was hardly recognizable."

Miss Morris looked queerly at me. "Some girls are very strong, and you never know what frenzy a woman may get into, especially a wronged woman, who has a grievance against a man."

"It's possible—a woman could have got out of the house easier than a man." I recalled what Margorie had told me.

"The stick was left at the Crown, you say," Miss Morris said with meaning. She took a cigarette and lit it. "The question is whether the murder was done to stop the wedding, or had it any connexion with the private life of Barton?"

"You mean it was the perfect murder—someone wanted to get rid of Barton for some unknown reason, and chose the opportunity and the hour, in order to have an absolutely damning case against Kenneth."

She leant down and patted one of her dogs. "With what object?"

"Either personal gain or revenge."

"Here, don't get melodramatic or filmy, for the Lord's sake. You've got something at the back of your mind."

"I have, but I'm keeping it to myself. I don't want to be laughed at for a fool. If anything comes of it, I'll tell you."

"You are going to try your hand at detective work—well, I hope you succeed. Have a glass of port. You'll find it on the sideboard."

It seemed to me that Miss Morris was disappointed with our interview and had expected something more—I was not quite sure whether she thought I had been telling her the truth.

"Look here, Dennis," she said suddenly when I had returned to my seat, "are you going on with this alibi of yours?"

She shot the question at me.

I sipped at my port before replying.

"If I am called as a witness, I shall certainly state exactly what happened."

"What in Heaven's name do you mean by that?" she asked testily.

"I have already told the inspector."

"I know, and he told me—I've heard all about it, and I don't care two hoots about your perjuring yourself, if it's the only way to get Kenneth off, but I'm afraid you'll make an ass of yourself in the witness-box, and do more harm than good."

Her statement coincided so accurately with my own thoughts that I could not feel anger.

"I hope not."

Miss Morris remained silent, drumming her fingers on the table, and I walked to the window, looking out on the greenery of Regent's Park, where the trees had wilted in the summer heat, and nursemaids were wheeling their charges slowly beneath the shady covering of the branches. I gazed idly at the scene, my mind only seeing a crowded court, and a stern-faced judge facing me. "Perjury," he was saying, and every eye was turned on me. And then I came back to realities, and saw a sight that was almost as terrifying. A man was lurking under the trees, half hidden but distinct, and I recognized the sallow face of Turnbull. He was watching the house, and when he saw me at the window he fixed his eyes on mine. Even at that distance I could see his cold, malevolent look. I turned back to the room, and met Miss Morris's eyes fixed on me.

"It may not come to that," she said quietly.

I started violently. "I beg your pardon."

"I knew what you were thinking about, but if we can only solve this mystery, there will be no necessity for you to give evidence."

"Quite so," I said vaguely, for the sight of Turnbull waiting outside like a venomous snake had put the other question right out of my head.

"Don't look so gloomy. I expect you want to go and keep your appointment. I am glad to have met you, Dennis. I wasn't altogether certain whether you were a fool or a criminal."

"And which have you discovered me to be?"

She smiled broadly at me, and took my hand.

"Neither, but a generous and loyal friend, and, I hope, one of mine."

I thanked her, wondering whether I could ask her if she had a back entrance through which I might make my escape, and then a wave of anger swept over me, and I put my hat firmly on my head and went down the front steps, determined to meet the little viper face to face.

I did not go to my car, but walked straight across the road, and hopped the railings. I think my deliberate approach disconcerted him, but he came to meet me.

"You have been watching Miss Morris's house," I said without preface.

"I happened to see you go in, Mr. Tracey," he replied in sleek tones that put me at once upon my guard. "I was waiting for you to come out."

"For what purpose! I have no desire to see you."

"Come, Mr. Tracey, I think there are several things that we have to discuss, and it is a more pleasant place here in the open park than at your own flat perhaps: I have already had experience of your methods." He laughed in a cringing manner, and I looked full at the man. Although he had been standing under the shade, his forehead was wet with perspiration and his hands were twitching. I realized two things—he was in mortal dread of me for some reason, and he had sought this interview for some unpleasant purpose of his own at a place where he could not be attacked.

"Let us walk a little," he said; 'the park is very beautiful at this time of year, and full of interest."

Unconsciously I fell into line with him, and we strolled across the grass in the direction of the lovely flower gardens, now rather past their prime.

"I understand, Mr. Tracey, from the most interesting talk we had yesterday, that you are proposing to do something in the matter of Mr. Darent's debts, while he is unable to see to things."

"That is a matter I propose to leave entirely to my lawyer," I said coldly, knowing full well that this was not the reason for his presence outside the house.

"Quite so! I understand that. Perhaps he and I could meet and discuss matters, some time—it would smooth the way to a complete settlement."

"I don't think I follow you. What do you mean by a settlement?"

"There are certain things, Mr. Tracey. For example, the assault you committed the day of your arrival—dear me, it was only the day before yesterday. Of course, I don't wish to go to extremes in the matter, and I am sure that you don't, either. Perhaps we could compromise by a small cash consideration instead of going to the courts."

"You won't get a farthing out of me." I laughed at him, for I was convinced that all this was only leading up to something more important, but he was bolstering his courage in this way.

"Well, if you are obstinate—but I should have thought a gentleman in your position would have made the *amende honorable* without being asked. It is a very ugly business at Crowfield—murder cannot be settled on such easy terms."

"Murder can only be paid for with the rope!" I looked him full in the face, and he winced.

"I agree entirely, but there are other crimes—perjury, for example—which are serious in the eyes of the law."

"I have been told so," I answered him, now completely master of myself.

"I see you take a sensible view of matters. Now, as you have probably guessed, I have been instructed to collect all the outstanding debts of Mr. Darent, and to take steps for the recovery of them. It amounts in all to a fairly large sum."

"Possibly—my lawyer will see all the accounts and check them."

He stopped in his walk, and laid his hand on my arm —a habit I detest. "But is it necessary, Mr. Tracey? Would it not be better for us to settle this between us? And you can give me sufficient to cover everything—I think, mind you, that it is most generous of you."

I shook his arm off. "Speak plainly. You want me to give you money; some to go on the debts and the rest into your pocket."

He made a movement—deprecatory—with his hand.

"There will be expenses, of course, and"—he looked round to see that no one was within earshot—"believe me, it will be your wisest course. You are anxious, I know, that your friend Mr. Darent shall get off."

"Is this blackmail?"

"Heaven forbid—what are you talking about? Certainly not. I merely wish to help you."

"You dirty little toad," I said, completely losing my temper. "You think you know something, and are trying to get money for your silence."

I had expected him to cringe, or show signs of fear, but he had braced his courage to the sticking-point, and his manner suddenly changed. The worm became a snake, and a poisonous one too.

"I know this," he said in that same vitriolic voice he had used at the Crown. "That your friend *did* leave the Hall and go to the Towers the night before last, and that the lie you are proposing to tell will land you in prison. I know that Barton, like a fool, had transferred the mortgage deeds on the Hall to Miss Browne, and that they are missing, and I know other things. Would you like to hear them?"

"I think it would be wiser for you to hold up there."

"Very good, Mr. Tracey; I give you fair warning. Where will your friend be if I, as a good citizen, go into the witness-box and simply tell the truth?"

"Rubbish—you know no more than the police have told you!"

"The police!" He laughed scornfully. "You are very simple, Mr. Tracey. You came into the lounge yesterday, and found me with two friends of mine, and jumped to the conclusion that they were bailiffs. Really! They are two men I employ in my work—two very useful men, and strong as well. I rather thought that something might happen on the eve of the wedding—something unfortunate, let us say—and after your attack on me, I got them to come over from Wickstead for my protection—you understand, for my personal safety—but they were useful in other ways, and I learnt a lot from them."

"My opinion of you goes up every time I meet you," I remarked scornfully, though my mind was full of misgivings.

"I am delighted," he replied with an ironic bow. "Then we begin to appreciate each other. It may interest you to know that one of my men" —he edged away from me warily—"was keeping a close watch on a certain young lady last night, and followed her to an assignation at the village church—a charming place to meet at ten o'clock."

He sprang backwards with an agility for which I had not given him credit, and his hand went to his pocket. "No, Mr. Tracey, physical violence will not do you any good, and there are too many people about." He produced a police whistle from his pocket instead of a revolver as I had expected.

"We can discuss these matters without heat. Think it over carefully when your temper has died down. I don't know what your friend Darent would think of you." He stopped and laughed. "All right, I'll say no more. There is no hurry for the moment, and I don't want to press you in any way, but I give you warning that if you repeat what I have said to a soul, I shall take action at once. What has been said here you had better forget. If we can come to terms, well and good. I give you a week, and shall expect to hear from you then. We can arrange a suitable place for a further conversation."

"I believe you did the murder yourself—you rat. You took Darent's stick from the Crown Inn, and—"

He grinned at me. "And then went to the Towers, where every one saw me, during the whole evening. That will hardly do, Mr. Tracey."

I saw it was no good bandying words with him. He had chosen his place and time cunningly. There were scores of people about, and a policeman on duty close by.

"Shall we have a look at the flowers?" he asked politely as a couple passed close to us.

"Go to hell!" I said, and strode away across the grass to the place where I had left my car.

CHAPTER XII

MABEL PETERS

IT was an enormous relief to me to see my friend Charles Erskine. As a lawyer I had no great opinion of his abilities, though he was no fool. He was more at home, however, on a golf course than in the office.

His father was far-seeing enough to make arrangements for that. He had insisted that Charles should take their old and trusted chief clerk into partnership, and he was in virtual control of the business, though Charles as a qualified solicitor was the nominal head, and had an unfailing remedy for all difficulties: he would touch a bell on his table and Mr. Smithers, grave and learned, would come to the rescue.

I received a warm welcome, and a terrific handshake when I entered his office in Bedford Row. Charles was a loose-limbed athlete, with a cheery manner and a way of getting on with people.

"Hallo, Dennis, my boy—I thought you would ring me up, when I read about the case at Crowfield. Been having a spot of bother there?"

"It's worse than that."

"What? Did you murder the man or just help your friend Darent bump him off?"

"Neither, Charles—I want you to be serious if you can for a moment. It's a mess—a proper mess."

Something in my appearance must have shown him that the matter was grave, for he sat down at the great desk his father had occupied for so many years.

"Now let's talk."

"It's not about the murder that I wanted to see you, at least not directly, but Kenneth can't look after his affairs while he's under arrest, and I want to help."

He gave a whistle. "My word, you're going to let yourself in for something. I didn't know you were so keen on Darent as all that, but you always were a quixotic sort of beggar."

He tapped his teeth with his pencil, a habit that always annoyed me intensely.

"We must save the old place for him," I said shortly—my nerves were on edge after the interview with Turnbull.

"Hello! Is there a woman in the case?"

"Nothing of the sort," I said indignantly. "At least there is, but nothing to do with what you think."

He gave me a laugh of that particular kind that suggests a hidden joke.

"Charles, I've come to a lawyer, not to a grinning puss-in-boots, so try to collect what wits you have and listen."

"O.K., old thing—what do you want me to do?"

"There's a lawyer—one of the worst blackguards in your disreputable profession, named Turnbull, from Wickstead."

"Turnbull! I know the beauty by name—he's got an office in London, I believe."

"A nasty piece of work, Charles you'll want all the small amount of brain you received from your father to tackle him."

"I'll see to him," he said airily. "I expect he was too much for you. What's he got to do with it anyhow?"

"As far as I can make out, he's got the right of collecting all the debts on Darent's estate."

"An old game, Dennis—the sort of thing he would do. He's always employed to buy up hopeless debts, and has a way of squeezing the money out of the unfortunate wretches who fall into his clutches."

"By blackmail," I said fiercely.

He looked at me seriously. "It's like that, is it?"

I dropped the subject—Charles is a nice fellow and a good friend, but I was not going to confide in him on this question; that would involve Margorie. I had determined to fight this out with Turnbull.

"All I want you to do is to go and see this man, and make the best terms you can with him; but you must stop him from selling up the place."

"They won't do that—don't get the wind up: I'll find out what the liabilities are. By the way, is the place mortgaged?"

"It was—but, well, as a matter of fact, Barton bought up the mortgage deeds and gave them to his fiancée, Miss Margorie Browne."

"Phew! That's going to complicate matters—and she's got them, I suppose?"

"As a matter of fact she destroyed them, but that's private."

"You know, Dennis, it's devilish hard to get anything out of you. The sooner I get down on the spot and see the young lady for myself, the better."

"Go when you like—I know you are not very busy here, and there are two golf courses quite near to Crowfield. There's a nice country inn called the Crown, and the girls are passably pretty for one with catholic tastes like you, only beware of Polly the landlord's daughter."

"And why?"

"If you try to kiss her, she'll box your ears very hard, and she's walking out, as they call it, with the local bobby, who's pretty tough."

"Sounds good—I shan't say that I have any connexion with you—I may find out more that way—but just make myself pleasant and see how the land lies; that's the idea, eh?"

"That'll do."

"Righto, but look here, Dennis, I don't know much at present, but with regard to your position, hadn't you better let us act for you?"

"I was going to ask you to do so."

He touched his bell, and a grey-haired, clean-shaven man of about sixty came in, with a face as hard and unemotional as a piece of parchment.

He took my hand like an undertaker come for an order, though he knew me quite well, and sat down at the desk beside Charles.

He listened in complete silence while I told the facts of the case as far as I wanted them known, and from time to time he took notes with a thin, gold pencil, that somehow looked out of place in his large, fat hand. When I mentioned the name of Beaton and Sykes—which Miss Morris had told me—as the solicitors for Darent, he looked up sharply with a frown on his impassive face.

"They are all right, aren't they?" Charles asked.

"In a case of this sort—the very best."

"Then what's the matter?"

"They are a firm," he said slowly, "that I would rather have on my side than against me—they don't stick at trifles." He closed his mouth like a rat-trap, and would say no more on that subject.

"This is not an easy case," he observed at length, "I think I had better see Mr. Deaken of Beaton and Sykes, and I must have a word with Detective-Inspector Pyke —I have met him over several cases, and he knows me."

"You take a serious view of the case?" I asked with a sinking feeling, for the skull-like head of the old clerk filled me with gloomy forebodings.

"I would not go so far as to say that," he replied in a manner suggestive of a doctor giving a death sentence to a patient.

"I think Mr. Tracey will be well advised to see no one without a representative of our firm."

I nodded in agreement.

"In the second place, I must find out whether they are going to try to implicate him in the actual crime."

This was cheerful hearing.

"Personally, I don't think, from what Mr. Tracey has told us, that they will, but they may call him as a witness for the prosecution."

"Is that what's called King's evidence?" I asked.

Smithers looked hard at me. "Not necessarily—that expression implies complicity in the crime—I had in mind an ordinary witness for the prosecution." He paused as though weighing each word. "I don't think they will do that."

"That's a blessing," I said.

"No, I should think that they will probably let Beaton and Sykes call you as a witness for the defence." His tone was so solemn that I felt alarmed.

"Why?"

"In order, Mr. Tracey," he said, fixing me with his piercing black eyes under beetling white eyebrows, "that the Public Prosecutor may be able to cross-examine you."

"All right," I said with more confidence than I felt.

"When I have more information, I shall probably want you here, Mr. Tracey, to get a statement from you. It would be better, as well as more regular, if we did it, Mr. Charles."

I remembered his remark that Beaton and Sykes would stick at nothing; I began to have a hearty dislike of Smithers and his ghoulish manner. I was certain that he believed my tale no more than Miss Morris had done.

"You carry on, Smithers," Charles said cheerfully, as though glad to be able to shelve the major problem on to the broad back of the chief clerk. I noticed the curious anomaly that although Smithers was a partner, the lifelong habit of 'Mr. Charles' still subsisted.

Charles drew a breath of relief when the other had gone. "Come and have a drink, Dennis; you look as white as a ghost after all this. Smithers positively frightens me, but if any one can help us he can."

"I'd not like to have him against me," I commented.

"That's all right—don't look so glum—there's a sporting chance for Darent."

"That's the way you look at it."

"We'll hope for the best; don't get ratty."

"I'm going to find the murderer," I declared angrily.

"Of course—that's the thing to do." He grinned at me, as though humouring a child.

The week that followed was a nightmare to me, and one I shall never forget. Charles had been resolute that I must not return to Crowfield, and I could sense Smithers behind this mandate. I wandered about London, listlessly, aimlessly, without the heart to go to my club or look up old friends. Their talk would have driven me to distraction. My only solace was the post, and I devoured each letter eagerly. Charles seemed to be treating the whole business as a huge joke, I gathered, and was playing golf most of the time. He had made the acquaintance of young

Barton, and they had struck up quite a friendship from what he told me. He had also called on the rector and seen Margorie which somehow annoyed me. He described her in terms of eulogy which I heartily agreed with, but hardly appreciated as coming from him.

He had, however, seen Turnbull, and it appeared that he was finding no difficulty with him, in fact he said he was pleasantly surprised to find him more agreeable than he had expected. In short his letter thoroughly upset me. Miss Morris wrote me a characteristic letter. She had seen Darent, who absolutely refused to discuss the question of the murder, and had told the lawyer who came to see him, to go to the devil. He said if the lawyer chose to defend him, that was his look-out, but he would take no part in the proceedings. He had been before the magistrates and had been formally remanded at the request of the police. The inquest had been a mere matter of minutes, as the coroner had adjourned it pending the police prosecution. Only evidence of identification was given.

No word had come from Margorie. I had written her a long letter, telling her quite frankly what had happened, except with regard to my interview with Turnbull—that I dared not write. For what was at the back of my mind in these troublous days? Not the question of my evidence, though that was serious enough, but the thought of that slimy brute carrying out his threat of letting Darent know of the meeting in the church. For myself I cared not in the least he could think what he liked of me, but that Margorie's name should be brought in, filled me with fury, and at times I felt that I would rather pay his blackmailer's price than risk this eventuality.

There was nothing that I could do, but think and think, calling back to my fevered mind the tumbled episodes of that visit to Crowfield; Darent lying drunk on his bed; Mary's brave self-accusation; and the moonlit scene in the church, for Margorie's face, wistful and beseeching, would rise salient and torturing over all. I know now that I was a fool to stay in Town, but then I did not dare to meet her.

One other occurrence I must mention; I met a man in the street suspiciously near my flat, who stopped me politely, and asked my name. On hearing it, he merely said that there were three days more, nothing else, and went off, but I recognized him as one of the men in the Crown with Turnbull, and could read the grim meaning. The net was closing in on every side, and it was not even a case where flight would be of any use. I knew I must stay and face it out.

On the last day of the week I could stand it no longer, and wrote a letter, sorely against my better judgement, to Turnbull, asking him to name the price he required for the "article he wished to sell." I was playing for time, and hoped to put him off for a few days at any rate.

And then at the end of this intolerable week, when I was almost at the end of my tether, my telephone bell rang, and I heard the voice of Peters speaking.

"If you are free, would you care to dine with us tonight?"

I almost shouted, for here was a chance of getting back to the problem that filled my whole life.

"Of course, you understand, Tracey," I heard him saying, "now that I have been actually briefed for the defence of Mr. Darent, we must not discuss that question at all, but we should all like to see you again, and I expect you are rather dull in Town."

I agreed with him on both points, and it was with a lighter heart that I set out in my car to his house in Hill Street. Mrs. Peters greeted me kindly, but I had a shock when I saw Mabel. The girl seemed much older, and had a look I did not like—I strongly suspected that she was taking drugs, for I had studied medicine in a desultory way when I had left the Service and found life dull.

I wondered whether her mother had noticed anything, but she gave no sign, and Mabel forced a smile when she shook hands, but her fingers were like icicles, and limp like dead things.

Mr. Peters was a very well-read man, of wide knowledge, and had travelled much. He told me much that I did not know about my father, and of his life in India. I listened, and at intervals made suitable answers, but all the time I was watching Mabel, and my mind was on the one topic of conversation that he had declared taboo. Mabel remained silent, eating practically nothing, but drinking furtively when she thought no one was looking, more than a girl of her age should take.

Peters asked me politely enough about my life and doings, and suggested that a young man should travel and see the world.

Most foolishly I told him I was very fond of mountain climbing.

"Don't!" Mrs. Peters gave a stifled cry. "I can't bear to hear of mountaineering—"

"Nonsense," Mabel interrupted roughly. "Thousands of people go every year, and there's only an occasional accident."

Peters adroitly turned the conversation, but the tragedy in Switzerland had suddenly come like a spectre at a wedding, and conversation became disjointed, and then sank to an uneasy silence.

"I'm going to leave you for a few minutes, Tracey," Peters said. "You can entertain my wife and daughter. I have a couple of letters to write, and then I thought you might care to go on somewhere—a cabaret or a nightclub; it will have to be respectable, as I am rather too well known by sight."

He closed the door behind him, and I determined that I would get at the root of the matter while he was out of the room.

"Mrs. Peters," I said, "I am going to put a very rude question to you; I hope you won't be offended. Why did your husband ask me here?"

"I think—and you too must not be offended—that he wanted to get to know you better, as we had such a short conversation at Crowfield."

"He wanted to study me at first hand, in view of the fact that I shall be one of the principal witnesses at Darent's trial?"

"Partly—I suppose—but he thought you were a lonely man, and he knew your father well."

"I think I understand," I said, with rage in my heart. He had had me on a pin like a butterfly, to find out the species. He wanted to know whether I was a liar or merely a fool, like all the rest. I was up against the same brick wall—these people were friendly enough, but like all at the village, they had a firm conviction that Darent had killed Barton and that I was screening him. I guessed that Peters had already had a talk with the solicitors, and that they were doubtful about me.

Mrs. Peters must have seen something of what I was thinking on my face.

"You have heard about the rector?" she said.

"I have been buried alive for a week, and know nothing," I said, rather shortly, I fear.

"He is going to resign his living at Crowfield."

"What! I've heard nothing about that. But why?"

"No one seems to know the reason, but there was some trouble over Sir John's funeral. It was rather unpleasant for every one. Robert Barton insisted on his brother being buried in the vault where Elsie is buried."

"It was disgraceful!" Mabel flashed out. "Fancy that man being buried with Elsie?"

"My dear!" Mrs. Peters said in gentle reproof.

"The rector buried him, I suppose?" I asked.

"He refused. A friend of the family came down and performed the ceremony. I can't understand it. He told Miss Morris, as the patron of the living, and came to Town to see his bishop, I believe."

"And Mrs. Browne?"

"She's furious, I hear, for, of course, the living is a very good one, and at his age it won't be easy for him to get another."

I was bewildered at the news, and cursed Charles for advising me to stay in London.

"I'll just go and see if Jim has finished his letters," Mrs. Peters remarked to Mabel, wishing to get away from further discussion. She rose hastily, and I held the door open for her, returning to the table. Mabel was helping herself to port, and looked at me as though she was frightened at being alone without her mother; she was smoking furiously.

"You can keep that one alight, Miss Peters," I said off-handedly.

"What do you mean?" She had a puzzled frown. "Oh, you are referring to the cigarette that went out at the Crown."

"No"—I leant forward and made her look at me—"I was referring to the cigarette-end that you dropped in your brother-in-law's car on the night of the murder."

Her face became livid, and her eyes were staring wildly at me. I waited for her to speak.

"I am afraid you imagine things," she said with an obvious effort, "and you are rather impertinent—I thought you were a gentleman, Mr. Tracey." She got to her feet.

"Please sit down—I wanted to talk to you alone, and I don't want your mother and father to hear—I don't suppose you do either. This is not a matter of impertinence, so don't play about it—I am trying to save my friend, and I want the truth."

"How much do you know?" she said, cowed at my words, and glancing anxiously at the door.

"I know that you left the Crown Inn about seven o'clock, and that you were riding in Barton's car when he was supposed to be receiving his guests."

"It was a personal matter—he wanted to see me," she said sullenly. "He chose his own time and place."

I made a shot in the dark. "Was it about something that you and he did not want Margorie to know?"

"Don't ask me any more questions; it had no connexion with what happened afterwards. It was purely a private matter, as I have told you once."

The door opened, and Mr. and Mrs. Peters came in. "It was very rude of me to leave you, Tracey," he said genially, "but you have been in good company. Why, Mabel, you don't look well, child! What's the matter?"

"I am afraid it's partly my fault." I came to the rescue. "My stupid reference to Alpine climbing has upset Miss Peters; it brought the whole thing back to her."

"Poor child," Mrs. Peters said, "she was devoted to Elsie."

"Well, do you feel like coming round with an old man like me?" Peters said.

I did not care for the prospect in the least, but could hardly refuse. The telephone came to my aid.

A maid came in to say that I was wanted on the phone, and I went out into the hall. The last week had made my nerves so jumpy that I was frightened at the least thing.

My man Hoad was at the other end. "There's someone to see you, sir," he said cautiously.

"Who is it, Hoad? You can speak freely."

"It's a lady, sir; she's been waiting quite a long time."

"What's her name?" I asked impatiently, for my heart gave a bound.

"Miss Browne."

"Tell her I will come at once," I said, replacing the telephone on the hook. I paused a moment to invent a story, and then returned to my hosts. "I'm very sorry, Mr. Peters, but I'm wanted at once—my friend Charles Erskine has just come to see me. I must go."

"Yes, we must not keep you in that case," he said with a curious smile.

I took leave hurriedly, and went out for my car, which I had left in a garage round the corner. I had not troubled to put on coat or hat, for the night had been sultry, but now tropical rain was falling in sheets, and lightning was flashing overhead. I was soaked through before I reached the garage, but it merely cooled my head. I took the car, and drove through streets almost flooded with the sudden downpour, with a strange foreboding of evil, though I am far from superstitious.

CHAPTER XIII

MARGORIE'S VISIT

PUT the car away, Hoad," I said, and ran up the stairs, not waiting for the lift. I opened the door and walked into my sitting-room, where Hoad had thoughtfully lit a fire, as the rain had chilled the air. Margorie had taken off her hat and coat, and was sitting staring into the flames, but looked up eagerly at my entrance.

"Margorie!" I exclaimed, taking her hand.

"I am so glad you have come; I have been waiting all the evening."

"But I didn't know—I would have come at once. Why didn't Hoad ring me up before?"

"I wouldn't let him—he told me you were with the Peterses, but it was getting late, so I told him at last to do so. He has been most attentive."

"Have you had some food?"

"That's so like a man—yes, Hoad got me all I wanted."

"When did you come?"

"Do sit down." She actually laughed. "You look so tall, standing there as though you didn't like my coming."

I obeyed her at once. Didn't want her here! Good heavens! If she knew what her presence meant—

"May I have a cigarette?"

"I am sorry. My wits are all scattered."

"That's better," she said when I had lit a match and she was puffing contentedly. Her hand had touched my sleeve, and she assumed a severe tone. "I am not going to tell you anything until you have taken off your wet clothes—you ought to be ashamed of yourself. Go and change, and I shall tell Hoad to get a hot whisky."

She hustled me out of the room, and I had time to collect my thoughts while changing into a lounge suit. When I returned I was steadier. Her sudden appearance had upset more than my nerves, but evidently something had happened at Crowfield that she did not care to put in a letter.

A jug of hot water had been placed at a table by an arm-chair, with whisky, lemon and sugar.

"Help yourself," Margorie said with complete assurance. "I came up with my father to London."

"I heard that he has said he will resign the living—Peters told me."

"I thought he would. There's been an awful row at home. Mother is impossible—she was at it day and night; of course she is quite convinced about Ken being guilty, and she went down to the Hall every day, and saw the Martins, till your friend Mr. Erskine told her that she must leave them alone, as they would be called as witnesses for the defence and must not be tampered with. Mother was furious, but my father said he was right; and then Miss Morris came round and gave mother a talking to that she will never forget."

"Good!" I could not help exclaiming. "But why has your father resigned?"

"I wish I knew—he's very strange in his manner, and won't tell me anything. The Peters came down for the funeral—you heard about that?"

"I heard that your father wouldn't conduct it," I said gravely.

"He did more than that—he refused permission for John to be buried in the vault, but Miss Morris came and saw him and they were together in the library for a long time. When they came out, he seemed very upset, but had withdrawn his objection."

"Was it then that he offered his resignation?"

"No," she said thoughtfully. "But on the day of the funeral Mabel came to see me, and she had a talk with my father. Dennis, what's the matter with the girl?"

"I'd give something to know—I saw her this evening."

Our eyes met, and an unspoken question was on the tip of my tongue, and, I believe, on hers.

I sipped at my hot 'toddy' and waited.

"It was after the funeral that he told mother and me he had written to Miss Morris."

"You needn't worry about that," I said cheerily. "I am certain that she will not allow it."

"You heard about his sermon?"

"His sermon—nothing whatever."

She looked at me strangely. "I wonder they didn't tell you. It's all over the village. It was last Sunday. He took as his text "Vengeance is mine, and I will repay, saith the Lord," and every one thought he was going to talk about the murder. There was quite a buzz among the congregation, and I felt awful. But he went on to say that if a man killed another, the punishment was death, but that there were worse crimes than murder, and that it was said that for certain offences it were better that a millstone were hanged about a man's neck, and he were drowned. And then, practically in so many words, he told us that in some cases murder was justifiable."

Silence fell between us—my mind went back to the rector's words, that if the murderer came into his room and confessed the crime, he would not give him up to justice.

"What is the meaning of it?" I whispered at last.

"Mother walked out of the church," Margorie remarked quietly.

"I don't wonder." The rain was lashing against the windows, and a storm was raging outside; I could not think coherently.

"Dennis," I heard Margorie say. "My father knows more of this than he will tell us. He came to London to-day, and I was only too pleased to get away. He said he had to see his bishop, and I know he was going to see the Peters, on business, I expect."

"I only hope that he is on the track of the murderer, as the time is getting short."

A frightened look came into her hazel eyes. "You have no further news?"

"The solicitors are working on the case, and I am told that Mr. Peters is the very best man in London for the defence," I said to reassure her.

"*He* wouldn't see me, Dennis." Tears gathered in her eyes, and she brushed them away angrily.

"He wouldn't see his lawyer either—don't worry about that. I can understand his attitude, and he must be going through an awful time. Please God it will soon be over."

"You are a good friend," she said simply. "But that brings me to the real reason for this call."

"I thought you came to see me," I said sadly.

"Of course I did, you know that, but this is very serious. I hardly like to tell you."

"You know you can trust me with anything."

"I know that, Dennis, it's not that, but I am afraid of what you will do. That man Turnbull."

I sat up straight, and I dare say my face was grimly set. "Yes," she said, "I'm afraid of what you will do to him."

"What has he been doing?" I could guess only too well.

"He has been threatening me—he met me in the street, and was so polite and slippery that I didn't know what he was trying to say, but I gathered at last. He knows about our meeting in the church, and says he feels it his duty to tell my mother and also to let Ken know."

"The swine," I ejaculated. "Leave him to me—I've seen him, too; he's trying to force my hand by threatening you."

"What will you do?

I told her of our meeting, and of what I proposed to do. "It goes against the grain to have to pay the brute, but there's nothing else."

"But if you pay, won't he come again and ask for more? I've heard that's what these people do."

"I'll put my lawyer on his track," I said to reassure her, for there was one thing that worried me at the moment—her presence here, if my flat was being watched

"Where is your father?" I asked abruptly.

To my astonishment she answered carelessly, "I don't know—he's stopping at some hotel. You see I left him when we arrived, and he thought I was going straight back to Crowfield."

"But where on earth are you staying, then?

She glanced calmly at the clock. "The last train has gone, and you can hardly turn me out in the rain. Your man told me you had a spare bedroom, and I brought a small handbag in case of accidents. He's put it in there."

I fairly gasped. "But would it do?" I managed to stutter.

"Don't be so old-fashioned, Dennis; are you afraid of me? If I don't mind why should you? With another it might be different, but I can trust you; you are far too loyal to Ken to try to play the fool, and I think you like me too much."

"Don't for God's sake," I blurted out like a hurt animal. "Of course you can stay here. If the house is being watched, it would, perhaps, be the wisest course."

"Now that's settled we can talk. I'm not in the least sleepy."

She settled herself down snugly into her chair.

"Do you know, Dennis, this is the first comfortable moment I have known for a week. I seem to feel that you will get things put right. I can't tell why."

"You are leaning on a broken reed," I said bitterly, but could have echoed the rest of her words. "By the way," I went on as casually as I could, "did Mabel Peters come to see you before or after the funeral?"

"Why do you ask? As a matter of fact she came before. Something seemed to have upset her, but her chief grievance was that John should be buried with Elsie; she was most indignant about it, and she tried to persuade me not to go—she had a perfect hatred of John."

Margorie never showed the slightest signs of regret at the death of her fiancé, but appeared to have blotted him out of her memory, though she was far from being a hard type.

The sound of the electric bell in the hall made me start to my feet, and dash for the door. Hoad was on his way to the front entrance when I stopped him.

"Wait a moment," I whispered, and turned back to the doorway. "Margorie, you mustn't be seen here; you'd better slip off into your room."

"You weren't expecting any one?" I think she was afraid that it might be Turnbull.

"No one—take your things with you."

She seized her hat and coat, and tiptoed down the short passage, with a whispered good night, and I returned to my seat.

The door was opened by Hoad, and Charles came in dripping wet. He handed his macintosh and hat to my servant, and advanced smiling. "Lord, what a night—I didn't expect to find you up at this time." He was glancing round the room in a most annoying way.

A cigarette still alight lay in Margorie's ash-tray, and the cushions showed clearly that someone had been sitting in the chair.

"I was having dinner with Peters," I said shortly. "Have a hot grog—it'll do you good."

He sank down on the seat vacated by Margorie, and grinned. "I thought the Peters always dressed for dinner," he remarked, looking up at the ceiling.

"So they do, you fool, but I got sopping wet and changed."

He laughed. "Instead of going to bed—Dennis, you are a wonderful quick-change artist; you seem to be always changing out of dress clothes." The hit was a shrewd one.

"What did you come for, at this time of night?"

He was not to be put off. "Had a visitor, I see!" He picked up Margorie's cigarette.

"A friend of mine called."

"Ah! These cigarettes do burn a long time, don't they? Am I in the way?"

"Not a bit," I said irritably. "I'm only too pleased, after being cooped up for a week."

He put the cigarette down carefully, and helped himself to whisky that Hoad held on a tray for him.

"I *was* going to ask you to put me up, as it's so late."

"You can have my room with pleasure. I've got a visitor here if you want to know; he's fast asleep now."

The smile broadened on Charles's face. "I wish I could do that—smoking one minute and asleep the next wonderful gift."

"Shut up and tell me why you came."

"To report progress, my lad. I've had a busy week down at Crowfield."

"Golfing?"

"Golfing with a purpose. Making friends with young Barton, the new Baronet, and taking his money."

He stretched his long legs to the fire and sipped the hot drink with obvious appreciation.

"Do you know, Dennis, old son, I got quite a lot of information out of young Barton—in fact he made quite a confidant of me when he'd had one or two."

"Birds of a feather," I murmured.

"It appears," he started off in a sententious manner, "from what I learnt from this youngster, that your sour-faced friend Turnbull came along on the morning before the murder with some papers for the late lamented baronet. There was the marriage settlement and the will, as well as the mortgage deeds on the Hall, about which you informed me."

"He said at the inn that it was a monstrous document," I observed.

"Most extraordinary, from what I hear. He had settled a very large sum on his wife at marriage, and had practically left her everything in his will, including the Towers; and cut his brother right out. But mark this point, Dennis, in your rather thick head—as he died before he married, the will is null and void, because he had made everything over to "his wife," and not to Margorie Browne, or even to Margorie Barton."

"What do you make of that?"

"It may be just that he was infatuated with Margorie, and wanted to show his love—for these commercial people appraise love in terms of money. But—and this is the very solid 'but'—it does afford a very powerful lever for getting rid of Barton before he got married."

"And now young Barton gets the whole lot?"

"His brother died intestate, since this will is null and void and he had made no former will—but that's a queer point about the whole thing. Young Robert told me that the will Turnbull brought down was the same that he had made out when Barton married Elsie Peters, identical in every particular except for the witnesses."

"You've been to the Towers?"

"As an honoured guest they seem to have taken up their residence there, young Barton and his cousin, which is rather cool cheek. They are a detestable pair, and I long to kick them."

We smoked on in silence, each absorbed in his own thoughts. From time to time he glanced to me as if about to ask a question, and thought better of it. Outside the wind was storming and howling, as though in sympathy with the dark business on which our thoughts were centred.

"The sooner we catch the man the better," he said slowly at last. "I don't like the look of things at all."

"I won't say that I am exactly pleased myself."

"I have had a consultation with old Deaken—that is, I took Smithers along with me, and they did the talking. We outlined your evidence to him, and he is very doubtful about calling you."

"He can't stop me," I said angrily.

"Don't get excited Dennis; to tell the bare truth he doesn't like this alibi of yours at all."

"He'll have to like it."

"What he said was: 'Dangerous—if that breaks down in cross-examination, our case goes.' "

"I'm quite satisfied that it won't," I said stubbornly. "Only, you know, Charles, I wish the thing would come on—this waiting is devilish trying."

"That's why it is important to get busy. I believe I am on the right line, but must get more evidence."

. I started. "You mean you think you know who murdered Barton?"

"I have a shrewd idea." He winked at me. "I'm not saying anything yet, till I've more data."

"You've settled everything with Turnbull?"

"I found him most agreeable. I think you've wronged the poor fellow; he spoke quite nicely about you, and said he was sorry you had quarrelled. He is letting me have a properly audited statement of the liabilities, and then they can be settled up, and I doubt very much whether Darent will even know what he owes. Apparently he used to throw all bills on the fire. He'll find everything ready when he comes back—if he ever does."

I swore forcibly.

"Naughty! I'm surprised at you, Dennis. Well, I must be going."

"I can put you up if you don't mind a shakedown," I said desperately.

"I wouldn't stay for worlds, my dear fellow." He grinned at my angry face. "Only I'm beginning to have doubts myself about your evidence. I don't believe you can tell a lie without giving the show away. All right, don't get ratty. Remember me to your visitor in the morning."

He put on his macintosh and hat, which Hoad had dried, and went out into the storm, whistling a tune.

CHAPTER XIV

IN THE GRIP OF THE BLACKMAILER

SAT on in the arm-chair long after Charles had gone, until the red flames had died down in the fire, and the coals had become a dull angry glow, and then merely dead white ash, and the room cold and cheerless. I cursed myself for having taken orders from Charles, or rather Smithers, and loafed about in London, when I should have been at Crowfield. That was the centre of things, and the only place where I could hope to obtain information. Charles had his own idea, and I felt I could leave him to follow that up, but to my mind the solution of the problem lay with the two clues I held. Who took the stick with which the murder had been committed, and whose pumps had been placed into my bag as an obvious attempt to throw the blame on to me? Why had the police not followed this latter question up? There would seem to be only one solution. Pyke must have found out to whom they belonged, and have been satisfied on the matter. And where were my own shoes?

I could not believe that Mary had put these into my suit-case at the Hall, so what remained? They must have been placed in the suit-case at the Crown, by someone who knew where my room was. Or was it by any chance done by someone who knew that the guilty marks on the lawn would fit his own pumps, and hoped that I should take the substituted shoes off to London without noticing anything wrong, and so remove an important piece of evidence? Yes, I must certainly go to Crowfield, and pick up the threads there.

I must have dozed off, and woke shivering, and with that miserable feeling that comes of sleeping in one's clothes. The storm had ceased, though thick black-clouds were racing across a dreary, leaden sky when I pulled back the curtains. A pale dawn was breaking, and a ghostly grey mist half hid the street beneath me.

Hoad would be coming in soon, and I retired to the bathroom, stealing quietly past the room where Margorie was sleeping. Her trust in me, and the thought that we were fighting together in the battle for Darent, was my one consolation.

I lingered long in a hot bath, and then in my room, dressing, to give Hoad a chance to get my sitting-room ready, and packed my suit-case myself, with the care that a faddy bachelor gives to these details.

And then I received a shock—small as it was in itself. Hoad always keeps my shoes in a special shelf in my compactum, every pair with trees inside. I selected what I wanted and then stopped suddenly. There were two pairs of pumps—for I always have a spare pair—in the line. I stared at them as though I had seen a corpse, and then made my way into the sitting-room, where Hoad had just completed his work.

"When you unpacked my bag," I asked him, "did you find my pumps?"

"Why, yes, sir," he said in surprise. "Did you think you had left them behind?"

I told Hoad that I had not been certain about it, but somehow this trivial discovery had filled me with a new hope. I remembered that in the state of mind I had been, with the crowded events of the day, and the prospect of my interview with Margorie in the evening, I had told Polly to fetch my case and put it into the car, and had left it at my flat before returning to Crowfield. Since then I had never dressed, till last night, and then, owing to the state of the weather, I had worn shoes.

Someone had entered my room again after Pyke had been there and had replaced my own pumps.

"I hope you slept well?"

I looked up and saw Margorie, looking as fresh as a spring flower, and smiling at me from the doorway.

"Hardly a wink," I answered. "I was talking with Charles Erskine for some time, and then I had a lot to think about. Margorie, I've made up my mind—I'm going to Crowfield."

To my surprise her face became radiant, and she impulsively seized my hand. "I'm so glad, Dennis—I wanted you to come ever so badly, but I didn't like to ask you. That was the real reason of my visit. It will make all the difference. Don't you see that if there is any chance of finding out the murderer, it must be there?"

"I know now—I ought to have gone there before."

"Do you know—it seemed so strange that you kept away—I almost thought you were afraid to come. I am so glad I was wrong."

"We'll go right away after breakfast," I exclaimed, feeling that a great load had been lifted off my mind.

"I shall have to lie like a trooper to mother. Of course, she will think I stopped with dad, at his hotel. Never mind—you can drop me at Wickstead, and I'll take the bus from there."

During that journey I saw what Margorie must have been like be-fore this shadow came to darken her life. She had thrown off her mis-givings of the night before, as the clouds had passed, and a clear sky took their place, and there was a freshness after the rain that made the day like spring. I had taken Hoad with me to drive, so that we could talk, and I learnt more of her life before the catastrophe of Lady Barton's death than I had known before. I could picture her as an eager schoolgirl, and Kenneth as I had known him in the old days, and the peaceful life in the village before Barton had come to defile it with his monied arrogance. Later on she told me something of the accident in Switzerland.

"We were just a party of eight—four of us girls and four jolly boys down from the 'varsity. We set out with two experienced guides from Meiningen for a three-day expedition, and a snowstorm came on. The guides thought we ought to try to make our way back, before it got too bad, and we were all roped together. The boys were all experienced Alpinists, and no one knows quite what happened. The snowstorm was very thick, and I felt a tug at the rope, and the next thing I remember was sliding down, faster and faster —it was a horrible sensation. I drove in my alpenstock, but there was no grip, and then we went over the edge, and I can't remember anything more till I woke in hospital all bound up, and with a shocking headache—I believe I was rather badly smashed. I was laid up in Meiningen for weeks, and dad came out and had a pretty anxious time. It was only after I had recovered sufficiently to be told that I learnt that Elsie and one of the boys of the party had been killed, and the front guide, all having fallen on the rocks."

"Your father brought you and Mabel back?"

"No—Mabel was not so badly injured, mostly bruises, and Mr. Peters came and fetched her. I came back later with dad, and John, who had come out to settle up all the bills, which he insisted on doing, and he gave a large sum to the hospital. Then he had a memorial stone erected at the place where he had found Elsie's body."

"I thought he wasn't there?" I said quickly.

"He wasn't when the accident happened, but when they cabled to him he came straight away. He organized a search party at once, to look for the others. The snow fell for days before they returned."

We were coming into Wickstead, and as we passed the police station and court I saw a look of pain come to Margorie's face.

"He is at Maidstone," she said sadly, answering my glance. "They bring him here for the hearings. I do wish it was all over."

"So do I," I agreed; "but don't forget that the longer these remands drag out, the longer time we have for our investigations."

"Here's the bus terminus. I'll just do some shopping and come on later."

She stepped lightly from the car and held out her hand, and I told Hoad to drive on to the village.

My second visit was like a homecoming. I had a warm welcome from the Willises, and especially from Polly. Charles had stayed there, and had apparently told a lot of lies about me, so that I had become a sort of mythical hero; and it had leaked out somehow that I had come to

Darent's rescue in the matter of finance. I shrewdly suspected that Turnbull had done that out of spite, hoping it would get round to Kenneth. I had imagined myself sneaking back to the village under cover of night, and my return was like that of a soldier from a successful campaign.

Even Oliver greeted me with a fine salute and a "Good morning, sir," which I attributed to Polly.

I took the first opportunity I could of getting hold of her and asking her the news. She took my suitcase to the room which the Peters had occupied—a large room in the front of the house. I waited to hear what she had to tell before I asked some vital questions. She was very verbose, but what she had to tell me, compressed into a few sentences, was as follows.

Oliver had been thoroughly turned inside out, and like a faithful swain had confided his information to Polly. Pyke had taken Oliver with Watson to the scene of the murder, and the constable, standing at a respectful distance, had kept his ears open.

Most of the lawn round the roped square had been trampled over by the guests. Only in the direction of the Hall the tracks had been visible, and from what the rector had said, when he saw the marks before the dew was off the grass, one set had frequently been superimposed over the other, either from one walking just behind the other or the second pair having followed the first. But there were no tracks from the Hall, and Pyke had suggested that perhaps the murderer had reversed his shoes or walked backwards. The next item was of greater importance. Pyke had followed the tracks, and then searched for the place where the man had crossed the high barbed-wire fence that Barton had erected between his property and Darent's. At a corner where a very strong support had been driven into the ground to take the double strain, with supporting strands of thick wire, the barbed wire had been broken down, and there were marks on the soft earth. Barton had had the ground just inside his hedge dug up, and had planted a row of quick-growing tamarisks to make a circular walk round the edge of his grounds. At this corner the impress of the first pair of pumps was clear and unmistakable, as they had sunk into the soft earth, as though the man had stood there, possibly listening for sounds from the lawn. The second pair, however, ceased, but there were faint marks of a man's walking shoes, going up the gravel path. It appeared, so Pyke thought, that the second man had changed from pumps to shoes at this point—but why? This fact, coupled with the discovery that the pumps were not mine, had evidently modified Pyke's first impression that I had been an accomplice.

Polly informed me that Oliver thought the second tracks were made by a woman, as they were small, but she thought that was absurd.

I thanked her for the information, sitting on the bed to listen, and then asked her whether she had any idea as to who had taken the stick from the room where it had been left.

She seemed surprised at the question, and said indifferently that as she had gone with Oliver to the Towers, only her father and mother had been at home, except the potman, who did not have any access to the sitting-room. They had both been busy after the opening hour.

It was useless to ask further questions on this subject, as I could see quite clearly that she thought Darent had taken it with him.

"One other question, Polly," I said, "as I mustn't keep you. Someone went into my room on the morning after the murder, while I was out."

"Yes, sir," she said, readily enough. "That detective went there—he said he had a right to do so, and came down with Inspector Watson. I don't know what they were up to."

"I know that, but someone had been there before, and taken my pumps out of my case."

"Your pumps, sir—them dancing shoes? I took them and gave them a clean, sir. When you asked me to fetch your bag I packed them."

So here was half the mystery of the pumps solved, but not all. I let her go then, and came down to the lounge, only to find my arch-enemy Turnbull sitting there, glowering like a great spider in his web waiting for flies.

I would have walked past him, but he rose and laid his claw-like hand on my arm, and asked me, politely enough, to sit down. I accepted the challenge.

"I hoped that possibly I might find you here," he said quite genially. "I suppose you came here last night?"

"I fail to see how my movements interest you," I retorted.

"Oh, I beg your pardon—I was not trying to be inquisitive. I must really express my admiration for the generous way in which you have come to the rescue of your friend Mr. Darent," he went on suavely, as though there were nothing for us to do but exchange compliments. "Your solicitors and I have been able to settle everything amicably."

He had learnt by some means that Charles had been acting for me—and was telling me plainly that he knew. I waited for him to speak, knowing exactly to what this conversation was leading.

"You will be going to the Hall?" he asked, searching me with his beady eyes.

"It is quite likely—I shall probably call there."

"I did not quite mean that. I meant that you might be taking up your residence there—keeping the place warm, so to speak, for your friend?"

I had begun to understand his ways and his tortuous method of approaching a subject, and was not angry now—only amused, in spite of the loathing I had for the man.

"That's quite a good idea of yours—it's worth thinking about," I replied.

"Do you think that it would be quite wise? Please don't get angry—I am not trying to interfere in your affairs—I was merely thinking of your friend Darent."

I felt a sudden misgiving—the words were plain enough, but I knew that intonation of his—a sort of intake of the breath—the hiss of a snake about to strike.

"I don't follow your meaning."

"Only—you know your Bible, Mr. Tracey—do you remember the text: 'Hast thou slain and also taken possession?' "

Had an avalanche fallen on my head I could not have been more completely stunned. Was the pestilent little beast gloating over something far more vital than the occupation of the Hall, of which I had no intention? Had he become possessed of the knowledge that Margorie had stayed the night at my flat, and had come down with me in my car? If so, the words of the text would indeed have a terrible meaning for Darent—evidence of falsehood and dishonour—if they ever came to his ears.

I heard Turnbull speaking in sleek, oily tones. "There is no reason, Mr. Tracey, why Mr. Darent should know anything, and you are quite right to look after *all his interests* while he is not able to do so himself."

Something of the horror I felt must have shown itself on my face. He had paved the way with infinite cunning.

"I got your note"—he gave a glance round the room in fear of eavesdroppers—"I am very glad that you are prepared to settle that little matter—it is really the best thing, and I am not an unreasonable man. But I am a poor man, who has been ruined by others, and I have lost a good client in Sir John Barton. Perhaps five thousand pounds might be a fair sum in complete settlement."

"I'll see you in—" I began.

He raised his hand in protest. "It is a fair offer, but you would like time to consider it. It must be in pound notes, remember, not bank-notes." His face was peering at me, and his hands clutching each other with the miser's greed for gold. I could have hit him without moving from my seat, but what was the good? He would have swallowed the insult and doubled his price.

"I will give you till to-morrow—no longer. That will give you time to get the money, and I will arrange where to meet. I don't want any third person there."

He rose abruptly, his courage, roused by desire of gain, having evaporated, and his face assumed that sickly green colour I had seen before.

"Till to-morrow then," he said, at the door, and went out.

The pleasure of the morning had gone, and I saw before me the prospect of being bled white by this vampire, or facing the consequences of his revelations. He had me in a strangle hold.

I sat on alone in the lounge, a prey to my thoughts. The door was opened noisily, and Charles burst into the lounge. I had half expected him, and was not surprised at his appearance.

"Hallo, Dennis, my lad. I called at your flat, but you and your visitor had flown. Splendid day, isn't it?"

"Glorious," I responded, without much enthusiasm.

"What's the matter? I saw that particular friend of yours, Turnbull, just now, as I was coming down the road. Been having words with him?"

The matter on which I had been conversing was not one that I could trust even to him.

"What are you doing here?" I asked instead.

"Just going down to the Hall, to have a look round, and then to Barton's. Like to come?"

"To the Hall, yes—but I don't think I should be very welcome at the Towers."

"Nonsense. Barton hasn't the sense to bear animosity, and now that he has been told that you had nothing to do with the crime he will be pleased to see you." He frowned, as though at an unpleasant thought. "To tell you the truth, I think he's so glad to have got the property that he would have welcomed you still more if you had still been suspected of having killed his brother in actual fact."

"I do want to go there to have a look round," I said.

"Then come along, and don't mope."

He drove me down to the Hall at a breakneck speed, for Charles was a road-hog of the worst kind, and drew up at the familiar old door.

The Martins had been allowed to return, and I could see that already the place was considerably altered. Two men were clearing the garden, and some workmen were supposed to be mending the roof, but when we arrived they were munching huge sandwiches in the shade.

John was pleased to see me, but his special welcome was for Charles, who had come to them like a good fairy and relieved all their anxieties.

"Lovely old place this, Dennis. It's a shame to let it go to ruin."

"You seem to be doing your best to save such a contingency."

"How's the bank balance?" He grinned at me.

"Pretty fair. Why?"

"I've got a scheme, Dennis—I'll tell you presently."

"Will Darent stand this?"

"He's not going to know. Wait till I tell you about it."

John had left us, to fetch refreshments, for Charles had told the old fellow to keep a careful check on anything we had, and it would be paid for.

I strolled to the familiar table where the decanter had stood on that momentous night, and my thoughts went back to Darent and his pitiful plight. But one could not be dull with Charles, whose vitality was infectious. As soon as we had finished our drinks he proposed a tour of inspection of the house, to which I eagerly agreed, suddenly remembering that I had seen nothing of it except the dining-room and library and my bedroom and Mary's.

Charles was evidently familiar with the house, and conducted me into the drawing-room, every article of furniture in which was covered with dust-sheets, and cobwebs were thick on the ceiling.

It was a long room, corresponding with the dining-room on the other side of the hall, and looking on to the lake.

"John told me about this room," Charles remarked. "On the very day that Darent heard of Margorie's engagement he told the old man to shut it up and never to open the door again."

I closed the door softly, as Darent must have closed it on his dead hopes, and we went into the other rooms—a smoking- or writing-room, which was doubtless meant for an office for the estate, a billiards-room, and a small drawing-room, all showing signs of neglect and disuse.

And then we ascended the stairs, and I entered the room I had occupied, Darent's own room, which he had vacated for me. It was exactly as I had left it, and I sat on the bed, recalling that terrible night.

Charles had strolled to the window and was looking out on the garden.

"Wonderful view from here," he said without turning his head.

"Yes, isn't it? But it's a pity the garden under the window is so neglected."

"How did you manage without gas or electric light? It must have been rather inconvenient for you."

"Gas?" My thoughts were far away at the moment. "I brought a candle up with me; there it is, over there." I saw the candle-stick standing where I had left it on that fatal night.

Charles left the window, and even in my semi-abstraction I noticed a change in his voice. "Let's have a look at the room you slept in on the night of the murder."

I saw I was caught—I hadn't the faintest idea which room Mary had made up for me after I had gone.

"Oh," I said in some confusion, "it was one of these round the gallery, but it was very dark and they are all so much alike."

"I see, and which was Mary's room, where Darent slept?"

I got up from the bed with relief. "I'll show you."

"There is no need to do so." His voice was quite unlike his usual gay tones; he came and put his hands on my shoulders. "Dennis, you are lying to me."

"What the hell do you mean, Charles?" I blustered.

His grip became tighter.

"Dennis! Before you had even looked out of this window you knew the state of the garden just below, and the view from the window, although when you were supposed to have put Darent to bed here it was pitch dark, and presumably the curtains were drawn. You let out that you had brought a candle here, although from your statement Mrs. Martin followed you with a lamp, and when I asked where you had slept you couldn't tell me, though you knew Mary's bedroom quite well."

"What a lot of rubbish," I said peevishly. "Let's go downstairs."

"Dennis, I want the truth—it's only fair to me as your solicitor. That alibi of yours is a pack of lies. What is the real story?"

"The truth is that Darent never committed that murder —that's all."

He looked at me long and earnestly.

"I don't know why you are doing this thing, Dennis," he said at last. "It can't be for a man you haven't seen for five years, and a drunken sot, from what I hear: quixotism can't go so far as that. I think you are doing this for someone else."

I ought to have been angry, but I could only hang my head. For the truth stood revealed to me—not only to him, but to myself. I am no hero—that surely is revealed in my narrative—and dozens of times during the last wretched week I had made up my mind to prevaricate and modify my evidence before the moment when I had to take the oath, but the vision of Margorie and of her scorn had strengthened my failing resolution. She looked on me as a staunch friend who would not desert her, as loyal—the thought was maddening—as the servants. In her heart she knew that Kenneth was innocent, and on me and these others hung the whole responsibility of getting him off.

"Come, old man." Charles linked his arm in mine and we went down the staircase with no more thought of exploring the other rooms. "I think I understand—You may rely on me to help all I can. I knew Margorie was at your flat last night—the panel of your door is of glass, and the curtain does not quite cover it. With any one else I might have thought things, but I know you, old man, and could guess that she had come to see you about this matter. If Darent gets away with this, and doesn't play the man about that girl, Heaven help him. And you?"

"Me! I shall go abroad for a time, I think. I couldn't stand the routine of London. It doesn't matter."

"We'll take a trip together," he said, squeezing my band. "But why not go now, Dennis? There's nothing to keep you. If you are travelling, they won't be able to subpoena you as a witness."

"And leave the Martins to face the music? No, thank you. Don't let's discuss the matter any more."

"Very well—come and have a look round the farm buildings." Not another word was said on the subject, and Charles eagerly discussed what should be done to improve the place, as though it belonged to him. Every time I asked him what his idea was about the Hall he put me off with some excuse, saying that he had arranged everything.

We returned to the library, and Charles, who had had the telephone put into commission again, called up the Towers, and asked for Sir Robert Barton.

To my annoyance, I heard him accepting an invitation to lunch for both of us, and he put the receiver up before I could protest.

It went sorely against the grain to accept hospitality from this man, though a mere formal call would have been a different matter, but after Charles had called me thin-skinned, pedantic and at last a prig, I gave way. It certainly looked as though my week of inaction was to be followed by furious action, which is reversing Newton's third law of motion.

During lunch I had a better chance of becoming acquainted with young Robert Barton than at my previous meeting. His manner had not improved since he had become a baronet and the inheritor of the property, and he showed much of the quality of a man about town of the modern type—blasé, drawling in speech, and with a hearty contempt for any one over the advanced age of thirty.

His face was long and cadaverous, almost vulpine, and the eyes were black and restless.

He had fallen under the spell of Charles's genial personality, but evidently considered me a very dull dog, and was patronizing in his manner. He ordered the servants about with that lack of taste that accompanies newly acquired riches without a sense of responsibility.

Young Vickers was a mere cipher, repeating everything that his cousin said, and, I judged, only too anxious to snatch some crumbs from his new-rich cousin, and to remain at the Towers.

The house was massive and vulgar, but there was a curious incongruity about the interior that suggested the influence of Elsie Peters. The walls were beautifully decorated in the ultra-modern style, in soft tones and straight lines, but the late baronet had ruined the effect by hanging expensive pictures out of keeping with the scheme.

The furniture was devastating, and I was not surprised to hear that Sir John had refurnished the whole place in honour of his new wife—poor Margorie!

Robert was honest enough to tell us of the change in his fortunes. He had been living since he came down prematurely from Oxford on a small allowance that his brother had grudgingly—the words were his—doled out to him, and which barely sufficed for a flat in Town, and golf club subscriptions, as well as a car. He had only been able to manage by persuading certain lenders of money that his brother being a widower, and not likely to remarry, he, as the next-of-kin, had reasonable prospects of funds in the future, but the news of John's engagement had crashed his house of cards, and the said lenders had been restive!

After lunch, which was an extensive meal, they insisted on taking me off to play golf at the course at Crawfold.

Charles mercifully partnered me, as I was quite out of practice, and as the other two had done themselves very well at lunch, we were able to win the match and a pound each, the stake having been fixed by Robert Barton. I was not over-happy in this matter. Charles, I could see, was studying Barton keenly, and getting to know him, but to me it hardly seemed playing the game to accept a man's hospitality for that purpose.

The visit itself would hardly have been worth chronicling, but for the strange discovery I made later, on our return to the Towers.

I would have taken my leave, but Charles was insistent on staying, and pointed out truly that I had nothing whatever to do, and that he had his own line of investigation to follow.

Robert was anxious to have his revenge for losing at golf by playing Charles at billiards, a game at which I knew, to my cost, my friend was an adept. Like most men of his type, Barton was a born gambler, and I could foresee that the huge fortune that had been built up by his father and grandfather, both worthy brewers, would soon vanish.

I found myself alone with young Vickers for a few minutes, and we strolled together along the terrace.

"Bob's a fool," he started fretfully. "If I had my way, with a place like this, I would settle down and enjoy myself. Don't you agree?"

"I thought that was what he intended to do," I answered.

"Of course, you and I understand these things." I was flattered. "He can't see it; says this place is dull. He's going to buy a yacht and go round the world with a party. All very fine, but it's going to cost him something."

"I suppose you will stay and look after the place?"

"No jolly fear—I shall go with them; but I think he's going to sell the Towers—he doesn't like it."

"I can quite understand that," I said warmly, though I could hardly believe his reason was the same as mine.

A soft warm evening was closing the day, and over the valleys the same filmy haze that I had noticed at my first visit was lending an air of unreality to the scene, making a vision of fairyland.

I stood and watched the bars of purple clouds gathering in lines above the setting sun, when his voice, a little petulant, broke the stillness.

"I'm going in for a drink—coming?"

"I think I'll stay here a little longer—I shall be coming in later on."

I was glad to get rid of him, and I am sure he wanted to go. He was one of those empty-headed creatures who must be for ever talking. The subject didn't matter in the least, but left alone, he was like a child without toys.

I think he found my company dull, and also was afraid that perhaps he had said too much about his precious cousin, on whose bounty he depended.

He was one who could never keep a secret, and I was convinced that Charles had already turned him inside out.

I made off across the lawn when he had gone, feeling a keen desire to see the grounds. There was no trace of the roped square, and I walked on to the dense shrubbery that had formed part of the old garden.

A twisted path led between flowering shrubs and rhododendrons, forming a sort of 'lovers' walk,' and leading to the newly made gravel pathway that encircled the whole of the gardens, of which Polly had told me. I was brought up abruptly by the wire fence, six feet high, that Sir John had caused to be erected with the meticulous care a rich parvenu always takes to exclude the dwellers on the land from intruding upon his newly acquired property.

The villagers had wandered freely for generations on Darent's estate, without picking flower or damaging fence, but this was a preserve for the baronet and his friends.

I longed to take a hatchet and hack the ugly barbed wire to pieces. I turned up the path towards the road, in idle curiosity, and suddenly came upon a summerhouse some few yards back from the pathway, in a part of the old garden. It was a rustic wooden building, almost hidden in a green drapery of trees and thick bushes. Somehow it seemed out of keeping with the wire fence, the yellow gravel, and the plain row of tamarisks. I made my way through the bushes, and opened the door, expecting to see dust and dirt, and a broken roof. To my surprise there were cushions on the seats, and signs of recent occupation. The tobacco ash on the floor was of recent date, and a small cupboard contained glasses, a siphon, and a cut-glass bottle half full of whisky.

I sat down at a round table and thought out the meaning of this.

In any ordinary circumstances the summer-house and its contents would have no sinister meaning—just a place for friends to come for a yarn and a smoke—but there was more in it than that. Pyke and his assistants had searched the grounds thoroughly, and would have undoubtedly found this place. They would have taken away the glasses and bottle for fingerprints; that was rudimentary. I deduced—to use the word of detective stories—that the drinking requisites had been brought here since the murder, and without the knowledge of the servants, for the place was unswept, and two of the glasses had been used, but not cleaned. Barton and his cousin had been in sole possession of the house, but why should they come here when they had the whole place to themselves? Women do not as a rule drink whisky, or it might have been used for a trysting-place, though the possibility could not be overlooked. I examined the floor as well as I could in the twilight, for under the trees the place was almost dark; one man had smoked cigars, and I found three ends that had been bitten off. The other had smoked a pipe and had knocked out the ashes on the floor several times, which seemed to indicate that the conversation had been a long one, or that there had been more than one, and of a secret nature; or why choose this hidden meeting-place? A hundred explanations came to my mind, but none that fitted in with the facts, and yet I felt that if I could only read this problem aright, I held in my hands a most important clue to the murder. The cigar-ends I had found in the car had been cut.

I found my imagination running away with me. I pictured a crouching figure in the dark of the night, creeping into the summer-house to meet the man who smoked cigars, to receive the reward of his foul crime, and the long argument over the ghastly payment.

Only a faint light penetrated into the summer-house, and pale stars were showing in the sky through the open door that swung slightly in the night breeze. I shivered, and had risen to go, when I heard a sound in the bushes, and a dark figure blocked the doorway. I started back, filled with a nameless dread, and the table creaked with my weight against it.

A voice came from the darkness—young Robert Barton was speaking in a cracked, dry voice. "That you, Turnbull? You're before your time, man, and it's infernally dark here."

A match flashed, and the white face of the man looked straight into mine.

He leapt back with a curse, and the match went out.

"Tracey! What the devil are you doing here, man?"

I gave him time to recover, and then laughed, and gave a mighty yawn. "Hallo! Who's that? By Jove, I'm stiff! I must have fallen asleep. I suppose it was playing golf."

"I'm sorry I woke you up, but your friend Erskine thought you had gone home. I thought I would just have a look round for you—fancy you finding this queer old summer-house." His voice was forced and feverish, but he had recovered his nerve. He struck another match, and went to the cupboard, taking out a candle, which he lighted.

I saw him cast a hurried glance round, and even look cautiously under the table.

"My brother used this place—I never knew what for." There was a sneering suggestion in his voice. "But it's never been used since his death. Come on, or your friend will have gone without you."

How did he know that it had never been used, and why did he fetch out the candle without hesitation?

He blew out the light and in silence we made our way along the dark track. I heard Charles shouting my name from the terrace, and 'halloed' to him.

"Come along, Dennis—I thought we'd lost you."

There was something unnaturally boisterous in Barton's tones as he told Charles that he had found me asleep in an old disused summer-house. "He might have stopped there all night," he added.

"Charles," I said, when we were speeding down the drive, "never ask me to that place again; the whole atmosphere, as Stevenson says, 'makes me sick at the stomach.' "

He chuckled to himself. "They are not a pleasant pair, but I have to find out all I can, and I think I'm on the track of something at last. Let's get to the Crown and have some clean beer—and watch out for squalls, Dennis, my boy."

CHAPTER XV

CHANCE OR DESIGN?

WE were sitting in the private sitting-room at the Crown—the same room in which I had talked with the Peters, as it seemed ages ago. That pleasant after-dinner feeling possessed us, and in Charles's cheery company I felt less pessimistic. The golf had made me just sufficiently tired to wish to sprawl at ease, with a cigar between my teeth.

"And now, Charles," I said, 'let's hear your wonderful plan about the Hall."

"Oh! the Hall—of course," he rattled on as though repeating a lesson; "you see I've rented it for a year, as I'm keen on shooting and golf, and as Mr. Darent, the owner, will probably want to go away for a bit to recover his health"—he looked slyly at me—"I thought later on I could bring my wife and children down for a breath of country air."

"Well—you say I can't tell a lie—of all the glib liars I have ever heard—"

He laughed boyishly. "An acquired habit, my boy—comes of being a lawyer. Rather neat idea, don't you think? Keeps you out of it altogether, and of course I shall have to do the place up before I can occupy it."

"But Darent—he will never consent."

"That's where you are wrong. We got his old lawyers to write saying they had received this attractive offer, and that it would mean that there would be no question of the place being sold up—that's what he was worrying about—and he actually agreed."

"I can't imagine him doing so."

"Well, it was good enough—he handed the letter to the officer who brought it, and said: 'Tell the damned lawyer to do what he likes,' so I suppose that's good enough to act upon. If he wants to repudiate the contract of course I shall have to clear out."

"How are you going to manage about the wife and children," I said sarcastically; "produce them out of your hat?"

"That's all right," he said airily, "I've got a friend of mine with a host of them—he'll be only too pleased to come along—he'll be the lessee, and I can stay with him—if necessary."

"You're a splendid friend to have, Charles, I admire your energy, and your vivid imagination. It sounds a good scheme."

"You see," he went on warming to his tale, "no one would take the place as it is, and the repairs can nominally be charged against the rent, though they will come to much more in actual fact, but Darent will never know. Why, bless my soul, if I had that place, I'd actually make it pay its way, now that the mortgage is gone and the debts paid. The Crown itself is a small gold mine."

I let him ramble on, for he had done wonders already and I did not wish to discourage him in the good work; but all the time I was picturing to myself Darent's face if he came to know of the way we had taken control of his place while he was away.

And then Polly came in with a message to say that someone wanted to see me, and would not give a name. My face went crimson as I saw Charles's grinning face, but I went swiftly out, fancying like him that I knew who the late-caller must be. Once the door was shut, however, I was undeceived. Polly whispered that Turnbull was the visitor and that he wanted to see me outside the house for some reason.

Anger and a sense of disappointment were mixed with a certain amount of relief, for Margorie had risked enough already.

The lawyer was standing under the trees in shadow, but in easy reach of the open window in case of danger, and the sound of men talking in the lounge came to our cars clearly in the still night.

"What do you want?" I asked.

"You would not care to talk in your private room, Mr. Tracey?"

"I have Mr. Erskine there—say what you want to and get off."

"I am sorry that you should be disturbed at this hour, but you see it will be necessary for you to go to London, to your bank to-morrow, and I thought you might forget. Circumstances have arisen that render it imperative for me to obtain a fairly large sum to-morrow. I have a sick wife who has to go into a nursing home, and my children—"

"You can cut that out," I said savagely, "I have a great mind to give you in charge."

"On what charge, Mr. Tracey?" he said softly, "I cannot conceive of anything that I have done that would render me liable to prosecution, but of course if you think you could make out a case?"

"I shall want a written statement from you that this is a complete and final settlement," I said desperately—knowing full well it would be valueless.

"Of course—everything shall be done in order. But now as to the place of meeting. I do not want any third person present"—his hard cackle that I had learnt to hate, sounded in the darkness of the yard.

"Choose your own place," I said, really more to gain time than because I had agreed to yield to his blackmail. I wanted to think.

"That's better, Mr. Tracey," he purred. "I knew you would see the reasonableness of my offer, but no monkey tricks, mind. Knowing your strength, I shall be armed." He came close to me, and would have pawed my coat had I not stepped back. "You know the Towers—anyway, the outside."

I held my breath. What on earth was coming next?

"Before you come to the wall under the trees, there is a gate that leads down a side path, and goes to the stables. It is a high iron gate that you cannot climb. Now follow me carefully, Mr. Tracey. That gate is usually locked, but at nine o'clock to-morrow night it will be open, and you can go down that gravel path. About a hundred yards down, on the left-hand side, you will find a summerhouse."

Every nerve was on the stretch, and I dared not trust myself even to speak. I waited in silence for him to go on. Again he gave that horrid laugh. "I can read what is in your mind. Such a secret place will suit you well—what chance would a poor feeble creature like me have against you there? I have taken precautions—you will come alone; otherwise you won't pass that gate. Bring the money with you, and I will give you a receipt, and the statement you want. At nine o'clock punctually, and not a word to a soul, or I shall not hold myself bound to secrecy, and you know what that will mean. Is that all clear?" I could feel that he was panting, for he had spoken quickly in one sentence, as though he still feared an attack.

I repeated his instructions to the letter.

"Good," he said, "I see you are a sensible man. By to-morrow night I hope your anxieties will be over. It is very worrying to have the thought of prison and disgrace hanging over one's head."

He turned so suddenly, and disappeared into the darkness, that I rubbed my eyes, wondering whether he had really gone, or was playing some trick; but only the sounds from within the Crown came to me, and Willis's voice politely telling his customers that it was time to order last drinks before closing-time. I shivered, though the night was close, and went slowly back to the sitting-room. I was in no mood to listen to Charles's banter, and told him at once that it was Turnbull who had called. He looked questioningly at me, but I answered that I had a matter to settle with the lawyer of a private nature. I had half a mind to tell Charles the whole story, but it was only the lawyer's word against mine, as to blackmail, and of course, he would absolutely deny everything, and then I could imagine the consequences. I had twenty-four hours, at any rate.

I pleaded sleepiness and wished him good night, but could see that he was puzzled at my abrupt departure.

The events of the next day were so utterly bewildering and unforeseen that I must set them down as calmly as possible in order to avoid melodrama. Charles was already at breakfast when I arrived, and deeply engrossed in his correspondence.

"It's a nuisance," he said, looking up at my entrance. "I've got to run up to Town to see Smithers. They are rather getting the wind up over some anonymous letter or other—it's no good taking any notice of these things. Some maniac has written saying he knows all about the murder, and so on. We always get these in murder cases. The fool wrote to Peters, who handed the letter to Deaken."

I had a fair idea as to the author, but kept my own counsel. "You will be back to-night?"

"I hope so. I've lots to do here. Oh, by the way, Dennis, there's a note come by hand from Robert Barton for you." He searched my face as he spoke. "You seem to have interested him."

"Barton?" I took the note from him. "Why on earth should he write to me?"

I waited till Charles was reading another letter before I broke open the envelope.

A silence fell between us, a heavy silence that sank and endured.

I heard Charles pick up his knife and fork at last, and the homely sound of toast being crunched between strong teeth. I sat there stunned, unable to think or speak.

I could only seize my cup and gulp down coffee to hide my face.

"What's the matter? You look as though you had seen a ghost."

I made a tremendous effort. "Sorry, Charles—I was thinking."

"Anything to do with that note from Barton?"

"Oh, no." I laughed, I am afraid rather harshly. "He merely asked me to come and see him to-night."

"Take care, then—he's got something up his sleeve. It's a pity he didn't ask us both. He didn't mention me?"

"Not a word." I crushed the letter into my pocket, and let Charles think what he liked. Luckily his own letters had given him food for thought, and he let the incident pass. Half-way through breakfast, I burst into a wild laugh.

"What's the joke?" Charles asked anxiously. I think he thought the strain of the whole position was telling on me.

"One of the funniest things I've ever heard," I said. "I'll tell you one day."

He had to be content with that, and went off to get his car.

I took the note out of my pocket and read it through, though every word was clear in my mind. The address and a crest were stamped on the thick vellum paper, but the writing was like that of a half-educated rustic, and the lines were irregular. This is what I read:

"DEAR MR. TRACEY,

"I have been thinking over our strange meeting in the summer-house last night. I believe I can help you, and give you information of the greatest value, but this must be in the strictest confidence. You have a dangerous enemy, let me tell you, who will stick at nothing. But I shall require your help as well, and hope you will be able to assist me. I think we are both rather in a hole. If you can manage it, I would like to have a talk, and suggest that you come to the summer-house—you know the way—at nine o'clock to-night, where we can have a quiet talk. It would be better than coming to the house. Please regard this as entirely between us two. I rely on your honour for that.

"Yours truly,

ROBERT F. BARTON (Baronet)."

By an almost unbelievable coincidence he had fixed the very time and place that Turnbull had arranged.

I had read a story somewhere in which a criminal had escaped by making two detectives who were both after him arrest each other.

All I had to do was to stay at home, and let them meet. It did not require much astuteness to guess that they had met before in the summer-house, for Barton's startled expression on seeing a dim form there had told me that; and I fancied that he thought I knew more about the place than I had told him.

Polly came in to clear away, and I went out into the fresh morning air, with a curious sense of relief, stifling an uneasy feeling that something might happen at that meeting that might solve my difficulties with Turnbull, and that I should prevent such a meeting from taking place.

"You are staying here?" Charles said, having brought his car round.

"Yes, I'm going to have a general look round."

"Calling at the rectory, eh?"

"I might do so, and I am going to see my friend Miss Morris; she asked me to call."

"You'll have a busy day, then—so long."

I watched him racing up the road, and envied his lighthearted, carefree nature. I was sure that he was enjoying the working out of this problem as a jolly experience.

Of one thing I felt certain—Turnbull would keep an eye on my movements, and the departure of Charles in his eyes might mean that I had commissioned him to get the money for him. Knowing as he did what I was doing for Darent, there would be nothing strange in my requiring a sum of ready money. Turnbull had worked out his plans cunningly.

The order of my projected calls was settled for me, for I had not gone fifty yards up the road before I saw the two huge hounds I had seen at Regent's Park lying peacefully at the gate of a cottage from which Miss Morris emerged and came to meet me.

"I thought you'd be down here, Dennis. Couldn't keep away. These people make me tired. I've just been to see a girl who has been practically excommunicated, indicted, accused, judged and condemned by the rector's wife, and all because she forgot the ceremony of marriage comes before and not after the producing of a family. I've fixed things up for her, and am taking her in my car with Bill Nokes, to whom I have administered a lecture, and they are going to get married if I know anything about it."

"And you have probably given her a fiver," I said, smiling.

"Damme, Dennis, they can't marry on nothing."

We strolled along together, and I could not help noticing the respect and friendliness paid to this strange being by the villagers who passed. In her weird costume—the same I had seen before—she would have been an object of derision among strangers.

"You heard about that ass the rector?" was her next remark.

"I heard he had handed in his resignation."

"Stuff and nonsense! I'm not a fool, Dennis. If he had been a miserable weakling, henpecked by his appalling wife, I would have accepted it like a shot, and glad to get rid of him, but you can take it from me, my boy, that he's nothing of the sort. He's got a powerful intellect and a strong will of his own, though he does give way to her too much. A good horsewhipping now and then would do her good. But as I was saying, he's got some other motive, a much more serious one. It's his infernal conscience."

"You mean that for some reason he feels that he can't go on as rector here?"

"You are bright this morning—but you've only got half the sentence; you should have added 'without revealing something that he has promised not to tell.' "

I was startled by her words; the rector's peculiar views concerning the secrecy of his office might conceivably have brought him information that he felt must be kept utterly secret, but if it had reference to the murder, I was certain that he would not let an innocent man be convicted.

We arrived at the gate of the rectory, and Miss Morris called her dogs to her.

"I am going to see whether he has come back," she said. "Come along."

"I don't think I should be very welcome—" I smiled at her.

"Fiddlesticks! Mrs. Browne can't eat you. I simply love the way she looks at me. A highly polished glare. The look Shylock must have given to the Duke. 'I'd bite you if I dared!' You watch her."

We walked up the drive, a weird quartet—Miss Morris scarcely reaching my shoulder, myself lagging nervously behind, and the two hounds with their red tongues hanging out, as though ready to back their mistress's word with solid bites.

Mrs. Browne came from the garden with a large bunch of flowers she had been cutting, and advanced on us with a tremendous smile. "How do you do, Miss Morris? I fancied you were still in London. I am so glad to see you. And you have brought Mr. Tracey with you, and your two dear doggies. That is nice of you. How do you do, Mr. Tracey? So you have come back to the village."

She shook hands and then patted the two dogs while she prattled.

"Any news of the dear rector?" Miss Morris asked when she had finished.

"He is coming back to-day—we are so glad. Of course, he never really meant to resign, and it was so good of you to take it in that spirit, Miss Morris. He was just overworked—you know how hard he labours in the parish."

"That's all right, then—don't let him make a fool of himself again, or his bishop may take him at his word. Resign forsooth—" I could see that the old-fashioned word was hastily inserted for something a good deal stronger, and smiled.

"And Margorie?"

"She is in the garden—she is bearing up wonderfully in the circumstances."

"It must be a trying time for her," I ventured to say.

"It's all over now, thank God, but of course at the time it was dreadful."

"I think Mr. Tracey was referring to the worry of Kenneth's position," Miss Morris remarked rather cattishly.

Mrs. Browne's face clouded over, and the artificial smile vanished.

"I trust she has got over all that nonsense by now," she snapped, and then she forced a laugh. "Of course, we are all anxious to see him get off." She turned to me. "Perhaps you would like to go and look for the dear child?"

There was no mistaking the arch expression, almost a simper.

"Good gracious!' Miss Morris exclaimed.

"I think I will." I looked steadily at Miss Morris's amused face.

"I know," I added as a parting shot, "Miss Morris wants to talk to you about Bill Nokes and his marriage."

Was this dreadful woman, having found out that I was a bachelor and fairly well off, already seeking for a substitute for the late baronet? The thought filled me with disgust, but it certainly gave me an opportunity of seeing Margorie openly.

I found her sitting on the same garden seat that we had occupied before, looking rather pensively on the ground, and she did not hear me coming over the soft turf. When she saw me she sprang up with a smile of welcome she took no trouble to hide.

"Dennis—I'm so glad to see you: I was just thinking of you when you came."

"That's very kind of you," I said. "What were your thoughts?" I took a seat beside her, and watched the light breeze playing with her brown curls, for as usual she wore no hat.

"I've heard all about the Hall, and what you are doing there. I think it's splendid of you."

"It's all over the village as far as I can hear, and I particularly didn't want Kenneth to know. I must get Charles to contradict the rumour as soon as possible."

"He ought to be grateful," Margorie said—as usual always using "he" for Kenneth.

"You know him better than I. He is extremely sensitive about this matter of the Hall, and money."

I told her of Charles's scheme, and saw her eyes sparkle with delight. It seemed to her such a fine ending to all Kenneth's troubles.

A triumphant return after an acquittal; all his worries over and a new, prosperous estate.

I felt a pang of jealousy, but I suppose a woman in love can only think of the happiness of her man.

"I want you to understand, Margorie, that my one hope is that when all this wretched business is over, the place will be ready for you and Kenneth."

I had taken her hand in mine to emphasize my words, and she turned her fearless eyes on me.

"I understand. And after that what will you do?"

I tried to smile at her. "That will be enough for me. If I can discover the author of this crime, and then see you both happy, I shall have done a good day's work, and can go away."

I saw the tears start to her lovely eyes, and she turned her head away.

I jumped up briskly. "We must be getting back—I came with Miss Morris, and she is now having a regular chin-wag with your respected mother."

We wandered past the flower-beds and came to the house by the farther side, where the windows looked over the valley.

It was the last moment of peace I was to know for many days.

Mrs. Browne had a red spot on each cheek when we found her. Her feathers had been properly ruffled by Miss Morris.

"Come along, Dennis, I'm going to take you to my house to lunch. Margorie, you look much better than when I saw you last—that's the best of being young. When you get to your mother's age, then it will be time to worry—rheumatics and all those jolly things. I know what a bother I had when my dogs had distemper."

Had we gone at once we should have missed the rector, but Miss Morris could not refrain from baiting Mrs. Browne, and continued the conversation until the rector himself appeared, coming slowly up the drive. He looked old and weary, and I fancied he was not pleased to find the group standing in front of the house, where we had moved on our way out.

He nodded to me and greeted his wife and daughter, and then he turned coldly to Miss Morris.

"I find that you wrote to my bishop, who is in London at a conference. He told me he had heard from you."

"Certainly I did. I never heard such nonsense in my life. I take all the trouble to select a really good man, and recommend him, and then he tries to slink off as though he had committed some crime. I told the bishop you were suffering from a temporary brain attack, but would be all right in a short time."

"So I understood," he said grimly. "He insisted on my taking a holiday and would not hear of my resignation."

"Good!" Miss Morris said, like a schoolgirl, and for the first time that morning I saw Mrs. Browne look at her with gratitude.

"Then you will be going away for a change, dear?" she asked, I fancied a little anxiously.

"Presently—when things are straighter. I cannot leave just yet."

There was something in the rector's manner that struck me as peculiar, and Miss Morris was quick to note it.

"You didn't spend all the time in London seeing that precious bishop, did you?" she asked him direct.

Instead of laughing or being offended, he replied gravely: "I did not! I had other things to do."

I was sure that he was going to say more, but his wife interrupted.

"Well—it's no good standing about. Of course you must decide for yourself, but I should have thought that this was the very best time you could choose for a holiday. Take Margorie with you and have a trip on the Continent."

There was no mistaking the meaning that underlay her words. It was a plain suggestion that he and Margorie should keep out of the way till the trial was over.

To my surprise—and I think Miss Morris's too—the rector turned sharply to his wife, his face white and hard-set.

"The last time I went on the Continent was not a happy experience. During my absence arrangements were made of which I should not have approved, and that may cause considerable trouble yet."

"I suppose you are referring to the Barton vault," Miss Morris said, looking strangely at him, while Mrs. Browne bit her lip in vexation at his outburst.

"I am referring," he said with icy coldness, "to what is in it, and the blasphemous desecration—"

"Don't use that ridiculous, extravagant language," Mrs. Browne cried indignantly.

We felt that it was time for us to go. I saw Margorie's white face and scared look, and Mrs. Browne's fierce, protesting attitude, and then Miss Morris touched me on the arm, and, collecting her two hounds, led the way down the drive without another word.

It was only when we had arrived in the road that she spoke.

"Something's very wrong." I had never seen her so moved.

"Has he gone off his head?" I suggested.

"Dennis, you're a fool!" she snapped at me. "He's the last man in the world to do that—but he's discovered something, you take my word, and whatever it is, there's going to be trouble. He's not a man to let a thing rest —especially not an injustice."

Like a flash of lightning part of the truth suddenly dawned on me.

"You know what he meant?" I said, with the familiarity she had taught me to use towards her.

"I don't know—if I did, I should have said so—I have merely a vague idea from what he told me, but have no facts, and it's only an idiot who makes statements that can't be substantiated."

And that was the last word she would say on the subject. "What a day!" I said to myself as I went off to wash before lunch.

CHAPTER XVI

THE SHOT IN THE DARK

LINGERED as long as I dared at the Crest, talking with Miss Morris on every subject under the sun, for I feared to be left alone with my thoughts. She showed me round her grounds, and I think she imagined that I was worrying about the general situation, for she was quick to notice my abstracted, nervous manner, and like a good soul kept me in conversation. She was a most amusing companion, and had every one in the village taped and docketed, and described them in humorous burlesque.

In her nature she had a curious blending of a rugged kindness and generosity with a certain bitterness, and on occasions she would refer to herself as a "lonely old woman." Her wealth and position had brought her no happiness, but she was one who would carry on to the end without a murmur. I wondered what her earlier life had been, and whether some tragedy had come to leave its marks on her.

At last I felt that I could stay no longer, and told her that I must get back to the hotel, pleading letters that must be written.

"I shall be going to London, Dennis," she told me. "I am on several committees, and have to attend the meetings, and there are other things. I want you to promise me something. I'm as certain as can be that Darent will be committed for trial—I speak as a magistrate. I want you to stay with me during the trial. It will be a nasty time for you."

"That's very kind of you," I said with a rather wan smile. "I am hoping that we shall know something definite about the crime before then."

"You mustn't bank on that. Dennis, it's a race—but there's too much to discover in a short time. Don't ask me any more." She took my hand and her manner became quite gentle for her. "You poor boy—even if Darent can be got off, there is danger for you. Keep your heart up, and we'll hope for the best."

With this cold comfort I took my way back to the Crown Inn, half dreading to find some note there for me, or even the sinister figure of Turnbull waiting under the shadow of the trees, but only the burly form of Hickmott was occupying the bench, and he grinned at me as I passed. I had no wish to speak to him, but he rose sheepishly and intercepted me.

"Good afternoon, Mr. Tracey—pleased to see you back. You are staying here at the inn?"

I told him sharply that such was the case.

"I wonder whether you would do me a favour, sir?"

"What is it, man?"

"Well, sir, it's like this—they don't open till six o'clock, and Willis is most particular about hours—too damned particular for me—and I thought as how you being there it would be all right for you to get what you wanted."

I laughed outright, only too glad of some comic relief. "All right, Hickmott; come along. I can get what I like."

"I don't want you to pay for it, mind," he said, with the stubborn pride of the farmer all the world over.

I took him to my private sitting-room and soon had a tankard for him, and something stronger for myself, as I felt in need of it.

It was a relief to talk to any one.

Under the influence of beer, the farmer became talkative, and naturally the conversation veered round to the subject of the murder.

The villagers had formed themselves into two parties —for and against Darent—and heated arguments took place on the subject. He had various theories to propound, and told me confidentially that he was certain that there was a woman in it—someone whom Barton had known before his engagement to Margorie, who wanted to stop the wedding.

He got so keen on his theory that he suggested that a brother or father had come with the wronged girl and demanded justice, and that on Barton refusing, a quarrel had ensued, and Barton had been killed.

It sounded very ingenious, but when I asked him who the woman was he was bound to confess that he had no idea, but added that Barton had been "hot stuff" when young. It all helped to pass the time, and I was almost sorry when he went. The sounds of clattering from below told that the bar was open, and I suppose he had gone to retail our conversation to his cronies, for I, too, had given a solution—that Barton had been attacked by a savage ape that was still hiding somewhere in the grounds and had been seen by several of the servants. I gave him such vivid details that his eyes were nearly starting from his head and his silly mouth was gaping wide before I had finished.

A sense of depression fell on me when he had gone. There was no sign of Charles, and the clock was relentlessly ticking out the seconds. I tried vainly to eat the dinner that Polly brought, but was compelled to wrap most of it up in a newspaper, for fear of offending her. Remembering Darent, I rigidly refrained from drink, only I put a flask in my pocket.

At eight o'clock I could stand it no longer. I put on a light greatcoat, for a thin rain was falling, and heavy black clouds were banked up in the south-west, causing a premature twilight.

I took the footpath that led to the Towers, and made a wide detour. I found that it was impossible to carry out my first intention of staying quietly in the inn and waiting events. I must be somewhere on the spot—unseen, but near enough to know what transpired at the summer-house. I had no thought of going to the iron gate, but would get near the barbed-wire fence. It was dark and the rain was heavier when I arrived across a meadow at this barrier and felt my way carefully along the wire. The hands of my watch, which had a luminous face, showed me that the time was a quarter to nine, and at the same time the quarter struck from the old church clock. I had no means of judging the exact spot where the summer-house stood, but could see the tall trees on the road very dimly as black shadows. By this time I was soaked through to the skin and shivering with cold.

Not a sound came from the other side of the fence, and I crouched down in the damp darkness of the meadow, waiting.

A faint flicker of light showed in the dense shrubbery in front of me, and went out as suddenly. By the appearance of the beam of light I guessed it was from an electric torch. Then there came the sound of bushes being pushed aside, and about thirty yards from where I was the light suddenly appeared like a glow-worm, seen only by reflection as the beam was flashed from someone whose back was turned towards me.

Then came darkness and silence. From the direction the man had come I knew that it must be Barton, for the summer-house was between me and the road. I crawled along the wire inch by inch, fearing a snapping twig or a sudden tear against the barbed wire.

I must have taken longer than I thought, for the hour struck when I was only half-way there. And then things happened with blinding rapidity.

The bushes were pushed apart, and I heard the door of the summer-house open creakily. From between the bushes I could make out the flash-lamp turned on, and voices raised in anger, the sound of a glass smashing and the table being overturned. The light had gone out, but from the darkness there came a cry, and then the report of a pistol-shot—I could make out the flash between the intervening foliage. I threw all caution to the winds, and dashed along the fence to the road, crashing through the hedge that was on Darent's property and not thick. A few yards from me was the gate that Turnbull had described to me, and as I stood panting and with my hands torn with brambles, a dark figure darted out and came along the road, crouching and sobbing as it ran. For a moment I stood motionless, struck with horror, but as the figure rushed past me I threw out a leg and he fell heavily to the ground. I was on him like a flash, holding him down.

He fought and kicked and tried to bite my hand, all the time making a snarling noise like a trapped puma, but I knew him.

"It's no good struggling, Turnbull," I said; "you won't get away."

I jerked the wretched man to his feet. There was no more fight in him.

He clung to me, trembling and whining. "Oh, Mr. Tracey, let me go—let me go! I haven't killed him! I swear I haven't!"

"So, Turnbull, you expected to see me and found Barton instead. I suppose that shot was meant for me?"

"Let me explain, Mr. Tracey—have mercy. I know I did wrong, but I meant no harm to you. You trapped me properly; I'll own to that." He was in abject terror and hardly articulate, but I was cool now, and saw my advantage. My first thought was to take him to the Towers and give him up, but I was not certain that this was the wisest course, for an animal at bay is a dangerous beast, and he could still tell all he knew.

"Let me go, Mr. Tracey, please let me go, and I swear I'll not trouble you again. Don't let's stay here —they will come and find me. I'll tell you everything —I will indeed, and you will be glad you let me go."

"I'll make no promise, but I would like a talk," I said, and led him to the gap, through which I pushed him.

"Where are you taking me, Mr. Tracey?" the shivering coward asked, clinging to me like a drowning man.

"Pull yourself together, man. Here, take some of this." I produced my flask and handed it to him.

"I am going to take you across these meadows, to a place where we can talk out of earshot," I said grimly.

There was more in this than I could fathom. If, as he had told me, he had only wounded Barton, the most he could expect was to be charged with assault, for, from what I had heard, there had been a struggle and Turnbull might have pleaded self-defence. His abject condition and his wish to get away suggested something more than that.

I made him tramp across the now sodden meadows till we reached a secluded spot under a great elm tree.

"Now, Turnbull—I want to hear your story, but I make no conditions, mind."

He was too far gone in fear to argue. In spite of the spirit he had swallowed, his teeth were chattering.

"I went there—" He spoke in jerks, as though even speaking were an effort. "I swear to God, Mr. Tracey, I'm telling the truth. I expected to find you, as we had arranged, but as soon as I got inside someone flashed a torch right in my face, and I thought it was the police."

"Ah, you were afraid of the police! Go on."

"I tried to get away, and then Sir Robert Barton spoke, and he took hold of me. "So it's you," he said, and struck me across the table. He gave me no time to explain, and before I knew what I was doing I had pulled out my automatic and fired at him. That's the truth, Mr. Tracey."

"It may be, but not the whole truth," I said sternly.

"It was only a flesh wound," he whined. "I picked up his torch and examined him. The bullet had only grazed his head, but he was unconscious."

"Then why didn't you go to the Towers and tell them—if it was as you say?"

"I daren't, Mr. Tracey—it would have all come out."

I was learning something at last. "Go on—I want to know everything, before I decide what to do."

I could just make out his writhing face in the darkness and the shifty, sullen eyes that would not meet mine, but gazed round as though fearful of pursuers.

"I daren't go to the Towers," he said hoarsely. "Sir Robert Barton has been to the police about me. I would have been arrested . . . they"—he licked his dry lips—"they are waiting for me at my office."

"So that's it." I felt a sense of triumph, for whatever happened now I was free from his clutches. "You have been to that summer-house before. Don't try to deny it. I know."

"I have been there," he said slowly. I think he felt by this time that his only chance lay in a clean breast of things to me.

"What did you go there for?"

"To meet Sir John Barton," he answered sullenly. What was coming out now from this pitiable wretch, who was only trying to buy his freedom from me at any price?

"We had business to discuss of a very private nature."

"Your usual business, I suppose—blackmail!" I said scornfully.

"Don't be hard on me, Mr. Tracey," he wailed. "I had done things for him for which he wouldn't pay."

"You met the present baronet—Robert—whom you have now shot, as well."

"Only once—I swear it's true. He wanted to see me, and took me there himself, after the detectives had gone. It was just a friendly meeting on family affairs."

"Then why were you so surprised when you saw him there instead of me? Come—no lies."

"You see, Mr. Tracey, I thought that you had gone to him and told him of our appointment, and he was there with the police."

I was beginning to see light.

"What you mean is that you have been trying to blackmail him, as you did his brother, but he would not agree to being fleeced, and was going to treat you as blackmailers should be treated."

"I thought he was going to kill me."

"I have no doubt you deserve it, but why should he want to do it?"

"Mr. Tracey," he said earnestly, "I know I can trust you. You remember our first meeting, when you—attacked me, and pushed me out of the door of the Crown Inn. All my papers came out of my dispatch-case and went all over the ground."

"I remember perfectly." I laughed at him.

He fiddled with his fingers, and seemed in doubt as to whether to proceed. "One of my papers—a very important letter—though of no value to any one else—was lost. I could not find it, though I came back to search. You did not find it, by any chance, Mr. Tracey?"

There was intense anxiety in his voice. "What was it?" I asked, to draw him on.

"A letter from me—it would mean nothing to you, but if it got into wrong hands— You did not take it to Sir Robert Barton?"

"I never saw any paper of yours, and I never looked for one," I said in sudden disgust. "If I had, I should not have taken another person's letter, in any case."

"Then I wonder who found it?"

"I'm tired of your letter. I expect some villager lit his pipe with it, or it got blown away. Now answer me this. What were you blackmailing Sir John Barton for?"

"I can't tell you—don't ask me!" he said fiercely, like a tigress defending its young. "Believe me, it will be better for every one not to know. It is all over and done with now, and it was not blackmail. It was merely payment for services rendered."

I was frankly puzzled. I could understand him blackmailing Robert if he had a hand in his brother's murder, as Charles seemed to think, but the elder brother was a different matter, and brought in fresh complications. I tried by threats and even promises to get him to, tell me, but he resolutely refused to say a word. I had a suspicion that he was possessed of a secret that he still hoped to make use of for some purpose. Perhaps he wished to keep this as his only asset, and continue his threats from a safe distance or through agents.

"I will tell you this," he said at last; "it had nothing to do with the murder of Sir John."

"How do you know? Do you know who did that?" I asked sharply.

"No, I don't, Mr. Tracey. I swear—"

I stopped him. "I've had enough of your swearing. Cut that out. Do you know, or have you any idea?"

"I have not—I wish I had."

Even in the middle of this ghastly interview I laughed. "I expect you do. It would have been another human body to suck dry, you vampire."

He began to whimper then. "I'm not so bad as you think, Mr. Tracey. Only give me a chance—I have a wife and children, and I am a ruined man."

I didn't care a button for Barton or his affairs, but I did care very much about Margorie, and I saw a chance to save her. I was conniving at a felony, but that troubled me little when playing for such high stakes.

"If I do let you go—though you don't deserve it—what are you going to do?"

"Oh, thank you, Mr. Tracey. I shall be grateful all my life to you."

I shook him like a rat, and he changed his tone.

"I shall go abroad," he said eagerly. "I have my passport on me now, and am all ready. I can cross at once."

"How did you come to have a passport all ready?" I asked him, my suspicions suddenly aroused.

"I frequently go abroad," he said evasively.

"Thank you, Mr. Turnbull," I said sarcastically. "You have told me just what I wanted to know. In other words, you were preparing to fly the country when you made the appointment to meet me."

"Then you will let me go?"

"I have no right to, but I am going to take the responsibility of doing so, but remember, although I can't trust to your word in the least, you have blurted out enough in your fear for me to be able to go to the police and tell all I know about you if you ever try to carry out your threats. Do you understand?"

A sickly smile came to his face that made me ill and almost inclined to retract my words, for he evidently felt he was making a bargain with a fellow-criminal and understood that sort of procedure to a nicety.

"I promise you, Mr. Tracey. One good turn deserves another."

I pushed him from me—feeling contempt for myself as well as for the loathsome toad.

To my surprise he did not rush off at once, but stood there bowing and scraping, his nerves restored to normal by my promise.

"Get off!" I said.

"You will excuse me, Mr. Tracey—I should not ask a favour, but I dare not go to Wickstead to get money. I have only a small sum on me—if you could—

I saw it all then. He had tried a gambler's throw. He had been prepared to bolt, and had reckoned on my blood-money to finance him. Sir John Barton had been his source of income, and he had tried and failed with the younger for some reason. In his despair he had turned to me. It was probably—though a long shot—to warn me and to find out how much I knew that Robert had made the appointment.

"If any one will get on by colossal cheek, you will," I said.

But I was now as keen to get rid of him as he to go, for if his affairs were so desperate, he might sell his knowledge to the police as a price of neutrality on their part.

I pulled out my pocket-book, and handed him all I had, which was quite a considerable sum, for I had brought it for expenses at the Hall.

"Take that, and make the best escape you can."

He grabbed the notes with a wealth of hypocritical thanks, so that I turned my back on him and was surprised when he laid his hand on my shoulder.

"Mr. Tracey, you have done me a good turn, but you don't know what you have done for yourself. I shall not be available as a witness at the trial." He grinned horribly at me. "You see what that will mean to you —and"—he paused, and I saw his mouth working—"I am going to tell you another thing. Go to the rector, your friend, and ask him to go to the vault where Sir John Barton and his first wife are buried and open the coffins. Don't forget—I have told you more than I should have done, but you have treated me like a gentleman, after the way I treated you."

He disappeared into the darkness before I could ask him another question, and I stood dumbfounded and shivering with the cold.

I stumbled back to the Crown through the storm. The lights of the place gave me a feeling of welcome after the vile business in which I had been engaged. I went by the back door, not wishing to pass through the lounge, but Polly was on the watch.

"Mr. Tracey," she said, "have you heard the news? Sir Robert Barton has been murdered in his grounds—just like the other one. Isn't it awful, sir? And Mr. Erskine has come back and wants to see you at once."

CHAPTER XVII

AT DEATH'S DOOR

CHARLES was waiting for me in our sitting-room, and, before the door had been shut, exclaimed:

"Hallo, Dennis! I hear you have been doing another murder."

I took off my dripping hat and greatcoat before replying to his outrageous allegation.

"I always make a point of doing two murders when I start—one is so dull. But what's happened?"

"Haven't you heard? We've been having thrills. First Oliver popped in to say that he had been summoned to the Towers, and, of course, Polly found out the reason. It appears that there's been a spot of bother there, and Robert Barton has been shot. So, of course, it was all over the bar in no time that he had been murdered in the same way as his brother. I called up young Vickers, and found that Robert had been wandering about the grounds, or something, and had received a slight wound from an automatic pistol in the head, but had been able to crawl back to the lawn, where he was found. Strange coincidence, wasn't it? Young Vickers said that it served him right for making assignations at night, and suggested that it was with a woman. He doesn't seem much upset about it."

Charles looked questioningly at me, but I was thinking deeply.

Of course, young Vickers was not to be relied upon to give a true version of the affair, but it struck me at once, after what Turnbull had told me, that it was quite likely that Robert Barton would try to hush the matter up or there might be awkward revelations. I took the opportunity of lighting my pipe—as I had not been able to smoke during the expedition—before I replied to his tacit question.

"What do you make of it?"

"Well, as you've been out all the evening, and come home soaking wet and covered with mud, I thought perhaps you might know something about it."

"I haven't even seen Barton, much less spoken to him," I replied truthfully. I felt I must give some explanation. "I have been seeing quite a different person—our friend Turnbull, the lawyer. You can be quite certain that he will trouble us no more."

"You're a rum bird, Dennis," Charles observed uneasily. "Have you bumped him off as well?"

"Try to be serious—I don't go bumping people off. I can't tell you the whole story, old man, because it involves other people, but you can take it from me that we have seen the last of Turnbull."

Charles, like the generous friend he always has been, refrained from asking more on that matter, though I could see he was puzzled. He remained smoking quietly, deep in thought, while I tried to get myself reasonably dry, and the steam rose from my trouser legs as I held them to the fire.

"In one way," he said, as though thinking aloud, "this will help us. If Turnbull is out of the way, he will not be able to give evidence. You are sure he has gone?"

"He has bolted to the Continent—by this time he will be on his way to Croydon, and will cross by air, leaving no address. He will certainly not be available as a witness."

"That's a very good thing, but you seem cocksure about it."

"I have just seen him off—look here, Charles, I promise one day I will tell you the whole thing, but don't ask me now."

"All right, lad—I had no intention of doing a third degree on you, but I'm just thinking. This may help Darent. If we could show some connexion between the murder of the elder brother and the attempted murder of the younger, it would look like a vendetta, and certainly Darent could hardly have done this, unless he's escaped from Maidstone."

If Vickers's scrappy account was true, it was obvious that Robert Barton had been as anxious to hide up the real story as I had been, and we met on common grounds. In that case he would prefer no charge, and I was eager to hear what he would make of it.

"I wonder who winged him?" Charles interrupted. "It's a devilish funny business."

He was frowning heavily, and I could not refrain from laughing. Somehow the departure of Turnbull had lifted a great weight from my mind.

"Why this merriment?" Charles asked crossly.

"Sorry, Charles, but I know what's worrying you. You are firmly convinced that Barton murdered his brother, or got some thug to do it. I have watched you working up a case against him, and now that someone has tried to murder Robert it doesn't look so good. Isn't that right?"

Polly knocked at the door, and entered.

"It's too late for dinner," Charles said; "we'll just have whatever you've got—anything will do, Polly."

"Yes, sir, but I came to see Mr. Tracey. Jack's outside and wants to speak to you, sir," she said to me.

Charles looked at me with an injured expression, as though I had been deceiving him.

"Ask him to come here, Polly, and bring him a drink," I said.

"What's the game?" Charles questioned when the door was shut.

"I don't know—you'll hear what he's got to say."

The constable entered, and removed his hat. I told him to sit down, and Polly came in with a large sliver of beer, and departed.

"My best respects, sir," Oliver said, burying his head in the foaming tankard.

Charles was relieved; a man who was going to be arrested, or even questioned, would hardly be treated with this deference.

When he had quenched his thirst Oliver turned to me. "I've been to the Towers, sir—rum go altogether. They phoned for me, and I thought it was going to be another murder, but when I got there the new baronet, Sir Robert, was sitting up in bed, with a bandage round his head, and the doctor had just gone. He seemed very angry that I had been sent for, and said that he had met with an accident—that was all. However, he gave me something for my trouble, and then sent me back in his car, and asked me to tell you that he would like to see you, and would you come back in the car. He seemed most particular about that."

"So he's not going to prefer any charge?" Charles asked.

"No, sir, and from what I gathered, he wanted the matter to be discussed as little as possible—seemed a bit snappy about it, and hoped I hadn't mentioned it to any one."

"Very good, Oliver; I'll go at once."

The officer finished his drink, and bade us good night—I rather guessed he would find some difficulty in making Polly refrain from talking.

Charles seemed a little surly, and I could hardly blame him.

"Wait up for me—I shan't be long—and I'll tell you all I can."

Things were moving fast this day, and I had a feeling of excitement that overmastered my fatigue as I sped along to the Towers.

The butler took me straight up to a huge bedroom, more like a dormitory, in which Barton was lying in bed, looking small and insignificant in this chamber. The windows were covered with crimson brocade curtains, and sofas and arm-chairs and weird-shaped settees were dotted about the floor. A feeling of disgust came to me as I realized that this display was meant for Margorie's delectation.

Vickers was sitting by the bed, and a table had been drawn up on which were glasses and champagne.

Robert summarily dismissed his cousin, and beckoned me to take his place and help myself.

He was propped up with pillows and his dark, swarthy face had an underlying pallor, while his head was swathed in bandages.

He was a sick man, and had no business to be speaking, but his restless eyes, and the twitching of his mouth, showed that he could not attempt to get to sleep till he had seen me.

"That was a dirty trick you played on me," he said in a feeble voice, without preface.

"I have come here at your request," I said stiffly, for I felt he had a grievance, "and I will listen to what you have to say, but don't let's start by an argument."

"I asked you to meet me at the summer-house, and you sent someone else instead."

"Look here, Barton, I'll tell you what happened. Before I heard from you Turnbull had made an appointment to see me at the very place and time of your appointment; it was a sheer coincidence, but honestly I had no idea that he was going to attack you."

"You seem to know all about it.' His feverish eyes were on me with a keen look.

"I was outside the wire—and heard the shot."

"What did he want to see you for?' he asked suspiciously.

"That I am afraid I can't tell you, but if you will let me know what you wanted with me, it may throw some light on the matter."

"I was trying to do you a good turn," he muttered. "I wanted to warn you against Turnbull."

"Let's be frank about it. When I was in the summer-house—the time you found me—you were expecting Turnbull there. He has been there before and has been trying to blackmail you. He told me so."

I thought he was going to faint, and handed him a glass of champagne, but he pulled himself together with an effort. "Are you in league with him? Do you know—" He stopped in the middle of the sentence.

"He is my worst enemy, but I don't think he will worry you any more. He has bolted abroad—you will be glad of that."

Far from being satisfied, I saw a look of horror gather on his face. "Abroad," he muttered. "God! I wish I'd killed him."

"Amen to that," I said fervently.

"You devil," he said slowly. "I believe you wanted me to do so, and then give me up for murder."

I laughed at him scornfully.

"I don't think you ought to be talking—that's ridiculous; but we are wandering from the point."

A cunning look came to his face, flushed with the effort of talking. "There is now no need to go into that—I just wanted to tell you what a dangerous man Turnbull is."

"You are telling a lie, Barton." I had waited for this all along, and was going to shoot my bolt—though it seemed unfair when dealing with a sick man. "What you wanted me for was to find out whether I knew the secret for the keeping of which your brother had paid blackmail to this lawyer, and for which he was trying to make you do the same."

I looked down at the man, and saw that he had fainted. I felt no feeling of compunction: Darent's freedom and Margorie's happiness were at stake; but I was sorry for him when I saw his bandaged head and the weak, tired look on his face. I touched the electric push beside the bed, and dashed some cold water into his face.

Vickers and the butler hurried into the room.

"Your cousin has fainted," I told Vickers. "I don't think he should have talked at all to-night. I'll just wait till he has recovered, and then go."

Vickers glowered at me, but made no remark. I think the happenings of the evening had scared him, and that he regarded me as a sort of gangster. I took Barton's pulse, and found it fairly strong; there was no cause for alarm. It was not his wound, but my words that had struck him senseless.

Presently he opened his eyes and gazed round the room with a vacant stare, and put his hand to his head, mumbling some words I could not catch. He looked at me in a puzzled fashion, as though wondering what I was doing in his room. Vickers was watching keenly, and I was anxious that Barton should not blurt out something in his state of semi-consciousness. I leant over the wounded man, and said, very slowly and distinctly: "I am sorry you are so ill. Thanks for telling me what you have done. I am leaving you now, but hope to see you when you are better. Try and get some sleep now."

He closed his eyes, though whether he had heard me or not, I cannot say.

"Shall I telephone for the doctor, sir?" the butler asked, standing a long way off by the door.

"There is no need—he'll be all right now, but don't let him talk." I made my way to the door, and felt a touch on my arm. Vickers had followed me.

"What is it?" His eyes were large with fear.

"Nothing that you need know—there is no danger for you. Good night."

I went out, preferring to walk, as I wanted to think before I met Charles, but my head was throbbing terribly, and I felt hot and cold by turns. I felt like a man who, reading an exciting detective story, finds that the last pages have been torn out and the solution missing.

Here was obviously a vital secret—a secret so deadly that John Barton had paid goodness knows what in money to Turnbull, sooner than expose him as a blackmailer. That was clear, but in that case what connexion, if any, had this with his murder—unless he had at last turned on his persecutor, and met his death? All my common sense was against that, for Turnbull was an arrant coward. He might shoot in desperation, but I could not picture him making that savage assault, unless driven absolutely into a corner.

But Robert Barton had also been approached by Turnbull for blackmail, and had resisted, though he knew this secret, or why was he so anxious to meet me secretly, when he feared that I was in possession of it? There came back to me the unguarded words of young Vickers, that his cousin was intending "to sell up and clear out." Was he temporizing with Turnbull until he could get beyond his reach, or was he going to defy Turnbull to do his worst? And then in a flash a wild idea came to me. If the brother was in deadly fear, the secret, whatever it was—would mean something dreadful for him, but if Robert merely knew it, the case was not so serious.

Then and there, on that lonely road, in the splashing of the rain that was still coming down heavily, and with the echoes of my footfalls sounding eerily in the darkness, the truth, as I saw it then, dawned on me, the whole ghastly truth, hideous as the worst nightmare.

At times—seldom, thank goodness, in this peaceful land —there emerges from hell itself some deed so foul, that the very thought of it blasts the soul.

I was worn out, and my mind was tired with thinking. Proof! Proof! Proof! My feet were beating out on the road, till the very sound was driving me mad. Faintness, and waves of giddiness came over me. I staggered to the inn door, and knocked—Charles had been on the look-out for me, and led me in. He gave one look at my face, and took my arm: "Come on, lad, you are done in. I've got a hot grog ready, and then bed for you."

He was as tender as a woman, and I am afraid I gave an hysterical sob, and clung to him. He half carried me to our sitting-room, and fetched my pyjamas, after mixing a stiff dose of brandy and hot water.

"You've caught a chill—no wonder—now just sit there till I come back, and mind, not a word of any sort."

I was half asleep with sheer exhaustion when he returned, and he must have undressed me and practically carried me to bed, for I remembered nothing more until I woke next morning with a splitting headache and a high temperature, and a doctor feeling my pulse. Charles was there, looking gravely at me, and I tried to laugh to reassure him.

Dimly, and from far off I heard the doctor say: "We can't tell at present—keep him in bed and warm, and above all no excitement. I'll look in this afternoon."

And then I drifted off into a feverish sleep.

Faces came and went in my delirious dreams. Sometimes the visions were delightful—Margorie's face bending over me, and smoothing the pillows, and the kindly vision of the rector, and of Charles. I seemed to hear Miss Morris in her deep tones telling me not to be a fool, but to get well quickly. But there were other and darker visions, and I was told afterwards that I had to be held in bed at times, when the sallow, evil face of Turnbull came to haunt me, and Barton with a splash of blood where his face should have been. And then I would see Kenneth with sad reproachful eyes, calling me traitor.

Worst of all, I saw him going to the gallows—the slow procession led by the chaplain; and I was being held back, when I could have saved him. I believe I shrieked and sobbed, and implored them to let me get up and give evidence.

But I have a strong constitution, and was able to get through the crisis somehow, and then it was merely a matter of lying still and recovering—though the process was tedious. At first I was too weak to think or worry about anything, only taking medicine and food obediently when it was offered.

I think the first person I recognized with proper intelligence was Charles, who was sitting in an easy chair reading a book.

I called his name, and he came to me at once.

"Hello, my lad, sane at last! You've given us a devil of a time."

He spoke hoarsely, and I noticed a tired look about him.

"Have I been ill long?"

"Long? Don't worry about that, old thing—get better. You'll be all right now. Sleep, and eat what's given you; we'll soon have you up again."

"But where am I?" I looked round the large comfortable room, totally unfamiliar to me.

"Now don't start asking questions or you'll have your temperature up again. You are at the Crest. When you cracked up, Miss Morris insisted on your being taken there, and her word is law. So here you are and here you remain." He grinned at me, but I could perceive, even in my weakness, that he was pleased to find me well enough to speak sensibly.

I took in the furniture of the room, as a sick man will, and then I asked nervously: "Tell me one thing, Charles —in my delirium I fancied once or twice I saw Margorie —did she ever come and see me?"

"Ungrateful wretch," he exclaimed playfully, "you owe your life—which isn't worth much—to her. She has nursed you all along, and only when you became violent, I, or the rector—whichever happened to be on duty—had to hold you down. My word, Dennis, you are strong. Margorie! Why, bless her heart, she's only lying down now for a rest while I take her place."

"But why," I asked fretfully, "didn't you have a trained nurse? She never ought to have wasted time on me."

"It was better not to have one," he said. "You were raving, and saying things."

They told me afterwards that Miss Morris had decided that they must not have a stranger in the room, but she had fetched Mary from the Hall, and she had turned out an efficient night nurse, while they had taken turns in the daytime.

I will not dwell on Margorie's coming, or what her presence meant to me. She was tired-looking and seemed thinner in the face, but came and sat by my side and read aloud to me till I dozed off to sleep with her hand in mine, for she treated me like a child.

They wouldn't let me ask questions; only when Charles thought that I was worrying, he informed me that nothing of any importance had transpired while I had been laid up, and that things were more or less as they were when I was taken ill. Barton had recovered, and had gone off somewhere, taking Vickers with him, and the Towers had been shut up.

Of Darent they would not speak, and I feared to ask, but the most they would say was that he was still in prison.

It would be tedious and egotistical to retail the story of my convalescence. My friends were all far too kind.

Margorie was sitting one day beside me, and I watched the worn face with a feeling of self-reproach. She was pensively staring out of the window, and was unaware, of my scrutiny.

"Margorie," I said softly, and she turned to me at once. "Tell me—how long have I been lying here?"

"Seven weeks," she said with a smile, "but you will be up again soon. The doctor says you are making a wonderful recovery after pneumonia."

"Good Lord—and you have been nursing me all this time!"

"I was glad to do it, Dennis. It—it took my mind off other things."

"What a selfish brute I've been!" I exclaimed somewhat irrationally.

"Of course, I came at once.' She smiled at me wanly. "Mother was only too pleased."

I read her meaning, and tried to smile with her.

I tried again and again to ask the one question, but simply couldn't get my lips to frame it—I suppose it was due to my weak state.

I think she saw in my eyes what I wanted.

"Kenneth was committed for trial by the magistrates." Tears, which she tried to dash away, filled her eyes.

"Tell me about it," I said firmly. "I am quite strong enough, and the worry of not knowing will do me more harm than the truth."

"There is little to tell," she said sadly. "There were repeated re-mands, and the prosecution brought out their evidence bit by bit, in a terribly slow way. At last they had finished, and Mr. Deaken, who had represented Ken at the police court, when every one knew that a committal was inevitable—reserved the defence."

"And Kenneth?"

"He has absolutely refused to say anything, even to Mr. Deaken, and sat in the dock as though the whole thing bored him. They wouldn't let me go, and I think they were right, but Miss Morris says there is a great change in him."

"I should think so after the time he has been through."

Margorie looked at me strangely. "It's not that, Dennis. He was firm and strong, and many years younger. They tell me he was much more like he used to be in the old days."

"I'm glad of that," I said earnestly.

"So am I, Dennis, but he was so stern, and like a man who has every one against him—that's what Miss Morris said." Her voice broke. "He thinks that every one has turned against him—even you and I."

I tried to cheer her. "Wait till he's free again, and we'll get that put right," I said.

"Oh, I do hope so, Dennis. I don't mind about myself, though it hurts, as long as we get him off."

The days went by, and I was allowed to sit up, and walk a little.

If it had not been for the gnawing anxiety of the situation, I should have tried to prolong those days, for as I got stronger Margorie's presence was no longer necessary as a nurse, though she came to see me every day.

And then I had a visit of more serious import. Peters came with his wife, and had a talk, though the subject of Darent was not mentioned. They were both exceedingly kind, but I was convinced that his real object in calling was to find out how far I had recovered, and whether I should be available as a witness in the forthcoming trial.

I asked after Mabel, and Mrs. Peters told me that she had been far from well, and was in a nursing home, with a temporary nervous breakdown. I asked no more, but from what I had seen of her at their house, I surmised that drugs were the cause of the trouble.

The following day I had a less pleasant visit, for Charles brought in Smithers and Mr. Deaken. After beating about the bush, as lawyers will do, Deaken came to the point.

"The assizes open next week, Mr. Tracey, and our case comes on first—that will be Tuesday. Do you think you will be well enough to be called as a witness?"

"Of course I will," I answered stoutly, for I did not like his manner, and sensed the reason for the question.

"Of course," he said, choosing his words, "the doctor is quite prepared to give you a certificate, and in that case your evidence can be taken on commission."

"What good will that do?"

Deaken and Smithers exchanged glances. 'It will save you the strain—which after your recent illness will be considerable—of cross-examination."

So that was it! They wanted me to remain behind while Margorie and the Martins faced the music.

"I am quite prepared to give evidence—you have my statement, Mr. Smithers."

"It is rather an ordeal," Deaken said doubtfully.

"I don't care a damn what it is," I exclaimed stubbornly. "I'm going through with it, and that's an end of it."

Deaken gathered up some papers he had brought with him and rose to go. "Very well, Mr. Tracey, if you take that attitude, we shall call you."

"And my blood be upon my own head," I said. 'That's what you are thinking."

He turned angrily at the door. "It is not a laughing matter, Mr. Tracey. It is my client I am thinking of, not you."

"He's gone to see the Martins," Charles said when the door was shut.

"Stupid old prig," I responded.

And then Smithers squared his shoulders and put me through my paces. It was sort of dress rehearsal. He took the part of the *advocatus diaboli*, and tried to turn me inside out. With Turnbull out of the way, for no traces had been found of him, though the police were after him, I felt more confident.

It appeared that the police would have arrested Turnbull on the night that I had last seen him, but were waiting for instructions from Barton, who afterwards withdrew the charge of blackmail that he had laid, before they could pounce on him.

I felt rather done up after Smithers had finished, but Charles told me that I had done well, with a queer quizzical expression.

The case had been sent to the Old Bailey for trial—I do not know why, not understanding the ways of the Law; but Peters had applied for it, and there was some question of dates of the assizes. We were all glad of that, as we had expected it to be heard at Maidstone; and Miss

Morris had insisted upon us staying with her, so we moved up to her Town house. During those dreadful days Miss Morris was splendid. Her extravagant slang and banter braced our nerves, and she would allow no one to mope, or leave food untouched.

The trial was right on us and absorbed all our thoughts, and I think this accounted for the fact that the tremendous and startling idea that had come to me on the night I had been taken ill, I kept to myself. I had been very ill, and delirious, and I had no shadow of real proof only conjecture, and the piecing together of the little hints and suggestions that had come to me during this period at Crowfield. Had I taken any one into my confidence, I am convinced that the person would have put the whole wild tale down to the result of temporary derangement.

But at the back of my mind I was certain that I had lit on the true solution. Which just goes to show how far one can be wrong.

CHAPTER XVIII

THE TRIAL OF KENNETH DARENT

EFORE the trial came on I had an opportunity of reading through the complete transcript of the proceedings in the lower court, with which Charles had supplied me. It was not pleasant reading, and my heart sank to my boots long before I had finished.

The prosecution had woven such a web of circumstantial evidence round Darent that I felt that he was like a fish caught in a net that was closing round him, and dart where he would there was no escape. I do not suppose that one in a hundred who had read the accounts in the papers would have any doubts about his guilt.

Most of the facts of the case are already familiar to the reader, but there were one or two new pieces of evidence that the police had brought forward.

The celebrated expert Sir Bertram Pillbeam had been called in to testify as to the cause of death, and on other matters. He agreed with the local doctor and the police surgeon that death was due to internal haemorrhage on the brain caused by laceration and fracture. There was one wound at the back of the head that alone, he said, would have been sufficient to have caused death, and a number of blows had been delivered in the face, which had been reduced almost to a pulp.

His theory was that the antagonist had attacked Barton from the front, and that, as he had turned to run, he had been struck a terrific blow from behind. Sir Bertram had then dealt with the stick, on which he had found traces of human hair, blood and skin, and had no doubt that the injuries were caused by this instrument. As plenty of evidence was forthcoming that the stick belonged to Darent, and that he had actually been seen walking with it on the day of the murder, the first nail was, so to speak, hammered into Darent's coffin.

Sir Bertram then went on, in that calm, confident manner that has brought many a man to the gallows, to say that he had examined an evening dress coat belonging to Darent, and found on the right sleeve stains of human blood. Attempts, he said, had been made to clean the marks off, but they showed distinctly on the lining of satin. Further, with the new micro-haematin test, the blood had been shown to fall into the same group as that of the murdered man. Pyke's evidence with regard to the pumps and the tracks that led in the direction of the Hall, which were identical with the measurements of Darent's pumps, seemed conclusive. No mention had been made of the second pair of tracks, and I concluded that the police were satisfied that one of the guests had merely strolled over the lawn during the search, and had been unable to find out the owner of the pumps. Their business was to obtain evidence against Darent, not to introduce extraneous matter.

As to motive, there were several busybodies in the village who had been only too willing to state that Darent and Barton had quarrelled, and that the accused had been heard to utter threats against Sir John.

Then evidence was produced with regard to Darent's financial position and the affair of the mortgage, to show that on the very day on which the murder took place Turnbull had brought the mortgage deeds on the Hall, which had been purchased by him for Barton, to the Towers, and that they were missing. It was shown that the accused was in desperate straits, and that the foreclosing of the mortgage would spell ruin.

In fact, carefully and relentlessly, the case had been built up, with the facts as I have told in this narrative. If anything there was *embarras des richesses* in the matter of evidence a damning indictment, rendered all the more imposing by the fact that Deaken had practically refrained from cross-examination of any sort. Motive, weapon, tracks, the butler's story of Sir John's words—everything was in order.

And against this there stood only our alibi!

The days before the trial were hard to bear. Miss Morris was unflagging in her endeavours to keep our spirits up. Charles, like a true friend, sat up half the nights with me, as sleep was well nigh impossible.

At last the dreaded day arrived, and I think we were all thankful that the waiting time was over.

The trial, as the papers said, was a *cause célèbre*, and the court was crowded every day, hundreds failing to gain admission.

The murdered man was a rich baronet, and the accused a member of an old county family, and a magistrate. There were also vague rumours of a romance behind the murder that brought crowds of hard-eyed and highly painted society women, and a number of actors.

Mr. Justice Pennyfold was the judge, a fine-looking old man with a wrinkled face, straight firm mouth, and piercing black eyes.

I had never been to a trial in my life, and in spite of my nervousness, I could not help being interested in the strange ritual of an English court of justice.

The splendid trappings of the judge, which would transform the most ordinary-looking man into a figure of awe and dread, and the three stately bows he gave to the jury, the counsel and the public—while we all stood up! There is a quiet yet stern dignity about an English court that one cannot find in any other country in the world.

The Crown prosecutor was Sir Herman Schultz—one of the hardest nuts at the Bar, Charles informed me gloomily.

And then the clerk of the court, a wizened little man, called the name of Kenneth Darent—which was echoed through the court as though they did not quite know where he was.

My heart missed a beat when I saw Kenneth enter the dock with two warders.

The clerk read the charge over to him, and asked him whether he pleaded guilty or not guilty.

"Not guilty," he said in a defiant voice.

I cast a furtive glance at him, and saw, as I had been told, that a great change had taken place in his appearance. He was neatly and quietly dressed in a tweed suit, and well groomed. The purplish, unhealthy colour had gone from his face, and his features seemed to stand out boldly without the fleshiness I had noticed before.

He showed no trace of nervousness, but gazed round the court with insolent, proud eyes, as though he held the crowd in contempt, and dared them to do their worst.

He looked like a man who has seen death face to face, and could fear no more.

The jury were sworn, and Kenneth was asked whether he wished to challenge any of them. He cast his eyes over them as though they were so many prize cattle at a fair, and shrugged his shoulders as he answered in the negative.

It would be tedious to re-tell the evidence for the prosecution. Sir Herman Schultz outlined his case in a perfectly fair manner, without the bitterness for which he was noted, and called his witnesses and we sat through that dreary day listening to all that we already knew. I felt more and more angry with Peters, as at the end of each witness's testament, he rose and said that he had no questions to ask, but Charles, who sat by me all through the case, told me that he was reserving his fire.

I had decided with Margorie that it would be better for us to sit apart, and she was with Miss Morris at the back of the court.

I do not know whether Darent saw her, but he made no sign, never once looking up after he had declared himself not guilty, and in fact appearing to be thoroughly bored by the proceedings.

We returned to Regent's Park very depressed, and Miss Morris ran us all off, much against our wills, to a picture-house, where, as luck would have it, a murder trial in America was being portrayed with great and vivid detail!

On the second day Margorie was called. She had already told me that she had been under subpoena to appear, and was glad of it.

When she stepped into the witness-box I saw Darent give one lightning glance at her, and then turn his head away with a contemptuous shrug. Having refused to hold any intercourse with the solicitor, he was ignorant of what was to happen, and, I think, was merely waiting for the farce to end.

Margorie was white, but perfectly cool and collected. She had felt that stab of Kenneth's look more than the staring, cruel eyes of the spectators; the gloating, wolfish eyes waiting to see a fellow being sent to a vile death.

Schultz was very suave with her, knowing that the average jury will not stand the bullying of a woman when she is young and good-looking.

After a few soothing preliminary questions, he purred at her:

"You were engaged to be married to Sir John Barton?"

"I was."

"How long had you been engaged?"

"Three months."

"When did you first hear of his death?"

"My father came and broke the news to me, at the Towers, after they had found him in the garden."

"It must have been a terrible shock to you?"

"Naturally."

Her quiet tones seemed to disconcert Schultz, and I saw his brow become puckered.

"Had you any idea that he was going out into the garden?"

"Not the slightest—he was wanted for the distribution of prizes, and could not be found."

"Was there any reason why he should have a special enemy?"

"None whatever," Margorie replied firmly.

"You have heard these witnesses say that there was a feud between your fiancé and the accused—can you tell his lordship and the jury anything about that?"

"I think it was grossly exaggerated by village gossip," she said scornfully. "I know that Mr. Darent was annoyed at the Towers being built, and Sir John was angry because Mr. Darent would not sell him some land, but that was some time ago. I don't think they saw each other for months before Sir John's death."

Schultz bent down and held a whispered conversation with the solicitors. Margorie's evidence was not going according to his brief and the instructions he had been given, and I could guess the reason. The prosecution had taken it for granted that she would testify against the supposed murderer of her fiancé, who had ruined her life and deprived her of a fortune.

"I am going to ask you a very delicate question, Miss Browne," Schultz said silkily, and all eyes were fixed on Margorie, who stood erect, icy cold, and proud.

"Was there any sort of rivalry between the two men?"

"Not the slightest. Mr. Darent and I had known each other since I was a child—we were just old friends, nothing more."

"You were never at any time engaged to Mr. Darent?"

"Most certainly not; there was never any suggestion of such a thing."

"You were fully acquainted with the position of the accused—financially, for example?"

"I knew very little. I really haven't seen anything of him for some time."

"You knew that there was a mortgage on his estate?"

"Yes. Sir John had bought it up, and Mr. Turnbull came to the Towers with it on the day of Sir John's death."

"On the day of his death—yes, and they are missing."

"They are nothing of the sort," Margorie answered in a clear, ringing voice. "Sir John gave them to me as a wedding present—he had told Turnbull to have them transferred to me."

Schultz looked up quickly from his papers, and I saw Peters give an anxious glance at Margorie.

"Wasn't that rather a singular wedding present?" Schultz asked with a slight sneer. "Can you suggest any reason?"

Margorie was equal to him.

"Yes, I can. My father and mother, and others for that matter, were very sorry for Mr. Darent, and that he had been compelled to raise a mortgage. Sir John wanted to help him, but he knew that Mr. Darent would not accept help from him, and chose this method which he knew would please us all."

I saw Darent's face go suddenly red with anger, and the veins stood out on his forehead. I thought he was going to break in on the evidence, but he controlled himself.

But Schultz was even more upset, and he looked like Barak when he turned in fury on Balaam and said: "I told thee to curse mine enemies, and behold thou hast blessed them altogether."

"Then if the deeds were made out to you, and given to you on the night when Sir John was murdered, where are they now?"

"I destroyed them," Margorie answered fearlessly.

"You destroyed them! May I ask why?"

"They belonged to me, and I knew that Mr. Darent would no more accept them from me than from any one else. Once they were destroyed the mortgage ceased, and the property reverted to him, without any fear of foreclosing."

"Did any one suggest that to you?

"No one at all. I had intended to do so when Sir John first mentioned the matter."

Schultz slapped his papers down on the table and turned to the judge. "M'lord, I shall have to treat this lady as a hostile witness."

I could almost see a look of amusement on the judge's face. "I fail to see why, Sir Herman," he said in a slow, deliberate voice; "I think she has given her evidence extremely clearly, and has certainly impressed me. Do you wish to put any questions, Mr. Peters?"

"In the circumstances, none, m'lord," Peters said, knowing that it was wiser to let well alone.

"Then I will ask one," the judge said. "Miss Browne, did you destroy these mortgage deeds before or after the death of Sir John?"

"Before, m'lord. He gave them to me in the afternoon at my father's house, with other presents. As soon as he had gone I burnt the deeds."

"It was a foolish thing to do, but, of course, you could not foresee the future. Thank you, Miss Browne."

Margorie stepped down from the box, and for the first time I felt that we had scored a point.

Schultz was on his feet again. "M'lord, one of the most important witnesses for the prosecution, Mr. Turnbull, a solicitor from Wickstead, was to have appeared, but he cannot be found—he has gone somewhere, and we are unable to trace his whereabouts."

"I hope," Peters said with an urbane smile, "my learned friend is not suggesting that we have spirited him away!"

"Certainly not," Schultz snapped, "but he cannot be called."

"Very well, then," the judge said, 'proceed with your case."

"In his absence, I shall call no more witnesses. That is my case, m'lord—gentlemen of the jury."

Margorie's evidence had cost her more than any one, except myself, in that crowded court could understand. I had seen fury and despair chase each other over Darent's face when she had almost scornfully repudiated him, and she had seen it as well, and every word must have been a sword-thrust through her own heart.

And then I realized that very shortly I had to stand in that witness-box, and a sick feeling came over me. But I vowed I would not fail her.

The day was wearing on, and the atmosphere in the court was stifling. I listened, hardly hearing a word, for my mind was absorbed with my own evidence, while Peters, in that beautiful silvery voice that had made his reputation at the Bar, outlined the case for the defence.

He was brief, but pointed out that he relied upon a complete alibi, which was worth more than any circumstantial evidence, however deadly it might appear.

And then came the shock of the day. Peters calmly said, "I am not putting the accused into the witness-box."

A gasp went round the court, and I could see a look of astonishment on the faces of the jury. Every one knew that those words are often the dreadful prelude to a conviction.

The only person who remained quite impassive was Darent himself, who had absolutely refused to give evidence.

I saw Schultz raise his eyebrows and smile at his solicitor, and then I heard Peters's voice: "Call Mr. Tracey."

Every face seemed to stand out like one of those composite photographs of a crowd, with an index to show the names of each. I felt like rushing from the court, but before I was fully aware of it I found myself in the witness-box, and an officer in a wooden voice was saying: "Take the book in your right hand, and repeat the words—hold it up." He thrust a Bible into my right hand and a printed card into my left.

"I swear by Almighty God to speak the truth, the whole truth and nothing but the truth." Though I spoke the words quietly, they seemed to thunder back from the corners of the place to my guilty soul like the accusing voice of God.

The officer had removed book and card, and Peters was looking anxiously at me. Charles told me afterwards that I looked like a ghost.

Then I heard Peters speaking; he led me gently along, with easy questions about my life and relations with Darent, to enable me to get accustomed to the atmosphere of the court.

He took me in detail through the story of my corning to Crowfield and meeting Darent, and then he became precise.

"When you returned to the inn, to get your car, Mr. Darent was with you?"

"Yes."

"Was he carrying anything?"

"He was carrying a heavy stick of holly that he told me he had cut out of the woods."

"Could you recognize that stick?"

"I think so."

Peters took what had been called "Exhibit 1"—the fatal holly stick—from the table, and handed it to me.

"Was that the stick? Look at it carefully."

"Yes," I said firmly, and heard a sort of murmur at such a statement from the first witness for the defence.

Strange as it may appear, now that I had started, all my fears had gone and my nerves were quite steady.

Peters very carefully replaced the stick on the table.

"You are certain that is the stick?"

"Positive."

"Did Mr. Darent bring it back with him?"

"No—he left it at the Crown Inn, and was grumbling about it on the way back."

"You are quite certain about that—there is no possibility of your having been mistaken?"

"I am absolutely certain. I afterwards went to look for it—I knew that whoever had taken it was the murderer."

Schultz was about to interrupt, but the judge said: "You must not make speeches or give opinions, Mr. Tracey; you must confine yourself to the evidence."

I knew that he had been informed that I had only just recovered from a serious illness, and was all through most generous to me.

I hastily apologized, and Peters said: "Go on with your narrative, Mr. Tracey, and keep to the facts."

My spirits were somewhat dashed, but I continued:

"We got back to the Hall, and had dinner."

"One moment. Did you dress?"

I had my tale ready—I had rehearsed it till it had become a reality to me. "No, we didn't—Darent didn't want to, and said his coat was being cleaned—he had cut his hand in the woods, I believe; and there was another reason."

"What was that?"

I made a pause deliberately, as though I did not wish to give my friend away.

"Well, I don't like saying it, but he had been drinking all day, and was in a surly mood and not a very pleasant companion. I had made up my mind to leave after dinner, and it didn't seem worth while dressing."

"Will you please tell his lordship and the jury what he had taken to drink?"

It went against my heart to have to expose him in front of that cold-hearted, gaping crowd, but there was no help for it.

"When I arrived at the Crown Inn, I was told by Mr. Willis, the landlord, that he had taken Mr. Darent home drunk a short time before. He had whisky at the Hall, and then at the Crown Inn, and at dinner he had champagne, and a good deal of port, and afterwards brandy."

The judge lifted his eyebrows and smiled grimly.

"I don't want to interrupt your evidence, Mr. Tracey, but are you quite certain you are not exaggerating a little?"

"No, m'lord." I was afraid he might mistrust the rest of my evidence. "If anything, I am understating the amount—John, the butler, knows."

"Please answer the questions. We shall hear what he has to say in good time," Peters said shortly.

My senses were sharpened up, and I could understand that Peters feared the suggestion of collusion by my remark.

"That is what he had to drink," I said doggedly, "and after dinner we sat and talked in the library."

"Now, Mr. Tracey, I am going to put this question to you, and I want you to be very careful in your answer."

I knew what was coming, and braced myself for the ordeal.

"Did Mr. Darent leave you at any time during the evening?"

"No."

"Now think carefully. Are you sure that you did not fall asleep or go out yourself?"

"He and I were talking the whole time—or, rather, towards the end it was I who was doing the talking, and he only answered in monosyllables, or meaningless words. It was five years since we had met, and I thought he would like to have a talk."

I took a rapid glance round the court and met Margorie's eyes fixed on me with grave approval, and then I saw Darent, who was leaning forward with an intent, puzzled gaze.

"Tell us what happened then."

"Darent went to sleep in the chair and was breathing loudly, and his face was very red. I was afraid he had had some stroke."

"What did you do?

"I loosened his collar and was going for help when John came in to ask whether we wanted anything before he went to bed."

"What time was this?" the judge asked sharply, like the crack of a pistol.

"I can't give the exact time, m'lord, but it must have been about eleven o'clock."

I saw the judge look at some notes he had before him and nod his head.

"What did you do then?" Peters went on.

"John and I carried him up to bed between us and undressed him. Mrs. Martin came with us with a lamp. We got him into bed and left him fast asleep, and I returned to the library."

"Did you hear anything after that?"

"I couldn't sleep. I was worried about Darent, and the change I had found in him. I pulled out several of his books and tried to read, and then I went to the room they had got ready for me, but I did not like the look of it, and thought that the bed was damp. I had almost decided to go off when I heard the police knocking at the door. I hurried down to see what was the matter."

"Yes, we know what occurred then," Peters said. 'You went up-stairs with the police and found Mr. Darent."

"He was in a drunken sleep—so drunk that we couldn't wake him up."

"In which bedroom did you find him—the one in which you had put him to bed?"

"He was in the maid's bedroom," I said, ashamed at the lie that was the naked truth—it seemed so mean.

"I am going to ask you this," Peters said severely. "It has been suggested in evidence that Mr. Darent went out and visited the Towers. What have you to say to that?"

"I say," I answered with some heat, "that no one but a lunatic could possibly imagine him getting up and walking in his condition. He couldn't stand."

"All right," Peters said, rather annoyed at the warmth of my answer. 'Now we come to another matter. I believe a pair of pumps were found in your suit-case at the Crown Inn, and that they were not yours. Can you account for that in any way?"

"Detective-Inspector Pyke showed me a pair which he said he had found in my suit-case," I replied. "He wanted to fasten the crime on to me, I believe, but they were three sizes at least too small, so he had to drop it like a hot brick."

There was a titter in court, and the judge leant forward, holding his pencil like a pointer. "You are a most extraordinary witness, Mr. Tracey. I make full allowance for the fact that you are hardly recovered from an illness, and are probably giving evidence for the first time, but I must warn you again to confine yourself to answering questions, and not to display such feeling. It does you no good."

I apologized most humbly, but was glad to see that the jury seemed by their faces to be favourably impressed.

"When you came from the Hall," Peters continued, "you took a room at the Crown. Did you unpack your things?"

"No. Polly Willis—the landlord's daughter—did so, and took my pumps away to clean, and packed them in my bag. Someone else must have put the other pair into my bag."

Peters shrugged his shoulders in despair.

"I will only ask you one more question. You stated that it was about eleven o'clock when you put Mr. Darent to bed. I suppose you could have said twelve or one just as easily?"

"Perfectly—only I was telling the truth."

Peters sat down abruptly, and I feared from his manner that my answers might have done harm to Darent.

Schultz rose slowly, and I knew the real crisis had come. He buttoned his coat under his gown, as though for a fight, and adjusted his glasses firmly on his Semitic nose.

Then he picked up some papers and cleared his throat. He may have thought to frighten me, but my blood was up now, and having once sworn my lie, nothing else seemed to matter.

"Mr. Tracey," he said very deliberately, "you are aware of the nature of an oath?"

"Perfectly."

"You realize that you are on your oath to tell the truth?"

"I have sworn to do so."

"Are you aware also of the penalties that are demanded for wilful perjury?"

"I believe they are very severe, Sir Herman," I said, with a coolness that astonished myself.

Schultz cast his eye at the jury, and then faced me like lightning.

"I am going to suggest that the evidence you have given is a tissue of lies from start to finish."

I suppose I was staggered by the shock—it was so unexpected. His glittering eyes, seen through his glasses, seemed blood-red in the ray of light coming aslant through a window.

"Well?" he said gloatingly.

"I can't help what you suggest," I said. "I am telling the truth."

"You say that you came to see your friend for the first time for five years, in answer to a letter from him. Was it for any special purpose?"

"None whatever. It was hot in London and I wanted a change—that is all."

Again a slight titter went round the court. I had been informed by Charles of the weak spot in Sir Herman's armour. He was well known as a bully of witnesses, but had a hasty temper himself, and if that could be roused, he lost something of his biting, effective manner.

"I suggest," he said, "that you came down to help the accused by purchasing the mortgage."

I thanked Heaven that the police had gone off the rails in some of their theories, and that I could tell the truth for a change.

"Nothing of the sort. I had never heard of the mortgage in my life."

"You say that your visit was not for the purpose of helping your friend, and possibly by that means preventing the wedding from taking place."

I laughed then—rather a raucous laugh—but I wanted to annoy him.

"I had never heard one single word about the proposed wedding, and I did not know of the existence of Sir John Barton, or of Miss Browne, until I went to Crowfield."

"There must have been some object in your going in that way, and on that particular date. What was it, please?"

"I have told you I had no particular object except to fulfil a long-standing engagement to come and see Mr. Darent. We had been together in the Service, you know."

"When you arrived—for no particular object," he sneered, "you started by picking a quarrel with Mr. Turnbull in the Crown Inn."

"I should put it the other way. I mentioned Mr. Darent's name, and Turnbull started blackguarding my friend with every epithet he could lay his tongue to. A man's got to stick up for his friend, you know."

I could have bitten my tongue out for my garrulity.

"Exactly, Mr. Tracey." Schultz pounced on me. "As you say, a man has got to stand up for his friend, but there are limits."

"I threw Turnbull into the road," I said, to hide my confusion.

"Exactly, and the dispatch-case came open, showing its contents. Is that so?"

"I didn't see them. He picked them up and flew up the road."

"And then you went and fetched your friend Mr. Darent, and brought him to the Crown with his murderous club."

"I came to fetch my car and suit-case."

"Was that the sole object? You didn't expect by any chance to find Mr. Turnbull there?"

He was so completely off the track that I was enjoying myself. It may sound a strange word to use, but a sort of exhilaration had come over me, and I was on perfectly safe ground now.

"I had no desire whatever to see him again," I said emphatically.

"You were disappointed not to find him?"

Peters leapt to his feet. "M'lord, I object to that question."

"I have finished with that point," Schultz snarled, and I noticed with pleasure that his face was getting red.

"Let us come to the evening at the Hall. You have told us of all the drinks that the accused consumed. I take it that you joined him?"

"He had a long start of me. I had my first drink at the Crown Inn when I arrived, and I am a very moderate drinker. In the evening I had nothing after dinner."

"I suppose it would not have been possible for you to have fallen asleep in the library, as the champagne and port and other drinks you have enumerated must have had some effect on a moderate drinker like you?"

"I've got a pretty strong head, and was fully awake the whole evening."

"If you were, as you say, so disgusted with your friend and with the place, may I ask why you did not leave either before you had accepted his liberal hospitality, the champagne and other things we have heard about, or after dinner, when you say he was getting drunk and objectionable?"

I saw the chance I had been waiting for. There was nothing Schultz hated more than to be reminded of his Teutonic ancestry. I paused for effect, and replied very politely:

"We English have rules with regard to hospitality and behaviour that are not perhaps understood in other countries."

I saw the blood rush to his head, but he could take no exception to my generalization.

"But you went later on?" he rapped out.

"I went for two reasons, Sir Herman," I answered blandly. "In the first place I did not want to catch pneumonia, and in the second place, when Inspector Watson had told me that the crime had been committed with Mr. Darent's stick, and I knew that he had not done it, I wished to ascertain who had taken the stick from the Crown Inn, for that undoubtedly had been done by the real criminal."

"You have been told already not to make speeches from the witness-box," he fumed. But I noticed the judge did not interrupt this time, but was searching my face with a keen, shrewd and, I fancied, almost puzzled gaze.

"You went to the Towers on the following day. With what object?"

"I have always understood," I said clearly, "that it is the duty of every citizen to assist the authorities in bringing a criminal to justice. I have been attempting to do so."

"I am glad you understand that duty," he thundered.

"I sincerely hope that success may crown my efforts." The long ordeal was telling on me, and I felt on the verge of a collapse. Had Schultz continued, goodness knows what I might have said. I was growing light-headed and wanted to insult him.

But he had done with me. He shot the final question at me with all the venom he could put into the words.

"I suggest to you that you and these servants concocted this alibi between you, and that you have been telling the court a pack of lies."

"You have suggested that before. It is not true."

He sat down with a glance at the jury, as much as to say: "The man's a liar."

Peters nodded to me, rather severely, I felt, and I was about to leave the box, when the judge spoke.

"Mr. Tracey, I do not know that I have ever heard a witness quite like you. I am going to put a very unusual question to you. You give me the impression that you know a good deal more than you say. Have you any idea as to the crime other than what you have told us?"

Peters was on his feet in a second. "M'lord, with the utmost respect, I suggest that the witness should not be asked to answer that question."

"Very well, Mr. Peters, if you object. Perhaps it would be as well."

I staggered rather than stepped out of the witness-box, the perspiration running down my back, and as I did so I happened to look at the clock. I had been in the box for over an hour!

CHAPTER XIX

THE VERDICT

JOHN MARTIN was called next and faithfully corroborated all that I had said. He was wiser than I, for he confined himself to monosyllables for the most part in his replies, and Schultz's feathers, already ruffled, were not smoothed down by the dogged obstinacy of the old butler.

He could only pin Martin down to the fatal hour of eleven, after which he declared he had heard nothing till roused by the knocking.

Mrs. Martin came next, and added her little bit about carrying the lamp while Darent was being conveyed to bed. And then there was a buzz of anticipation as Mary was called. Some rumour must have got about as to the nature of her evidence, and I could see the necks of the spectators craned forward to catch a glimpse of the girl as she stepped into the box.

It was a tense moment and seemed to affect even Peters. He asked her some quiet, unimportant questions, as he had done with me, to give her confidence, for the girl was feeling her position acutely.

Then he led up to the scene at the Hall.

"You told Inspector Watson that Mr. Darent had come to your room that night," he said in sympathetic tones.

The girl hung her head in a very natural way. "Yes, sir, he was drunk."

Darent's head went back as though he had been hit from behind, and he half started from his chair. A warder laid his hand on his shoulder and pushed him back in a kindly manner.

"What time was that?

"Just after twelve o'clock. I had heard them carrying him to bed. I couldn't sleep, but I had heard the clock strike twelve. It was after that."

"And then he came into your room?"

"Yes, sir. I think that he was so drunk that he mistook—"

"We don't want opinions—we want facts only," Schultz cried, leaping to his feet.

I smiled at Charles, for my baiting of Schultz had told on him. A jury of men—as this was—are always on the side of a woman, and against browbeating. It was a tactical error on his part.

Peters saw his advantage. "Of course, Miss Martin, we are all in sympathy with your position, but I am bound to ask you certain painful questions." His smooth polished voice contrasted to our advantage with Schultz's, which had a way of becoming guttural when he got excited. "What did you do?"

"I was so frightened, sir, that I didn't know what to do. He—he went fast asleep."

"You did not cry out or attempt to get away?"

"I was afraid to move, and I didn't like to call out because of Mr. Tracey, who was a stranger, being in the house"—a smart touch that, Mary!—"I didn't know what to do. He was quite quiet, and I was crushed against the wall. I slipped out as quietly as I could and sat in the arm-chair."

"I am sorry to ask the next question. Did he try to molest you in any way?"

"Oh, no, sir! He just slept on and snored."

"What happened then?" Peters asked in a more cheerful voice.

"I heard loud knocking, and ran downstairs to the hall."

"And that is all that you can tell us?

"That's all, sir."

Peters sat down, feeling that the proper effect had been made, and Schultz rose.

"I suggest to you that you are making up the whole of this story to try to shield your master?

"Oh, no, sir."

"Who suggested this tale to you?"

"No one, sir."

"You would have the jury believe that on this particular night of all nights, Mr. Darent happened to pay a visit to your bedroom?"

"The inspector found him there," she answered candidly.

"I am not asking that. Was this the only occasion that he had been in your room?" Schultz asked brutally.

It was the question I had been dreading for weeks, and I held my breath. If Mary said "yes" it would make the whole of our evidence look suspicious. If she said "no" her story would be doubtful, and her reputation gone. Further, I was certain that Darent would make a scene, and shout from the dock that it was a lie. It was one thing that a drunken man should make a mistake, however improbable it might sound, but it was quite another that there had been a liaison for some time.

The judge saved us: whether he had been impressed with Mary's evidence, or was annoyed with Schultz, I cannot say.

"You need not answer that question if you would rather not."

"Thank you, your lordship," Mary said in a low voice.

"I shall not put any further questions," Schultz said angrily, and sat down.

"That concludes the case for the defence," Peters said gravely, and I think he felt that everything hung on a straw.

The judge rose and the court was adjourned till the next day. We streamed out of that stifling place, and went to a little room reserved for witnesses, where we waited until the 'camera men' had departed. I felt as limp as a rag, and was suffering from reaction, and was never more glad of a drink than when. Charles produced a flask from his pocket. I saw Margorie sit down beside Mary, who was crying, and place her arm round the girl, and the sight did me good. We didn't talk much that evening, and Miss Morris packed us all off to bed, taking Margorie with her.

"How's it going, Charles?" I asked when we had retired to my room.

"I don't know, old lad—not too well. It depends a lot on the summing up."

My heart went to zero. "Is it as bad as all that? Did I give my evidence badly?"

He clapped me on the back and laughed. "My dear boy. I've never heard anything worse in my life." I was hurt and depressed by his tone.

"Why?" I asked.

"I told you some time ago that you would never make a liar. I could see through you, and I am sure both Schultz and old Pennyfold did, too. Whenever you were telling the truth, and fortunately you had quite a lot to tell, your manner was quite different: you spoke with a sort of relief, and without hesitation. It was a good thing that the prosecution had been misled about same of the facts. When you were lying, you were wooden, unnatural, and as though you were picking your answers carefully. I think old Peters saw it—let's hope the jury didn't."

"There's nothing like a candid friend. How do you know that I was lying?"

"My dear old fellow, I found you out at the Hall, and I admire you for what you have done for a friend. Perhaps I may be only imagining that the others guessed that there was anything wrong." He spoke soothingly, but the thought was disturbing.

"The Martins were splendid," he went on, "but of course they are only servants, and if the alibi has been concocted, in the opinion of the jury it would be obviously your doing."

"Thanks—you're a nice Job's comforter."

"You must try to take your mind off this business, and get some sleep: remember your evidence is over, and nothing we can do will have the slightest effect now on the issue."

"One more question, Charles, and then I won't worry you. Why didn't Peters put Darent in the box?"

"I think that is easily explained." Charles looked at me with a queer smile. "As I see it, Peters is relying entirely upon the alibi. As, from the evidence, Darent was dead drunk, he couldn't possibly throw any light on what happened that evening, or confirm or deny Mary's story. He had refused to see the solicitors, and there was no knowing what he might say—no, I think he was wise, but it is a dangerous proceeding."

There was a tense atmosphere in the court on the next and last day of the trial. Dark clouds had appeared after a spell of great heat, and the papers predicted thunder. The heavy expectancy of Nature had communicated itself to the eager crowds that had waited in queues for hours to get a seat in the gallery somehow. They knew that this day would see the end, and that by six o'clock at latest a fellow-man would be sent to his death, or walk from the court a free man. Many of them were *habitués* at murder trials, and obtained a depraved thrill when the chaplain laid the small black square on the judge's wig, and the death sentence was pronounced. Decadent authors attended, claiming that the psychological interest attracted them, and society women, who frankly came for 'thrills'; yet none of these people would have gone out of their way to listen to a case concerning a difficult dispute over company law, though the cut and thrust of counsel, and the neat points gained, were just as interesting 'psychologically.'

A feeling of disgust and anger came to me as I waited with Charles in the court. I will own that for my part I was in a blue funk. The most vital matter, of course, for all of us, was the acquittal of Kenneth, but behind that lay the lurking fear, bluntly imparted to me by Smithers when I had made my first statement to him, that should Darent be found guilty, speedy arrests of myself and the Martins would follow on a charge of wilful perjury, and the thought was one upon which I did not like to dwell. I thought the judge looked very stern and cold when he took his seat. Schultz had been talking in an animated way with his solicitor, and glanced at me from time to time, as a lion at the zoo when a plate of meat is passed along before his cage. Peters shuffled with his papers, anxious and, I thought, over-nervous for a King's Counsel of his standing. He looked at the clock from time to time in a worried manner.

Kenneth was brought in, and somehow his appearance reassured me.

He was perfectly calm and collected, and his face showed quiet resolution. I could not help thinking that only a man who knew that he was innocent could wear such a look. He bowed courteously to the judge, who told him he might be seated.

Peters had to open, as he had called witnesses for the defence, and had thereby forfeited the right to the last word. His grave, slow words, brought a dead hush to the court, till one could hear the noises of the street outside, and the buzz of a bluebottle.

He threw down the gauntlet boldly.

"It was," he said, "in some ways a case unique in his experience. The prosecution had built up a tremendous case on purely circumstantial evidence, which he was not denying was, by itself, overwhelming.

"But there was not one shred of direct evidence, and he was fortunately able to place before the jury a complete alibi. In how many cases," he said, facing the jury, "had a man been condemned or run the risk of being found guilty on circumstantial evidence, when one single word of direct evidence would have shattered the whole case? The vital and essential question for the jury to decide was whether they believed the evidence for the defence. This had been given by four perfectly respectable persons, and one—Mr. Tracey—an educated gentleman of unblemished character, who had no axe to grind, and who had, in fact, a very definite grievance against the accused. Further, this evidence was strongly corroborated by Watson and the constable, who had found the accused in the very bed, and in the condition that had been described by the other witnesses."

He claimed that this testimony had been unshaken in cross-examination. He dwelt at some length on myself, my character and past record, until I felt that I must be a much finer fellow than I had ever realized. He stressed the fact that I had come forward after a very serious illness, and solely in the cause of justice.

Then he turned on the evidence for the prosecution and tore it to pieces in a masterful manner. If my evidence was to be believed, the actual weapon with which the crime had been done had been left at the Crown. If it had been found there by any one who bore a grudge against the dead man, what better chance could there be of fixing the crime on Darent? "What real murderer," he said contemptuously, "would leave the weapon on the spot for any one to find?—it was out of all reason."

With regard to Barton's butler's statement about the note—again, a man wishing to fasten the crime on another would employ such a device, but no sane man would give himself away like that. The footmarks he brushed aside, remarking that they were only visible when the dew was on the grass and that measurements in that case were quite unreliable.

And so he went through the whole of the evidence until I began to feel that we really were winning. It was a masterly effort, and when he sat down, I thought the jury were impressed.

But Sir Herman Schultz was no fool, and had completely recovered his equanimity. I could understand from what Charles had told me, that it was not my answers that had annoyed him, but the fact that he be-lieved I was lying, and yet could not catch me tripping.

In his rasping, incisive voice he was soon at it, tearing to pieces Peters's points, like a dog with an old rag.

He went coldly through the whole chain of evidence, building up step by step, and asked why the accused had not been put on oath and given evidence. Then he concentrated on the alibi which he charac-terized as a loyal and quixotic, though criminal, attempt on the part of a friend and servants to save the accused man from the gallows.

He was clever enough not to attack me or Mary: he suggested that we had concocted this tale, and that the girl, far from being the de-praved woman she had made herself out to be, was a misguided but loyal retainer. And I, far from being disgusted with Darent, was a real friend who had come to the Hall deliberately to help him in his trou-bles.

It was a smashing speech, delivered with terrific force, and yet with a sense of fairness and even toleration. And then Mr. Justice Penny old began his summing up, and we leant forward to catch every word, for thunder was growling outside, and the court was in semi-darkness. Only the white face and wig of the judge seemed to stare at us, like some vast and imperious phantom, implacable, intolerably just.

He never used a note, but in a clear, solemn voice, like the tolling of a bell, summarized the whole of the evidence on both sides. He pointed out to the jury that the matter was a simple one: they must either accept our alibi or not, nothing else was of any importance. If we were telling the truth, all the circumstantial evidence in the world would fail to convict, for the accused had been in the Hall asleep at the time of the murder. But if they did not accept it, then there was ample evidence even though circumstantial. And then he paused as though weighing his words carefully. "I have already had occasion to comment on the witness, Mr. Tracey. He was a very remarkable witness. You must bear in mind that the evidence with regard to the stick having been left at the inn, rests solely on his word, but it was a most daring statement to make if an invention. He appeared to me, and perhaps to you, gen-tlemen of the jury, to be convinced that he *knew* who he thought was the murderer, but—that does not dispose of the question as to whether he was telling us the whole truth."

I felt my face go scarlet at these cryptic words, and I am sure the jury were puzzled.

At last it was over, and I could not have stood much more of it, for my nerves were on the stretch. The jury retired, and then ensued the most awful waiting time I have ever had in my life.

I walked across the court and sat with Margorie and Miss Morris, but talk was out of the question. I could only take Margorie's hand and her reassuring squeeze told me that she was bearing the strain bravely.

"I would like a smoke badly," I said, "but goodness knows how long the jury will take."

"Go out," Miss Morris said, "I'll fetch you at once if there are any signs."

I thanked her and wandered into the corridor, where a number of people were pacing up and down, and stared at me as I passed. I was going to the door when Detective-Inspector Pyke approached me.

"Excuse me, Mr. Tracey, but no witnesses are allowed to leave the premises."

I knew what he meant quite well—they were not going to let me go, in case they *wanted me.*

"I want a drink, Mr. Pyke," I said with a grin.

"Come along with me," he said in a friendly voice, and took me to the private room of the detective branch. "It's a bit of an anxious time for you, Mr. Tracey." He handed me a whisky and soda.

"What do you think of it—you've had a long experience?"

He eyed me in a questioning way, and with an amused smile took a coin and tossed it in the air.

"Like that, is it?" I said ruefully.

"Touch and go. I wouldn't like to bet on it."

I thanked him for the drink, and turned to go.

"I may see you later," he said cheerfully as I went out.

Back in the court, I sat by Charles, and the slow minutes dragged on. One hour had grown to two, and the clock was showing another terrible half-hour, when there was a rustle in the court, and people began flocking back hurriedly.

A messenger came quickly in and whispered to the clerk of the court, who walked over to the solicitor for the prosecution.

While every one held their breath, and watched every movement, there was a whispered consultation, and the solicitor searched among his papers, and then handed a document to the messenger. Charles went and spoke to Deaken and then told me that the jury had asked for a plan of the Hall.

"Whatever for?" I asked fretfully.

"I expect they want to see exactly where the bedrooms were."

Again we waited, and the talk went on like a faint murmur of bees round a hive. Just as I felt that I could bear no more, the usher called for silence in court, and the judge entered and took his seat. The talk died away like the closing of a door, and a deathlike stillness took its place. I saw the chaplain unobtrusively slip in and take his stand behind the judge, and Darent standing erect, while three warders closed in on him.

The jury filed in, flushed and self-conscious. There was a heavy silence as the clerk rose.

"Gentlemen of the jury, have you considered your verdict?"

A weak-looking little man—very nervous, and fluttering a paper in his hand, had risen from the jury box.

"We have," he said in a low voice.

"Do you find the prisoner at the bar guilty or not guilty?"

"Not guilty, m'lord."

"Is that the unanimous opinion of you all?"

"It is, m'lord."

There was no excitement or cheering, or any exhibition such as one reads of. Dimly I heard the judge telling the jury that they would be exempt from service for so many years, but only five words rang in my head—the sharp clear words spoken by the judge.

"Kenneth Darent—you are discharged."

Darent bowed politely to the judge, and cast a withering glance of contempt round the court. Then he went below, a free man.

CHAPTER XX

A TERRIBLE SUGGESTION

COME, old lad, pull yourself together—it's all over now."

I heard Charles speaking, and looked round the almost empty court.

"Yes, of course we must go," I said mechanically. "Sorry to be so stupid, but I feel done in completely. What about Kenneth: oughtn't we to go and see him?"

"I think not, Dennis—not now. He went down to avoid us. You know his temperament, he'd think we were coming to receive his thanks and he would resent it badly. Margorie and Miss Morris have gone to look for him, but I think he'll bolt from the court as soon as he can get away from Pressmen and photographers. Best leave him alone. He's such a queer fish you never know how he will take things."

Peters was talking with another barrister in the body of the court, and saw me going out. He called me to him, and shook hands quite warmly for him.

"Well, Tracey, that's done with, and I must confess it was the toughest case I've ever had to handle."

"I thought your speech was splendid," I said enthusiastically.

He made no answer, but drew himself up straight, with half-closed eyes, and a look almost of pain. It annoyed me, and took away all sense of gratitude. I have seen minor poets and actors assume just such a pose when someone has given them flattery.

I was turning away in disgust when he said:

"Do you know what got Darent off? You, Erskine, should be able to say."

"I suppose because he was not guilty," Charles replied with a shade of irony.

"You are *nearly* right—it was because he looked not guilty. I have seen many people in the dock, and the judge has seen more, and there is an indefinable something about a man or woman—difficult to analyse—that marks the innocent from the guilty. A man may be defiant, trembling, furtive or stoical, but there is a difference between the man who knows he is innocent, and one who knows he is guilty. That is why some verdicts cause the outside public to gasp—if they had been in court they would have understood. I believe the jury felt that his manner was not bravado, but a sense of complete innocence."

I was astonished, because up till then I had been under the impression that Peters had believed Darent guilty, and distrusted my evidence.

"It's rather presumption on my part," Charles remarked, "but in that case I wonder you didn't put him in the witness-box."

Peters smiled grimly. "You wouldn't wonder if you had talked to Deaken. He was so angry that he threatened to throw up the whole case. Darent not only refused to see him, but when he went to the prison, he got the message by a warder: 'Tell the damned lawyer to go to hell.' If I had called him, I had no summary or précis of evidence on which to question him, and as like as not he would have told the jury that he was glad Barton was dead, and congratulated the murderer, or something of that sort. I am certain Schultz would have made him lose his temper. It was a dangerous policy that I adopted, but the only possible one in the circumstances."

"May I ask you one question, Mr. Peters?" I inquired meekly.

"Why certainly, Tracey, if I can answer it."

"Why did the prosecution never mention the second pair of tracks found on the grass, and the ownership of the pumps?"

He laughed easily. "That is soon explained. You see there are a great number of minor points that are settled between the lawyers, in cases like this, before the trial comes on—points that would only confuse the issue, and do not have any direct bearing on the guilt or otherwise of the accused. In this case, we had ascertained that the pumps belonged to one of the guests, who had been scouring about and had followed the tracks without knowing it, and for no special purpose. He was a complete stranger to all of us, and could throw no light on the matter."

"That explains it then," I said, "but not how they came to be in my suit-case."

He seemed to show signs of impatience. "Really, Tracey, I think we should be satisfied that we have won the case, and a small thing like that is not of vital importance. Very likely Polly made a mistake."

"The thing to do now," I said hastily, "is to find the murderer."

"I am afraid then," he said with a smile of superiority, "you will have to do it yourself. I am sure the police still think that Darent was guilty, and will only make half-hearted attempts now that they have had such a nasty set-back. They will be glad to have the whole case forgotten. Besides, I should have thought, Tracey, that you had had enough of it yourself. You might find yourself in an even more difficult position than you were, if you try to stir up mud. Don't forget that your friend Turnbull has bolted."

He shook hands abruptly, with a smile that mitigated the rudeness of his dismissal, and turned away to speak with his colleague who had been waiting.

We took a taxi to Regent's Park, and found that Margorie and Miss Morris had not returned. Now that everything was over, an intense reaction seized me. I pictured to myself Darent free and happy at last, journeying to Crowfield with Margorie, their troubles over, and all life before them. I could quietly drop out of their lives, and pursue my own line of investigation. I tried to cheer myself with the thought of her happiness, but am of too selfish a nature for such altruistic thought.

Charles did his best, but I think he understood, and we smoked in silence until we heard the sound of a door opening and voices in the hall outside.

I sprang to my feet, wondering if they had brought Kenneth here, but only the two women entered.

On Margorie's face was a look of quiet satisfaction, and her wonderful eyes shone steadily. Miss Morris, on the other hand, was in a state of extreme irritation. She haled us into the garden, the night being warm, and the stars shone down, steady and eternal, above the trees.

"We can talk here till dinner is ready." She lit a cigarette and smoked furiously.

"I've no patience with that man," she exclaimed angrily, "and, Margorie, you are nearly as bad. Dammit, one would think he had just done us an enormous favour. Pride is all right in its place—I could have boxed his ears."

"What happened?" I ventured to ask.

"Happened? He was rude as a man could be, and asked us what we had come for. Then he turned on me of all people, and said: 'I suppose you have come to congratulate me on my lucky escape from being hanged? I am sure I ought to be grateful and grovel duly, but I don't feel like it. Some people can never mind their own business. We shall have Dennis round here next with his silly grin, expecting my thanks for all he's done.' That's the way he went on."

Charles burst out laughing, which relieved the situation.

"I expected that—it's so like him. That's why I kept Dennis away. He's the sort of man that can always forgive an injury but never a kindness. It galls him to think that we have been working for him, while he's been in 'choky', and that we have got him off between us. Peters defended him for nothing, and you, Miss Morris and Margorie have been working like Hercules, and old Dennis here testifying for him like a Briton. It makes him feel a worm, and Darent hates to feel a worm above everything else. He'll get over it in time."

"I quite understand his feelings," I said, and was rewarded by a grateful look from Margorie.

"Well, if you men take that line, I suppose I'm only a foolish old woman," Miss Morris fumed. "He hadn't a word for Margorie, and she was as quiet as a mouse and took everything lying down; and now he says he won't go near Crowfield, and as he's let the place, he's going off on his own for a trip, and be damned to us all."

"I don't mind," Margorie said softly; "he's free now, and he looks so different—strong and self-reliant, and as he used to be."

"You make me tired, Margorie. He ought to have gone down on his ham-bones and told you he had been an ass and a cad to you."

"I should have despised him if he had," she answered with spirit. "I shall just go back to Crowfield—my father wants me there, as he is not well, and mother is rather trying at times."

"Dennis, you had better come golfing with me—you haven't got over your illness yet, and I feel like a holiday. It's been a pretty good strain for all of us." Charles interrupted the conversation—deliberately, I am sure.

But my mind was full of dreadful thoughts—I suppose he was right—I hadn't got over the illness. The stillness of the night, the tangible darkness that wrapped us round like a pall, contributed to my feeling that the living presence of death was somewhere behind the trees, whose black branches were like menacing arms. In that sudden hush, for silence had fallen between us, there came again to me, as on the road to the Crown, like a stab of an electric needle through my brain, the elusive, maddening half-truth. The surmises, the guesses, the little suggestions here and there, were gathering themselves together like pieces of a jigsaw puzzle, fitting into their places, until I shrank from the awful picture that was growing before my eyes. A sudden cold, like a breath from the Scandinavian hell, took hold of me. I must have given some strange cry, like a sob of pain. Margorie quickly came to me, and laid her hand gently on my arm.

I thought she had misinterpreted my emotion, and the thought maddened me.

"I am going to Crowfield," I said in a voice I knew must have sounded hoarse and unnatural.

It was not the words, but the voice that startled them.

"Of course," Miss Morris said soothingly. "You shall come and stay with me; you are always welcome."

"It's not that," I cried. "You are very good—you don't understand. I intended to go right away if things had turned out right—I mean if Kenneth had gone there; but I must see your father, Margorie."

I could feel that she was breathing hard, close to me, and a shudder passed through her. I pulled myself together. "I shan't rest till I've seen you and Kenneth happy together, and the only way is to bring the criminal to justice—then Kenneth will come back."

I was desperately afraid that they might think I was going to try to take Darent's place.

"Yes! Yes, of course, my dear," Miss Morris said. "We can discuss all that when we have had a good rest."

"You don't understand," I exclaimed hysterically. *"I know who murdered Barton!"*

Silence greeted my words; not one of them spoke. Only Margorie slipped her arm into mine. A black form was stealing down the path that, to my imagination, assumed the appearance of a dead man crying for vengeance. I could stand no more—I sprang to my feet. And then the unbearable strain was relaxed, when the butler came forward and announced that dinner was ready.

"Thank you," Miss Morris said in a matter-of-fact voice.

She rose and patted me affectionately on the back. "You are tired, Dennis."

Not another word was said, and we walked along the gravel path to the house. Margorie took my arm with a little laugh, to relieve the tension. They all thought, to put it plainly, that I had temporarily gone off my head.

Miss Morris was a true friend to us all that night. She insisted upon celebrating the victory, as she called it, in her best champagne, and exerted herself to keep our minds off problems of the future. She argued with Charles, who took his cue from her, on every conceivable subject—cubists and nudists, Bernard Shaw and the young atheists of modern production—and finished by sweeping us all into the billiards-room, where she paired off Margorie and myself against herself and Charles at snooker pool. She plied me with a very stiff brandy, being shrewd to discern that in my present state it was either that or drugs, and these she abominated whole-heartedly.

At any rate, I slept that night the dreamless sleep of exhaustion—the first real rest I had known since the beginning of the trial.

The next day Charles left us, and we three motored down in my car to Crowfield. My outburst of the night before was completely ignored by the others, though I noticed Miss Morris frequently cast apprehensive glances at me when she thought I was not looking.

Naturally the news was all over the village, though, strange as it may sound, I am sure that half the villagers still firmly believed that Darent had killed Barton in a moment of temper, and thought it 'a jolly good job, too.' There is a considerable strain of primitive savage justice in the old places of England. To me it had become a haunted village—haunted by the awful discovery I had made, and which I dreaded to put to the test. Haunted—aye, and haunted also by 'the starry head of her whose gentle will had changed my fate.'

I saw much of Margorie in those few days, and learnt to understand what really unselfish love must be. She threw off her sadness like a cloak, and was kind and even merry, and seemingly happy. And all because the man to whom she had given her love was again a free man, able to face the world. She must have been deeply hurt at his conduct, but her attitude was that she deserved it all, and she asked no other reward than that one day he would come back to the Hall and take up his duties there. Her nobility made me ashamed of my petty heartache.

The year was dying, and the beautiful autumnal leaves, brown and yellow and crimson-red, filled the lanes and fell regretfully from the trees.

No news came from Darent. He had gone off somewhere, restless and untamed, with two of the furies that drove Orestes goading him on—the stigma of the trial and its disclosures, and the thought that Margorie had thrown him over, or had never really cared for him.

And then one evening I set my face steadfastly to call on the rector, calling myself a coward because I had not been able to face the interview before, but had been lingering and procrastinating. I was a welcome guest at the rectory, even Mrs. Browne having thawed and become so polite that I avoided her as far as possible.

I was fortunate in finding the rector alone, and received a warm greeting. Ever since his attempted resignation he had been very quiet and worried, going about his duties as though care sat heavy on his shoulders. He conducted me to his study, and closed the door.

"Sit down, Tracey. You have something about which you want to consult me?"

"For the second time," I answered. "You helped me before, and perhaps you can now. I have wanted to see you ever since I came back to Crowfield, but haven't plucked up sufficient courage."

"Then the matter is important."

His manner was very grave; he knew the reason for my coming.

"I am going to make a very strange request, Mr. Browne, but first I want you to believe that I am neither mad nor suffering from delusions."

"I am sure of that." He smiled a little uneasily at me.

"I want you to open that coffin in the vault that Barton constructed for his wife, and which is supposed to hold her body."

He never moved a muscle—nor did he show any signs of surprise at my bizarre request.

"You have some urgent reason for that?"

"I believe that if you do, you will find that there is no body inside."

He remained a while thinking, his brows knit, as though trying to grapple with some problem, and at last I saw his face clear, and he spoke firmly.

"You know, Tracey, my views with regard to communications made to me—I have already told you. This is the second time that this extraordinary suggestion has been made to me, and by one more insistent than you. I took no action in that case, and would never have mentioned it to a soul, but you have now come with the same request. You will agree that I must have reasons, and very cogent ones—before I could even attempt to give you an answer."

"Was this the cause of your resignation, Mr. Browne?"

"I felt that I could no longer remain in this village after what had been imparted to me."

"Then let me start from the beginning. From the first moment when I saw that vault I felt that there was something wrong about it, beyond its mere vulgarity. Call it instinct, or what you like. It was erected while you were away from the parish, and the funeral of Lady Barton was a past event when you returned. But why a vault? I know, of course, that Barton was a vulgarian, and liked to imitate the manners and customs of great families, but vaults are not built nowadays, and this is the only one in the churchyard."

"What are you hinting at, Tracey?"

"I am coming to that. I have given days and weeks to this problem, and my conclusions are not hastily drawn. I believed at the very beginning, and everything has strengthened my suppositions, that the mystery of the death of Sir John Barton is closely connected with the death of his wife in Switzerland."

I saw the rector start. "You are not suggesting that Barton killed his wife—he was not even there."

"It would have been more in keeping with his character to have employed agents if he had wished to do that. But let me ask you this: Did any living soul see Lady Barton after she was dead?"

"Really, Tracey—I suppose the doctor out there must have seen her and given the certificate, and the guides who found her, and besides, why on earth should he want to get rid of his wife?"

For the first time in our conversation the rector's voice had lost its firmness of tone.

"You know better than I do," I said, annoyed at his subterfuge. "He was in love with Margorie and wanted to marry her."

"This is a very serious charge you are bringing against a dead man who cannot defend himself."

"You know it is true, and so does Margorie."

"But aren't you letting your imagination run away with you, Tracey? If, as you seem to be hinting, Barton caused his wife to be murdered—mind, I am not agreeing with you—what object would he gain by having her buried out there in Switzerland? The accident was vouched for by those who survived, and he could just as easily have brought the body back."

"Mr. Browne," I said sternly, "you are fencing with me instead of helping. I am perfectly aware from whom you got your other demand for that coffin to be opened—it was Mabel Peters when she came to see you."

With all the control of his powerful will, he started.

"Mabel saw Barton on the night of the murder—they were riding in his car for some reason, while the guests were actually arriving. Why? The girl has been ill ever since, and when I saw her last she was taking drugs and in a terribly nervous state. She has some secret that is tearing her to pieces. She came to you and told you something—I am not asking you to tell me—but among other things she implored you to open that coffin, and she was most anxious that Margorie should not go to the funeral, which you refused to conduct. Now tell me that you are not concealing something from me!"

Instead of being offended at my outburst, he rose and paced the floor with uncertain, nervous steps. "Facts! Facts! All this theorizing and suggestion takes us nowhere. Give me proof."

"I found out, by accident, that Turnbull had been persistently blackmailing Barton—Sir John. You know that the laws concerning this foul crime have been tightened up, and that a man can prosecute, even if he has been guilty of the crime for which he is being black-mailed, and be immune, and have his name kept out of court. That is happening every day."

He stopped in his walk and nodded in agreement.

"It must have been a very grave crime, Mr. Browne, to cause Barton to pay up without giving Turnbull up to justice."

"You know that for a fact?"

"I do, and I will tell you the whole story presently. But Barton was murdered, and Turnbull turned his attentions to the new baronet, the younger brother, but here he met with a flat refusal, and when the two men met, Turnbull was so scared at seeing Robert Barton that he was in mortal dread of his life and shot Barton."

"What are you saying, Tracey? How do you know all these things?"

"I do know, and you shall, too; but let's stick to this point for a moment. The younger Barton was so afraid that I also knew this secret, that he made an assignation to meet me alone in secret in the sum-mer-house in his grounds—possibly to try to make terms with me. But mark this—he was not paying the blackmailer."

"What do you deduce from that, Tracey?" the rector said with an amused smile, that struck me as unnatural and assumed to hide his feelings.

"I don't think that is very hard to guess. The secret was one that would have landed John in the dock, but would have merely caused Robert extreme inconvenience —he had arranged to sell the Towers and clear out. Robert Barton sent for me to come and see him, after he had been wounded by Turnbull—he would not prosecute or tell any one, and, of course, I was taken ill the very next day, but when I told him that Turnbull had gone abroad and would trouble him no more, he was terribly upset—one would have thought that he would have been pleased. Why?"

The rector's face had gone very white, but there was a set look about his mouth as though he had made up his mind now that this thing must be probed to the bottom.

"You are asking riddles that I can't answer," he said coldly.

"Then I will. There can be only one explanation, to my mind. You said just now that there was no object in bringing back an empty coffin. Did he dare bring one back with a body in it? Turnbull himself suggested the opening of the vault before he went away."

"What are you hinting at, Tracey? Do you mean that they never found the body? But that is absurd."

"That is what we have to discover. The mystery lies in Switzerland, but we must start here."

A low cry came from the doorway. The rector had not turned the key in the lock, and Margorie, thinking that he was alone, had come in unseen and unheard by us, in the intensity of our absorption.

She came forward now, and took a seat quietly.

"I'm glad you've come," I said, looking defiantly at the rector. "I want you to support me. How much have you heard of our conversation?"

"I heard several sentences, Dennis, but it was not a surprise to me, as I knew you had this idea in your mind, from what you used to say when you were delirious. But it's not fair to take advantage of what a sick man says, and I never mentioned it."

I felt the time had come for revelation, and told them the whole story of my dealings with Turnbull, and of the events on the night before I was taken ill.

"It's a wild, fantastic story," the rector said when I had finished. "We must, of course, keep this entirely to ourselves until we have verified the facts. You both agree with that?"

We signified our assent, and he went on: "You know that I never reveal anything that is imparted to me when someone comes and seeks my advice. But you have guessed that Mabel was the person who asked me to have that coffin opened. She was half hysterical, and I did not attach great importance to the matter. I could hardly act on a girl's fancy."

His manner suggested that there was nothing more to be said on the subject, but I was not going to be put off. Before I could speak Margorie intervened: "Dad, we must get permission to have that coffin opened; we shall have no peace till we do."

"That is a matter that will require the most serious consideration," the rector said, with a hesitancy unusual with him. "It is desecration of a tomb, none the less because it is a vault and not a grave. If we applied to the Home Office for permission, the whole story would come out, and might involve consequences you cannot foresee. If you are completely wrong in your ideas, a scandal will have been caused for nothing."

"Mr. Browne," I said in heat, "we have gone too far to draw back—it only requires a screwdriver."

He looked at me in horror. "You don't understand. I could not possibly sanction such a thing."

"Then I shall lay the whole of the facts before the Home Office. Here's a great wrong to be put right—we hold the key, not only of John Barton's secret, but perhaps of his death, and you boggle about a few screws from an empty coffin."

"You must do what you like, Tracey, about going to the Home Office," he replied gravely, "but I warn you, you may deeply regret the step you are contemplating."

To my amazement Margorie took her father's side. "We must not do that, Dennis. Once tell them, and the whole thing is out of our hands. In any case it is a matter for careful thought, isn't it? We don't want to do anything in haste."

"Very well," I said, hiding my annoyance, but determined to resume the conversation when I had the rector alone.

"Don't forget that I am dining with Miss Morris to-night. You might go off somewhere and leave me alone with her." Margorie smiled at me, but I read a message in her eyes, and checked my surprise at the announcement.

"That's the first I've heard of it," the rector said heartily, relieved I could tell, at the dropping of the other matter. "But you girls nowadays never consult your parents."

"You don't mind, do you, dad?" she asked innocently.

"As a matter of fact, I am rather glad, because your mother and I are running up to Town, and I don't think you would care to come. I was afraid you would be all alone."

"Then it will all fit in quite well," Margorie said.

"I must go, or I shall be late for lunch," I remarked, looking at my watch.

"I'll come with you a little way," Margorie said. "I want to go to the village. I shan't be long, dad."

We walked down the drive in silence, but as soon as we were in the road, I turned to her. "What's the game, Margorie?"

"Dennis, couldn't you see? I was afraid you would spoil everything by showing surprise at what I said. My father will never give his consent to the vault being opened. I know him, and when he has made up his mind, there is no changing him. We can't go to the Home Office, and you know it."

I stopped dead in the road and looked at her in wonder.

"What do you mean?"

Her clear eyes met mine fearlessly. "Because, Dennis, you said a good deal more when you were delirious than you know, but I am not telling you anything about it."

"Good Lord—did any one else hear?"

"Only Mary, when she took her turn at night. That is why I got Miss Morris to send for her. She will say nothing."

"But," I said in a puzzled tone, "why should your father refuse to go on with the matter?"

"Surely you can guess—he does not want the truth to be revealed."

"Ah! Then what are we to do?"

"Dennis, your usually bright wits are dull. What did you think I invited myself to Miss Morris's to dinner for? I knew that my respected parents were going to Town, and would not be back till late. Dad will not give his consent, but what do people do when consent is denied?"

"You wouldn't dare do that?"

"I would dare more than that to get at the truth," she said bravely. "I can get the key of the vault—dad has one and the Bartons have the other. I know where he keeps it, because the sexton brought it back after the funeral. We can go from the Crest, and of course, you will see me home—we will go to the vault."

She shivered in the hot sunshine, and I could perceive that for all her calm manner, the horror of the proceeding had gripped her.

"I'll go by myself," I said; "it's not a job for a girl."

"I am coming too, Dennis. If any one should find out, it will be far better if there are two of us. They might doubt your motives."

Margorie turned back, and I went thoughtfully to the Crest, and told my hostess that Margorie was coming to dinner.

"Always glad to see her, Dennis. You haven't asked the mother, I hope."

I explained the situation—that Margorie would be all alone.

"It fits in very well"—she regarded me with amusement—"because I was wondering what to do with you. I shall be away myself. I've had a letter from Kenneth. He's in London and wants to see me—that's between ourselves."

CHAPTER XXI

THE OPENING OF THE VAULT

A CHILL wind was blowing, for autumn had come with a suddenness that formed a strong contrast to the brilliant summer, and the good folk hugged their fires, and the housewives got out the spare blankets.

It was an ideal night for the grim business on which we were employed. I had provided myself with tools from the gardener, and a lantern, as well as an electric torch. Dinner had been a nervous, uneasy meal, with the old butler hovering round, ministering to our wants, and doubtless wondering in his mind why we were so dull and listless. Conversation sprang up in broken gusts that died away, for neither could concentrate on any subject, and we were both heartily glad when the meal was over and we could retire. The wind had got up and was howling dismally round the old house, and a thin chilling rain was beating against the windows.

After coffee had been served, Margorie sprang up. "Dennis, I can't stand any more of this—let's go."

"I'm ready—but please let me go while you wait here."

"I am coming, don't argue about it," she replied almost angrily.

Margorie had brought a thick, dark cloak, and a pair of walking shoes.

We went out into the night, and I confess I was glad of Margorie's company on this grisly adventure.

She led me silently across the garden, and through an iron gate to a meadow. The pitchy darkness made going difficult, and the ground was sodden with the rain. I had no idea of the way, but Margorie took my hand and walked steadily forward, without hesitation. We had to climb a fence, and dark forms of trees loomed ahead, seen only as darker shadows against the universal blackness.

And then I recognized the pathway up which I had climbed to meet Margorie in the church, and the recollection of all that had occurred since that night came to me with crushing force.

"We are nearly there," Margorie said, speaking into my ear, for the howling of the wind drowned all sound. We came to the low wall, damp and slippery, and I picked the girl up bodily and placed her on the other side. "How strong you are," she said, with a nervous laugh, as I stood beside her.

The yew trees groaned and creaked above us with a melancholy, dirge-like sound, and the dim tombstones stood out like warning fingers of dead giants.

"Here it is." Margorie halted, and I saw the ghastly edifice looming in front of us, the beating rain making it appear as though it were receding and approaching us as we gazed in awe. Margorie's teeth were chattering and her hand was icy cold as she handed me the key.

All the horrible stories I had read of vampires and ghouls came crowding to my brain as I placed the key in the lock after descending the slimy steps that led to the grim doors.

The key turned, and I flung back the door. A damp, horrible smell greeted us, but I resolutely entered.

"We must shut the door, or the light will show," I whispered, and Margorie pressed my hand. The wind ceased, and only the dead darkness wrapped us round as I pushed to the thick, heavy door, and, striking a match, lit my primitive lantern. The light grew brighter as the wick caught, and we could see the inside of the place. It was not large, but gaudily decorated, either painted or with mosaics, but our attention was not focused on the ceiling or walls, but on a trestle laid across the end, on which there rested two coffins—one obviously recently placed there, and the other already showing signs of age. The brass plate was covered with verdigris, and the inscription was unreadable, but we dared not touch it.

I flung off my coat, for I was steaming with perspiration, and the place held the damp warmth of decay, as only two small gratings let in the air.

I pulled and tugged at the coffin, for there was no room to work on the trestle.

"You will have to help me," I whispered hoarsely.

I nearly had the dreadful thing off the trestle and feared that it would crash on the stone floor.

Margorie took the other end without a word, though I knew her mind was filled with the same overwhelming horror that possessed me.

We lifted it to the floor, and I seized my large screwdriver, with a feeling that if I did not act at once I should rush from the place.

I worked feverishly, exerting all my strength, for the screws had rusted in, and the foreign-made coffin had been constructed for the journey overseas.

One by one I laid the screws beside me on the ground until all were taken out. I wiped the grime and sweat from my eyes, and looked up at Margorie, who was holding the lantern over my work.

"Margorie—you had better not look."

She shook her head without replying, and her face was set and determined, like a mask of tragedy.

I prised up the lid and turned it back. It slid off with a hollow sound. We stared at what lay within. A silk shroud tied with white satin ribbons, now stained and faded, hid what was beneath. I pulled this gently off, and started back with a stifled cry of terror.

A dead face was looking up at us—the face of a beautiful woman, with tresses of hair almost hiding the contours and a death robe high set round the chin. The long eyelashes fell over the cheeks.

I looked up and saw Margorie's eyes wildly distended and she was holding her head in her hands. I was afraid she would shriek, and got to my feet, taking hold of her almost roughly.

"For God's sake, don't make a noise."

"It's Elsie—" she wailed piteously.

Common sense had come to my aid. I had never known the woman, and perhaps for me the shock was not so great.

"The cunning rogue," I said as naturally as I could. "Don't you understand?" I did not want to go into details with her, but it was quite clear to me that no woman's face would remain in that state. I dropped to my knees and tore away the shroud, while Margorie gave a suppressed cry. Beneath the waxen-like face was nothing but a long sack—already rotting and showing the sand within—shaped to a human form!

"You see," I said then, with a sudden revulsion of feeling now that the truth was revealed. "Barton had this wax model of her face made. In the dim light of a chapel somewhere in Switzerland, the face would look real enough to strangers, and there were no friends or relations to inquire too closely. When a very rich man turns to crime there are no limits to what he can do with his money."

"But if any one had opened the coffin here—?"

"Of course they would have known, as we do now, but this trick was not meant for England, but merely for some nuns perhaps who watched the bier, and only then for a brief glance from some distance, and not too close an inspection."

I had been talking deliberately to restore Margorie's nerves, but at the same time I had covered the face again and replaced the silk cover, and was vigorously applying my screw-driver.

At last it was done, and we lifted the coffin back to its place. I rubbed some dust and dirt over the screw holes, and dusted my hands on my handkerchief.

"We must go!" I said sharply.

"Yes, Dennis, we must go," Margorie said in such a queer voice that I was afraid the shock had affected her.

"Come on. Open the door, and I'll put the lantern out."

She gripped my arm—urgently. "Yes, we must go, but where, Dennis?"

"Why, back to your house, of course. Unless we go and have a clean-up at the Crest first."

"Yes, yes, of course—but after that—don't you see, Dennis? We must go to Switzerland—you and I—no one else must know. We only can find out there, and we must find out! We dare not tell my father of what we have done."

I knew as soon as she had spoken that her plan, formed in a flash, was inevitable. There was nothing else to do. Whatever difficulties it might present, and however doubtful our going together might appear, the risk must be taken.

"You are right, Margorie—we must go together, and as soon as possible."

We passed out of the vault, and closed and locked the heavy door. The beating of the storm in our faces was like a sea breeze to a sick man, and the good smell of the damp countryside was fresh to our nostrils, like the smell of flowers after rain.

A mighty load was lifted from our minds, even though the mystery lay before us still unsolved, but I believe that had we delayed our visit to that awful place we should have never screwed up our courage for the venture.

On the way back to the Crest, Margorie was able to explain one puzzle in this gruesome business. Sir John Barton, when he married Elsie Peters, had arranged with a well-known sculptor to have a bust made of his bride, and had placed it in the Towers. It was a life-like image, and he had been proud to point it out to his friends, and to tell them how much it had cost.

After Elsie's death, Barton had taken it away from its place in the hall, and told Margorie that he could not bear to look at it.

The artist, when sending the completed bust, had also given Sir John a beautiful wax impression, in a leather case, but it was too much like a death mask for Barton's taste, and he had put it away, after showing it to Elsie and Margorie.

There was no doubt that this mask had been used for the 'dummy' in the coffin, but for what foul object we could not guess. Only an ugly thought came to us that he must have taken this with him when he went to, Switzerland—for what purpose we could only guess.

I do not propose to tell of all our scheming and the lies we were forced to tell before we could arrange to set out. I had to feign a relapse of my illness, which was not altogether untrue, as I caught a snuffy, uncomfortable cold on our night expedition, and returned to London the next day, urging important business. My 'illness' led to three curious results. Miss Morris, loyal friend as she had shown herself to be, came to Town immediately and implored me to return to her house. It went against the grain to refuse, and must have looked like rank in-gratitude, but I was playing for high stakes. In the second place Charles came round, and told me I didn't know how to take care of myself, and that he was going to stay and look after me. He went away grumbling and a little hurt, when I declined his services.

The third event was the arrival of the rector of Crowfield, with Margorie. My sudden departure, which was perhaps a tactical error on my part, had aroused his suspicions with regard to our last conversa-tion, and he was much relieved when I assured him that I had given up all idea of going to the Home Office, and had, in fact, abandoned my notion of asking him to sanction the opening of the vault. I told him that I was now quite satisfied that no good purpose would be served by so doing, and the sincerity of my tones convinced him that I was telling the truth.

I received all my visitors in my bedroom, propped up with pillows, and surrounded by medicine bottles and sloppy drinks of the arrowroot species.

Margorie, who, of course, was in the secret, brought a huge bouquet of flowers for my room and was duly sympathetic.

I told them that there was nothing really wrong, but that—Heaven forgive me—the doctor fancied that one lung had been affected by the pneumonia, and that it was essential for me to go abroad.

The difficulty about going, I told them, was that the doctor did not consider that I ought to go alone, and I did not care for a stranger for a companion.

"If I could only leave my parish I would have come like a shot," the rector said. "What about Erskine?"

"He is too busy with his work. He's got one or two important cases coming on."

"Why shouldn't I go, if Dennis would care for my company?" Margorie spoke as though the idea had come to her at that instant.

"My dear—I doubt if your mother—unless you took her, too—"

"Oh, nonsense. No one nowadays minds that—we have long passed the day of chaperons. Dennis and I are like brother and sister, and I have helped nurse him through his illness. There's not the slightest reason why we shouldn't go together. You don't object, do you, Den-nis?"

"There is nothing would please me better," I said, with more truth than the rector guessed. "We could join one of these liner trips, and the sea air will soon cure my lung."

In the end we had our way. Mrs. Browne, I think, secretly hoped that we should return an engaged couple, and raised less objection than I expected. Charles was mortally offended—or pretended to be—and told me frankly that if I preferred 'poodle faking' with a girl to his manly company, I could go and be damned, but he would never meddle in my affairs again.

I took tickets on the *Latvania* for a trip in the Mediterranean, and Margorie and I planned to leave the ship at Genoa, and proceed on our quest from that place.

The urgency of our departure was emphasized by Miss Morris's account of her meeting with Kenneth. He had changed very much, she told me, and had lost much of the arrogant pride of their former meeting. He was now very depressed and subdued, thinner than before, and with a sad, haunted look about his eyes. He had not much to say, but I judged that Miss Morris had pitched it into him hot and strong about the whole case, and especially concerning the parts played by myself and Margorie. He had sent a characteristic message to me: "Tell Dennis I've been a damned fool," but no word for Margorie.

He was off again, having come back for money and clothes, and had asked Miss Morris to meet him for news. He had declared that he would never set foot in Crowfield again until the murder was cleared up, and pointed out sensibly that as the Hall was let he had better stay away, as the money would help to put the place in a proper condition.

I was not to say a word to Margorie—a promise I kept faithfully.

I need not dwell upon our voyage together. The 'lung trouble' disappeared as soon as I stepped on the deck of the vessel, and we had definitely made a compact that not a single reference should be made to the problem until we had left the ship. There was a ship-load of jolly people, all determined to enjoy every hour to the full, with games and dances, and frolics of every kind, into which Margorie and I entered with all the more zest after the grim months that had passed, and I am proud to think that my athletic prowess, though only moderate, gave great pleasure to Margorie, and made us quite celebrated. We were sorry when it all came to an end and we had to inform our newly made friends that we had been called back by cable and must cut the trip short. I have no doubt that half the passengers, and especially the female part, had constructed a romance, and weaved a happy ending for us both.

We parted with a feeling of intense regret. Those few crowded and fortunate days on the vessel had revealed to me a new phase of Margorie's nature. She had again become a laughing girl, utterly unlike the Margorie I had met when I first came to Crowfield. She had been acclaimed by her fellow-passengers on the liner a 'good sport,' and the most beautiful among many pretty girls. And yet I knew that this dancing, fascinating creature, vivacious and entirely without pose, possessed a strong, generous nature; a soul that, like a lamp behind a stained-glass window, illuminated her whole being, and a capacity for heroic self-sacrifice.

"And now, Dennis?" Margorie interrupted the train of my thoughts, as we watched the hull of our liner disappear in the distance.

"And now for our quest, Margorie. 'The bazaar is closed, the lights are put out, and you and I must go into the dark!' " I quoted.

We took the train for Geneva, and arrived at the small town of Meiningen (which is not its real name).

It was a typical Swiss town, owing everything to tourists, and forming a starting-place for many of the well-known resorts for Alpine sports. The hotels of many stories that bulged out like topsy-turvy toys, with roofs so big that they looked like comic covers, and the ancient market-place with its statue of William Tell in the centre, brought back to Margorie the memory of her former visit, when the party of young men and girls had laughed and danced, unconscious of the terrible fate awaiting them.

I would have suggested another hotel, but Margorie insisted on going to the Hotel Splendide, where she had stayed on her former visit, saying that we had better try to pick up the threads of the skein from that point.

New waiters had taken the place of those she had known, and even the management had changed, but the old register showed the names of the party, and with a feeling of interest I saw the signatures—Elsie Barton, Margorie Browne, Mabel Peters, and the others.

We were severely handicapped, for owing to the fact that Margorie had been brought back from the scene of the accident unconscious, she had no idea of its locality, or of the names of the guides. We sought the help of the local prefect of police, a worthy, bearded man of many words. Fortunately both Margorie and I were good linguists.

He remembered the accident quite well—a terrible affair. He could find one of the guides who was with the party—Johan Smidt—who was still working, but just now waiting for the winter season. And the hospital where madam, as he insisted on calling Margorie, was lying very ill. He even turned up his records for us, and a file of the local papers of the time, where an account was given in full.

"Sir John Barton," he said, speaking in German. "I recall him very well. He came from England as soon as the cable reached him, and saw me in this very room. A fine man, and deeply distressed. He organized a party of guides, though a great storm was raging, and insisted on going with them himself to look for the bodies. Up in the Grimmi Pass."

He pointed through the open window to the mass of mountains above the town, pine-clad on the lower levels, but snow-clad above, where the peaks lifted their heads into the blue sky.

"Sir John Barton brought his wife back here?" Margorie asked.

"It was after some days. They searched in the snow, and it took time. Then they were snow-bound in a chalet half-way down the pass. Yes—he brought the body of the poor lady here, and she was taken to the Convent of Our Lady of Pity, and from there he took her back to England."

I thought it strange that Barton should have taken the body of his wife to a Catholic convent, but perhaps it was the only resting-place he could find. At any rate, we obtained the address, and thanked the prefect. He promised to give us any further information we required, and we were about to take our leave when he said, with a genial smile:

"You will pardon me, madam, but do you know the other gentleman who was also making inquiries?"

"What gentleman?" I asked, with a sinking feeling of dread.

"Some weeks ago—a small, thin man with a yellowish face and black hair. His name was Davies. He had a nervous manner, and—pardon—I did not trust him. He offered me money—me, the prefect of police!"

Margorie's lips tightened and her hands clenched, but she gave no other sign.

"I think I know the man," I said in a level voice. "You were right not to trust him. What did he want to know?"

The prefect shrugged his shoulders.

"He, too, was inquiring about this accident, and was asking questions about Sir John Barton. He was anxious to know where the chalet was situated to which they carried the bodies, and where the rescuers were snowbound. I referred him to Johan Smidt, who is the only man living who knows. Two are dead, and the others left the village soon afterwards and have never returned."

That was all we could get from him, but the news was alarming. Turnbull was on the same quest. That was why Robert Barton had been so disturbed when I had told him that the lawyer had gone abroad. For what sinister purpose had this blackmailer come to the scene of the accident if not for conclusive evidence on which he could abstract blood-money from Robert?

In the evening a waiter told us that Johan Smidt was waiting to see us, and it was with beating hearts that we told him to show the guide up to our private sitting-room.

The old guide came in, as picturesque a figure as an artist could desire to see. His grizzled hair was tightly curled and his hard-bitten, gnarled face was seamed with lines, and of a dark mahogany colour. He must have been sixty years old, but his massive shoulders and upright carriage denoted strength and the hardness of his native pines.

He wore a faded green coat almost reaching to his knees, buckskin breeches and stockings.

I told him to be seated, and ordered him a drink. Rather to my surprise, he asked for Scotch whisky, which seemed out of keeping with his appearance.

He evidently expected that we wanted to secure his services for the coming season, as he was much in request, and his manner became reserved and as though he were on his guard when I told him we wanted him to take us to the scene of the accident.

"Do you remember me?" Margorie intervened. "I was one of the party, and badly injured."

His old face immediately cleared. He looked searchingly at Margorie.

"I remember your face now," he said slowly. "It is seldom that I forget any one I have seen once." He turned to me with a queer old smile. "Madam is older, and more beautiful now. Yes, I remember. We brought you back here and took you to the hospital, and your father, the priest, came and fetched you. And there was the baron—Sir John Barton."

He stopped and picked up his glass.

"You went out with him to show him the place?" I asked quietly.

"He went to look for the body of his wife—yes. We searched in the snow for days—it was hopeless in that blizzard. We brought them back here at last, and Sir John took the body of his wife back to England. The others were buried here in the cemetery."

"There were three?" Margorie asked, and I glanced at her in surprise and the old man looked puzzled.

"Three, madam? There were only two—Zwengle, the guide, and a young Englishman. You can see their graves in the cemetery. Sir John Barton paid for everything—he was a most generous man."

I am afraid that in the translation much of Smidt's picturesque diction is inevitably lost.

"I must have forgotten," Margorie said. "I was very ill at the time."

I saw the reason for the question, but could hardly imagine that Barton would have the effrontery to have his wife buried under another name possibly, as though three had perished.

"You took refuge in a chalet while the storm was too severe for you to get back?"

A sort of mask fell over the old fellow's face—the cunning, secretive look of the peasant.

"Yes, we were forced to wait," he said thoughtfully, and picked up his empty glass, which I promptly refilled for him.

"I suppose," Margorie said gently, "you could take us to that chalet?"

"I could not find it," he mumbled, his cunning old eyes sunk to pin-points. "I do not know where it is situated—it may have been destroyed by now."

"Come now, Smidt," I said sternly. "You have lived here all your life, and I am told that you are the very best guide in the whole district, and you ask us to believe that you don't know?"

He shook his head with stubborn determination. "I do not know."

"Well, it really doesn't matter," Margorie remarked, with a glance at me. "It would have been of interest to me, as I was a great friend of Lady Barton, but we would like to see the place where the bodies were found and the monument that Sir John put up on the spot."

His face cleared at once. "I can take you at any time, madam," he said genially. "At this time of year there is no snow at the place, only on the rocks above. If you had fallen at this time, you would all have been killed—you would have been dashed on rock instead of soft snow."

"You haven't had another person asking questions about this affair, have you?" I inquired, thinking of Turnbull.

He looked surprised. "No, sir, no one at all."

Here was another mystery, but one soon to be cleared up.

We dismissed Smidt, having arranged for him to take us to the spot on the next day but one, as we wanted to make some further inquiries in the town.

When he had gone Margorie explained that she thought if we had gone on with our questions about the chalet too insistently, he might have suspected something and have refused to take us at all. Already we had learnt sufficient to render us deeply engrossed in the venture, and the fact that Turnbull was hard on the track of the same problem urged us on.

The following day we paid a visit to the Convent of our Lady of Pity, which was outside the town—an old building surrounded by a high wall and built round a courtyard with the windows facing inwards.

The appearance of the place suggested that in the hard days of old such protection was necessary. Its very isolation and atmosphere of secrecy showed us the reason for Barton's choice of such a resting-place for the coffin.

A great door was set in the wall, before which stood a Calvary, and a bell jangled within when Margorie pulled the heavy bell-pull.

A grid was opened, and the face of a woman peered out. Margorie asked for the Lady Superior, and the grid was closed. Presently the noise of bolts being shot back announced the fact that we were to be admitted, and a small door that formed part of the larger gate was opened.

Margorie was admitted, but it was only after some considerable time that I, as a male being, was allowed to pass the portals, and then we were conducted through a garden, bare and desolate now in the autumn, to the inner gate. A door opened on the right, for all the world like the guardroom of my regimental barracks, and we were ushered into a visitors' room, warm and well furnished.

A dignified, white-haired lady entered from the other side, and introduced herself as the Mother Superior of the convent.

I let Margorie do the talking, and she explained that we had come to visit the scene where she had so nearly lost her own life and her friend had perished.

"I remember," the Mother said, in a clear, calm voice, used to give commands. "The poor gentleman brought his dead wife here, asking whether she could rest awhile in our chapel, until he took her back to England."

"Why did he bring her here, Mother?" Margorie asked.

The Mother Superior turned on her a glance that I felt was one of suspicion. "The party were exhausted and could go no farther, and although he told me that he was not of our religion, his wife was a Catholic."

Truly John Barton was not one to stick at a few lies!

"Forgive me asking," Margorie said meekly. "The matter is of greater importance than you think. I do not know the customs of your country. Was it not necessary to hold an inquest, as we call it—an inquiry?"

"I am fully acquainted with the customs of England—I have lived there. It was not necessary—the doctor gave a certificate, and there was no doubt about the cause of death."

"I was one of the party—" Margorie reminded her.

"An English doctor came with Sir John Barton. He, poor man, was nearly broken-hearted, and stayed by the body night and day, refusing food, and kneeling in prayer."

"An English doctor—we had no doctor in our party?" Margorie said, with a sudden catch in her voice.

"He came out with Sir John from England," the Mother Superior said, as though impatient at our questions.

"What was he like—this doctor?" I asked, with a sudden misgiving.

"A smallish man, very pleasant in manner, and devoted to Sir John. He would relieve him at times in the vigil by the body."

"In appearance?" I cried, on edge at her slow, deliberate manner. "I beg your pardon," I added, as she turned a cold look on me; "the matter, as this lady will tell you, is very important—a question of life and death."

"He had a rather sallow, yellowish face, and black hair, and heavy, dark eyebrows. His name was Dr. Richard Seagrave—we have his name in the visitors' book."

And so the secret was out at last! Barton had brought Turnbull with him—it may have been for some quite innocent purpose, at first, and the lawyer had become a doctor, and a party to his secret, though not to the method of his crime, or why was Turnbull out here now?

No wonder he had obtained a strangle hold on Barton, and sucked money from him; no wonder he would not see Smidt, when he had last seen him as a doctor. Something desperate must have made him take this step.

But this did not explain all. Was young Barton implicated in the murder of his sister-in-law? I could only conclude that there must have been murder done, or why had Barton employed all these elaborate means to take a false body back to England and bury it there?

My thoughts were interrupted by the voice of the Lady Superior. Something of our amazement at her words must have shown on our faces.

"If I can give you no more information, perhaps you might care to see our chapel."

She led us through stone passages and into a small, enclosed courtyard surrounded by cloisters, where white-robed nuns flitted away at our approach, and into a small chapel, beautifully decorated by the nuns themselves during the course of centuries, and where the vulgarity of the Reformation builders had not penetrated.

The place was dimly lighted, and only the candles on the high altar burned steadily. The Mother Superior bowed low to the Presence of Christ in the Pyx, and Margorie and I followed her example.

"It was here," she said in a hushed voice, "that they brought her. She lay on a catafalque, before the altar—her body completely covered in flowers, and with a veil spread over her face, through which the features could be faintly seen—a sweet face. And her husband stood or knelt at her head, guarding her as though jealous that any eyes but his should see for the last time her beauty. It was in this chapel that they placed her in a shell, the doctor helping Sir John, and carried her out, for we do not allow men to come here—only he had implored me. He must have been very devoted to her: he left a very large sum for masses for the repose of her soul."

I could not stand any more of the story of this arch-hypocrite, and signed to Margorie to come out of the place.

We thanked the Mother Superior, and left her at the door of the visitors' room.

CHAPTER XXII

THE SECRET REVEALED

A LARGE yellow barouche of ancient date, drawn by two horses, stood at the door of our hotel, and as the steeds moved their heads the musical tinkle of a bell sounded. When the snow came the wheels would be removed and runners attached, and the vehicle would become a sleigh, Smidt was waiting, and we stepped into the equipage, while the driver whipped up his unornamental but useful horses.

The sky was of unclouded blue, and the cold air from the mountains blew the vapours from our minds. I tucked Margorie up with rugs and soon we were on the road that led up a ravine, closed in on both sides by rocky slopes. At first chalets were plentiful, on both sides of the crystal-clear stream that raced down the centre of the valley, and cattle were still grazing in the fields, making the most of their time before the long winter shut them into their byres.

Their bells sounded faint and fairylike to our ears. The pines came lower, and the slopes more steep, as we ascended, and the chalets more scattered, and scarcer. The valley narrowed, and took a turn to the right, becoming a defile, the rocks almost overhanging in places; and filled with huge boulders that had fallen from the snow-clad heights above. The road had become a mere track, but the horses trotted cheerily along, by the bank of the stream. At last we stopped, and Smidt bade us get out, as we had to proceed on foot. We left the steaming horses, and plodded along between the stones which I fancied formed part of the bed of the stream when it was in spate. Smidt led us towards the cliff-side and pointed to a large granite cross.

“That is the memorial that Sir John erected,” he said shortly. We approached the monolith with feelings of awe. Margorie gazed up at the cliff above, which formed a ‘V,’ almost as though scooped from the hill-side.

“It was there that we fell,” she said, clutching my arm. “Of course, I remember nothing about it, but you see how we got into that groove, and slid down, and then over the edge.”

I was looking at the stone cross; Barton’s mockery and cruel joke.

It bore the simple inscription:

"At this spot the body of Lady Barton was found by her bereaved and sorrowing husband."

And then followed the date.

"It's a wonder any of you escaped," I remarked for something to say, for the place depressed my spirits. We seemed to have come to a dead end—a blank wall. It was all so perfectly fitted together—the long search in the snowstorm, the finding of the dead and frozen bodies, and the return to the town. Only that ghastly object in the vault at Crowfield reminded me of the mystery that lay behind.

A crime that John Barton had planned—in which his brother was not actually implicated, but of which he feared the revelation—and one in which Turnbull had taken a part, by forgery and as an accessory.

And then I cast a look at the beetling cliff above me, and an exclamation burst from me before I could prevent it. Margorie followed the direction of my glance, and I saw her turn pale. Standing on a jutting rock above us, and clearly outlined against the snow behind him, the sinister figure of Turnbull stood, rigid and motionless, his arms folded. His face I could only make out as a pink speck, but I am certain that he recognized us, and conjectured that he had been aware in some strange way that we were coming to this spot. There was no mistaking the figure, and Margorie turned to me.

"He's followed us here," I said quietly. "Well, if he was down here, I should have something to say to him."

Old Smidt was shading his eyes with his hands—eyes that could see farther than any other man in the town.

"It is the herr doctor—" he said, and cast a suspicious glance at us.

"You know him, then?" I said in feigned surprise.

"He met Sir John Barton when we had brought the body of his wife to the convent from here." He spoke with slow deliberation, weighing each word, and still with a half-doubtful look, as though he were trying to work out something in his mind.

The figure had vanished from the pinnacle, like an evil vulture from its watching-place. But for the fact that all of us had seen him, I should have imagined that my brain had tricked me.

"Have you seen enough?" Smidt asked. "Or perhaps you wish to take a photograph?"

He had furtively taken a small crucifix from his neck, where it hung by a cord, and I saw his lips moving as though in prayer.

He was powerfully built and tough, but older than I, and less active. I made one unexpected spring and tore the crucifix from his hands, snapping the cord.

His old eyes shot fire at me, but he only stared, waiting for me to explain myself. I wondered whether he thought I belonged to some hated protestant sect to whom the holy symbol is accursed.

Even Margorie gazed fearfully at me.

"I'm going to settle this matter now," I muttered between my clenched teeth.

"Smidt," I said sternly, holding the crucifix before his eyes, "will you swear on the cross that you do not know where this chalet where you took shelter is to be found?"

He trembled as though an ague had seized him, and looked uneasily round.

"Will you swear?"

"I will not tell—it does not concern you," he muttered.

"Then you know, and will not tell—that is so?"

He only shuffled his feet, and would not look up from the ground.

"I do not betray when I have promised," he said doggedly.

I lost all patience. "You saw that man—he has been getting money for a long time from Sir John Barton because he knows something that took place after the accident. He has come here to find out, and he is"—I sought for a suitable word in German—"*der teufel*—you had better tell us—"

A flash of inspiration came to me—I was intensely excited, and knew that we were on the verge of a discovery. "Man—do you not know that Sir John Barton is dead. He was murdered in England."

His old, puckered eyes went wild with horror. "Murdered!" he gasped, and his gaze wandered up to the spot where Turnbull had stood.

"Yes, murdered—and so your promise no longer holds good, for no one else in the world knows where this chalet lies. And,"—I played my trump card—"you will get no more money for keeping your secret. Do you understand? No more money. He will not come any more to see this monument—it was a cunning excuse."

My words were more than half bluff, but his face showed me that I had hit the target with a bull's-eye.

A complete change came over the old fellow, and his hands opened and closed, as though gold coins were filtering through his fingers.

A cunning miser's expression took the place of his recent fear. "Will you swear that what you have said is true—on the cross?"

"I am not a Catholic, but I give you my word, and that is sufficient, and this young lady will do the same."

"And I shall not go without reward?"

"I will give you what I think fit, and it will be sufficient. If not, I shall take you to the prefect of police and he will soon have the secret out of you, and you will only get prison, and a lot of it, and no money."

Whether it was the threat, or his avarice, my words seemed to settle the matter.

"Come," he said firmly, and turned back to the carriage. We drove back about a mile, and then he told us to alight once more.

We were still in the narrow defile, and he led us up the rocks on the other side of the stream, scrambling like a mountain goat. Excitement drove us on, and I held Margorie's hand tightly as we struggled over the boulders. Smidt took a turn where there seemed to be no outlet, and before us was a tiny valley, nestling between high walls of cliff—a little green basin, surrounded by pine trees.

Strangers wandering up the main ravine would never have noticed this entrance that looked like a mere cleft from the track below.

In the valley was a neat chalet, with overhanging roofs, and built over the cattle-byre. An outside ladder led to the living-rooms above. We took in the scene, glad of a moment's halt after our climb. The old guide gratefully took back the crucifix that I handed to him, and began speaking in a singsong voice.

"When we found the bodies of those who were dead we would have taken them back to Meiningen. It would have been possible. There was Hans and Peter and Sir John and myself. They grumbled, because a storm was coming on and there was no use, they said, in carrying dead bodies—they could be fetched later. But Sir John was carrying his wife, and I was holding the other end of the rough stretcher. He told me to put her down, and beckoned me to him. The others were ahead and the snow was getting thicker. I looked at the woman, and then I was on my hands and knees, and was chafing her hands and face. And Sir John pulled out a flask and held it to her lips. She opened her eyes. She was not dead, and not even badly injured. She had fallen in deep snow, and that had kept her alive, but the others were broken on the rocks."

He began slowly to descend and we walked on each side, hanging on every word. "That is my house where I live in the summer, but I go to Meiningen for the winter to act as guide to tourists. I was telling you—Sir John said: 'Not a word to the others; we must get her to some place of shelter.' So I brought him here, and the others left the dead men, who would take no harm, and came with us to the house."

"What happened there?" I asked, as he had ceased speaking.

"The storm kept us there—we could not get away for days! The others we put down with the cattle with a fire of dried dung, and plenty to drink—Sir John saw to that. My wife put the lady to bed, and nursed her, and then one day she came to me and said: 'Johan—the lady is better, but she is bewitched.' I laughed at her, but she boxed my ears—she has a bad temper. 'She will recover,' my wife said, 'but she will never get back her reason—she knows nothing—who she is or where she is, and does not even know the herr baron.'

"Then Sir John came and told me that this was so, but it must never be known. He would leave her with us, and would give a large sum each year for her safe keeping and for our silence. He was a very generous man, and we are poor folk. We have been expecting him to come as he had promised."

A woman was standing at the head of the stairway, a muscular creature with huge arms, but deformed by the terrible goitre that is the scourge of Switzerland. Smidt went forward, muttering some excuse, and we heard them talking rapidly, though the words were inaudible. They seemed to be having an argument, but at last she appeared to agree with him, and he signalled us on.

We ascended the stairs, Margorie going first, and entered a squalid living-room of rough timber plugged with mud. Margorie gave one cry of joy and rushed forward. I saw for a moment the face I had seen in the coffin in the vault, but changed, and less beautiful. I heard a sob, and Margorie's voice: "Don't you know me, Elsie?"

I signed to the two who stood staring stupidly at the girls, and we went out. "Leave them alone together," I told them. "No harm shall come to you for this—you only carried out orders, and knew nothing more."

"Johan tells me that the herr baron is dead," the woman said in a slobbering, guttural voice. "We want the money."

"You shall have the money," I said, only too pleased to have the matter settled without fuss or scandal. "How is she?" I nodded towards the house.

"She is well," the woman answered volubly. "She eats and sleeps, and walks as far as she is allowed, and cooks for me. But"—she touched her head—"she knows nothing—she is as a little child. She can only speak the German that we have taught her. She did not know the herr baron when he came to see her. We were expecting him now—he should have been here a month ago—it will be difficult when the snow comes."

The woman was very stupid and slow—I turned to Smidt, who had his wits about him.

"At Meiningen you shall have the money, but no more—there will be no more payments. You understand that? And we shall take the lady with us, so you will have no more expense." I saw that he was going to protest, and took him by the shoulder. "You are fortunate not to be sent to prison for what you have done. Listen to my advice—for your own sake you will forget this altogether, and tell your wife to do the same. You have made much money already—let that content you."

He shrugged his shoulders and walked off grumbling to impart the news to his wife.

Margorie came down the stairs—her eyes full of tears.

"Dennis, it's pitiful poor Elsie. Do you think that she will ever recover?"

"Of course she will," I said, eager to reassure her. "If she had been taken straight to the town, and put under proper treatment, I think she would have been cured long ago. With friends around her, and English being spoken, her memory would have come back. But the shock, and some lesion of the brain, affected her so greatly that when she recovered consciousness, and found strange surroundings and an unknown tongue being spoken, the brain could not recover. The great thing is that we have found her, and that she is alive and well—physically."

"Dennis—what a foul brute that man was. When I think of it I feel utterly ashamed of myself."

I knew what was in her mind—the thought that she could ever have become engaged to such a man.

"It was not your fault—he was a cunning, plausible ruffian. Remember how he took in the Lady Superior, and your father, and many more. That is all past and over."

Elsie came with us, docile and gentle as a child. Johan would have had us stay for food, but we were impatient to be gone, and I emptied all the ready money I had with me on the table. The woman eagerly grabbed it up with subservient thanks.

It was strange to see the apathy with which Elsie took farewell. She smiled vacantly as the woman kissed her. I believe the creature had really become fond of her, and had been glad of her companionship while her husband had been away, for, of course, they had not dared to have any visitors to the lonely chalet while Elsie had been there.

We reached the carriage, and Smidt and I walked, while the two girls rode inside. The driver only stared when he saw Elsie, but made no remark and walked his horses, for we dared not let them go on in front of us.

Johan was more communicative now, and told me further details. Barton had unfolded the plot to him, and with promise of much gain had obtained his agreement. Together, he and Barton had made up a dummy, and told the men below that the lady had died. As they had been plied with drink and given a handsome reward for their services, it was none of their business, and the husband's distress was so sincere.

They had picked up the other two bodies, and had gone down the pass with great difficulty owing to the storm that had flooded the stream and loosened a number of boulders.

Barton had sent the other guides on to Meiningen, with the bodies of the two men, with a note for Turnbull, who was waiting there.

He had arrived at a small chalet where Barton and Smidt had halted. It had been impressed upon Smidt that on no account was he to say a word to Turnbull concerning the truth, but he had seen the two men in earnest conversation, and what Barton told Turnbull will never be known. He had arranged the plot with him, being unable to carry it through without his aid, but he had undoubtedly kept the fact that his wife was alive from the lawyer, and let him draw his own conclusions.

He had tried to get information on the subject from Smidt, but the old fellow had kept his secret, as he had from us. I fancy that Turnbull's acute brain had fathomed the mystery, and that he had come out to discover where Lady Barton had been hidden. If he could actually prove that Elsie was alive, he would have as strong a hold over Robert as he had over John, for Sir John Barton's will, leaving everything to his wife, would then be valid, and Robert would be disinherited.

Smidt told me that Sir John had cut off all his wife's hair before leaving her, and I guessed for what purpose. Somehow it gave a devilish touch to the foul crime.

There was little more in Smidt's story. He and the other guides had been paid off with very liberal largess, and Barton and 'the herr doctor' had taken the 'dummy' to the convent, craving leave to have the 'body' placed in the chapel until arrangements could be made to take it to England.

The doctor's certificate and the testimony of the whole party provided sufficient evidence.

We reached the town in the late afternoon, and drove to the hospital in which Margorie had been a patient.

I had to take the senior doctor, a very clever young German, into my confidence to a certain extent, telling him that we had been searching for the missing woman for a long time, and that her relatives had given her up for dead. He was intensely interested in the case, and promised that he would have the very best specialists, both surgical and theuropathic, to examine her.

My mind at rest on that point, we returned to the hotel, footsore and tired out.

Dinner restored us both, and we were able to make plans for the immediate future.

It was a bitter moment for me, and one that I had dreaded ever since we had started on the quest. I do not think that Margorie had thought of it, for her mind had been entirely taken up with the venture.

The hour was getting late, and there were few people in the lounge.

"Let's go and have a breath of air on the veranda," I said unsteadily.

A clear full moon was shining down, and the white peaks of the mountains gleamed like pure silver, pointing to heaven. It must have been from such a vision that the first dreamer evolved the Gothic spire, the symbol of aspiration and faith.

The cold, dry air blew from the mountains, and the lights of the town lay below us.

I found it hard to begin, and we spoke softly of the night and its magic, and of the sense of the eternal conveyed by the wonderful scene.

And then we spoke of all that had gone by in the feverish weeks through which we had lived—of my first coming to Crowfield, and of the crowded events that had followed.

A silence fell between us and I think Margorie realized what was coming, for she drew close to me, and I felt the touch of her hand on my arm.

"Margorie," I said huskily, "you must stay here with Elsie—she must not be left alone on any account with complete strangers. Talk to her every day—and perhaps, slowly, a glimmering of the past will return. She must not come to England until she is better; the shock would be too great."

"I think you are right," she said in a dreary voice. "It will be better so. And you, Dennis?"

"I must go. My work is nearly done, Margorie—the task I swore to carry through. I dare not write. I must go to England and tell your father. I somehow fancy it will not come as so great a surprise as we imagine. And then I must break the news to the Peters, and to Mabel."

"Yes, I see that—I shall be quite all right here, and will let you know how things are going on." She spoke calmly, but there was a catch in her voice, and her grip of my arm became firmer.

"And after that I have something to do that no one else can do. Something that must be done, and you know it."

"Yes, Dennis, I know it—now."

"That is why I want you to stay here—you must not be in England—it will be better so."

"And then, Dennis—after you have done all that—you will be coming back here?"

"I have one more thing that I have to do," I said firmly, though my heart was beating fast. "Miss Morris has his address, and knows where to find him. I will send Kenneth out to you. You can be married quietly here at the English church, and when Elsie is fit to be moved, or before if her parents take charge of her, you can have a voyage together, to forget the horrible past, and come back to the Hall in the spring, when everything is over and the flowers are out. It will be a happy home-coming for him—his troubles over, and the dearest, best girl in the whole world as his wife at last."

She was crying, and I dared not look at her. The tears were falling from her beautiful eyes unchecked, and she could not speak.

I forced myself to talk in a practical, normal way—I would not part with her letting her think I was a maudlin, sentimental fool.

"You see, it has all worked out right at long last, though you have been through a terrible time. Kenneth will understand what you have suffered, and now that things are settled with regard to the Hall, and he has no money anxieties, he will be a different man—"

"Don't, please, Dennis"—she gave a piteous cry like a child in pain— "you hurt me—it is all so unfair—I know, dear. It has all been through you, and I cannot speak of gratitude. If ever two people had a staunch friend . . ." She smiled sadly at me. "Perhaps if we had met years ago it might have been different . . ."

"Then I will go now, Margorie. I shall not see you in the morning. You will arrange with Smidt, and I have left everything ready—you have only to go to the bank. Take care of yourself. It will only be for a few days."

I could stand no more of this. I think I should have broken down like a weak child.

"I shan't see you in the morning?" she cried piteously.

"You will not see me again—this is the end," I said, I am afraid with a note of bitterness I tried in vain to keep from my voice. "It is better so. Don't ask me—I shall go away—I have no ties, and no relatives. I shall travel—"

"And forget?" she said very low.

"Never, Margorie—don't insult me by the suggestion. As long as you and Kenneth are happy that's all that matters—good-bye."

I held out my hand, which she took in her own and drew me down to her. I dropped my head wearily, like a dying man, and felt her lips momentarily pressed to mine.

"Good-bye, my dearest brother."

She released her hold and fled away into the lighted room behind us, leaving me with the calm white mountains and the cold, unpitying stars.

CHAPTER XXIII

THE CROWFIELD MURDERER

I WILL not dwell on my journey back, for my affairs are not of interest to the reader, but must hasten to the end of my story.

A dull pain was gnawing at my heart, but I tried to banish it by going through in my mind the events that had taken place, for the jig-saw picture was now complete, and the puzzle over. I had made one big mistake—I had thought that Barton had murdered his wife—but murder for the sake of another woman, foul though it be, lacked something of the cold brutality of what he had done. But for us his miserable wife would have been condemned to a living death, and I shuddered to think of this fiend waiting for the end, when perhaps he could smuggle the real body back to that vault already prepared for such a purpose, and after a proper interval could defy Turnbull to do his worst.

I arrived in London and went to my flat, where I found Hoad almost in despair, with an accumulation of letters waiting attention.

I had no time or patience to open them, but merely glanced at the writing, and left them. A fever was consuming me, a feeling that I must get the thing done, before my resolution failed me.

I got Hoad to fetch my car, as I did not feel up to driving in London streets in my present state of mind.

We went to Peters's house, where I had dined—so many years ago it seemed.

He had just returned from the courts, I was informed, and was very tired, but I insisted, and was shown into his study.

After a few minutes he appeared, and greeted me warmly.

"What, back already, Tracey? I thought your ship had only just touched at Alexandria. I had imagined you and Margorie climbing the Pyramids."

"We left the ship. I came back to speak to you about the murder."

"Haven't we had enough of that?" he frowned. "We got your friend Darent off between us, and the best thing now is to let sleeping dogs lie."

"Unfortunately we can't do that, Mr. Peters—they have a way of rising up to confront us when we least expect it."

"Well, what's the latest discovery?" he said indulgently.

"How is Mabel?"

"Mabel? I am glad to say that she has made a very good recovery, and has completely shaken off that nervous attack. She is back with us now."

"Then, Mr. Peters, might I ask whether you would mind fetching her in here?"

"In here? Really, Tracey—what do you want with her?"

"I will tell you when she comes. I have some news for you both. I have just returned from Switzerland."

"I'll fetch her if you want her," he said with a certain uneasiness of expression, "though I don't understand you, Tracey."

I waited while he went out, and had half a mind to follow, but the girl was only in the drawing-room, and returned with him. I had barely time to resume my seat when he came in.

"You wanted to see me?" Mabel asked, and I saw the vast change the last few weeks had wrought in her. The nervous, frightened manner had gone, and she was self-possessed, and almost contemptuous in her attitude towards me.

I pulled out a precious note-book that I had concealed from every one, and opened it.

"Mr. Peters, I have at last discovered the murderer of Sir John Barton, or perhaps I ought to say I have known for a long time who killed him, but I have now obtained the last link in the chain of evidence."

"Indeed, Tracey," he sneered; "and who may that be?"

"Yourself, Mr. Peters."

He gave a scornful laugh. "You are either joking or raving."

But if any lingering doubt rested in my mind, the sight of Mabel's face would have banished it. Every vestige of natural colour had left her face, and the make-up of lips and cheeks showed up in startling tints like a wax doll.

She clutched the sides of her chair, and stared in horror at her father.

"I expected that you would deny it. I don't blame you, but to save time I will tell you how I came to know it."

"Who told you this ridiculous yarn?"

"You did—you gave me the facts, and I only wanted a motive. That I found in Switzerland."

Some of his assured manner vanished at the word. "Let's have your tale if it interests you. I suppose you have been doing some amateur detecting, and are rather proud of your deductions."

"Very well, Mr. Peters, since you will have it so. I am not a detective—far from it—but the facts came to me and pieced themselves together. You will remember when we first met in the lounge at the

Crown Inn, you told me the story of your daughter Elsie and her death. You mentioned that your wife and daughter had gone to the Towers for the evening, but that you had stayed at home, not wishing to go. You were in a lounge suit, and wore brown shoes. You said you had not been out all the evening, yet your shoes were wet and covered with mud and some had caked on your trousers—a small matter and of no importance in itself."

Neither of my listeners interrupted, but gazed at me during my recital as though fascinated.

"Then later when we talked, you made a remark that startled me completely. It was just before you went to bed, and I had told you I had informed the inspector about the alibi. You said: 'Heavens, and Darent's footprints were on the grass!' No wonder I was dumbfounded and unable to speak, for no one at that time except those actually at the Towers knew anything about the tracks. I did not myself, and only learnt the next day. You had not been out and had seen no one who did know, and yet you told me that Darent's tracks were on the grass. There was only one possible meaning—you must have seen them.

"That did not necessarily mean that you had any hand in the murder, but your insistence on my not going on with the alibi, and on my going away, assumed a new light if you knew that the alibi was false."

"You own up to that, then," Peters said fiercely.

I was not to be drawn aside from my accusation.

"You astonished me the next day by saying that you were going to defend Darent without charge. He was no friend of yours, and was accused of murdering your son-in-law. Why this extraordinary act of generosity? It was only later, when other facts had come to light, that I realized the reason. You would defend him with all your skill for one reason—because your freedom and perhaps your life depended upon getting him off."

"You are melodramatic, Tracey. I am afraid I don't follow your argument."

"And yet it is perfectly clear to any one who knows you, Mr. Peters," I said earnestly. "You would not have let Darent go to the gallows, or even be convicted, without telling the truth. I watched you during the trial, and if ever a man was in mortal agony when the jury had retired, you were that man. Shall I go on?"

"Do—it is most interesting."

"I began to have suspicions that you knew more than you would say at the Crown, and started to find out what I could. For example, I was trying to find who had taken Darent's stick, which was vital.

"Polly had gone to the 'show' at the Towers, and your wife and daughter had gone. That would mean that Mr. and Mrs. Willis would have all the work thrown on to them. The private sitting-room of theirs would be deserted.

"Now, an ordinary casual visitor would not go down the passage to their room, or up the stairs while the Willises were in the lounge and in the downstairs parts. But you had a private sitting-room, and were a man of great position, and suppose you had rung the bell and received no answer, you would naturally walk along the short passage from your room to theirs. When you paid the bill the next day you went there without hesitation, knowing where it was; and I found out from Polly that you had actually been in there to arrange for rooms when you first came. Very well. I had already discovered that you had been out, though you had said you hadn't; that you had seen the tracks yourself, and that you had access to the stick with which the crime was done. You would naturally have gone out by the back way, and not through the bar.

"I had got as far as that in a vague way when I discovered that Mabel had been out in the car with Sir John before dinner—why?

"When I faced her with it she told me that it was a personal matter that did not concern me. It was surely something of the utmost importance to make her seek an interview secretly, on the night before the wedding, and so serious that it led to a complete nervous breakdown, only cured when the danger, as she thought, was averted."

"You are lying," Mabel burst out. "I was going—"

"Hush, my dear—let him finish his absurd statement."

"I am not lying, and you know it, Mabel so why keep up the farce? You went to the rector, and asked him to have Elsie's coffin opened."

Mabel remained silent, her lips quivering, and she glared like a young tigress at me.

"I found out that Turnbull was blackmailing both the Bartons and that there was some guilty secret that Turnbull knew connected with the past. We will come to that in good time—" I referred to my note-book, as I had been led off the track.

"Polly had told me casually that when you had strolled down to dinner you had been wearing pumps, evidently not intending to go out, but you had changed to shoes later. You had taken your pumps with you because you meant to see Barton and did not want any tracks of your shoes showing on the grass. Suspicion was growing in my mind, but I could not bring myself to believe that you had murdered Barton, until after the trial, when you told me that the question of the second track on the grass was unimportant, and that you had been able to clear up the point satisfactorily. I was amazed that a brilliant lawyer like you should have entirely ignored this vitally important piece of evidence, when it was fairly obvious that the second pair belonged to the murderer. There could only be one explanation, since Pyke told me he knew nothing about the pumps, and had never discussed the matter with any one. They belonged to you. You rather cruelly used Darent's name to fetch Barton out."

"I did nothing of the sort! But go on." Peters's face had lost its air of assurance, but his mouth was grimly set.

"There is nothing more to say, except that you killed Barton because you thought he had murdered your daughter, and then you saw Darent come, and followed him to the bushes, where you resumed your shoes."

His calmness vanished instantly, and he started to his feet. I feared he was going to do something desperate.

He glared at me. *'Thought?* I knew he was a cold-blooded murderer." All pretence had gone, and we faced each other across the table, while Mabel was lying back in her chair, panting hard, and with a look of horror on her face.

"Yes, *thought*," I said sternly. "You were wrong; he did not murder his wife—she is alive at the present moment. I found her in Switzerland."

He never thought of doubting my word. He clapped his hand to his head and gave a gasping cry: "My God—then I am a murderer myself."

"Sit down, Mr. Peters; things are not so bad as you think. I wanted to force a confession from you. Now we can discuss matters calmly. You did kill Barton?"

"Yes, I killed him, and if what you say is true, I deserve to be hanged, though it was only because he would not tell me the truth, or agree to break off the wedding. I lost all control at his sneering face, daring me to prove my statement. And he struck me first, but I am making no excuses."

"Listen," I began, and told them the whole story of our expedition to Switzerland, beginning with the opening of the coffin, and the discovery we had made.

Both he and Mabel were frantic with delight at the news that Elsie was alive, and for the moment forgot the matter of the murder.

"Tracey," Peters said at last, "you have been a brick. You have come to me instead of going to the police, and all through you have acted as a true gentleman should. I place myself unreservedly in your hands. You have so accurately described what took place, that there is little that I can add, but in two matters I must correct you. I did not use Darent's name when asking Barton to come out and see me. I used my own, but he, I suppose, wanting to put people off the track, and being uneasy after his interview with Mabel, must have used Darent's name as a blind. He feared the interview with me, but did not expect any physical violence.

"The other point is this: I waited in the shrubbery, and saw Darent come, and followed him as you have said, but it was only when I saw him get over the fence that I recognized him, and then did all in my power to get him off. I've been a coward, Tracey. There was my wife and daughter to consider, and my whole career. I could not face the disgrace."

"But I don't understand now," I said, turning to Mabel. "What was your object in going to see Barton on the night before the wedding, and what happened to make your father go to the Towers afterwards?"

"I thought you knew," she answered in astonishment. "When John Barton brought Elsie's body back to England, he took the coffin to the church while they built the vault—the rector was away you know, looking after Margorie. I had an overmastering wish to see my sister once again. I could not get it out of my head. They had told me that she had been found in the snow, frozen and dead. I asked John to open the coffin and let me have a look, but he refused with such violence that I gave it up. If he had just told me that it was not a sight I could look on, I should have been content, but he seemed like a man in the last stage of fright. I never gave the matter another thought, until he became engaged to Margorie, but you remember that on the day before the wedding you threw Mr. Turnbull out of the Crown, and all his papers scattered all over the place. The wind must have blown one of them behind the bench, and when we came, I saw it lying there, and picked it up.

"It was a note that Turnbull had written to Sir John, and merely said: 'I have the note. If you don't keep your agreement, I shall be compelled to request that the vault, said to contain the body of your first wife, be opened and the coffin examined. You will then have to give an account of what you did with her in Switzerland.' That is as near as I can remember. I didn't know what to do—all my fears came back, and I went to see John to face him with the note and ask him what it meant. He drove me in his car, to avoid being seen, and was furiously angry, telling me the whole thing was a hoax, and written to get money out of him. I couldn't wait longer to argue, as I was afraid of being missed, and I got hold of father and told him. He took the note and said he would think about it. Then I had to go off to the Towers. When the murder took place I feared the worst."

"Did you know your father had killed John Barton?"

"I didn't know—I feared that it was so—when I came back I went to his room and found his pumps all stained with grass and wet through, and I didn't know what to do with them. Honestly I had no idea that it was your room, I had never even heard of you, Mr. Tracey, but I dashed into the first room I could find unoccupied, and put them into a suit-case, hoping it would be only put down as a mistake, and afterwards I could take them back to London. After the murder I dared not say anything about that note for fear of implicating my father. I thought you were on the track by your questions. It knocked me over. But I did ask the rector to have the coffin opened, in the hope that I might be wrong. I told him all I knew in confidence."

We talked on regardless of time, for Mrs. Peters had wisely refrained from interrupting us. I think she suspected more of the truth than either Peters or Mabel had imagined.

The whole truth was revealed at last, and the problem solved, but I had given many anxious hours of thought with regard to my right course of action.

"Mr. Peters," I said, and he and Mabel hung on my words. "I am going to ask you one question, and I want a truthful answer. When you took that stick from the Martins' room, did you know that it belonged to Darent?"

"I hadn't the remotest idea to whom it belonged. I saw it there as I went in to see Martin's wife, to tell her that I should be going out, but she was not there. And then I saw a rough country stick, unlike any walking-stick, and took it with me, with no ulterior object. That is the truth. You see I *knew* that Darent had not done the murder, and as soon as I had seen his figure in the dark, and traced him to the fence, I thought he would be safe. I never dreamt that the marks would be visible. From that moment, as you know, I did everything in my power to get him off. I am not exonerating myself—of course I should have made a full statement, and stood the consequences, but it meant the end of my career in any case, and I could not see that suicide would help my family."

"That clears up the point I wished to make certain about," I said sternly, for when I thought of the suffering he had brought on us—and if the truth were known I had been the worst sufferer—I could not think lightly of his crime.

"I shall make a full confession and send it to you," Peters said, "and I shall immediately resign my position. After that I shall know what to do, and you can rely on me."

Mabel seized his hand and looked wildly at me: "Have pity, Mr. Tracey—it will kill my mother."

"It is not for me to judge or condemn." I spoke as I knew Margorie would have me do. "Of the actual crime, I do not hold you greatly to blame. Any decent father, believing that his daughter had been murdered to make way for another woman, might have acted as you did—I am certain that I should have done. But the other crime, of allowing Darent to be accused, and go through all that terrible trial, and the suffering you brought on others, I find it hard to forgive. On the other hand, I cannot see that any useful purpose, other than sheer revenge, could be served by making the whole story public. No, Mr. Peters—let the dead past bury the dead. I think you are right to retire from the Bar, and that will be punishment enough, but I must insist that you tell Darent the whole truth, for he will not come back to Crowfield until he has learnt that, and it will be hard enough for him to live down the accusation, which is still believed to be the truth by many in the village. Your confession you will send not to me, but to the rector, in confidence, and he will regard it as such. There I think we can leave the matter. Darent, I am quite certain, will take the same line as I have done—and will probably congratulate you. I shan't see any more of you. I shall be starting off to-morrow morning, first to see the rector and Miss Morris, and then on a trip somewhere—I don't know where I am going at present."

"I think, Tracey," Peters said with strong emotion, "you have acted very generously over this—far more than I have deserved. I will do exactly what you have told me, and if Darent wishes to make the matter public, I must submit."

"I fancy," I said with a wry smile, "he will be only too pleased at the ending of the story, and will have other things to think of."

He held out his hand diffidently at parting. "Do you mind shaking hands with a murderer?"

"Not in the least, when you have acted as you have."

I smiled ironically, for although he had killed a man, I had committed wilful and deliberate perjury, and in my heart had been a traitor to my friend, for had loved the woman who loved him only, and nearly—how nearly I alone knew—had left him to his fate in order to supplant him in her affections, which could never be. Thank God we are judged by what we do, and not by the evil thoughts that come to us and do not find expression in deeds.

On the following day I went for the last time to Crowfield. After the tremendous strain of the last few days, and the clearing up of the mystery that had hung about us, I was feeling the reaction—a bitter aftermath—and was in terribly low spirits.

I drove straight to the rectory, and found the rector very anxious and puzzled over a cable he had received from Margorie, saying that he was to come out to her, and that I would explain.

When we were sitting in the old familiar study, smoking as before, I again reminded him of his habit of regarding matters imparted to him as secret, and on receiving his promise, I unfolded the whole story from the beginning, when I first began to suspect Peters, till the interview of the night before.

He listened in silence, never once interrupting, only when I came to Peters's name I saw a furrow appear between his eyes and his lips closed tightly over his pipe-stem.

When I had finished he remained in thought for a while, and then spoke deliberately.

"You have done well, Tracey—you and Margorie together. You already know my habits with regard to 'confessions.' If anything were needed to show how right I am in this matter, this mystery has proved it. I will confess to you that when Mabel came to me with her strange request, and in the condition she was then in, I formed the conclusion that she had killed John Barton. That was why I was not anxious for you and Margorie to go on with your investigations. It only shows how wrong one can be, and how wise one is to keep one's own counsel."

"I had my suspicions of her at one time," I remarked dryly.

"You remember, Tracey, you told me about that strange fancy you had at the Hall of opening the Bible and reading a text."

He glanced at me in a half-serious and half-amused way.

" 'Who knowest whether thou art come to the kingdom for such a time as this?' " I quoted.

"Exactly, Tracey—and it was true."

That was all that he would say on the subject, but kindly asked my plans, and was too big a man to suggest that I should come back to Crowfield. I think he knew my feelings, and that such a visit would be one long torture for me, and perhaps for others.

"I hope we shall meet in London some time," he said at parting. "I should not like to think that we shall not meet again." Then he smiled. "If ever you want advice again—you will know where to come."

I had one last task. I told Miss Morris the mere fact that we had found Elsie, and of her condition, and of my plan with regard to Margorie and Kenneth.

She promised—rather grudgingly—to send for him, and dispatch him out there.

"You're a fool, Dennis, as I've always said, but I like your folly. I wish there were more fools like you, but you and Margorie were skating on thin ice." She wrung my hand warmly and I went my way. What lies before me, I cannot see, and do not greatly care. Her image will for ever haunt me, but the thought I shall carry away with me in my wanderings is one of profound gratitude to Heaven that I was enabled, by luck rather than any cleverness on my part, to set matters right, and to bring happiness at last to Crowfield Hall, at the mere expense of a shattered heart and a perjured alibi.

THE END

RAMBLE HOUSE's

HARRY STEPHEN KEELER WEBWORK MYSTERIES

(RH) indicates the title is available ONLY in the RAMBLE HOUSE edition

The Ace of Spades Murder
The Affair of the Bottled Deuce (RH)
The Amazing Web
The Barking Clock
Behind That Mask
The Book with the Orange Leaves
The Bottle with the Green Wax Seal
The Box from Japan
The Case of the Canny Killer
The Case of the Crazy Corpse (RH)
The Case of the Flying Hands (RH)
The Case of the Ivory Arrow
The Case of the Jeweled Ragpicker
The Case of the Lavender Gripsack
The Case of the Mysterious Moll
The Case of the 16 Beans
The Case of the Transparent Nude (RH)
The Case of the Transposed Legs
The Case of the Two-Headed Idiot (RH)
The Case of the Two Strange Ladies
The Circus Stealers (RH)
Cleopatra's Tears
A Copy of Beowulf (RH)
The Crimson Cube (RH)
The Face of the Man From Saturn
Find the Clock
The Five Silver Buddhas
The 4th King
The Gallows Waits, My Lord! (RH)
The Green Jade Hand
Finger! Finger!
Hangman's Nights (RH)
I, Chameleon (RH)
I Killed Lincoln at 10:13! (RH)
The Iron Ring
The Man Who Changed His Skin (RH)
The Man with the Crimson Box
The Man with the Magic Eardrums
The Man with the Wooden Spectacles
The Marceau Case
The Matilda Hunter Murder
The Monocled Monster

The Murder of London Lew
The Murdered Mathematician
The Mysterious Card (RH)
The Mysterious Ivory Ball of Wong Shing Li (RH)
The Mystery of the Fiddling Cracksman
The Peacock Fan
The Photo of Lady X (RH)
The Portrait of Jirjohn Cobb
Report on Vanessa Hewstone (RH)
Riddle of the Travelling Skull
Riddle of the Wooden Parrakeet (RH)
The Scarlet Mummy (RH)
The Search for X-Y-Z
The Sharkskin Book
Sing Sing Nights
The Six From Nowhere (RH)
The Skull of the Waltzing Clown
The Spectacles of Mr. Cagliostro
Stand By—London Calling!
The Steeltown Strangler
The Stolen Gravestone (RH)
Strange Journey (RH)
The Strange Will
The Straw Hat Murders (RH)
The Street of 1000 Eyes (RH)
Thieves' Nights
Three Novellos (RH)
The Tiger Snake
The Trap (RH)
Vagabond Nights (Defrauded Yeggman)
Vagabond Nights 2 (10 Hours)
The Vanishing Gold Truck
The Voice of the Seven Sparrows
The Washington Square Enigma
When Thief Meets Thief
The White Circle (RH)
The Wonderful Scheme of Mr. Christopher Thorne
X. Jones—of Scotland Yard
Y. Cheung, Business Detective

Keeler Related Works

A To Izzard: A Harry Stephen Keeler Companion by Fender Tucker — Articles and stories about Harry, by Harry, and in his style. Included is a compleat bibliography.

Wild About Harry: Reviews of Keeler Novels — Edited by Richard Polt & Fender Tucker — 22 reviews of works by Harry Stephen Keeler from *Keeler News*. A perfect introduction to the author.

The Keeler Keyhole Collection: Annotated newsletter rants from Harry Stephen Keeler, edited by Francis M. Nevins. Over 400 pages of incredibly personal Keeleriana.

Fakealoo — Pastiches of the style of Harry Stephen Keeler by selected demented members of the HSK Society. Updated every year with the new winner.

RAMBLE HOUSE's OTHER LOONS

Strands of the Web: Short Stories of Harry Stephen Keeler — Edited and Introduced by Fred Cleaver

The Sam McCain Novels — Ed Gorman's terrific series includes *The Day the Music Died, Wake Up Little Susie* and *Will You Still Love Me Tomorrow?*

A Shot Rang Out — Three decades of reviews from Jon Breen

Blood Moon — The first of the Robert Payne series by Ed Gorman

The Time Armada — Fox B . Holden's 1953 SF gem.

Black River Falls — Suspense from the master, Ed Gorman

Sideslip — 1968 SF masterpiece by Ted White and Dave Van Arnam

The Triune Man — Mindscrambling science fiction from Richard A. Lupoff

Detective Duff Unravels It — Episodic mysteries by Harvey O'Higgins

Mysterious Martin, the Master of Murder — Two versions of a strange 1912 novel by Tod Robbins about a man who writes books that can kill.

The Master of Mysteries — 1912 novel of supernatural sleuthing by Gelett Burgess

Dago Red — 22 tales of dark suspense by Bill Pronzini

The Night Remembers — A 1991 Jack Walsh mystery from Ed Gorman

Rough Cut & New, Improved Murder — Ed Gorman's first two novels

Hollywood Dreams — A novel of the Depression by Richard O'Brien

Six Gelett Burgess Novels — *The Master of Mysteries, The White Cat, Two O'Clock Courage, Ladies in Boxes, Find the Woman, The Heart Line*

The Organ Reader — A huge compilation of just about everything published in the 1971-1972 radical bay-area newspaper, *THE ORGAN*.

A Clear Path to Cross — Sharon Knowles short mystery stories by Ed Lynskey

Old Times' Sake — Short stories by James Reasoner from Mike Shayne Magazine

Freaks and Fantasies — Eerie tales by Tod Robbins, collaborator of Tod Browning on the film FREAKS.

Five Jim Harmon Sleaze Double Novels — *Vixen Hollow/Celluloid Scandal, The Man Who Made Maniacs/Silent Siren, Ape Rape/Wanton Witch, Sex Burns Like Fire/Twist Session* , and *Sudden Lust/Passion Strip.* More doubles to come!

Marblehead: A Novel of H.P. Lovecraft — A long-lost masterpiece from Richard A. Lupoff. Published for the first time!

The Compleat Ova Hamlet — Parodies of SF authors by Richard A. Lupoff– New edition!

The Secret Adventures of Sherlock Holmes — Three Sherlockian pastiches by the Brooklyn author/publisher, Gary Lovisi.

The Universal Holmes — Richard A. Lupoff's 2007 collection of five Holmesian pastiches and a recipe for giant rat stew.

Four Joel Townsley Rogers Novels — By the author of *The Red Right Hand: Once In a Red Moon, Lady With the Dice, The Stopped Clock, Never Leave My Bed*

Two Joel Townsley Rogers Story Collections — Night of Horror and Killing Time

Twenty Norman Berrow Novels — *The Bishop's Sword, Ghost House, Don't Go Out After Dark, Claws of the Cougar, The Smokers of Hashish, The Secret Dancer, Don't Jump Mr. Boland!, The Footprints of Satan, Fingers for Ransom, The Three Tiers of Fantasy, The Spaniard's Thumb, The Eleventh Plague, Words Have Wings, One Thrilling Night, The Lady's in Danger, It Howls at Night, The Terror in the Fog, Oil Under the Window, Murder in the Melody, The Singing Room*

The N. R. De Mexico Novels — Robert Bragg presents *Marijuana Girl, Madman on a Drum, Private Chauffeur* in one volume.

Four Chelsea Quinn Yarbro Novels featuring Charlie Moon — *Ogilvie, Tallant and Moon, Music When the Sweet Voice Dies, Poisonous Fruit* and *Dead Mice*

Four Walter S. Masterman Mysteries — *The Green Toad, The Flying Beast, The Yellow Mistletoe* and *The Wrong Verdict,* fantastic i mpossible plots. More to come.

Two Hake Talbot Novels — *Rim of the Pit, The Hangman's Handyman.* Classic locked room mysteries.

Two Alexander Laing Novels — *The Motives of Nicholas Holtz* and *Dr. Scarlett,* stories of medical mayhem and intrigue from the 30s.

Four David Hume Novels — *Corpses Never Argue, Cemetery First Stop, Make Way for the Mourners, Eternity Here I Come,* and more to come.

Three Wade Wright Novels — *Echo of Fear, Death At Nostalgia Street* and *It Leads to Murder,* with more to come!

Six Rupert Penny Novels — *Policeman's Holiday, Policeman's Evidence, Lucky Policeman, Policeman in Armour, Sealed Room Murder, Sweet Poison,* classic mysteries.

Five Jack Mann Novels — Strange murder in the English countryside. *Gees' First Case,*

Nightmare Farm, Grey Shapes, The Ninth Life, The Glass Too Many.

Seven Max Afford Novels — *Owl of Darkness, Death's Mannikins, Blood on His Hands, The Dead Are Blind*, *The Sheep and the Wolves* , *Sinners in Paradise* and *Two Locked Room Mysteries and a Ripping Yarn* by one of Australia's finest novelists.

Five Joseph Shallit Novels — *The Case of the Billion Dollar Body, Lady Don't Die on My Doorstep, Kiss the Killer, Yell Bloody Murder, Take Your Last Look.* One of America's best 50's authors.

Two Crimson Clown Novels — By Johnston McCulley, author of the Zorro novels, *The Crimson Clown* and *The Crimson Clown Again.*

The Best of 10-Story Book — edited by Chris Mikul, over 35 stories from the literary magazine Harry Stephen Keeler edited.

A Young Man's Heart— A forgotten early classic by Cornell Woolrich

The Anthony Boucher Chronicles — edited by Francis M.Nevins
Book reviews by Anthony Boucher written for theSan Francisco Chronicle, 1942– 1947. Essential and fascinating reading.

Muddled Mind: Complete Works of Ed Wood, Jr. — David Hayes and Hayden Davis deconstruct the life and works of a mad genius.

Gadsby — A lipogram (a novel without the letter E). Ernest Vincent Wright's last work, published in 1939 right before his death.

My First Time: The One Experience You Never Forget — Michael Birchwood — 64 true first-person narratives of how they lost it.

Automaton — Brilliant treatise on robotics: 1928-style! By H. Stafford Hatfield

The Incredible Adventures of Rowland Hern — Rousing 1928 impossible crimes by Nicholas Olde.

Slammer Days — Two full-length prison memoirs: *Men into Beasts* (1952) by George Sylvester Viereck andHome Away From Home (1962) by Jack Woodford

Murder in Black and White — 1931 classic tennis whodunit by Evelyn Elder

Killer's Caress — Cary Moran's 1936 hardboiled thriller

The Golden Dagger — 1951 Scotland Yard yarn by E. R. Punshon

Beat Books #1 — Two beatnik classics,*A Sea of Thighs* by Ray Kainen andVillage Hipster by J.X. Williams

A Smell of Smoke — 1951 English countryside thriller by Miles Burton

Ruled By Radio — 1925 futuristic novel by Robert L. Hadfield & Frank E. Farncombe

Murder in Silk — A 1937 Yellow Peril novel of the silk trade by Ralph Trevor

The Case of the Withered Hand — 1936 potboiler by John G. Brandon

Finger-prints Never Lie — A 1939 classic detective novel by John G. Brandon

Inclination to Murder — 1966 thriller by New Zealand's Harriet Hunter

Invaders from the Dark — Classic werewolf tale from Greye La Spina

Fatal Accident — Murder by automobile, a 1936 mystery by Cecil M. Wills

The Devil Drives — A prison and lost treasure novel by Virgil Markham

Dr. Odin — Douglas Newton's 1933 potboiler comes back to life.

The Chinese Jar Mystery — Murder in the manor by John Stephen Strange, 1934

The Julius Caesar Murder Case — A classic 1935 re-telling of the assassination by Wallace Irwin that's much more fun than the Shakespeareversion

West Texas War and Other Western Stories — by Gary Lovisi

The Contested Earth and Other SF Stories — A never-before published space opera and seven short stories by Jim Harmon.

Tales of the Macabre and Ordinary — Modern twisted horror by Chris Mikul, author of the *Bizarrism* series.

The Gold Star Line — Seaboard adventure from L.T. Reade and Robert Eustace.

The Werewolf vs the Vampire Woman — Hard to believe ultraviolence by either Arthur M. Scarm or Arthur M. Scram.

Black Hogan Strikes Again — Australia's Peter Renwick pens a tale of the outback.

Don Diablo: Book of a Lost Film — Two-volume treatment of a western by Paul Landres, with diagrams. Intro by Francis M. Nevins.

The Charlie Chaplin Murder Mystery — Movie hijinks by Wes D. Gehring

The Koky Comics — A collection of all of the 1978-1981 Sunday and daily comic strips by Richard O'Brien and Mort Gerberg, in two volumes.

Suzy — Another collection of comic strips from Richard O'Brien and Bob Vojtko

Dime Novels: Ramble House's 10-Cent Books — *Knife in the Dark* by Robert Leslie Bellem, *Hot Lead* and *Song of Death* by Ed Earl Repp, *A Hashish House in New York* by H.H. Kane, and five more.

Blood in a Snap — The*Finnegan's Wake* of the 21st century, by Jim Weiler and Al Gorithm

Stakeout on Millennium Drive — Award-winning Indianapolis Noir — Ian Woollen.

Dope Tales #1 — Two dope-riddled classics; *Dope Runners* by Gerald Grantham and *Death Takes the Joystick* by Phillip Condé.

Dope Tales #2 — Two more narco-classics; *The Invisible Hand* by Rex Dark and *The Smokers of Hashish* by Norman Berrow.

Dope Tales #3 — Two enchanting novels of opium by the master, Sax Rohmer. *Dope* and *The Yellow Claw.*

Tenebrae — Ernest G. Henham's 1898 horror tale brought back.

The Singular Problem of the Stygian House-Boat — Two classic tales by John Kendrick Bangs about the denizens of Hades.

Tiresias — Psychotic modern horror novel by Jonathan M. Sweet.

The One After Snelling — Kickass modern noir from Richard O'Brien.

The Sign of the Scorpion — 1935 Edmund Snell tale of oriental evil.

The House of the Vampire — 1907 poetic thriller by George S. Viereck.

An Angel in the Street — Modern hardboiled noir by Peter Genovese.

The Devil's Mistress — Scottish gothic tale by J. W. Brodie-Innes.

The Lord of Terror — 1925 mystery with master-criminal, Fantômas.

The Lady of the Terraces — 1925 adventure by E. Charles Vivian.

My Deadly Angel — 1955 Cold War drama by John Chelton

Prose Bowl — Futuristic satire — Bill Pronzini & Barry N. Malzberg .

Satan's Den Exposed — True crime in Truth or Consequences New Mexico — Award-winning journalism by the *Desert Journal*.

The Amorous Intrigues & Adventures of Aaron Burr — by Anonymous — Hot historical action.

I Stole $16,000,000 — A true story by cracksman Herbert E. Wilson.

The Black Dark Murders — Vintage 50s college murder yarn by Milt Ozaki, writing as Robert O. Saber.

Sex Slave — Potboiler of lust in the days of Cleopatra— Dion Leclerq.

You'll Die Laughing — Bruce Elliott's 1945 novel of murder at a practical joker's English countryside manor.

The Private Journal & Diary of John H. Surratt — The memoirs of the man who conspired to assassinate President Lincoln.

Dead Man Talks Too Much — Hollywood boozer by Weed Dickenson

Red Light — History of legal prostitution in Shreveport Louisiana by Eric Brock. Includes wonderful photos of the houses and the ladies.

A Snark Selection — Lewis Carroll's *The Hunting of the Snark* with two Snarkian chapters by Harry Stephen Keeler— Illustrated by Gavin L. O'Keefe.

Ripped from the Headlines! — The Jack the Ripper story as told in the newspaper articles in the *New York* and *London Times.*

Geronimo — S. M. Barrett's 1905 autobiography of a noble American.

The White Peril in the Far East — Sidney Lewis Gulick's 1905 indictment of the West and assurance that Japan would never attack the U.S.

The Compleat Calhoon — All of Fender Tucker's works: Includes *The Totah Trilogy, Weed, Women and Song* and *Tales from the Tower,* plus a CD of all of his songs.

RAMBLE HOUSE
Fender Tucker, Prop.
www.ramblehouse.com   fender@ramblehouse.com
228-826-1783   10329 Sheephead Drive, Vancleave MS 39565

www.ingramcontent.com/pod-product-compliance
Lightning Source LLC
Chambersburg PA
CBHW020736020826
48980CB00018B/514/J